The Sisters
of Sea View

Books by Julie Klassen

ON DEVONSHIRE
SHORES ♦ 1

The Sisters of Sea View

JULIE KLASSEN

BETHANYHOUSE
a division of Baker Publishing Group
Minneapolis, Minnesota

Published by Bethany House Publishers
11400 Hampshire Avenue South
Minneapolis, Minnesota 55438
www.bethanyhouse.com

Bethany House Publishers is a division of
Baker Publishing Group, Grand Rapids, Michigan

Printed in the United States of America

Library of Congress Cataloging-in-Publication Data
Names: Klassen, Julie, author.
Title: The sisters of Sea View / Julie Klassen.
Description: Minneapolis, Minnesota : Bethany House, a division of Baker
    Publishing Group, [2022] | Series: On Devonshire shores ; 1
Identifiers: LCCN 2022029122 | ISBN 9780764234262 (trade paper) |
    ISBN 9780764234279 (hardcover) | ISBN 9780764236228 (large print) |
    ISBN 9781493439096 (ebook)
Subjects: LCGFT: Novels.
Classification: LCC PS3611.L37 S57 2022 | DDC 813/.6—dc23/eng/20220623
LC record available at https://lccn.loc.gov/2022029122

The Scripture quote in chapter 1's epigraph is taken from THE MESSAGE, copyright © 1993, 2002, 2018 by Eugene H. Peterson. Used by permission of NavPress. All rights reserved. Represented by Tyndale House Publishers, Inc.

All other Scripture quotations are from the King James Version of the Bible.

The quotes in chapter 13 are adapted from *Natural History and Antiquities of Selborne* by Gilbert White (London: MacMillan and Co., 1875), 70, 231–232.

The quote in chapter 27 is from *Belinda* by Maria Edgeworth (London: MacMillan and Co., 1896), 67–68.

Cover design by Jennifer Parker
Cover photography by Todd Hafermann Photography, Inc
Victorian Bathing Machine photo by Mal Bray
Map illustration by Bek Cruddace Cartography & Illustration

Published in association with Books & Such Literary Management,
52 Mission Circle, Suite 122,
PMB 170, Santa Rosa, CA 95409-5370
www.booksandsuch.com

Baker Publishing Group publications use paper produced from sustainable forestry practices and post-consumer waste whenever possible.

22 23 24 25 26 27 28   7 6 5 4 3 2 1

In memory of Walt McCoy,
who shared with me his mother Viola's story,
which inspired a character in this book.

≽ Old Sidmouth ≼

Sidmouth is celebrated for its mildness of climate. It
agrees very well with me.
My cough is no cough now, and I grow fatter & stronger
every day.

—Elizabeth Barrett (Browning)

O satisfy us early with thy mercy; that we may rejoice
and be glad all our days.

—Psalm 90:14

The prospect of spending future summers by the sea
. . . is very delightful.

—Jane Austen

1

GOD, pick up the pieces.
Put me back together again.
—Jeremiah 17:14

APRIL 1819

Sarah Summers carefully lifted the family heirloom, a warm mantle of nostalgia settling over her. The porcelain plate rimmed in gold had been painted with a colorful image of three sisters in Chinese robes, clustered close as a fourth read to them. Papa had given it to their mother long ago.

Sarah ran a gentle finger over the figures, a lump forming in her throat. Spying a streak of dust, she pulled a handkerchief from her sleeve and began wiping the plate.

At that moment, two of her sisters burst into the room, as different in looks as in temperament.

"Sarah, tell Vi to give back my straw bonnet."

Viola scowled. "It's not even yours. It belonged to—"

Realizing Viola was about to say the forbidden name, Sarah's heart lurched and her hand with it, and there went the prized plate, crashing to the floor.

Oh no. Sarah knelt and began to frantically gather the scattered shards, inwardly chastising herself. *Clumsy fool.* . . . Sliding forward on bombazine-clad knees, she stretched to reach every last fragment.

Could the broken pieces ever be put back together?

Standing nearby, Emily berated her twin. "See what you did."

Sarah murmured, "Not her fault. Mine."

Emily huffed. "Right. Nothing is ever Viola's fault. She can do as she pleases, and we are all to feel sorry for her."

"That is quite enough. Ow!" Sarah raised a pricked finger to her lips, tasting blood. "Now, would you both go and do something useful while I clean this up?"

With another huff, Emily turned and strode from the room in a flutter of pale muslin, Viola in her wake.

Her younger sisters had laid aside mourning gowns late last year. Sarah, however, was mourning more than one loss. She had worn black for nearly two years, even though she had never been married, and their father had been gone for less than a year.

She carefully settled the pieces into a glove box, planning to try to arrange them back into place and glue them together. Most of the fragments were fairly large, except . . . *Oh no.* Three pieces had all but crumbled.

Pain knifed through her at the melancholy sight—a grim reminder that her family would never be whole again.

Retrieving a broom, she swept up the remaining dust. Then she went to confess to her mother.

Sarah found her in her room as usual, lying in a canopied, French sofa bed, her back propped with bolsters. Today, she was fully dressed in black crepe.

"I am so sorry, Mamma. I've done something clumsy and stupid."

"What is all this fuss about?"

"I broke your plate."

"My plate? Which?"

"The china plate, with the four girls?"

Sarah lay the box on her lap. Her mother's soft eyes misted as she regarded its contents. "Oh, that is a shame." She gingerly picked up a fragment.

"Careful," Sarah warned. "I cut myself on one of those."

Her mother didn't seem to hear. "Your father was so proud of this. He found it in a shop in Bond Street. Said it reminded him of our four girls—before Georgiana came along, of course. He insisted we display it in the drawing room, although it matched none of the other furnishings." She shook her head, a slight tilt to her lips. "Such a sentimental dear he was . . . then."

Sarah's throat thickened. "Yes."

Her once-benign papa had become angry and bitter during the final two months of his life. Her fault as well, at least in part.

"What a pity." Her mother replaced the piece with a sigh. "You really loved it, I know."

"Me? I thought you treasured it."

Eugenia Summers looked up at her. "Oh, I liked it well enough, because your father gave it to me. But I don't break my heart over its loss, and neither should you."

"Thank you, Mamma. You are very kind."

"And you, my dear girl, take too much on yourself. Always have. Especially since . . . Well, we shan't speak of that now." Mamma forced a smile and changed the subject. "We expect Mr. Alford soon, do we not?"

"Yes. Tea will be ready in a few minutes. I hope he brings good news."

Mamma pressed her hand. "Somehow, my dear, I doubt it."

Since Papa's death, their Gloucestershire estate, entailed through the male line as it was, had gone to a relative they barely knew.

Thankfully, their father had purchased this house with money inherited from a maternal uncle. Therefore Sea View was not included in the entail, and he was able to leave it to his wife in his will. He had also agreed to a jointure for her in the event of his death, although they had yet to learn the particulars. They hoped the funds would be enough to live on.

Since moving to Sidmouth six months before, they had been paying expenses from Mamma's dress allowance and pin money, which she had saved for years. But that nest egg was rapidly dwindling.

Sarah glanced around her mother's room. "Shall I bring in a few extra chairs, or . . . ?"

"No, let us meet him in the drawing room. I think I can manage it. I don't want the man to see how weak I've become."

"Very well." Stepping from Mamma's room into the nearby parlour, Sarah set the glove box on her worktable and then went belowstairs for the tea things.

While she poured the hot water, their cook added a plate of currant cakes to the tray. "Made these myself. That baker charges too much in my view."

Sarah glanced at the plate. The thin icing did not quite conceal the burnt edges of the lopsided cakes. Baking had never been Mrs. Besley's forte, but they would have to do.

She thanked the cook and returned to the main floor. There Sarah and Viola helped their mother into the drawing room just as the family solicitor, Nigel Alford, arrived as scheduled. They had seen the man shortly after Papa's death, but this was his first visit to Sea View.

Emily and Georgiana joined them, and Sarah poured the tea while Emily passed the plate of cakes. The solicitor took one small bite, wrinkled his nose, and set the cake down.

After sipping his tea, Mr. Alford cleared his throat and addressed his former client's wife.

"Your husband's will has been proved and the bulk of the estate gone to his heir, as expected. I have paid the outstanding debts and am afraid I must tell you that your financial situation is rather bleak." He focused on Mamma as though the girls were not even there. "The jointure agreed to in your marriage settlement is in the form of an annuity, the interest to be paid annually. Unfortunately, the interest shan't be sufficient to support such a large family. I suggest you sell this house, as it will be beyond your means to maintain for long."

"W-we shall live simply," Sarah interjected, hearing the note of desperation in her voice. "Economize."

He frowned. "I doubt you shall be able to pay the taxes, let alone the other expenses, living frugally or not."

Incredulity flared. "If we sell this house, where are we to live?"

He lifted narrow shoulders. "You might rent a pair of rooms and live far more cheaply than in a big house like this."

Sarah bristled. "There are five of us here, Mr. Alford, not including our loyal retainers. Jessie is young and could easily find another place, but our cook and manservant are too old to secure employment elsewhere."

At last, he looked from sister to sister. "Then perhaps you ladies might consider taking situations yourselves. Genteel situations, of course, befitting your upbringing. Governesses, perhaps."

"Horrors," Mamma retorted. "You clearly have never had a beloved daughter or sister in such a role. Never received their letters describing their miserable, lonely plight, scorned by society, isolated from family, and left with only a few spoiled children for company."

The solicitor blinked, his Adam's apple rising and falling in his withered neck. "No, I . . . Well, it was only a suggestion."

Sarah said, "We wish to remain together, sir. If at all possible."

He nodded gravely. "I understand. But wishes do not always come true." He rose to take his leave. "Well, please consider my advice, and do let me know if I may be of assistance in selling the house."

Had he even listened? Clearly, the man would not be able to help them. If they were going to stay together, Sarah realized, it was up to her to find a way.

After Mr. Alford left, Sarah retreated into the library and took a closer look at their finances herself, comparing their expenditures over the last several months against the estimated income from Mamma's jointure. As much as she hated to admit the solicitor was right, once Mamma's nest egg was gone, the funds would not stretch far enough. Besides the land and window taxes, the government also taxed them for keeping a male servant and for many other items as well: salt, newspapers, soap, candles, tea, pins, sugar, coffee, carriages, wallpaper, and more. Then there was the church tax above the tithes and the county rates. And all of that was before ongoing expenses like food, fuel, clothing, et cetera. Not to mention doctors and medicine for Mamma.

The carriage and horses would clearly have to be sold. What else could they do? She had hoped to engage a dedicated kitchen maid to assist their overworked cook and sole maid, but that was out of the question now. Sarah wondered if she might attempt some of the baking herself, both to help Mrs. Besley and to reduce the amount paid to the local baker.

While she sat at the desk over the ledgers, someone knocked on the open doorframe. Sarah looked up and saw Miss Fran Stirling, and some of her tension immediately eased.

"I did not hear you arrive."

"Jessie let me in."

Mamma's former lady's maid was a thin brunette in her thirties with a pretty face apart from a rather sharp nose. She had saved her wages, and those savings coupled with a small inheritance from her grandfather had allowed her to leave service a few years ago and purchase a modest boarding house in eastern Sidmouth. Since then, Miss Stirling had maintained a friendly correspondence with her former mistress and had been the first to welcome them when they moved to Sidmouth.

Now the neatly dressed woman tilted her head to study her. "What has you looking so forlorn?"

With a sigh, Sarah explained the situation in bald terms, trusting the woman enough not to gloss over the facts.

Miss Stirling nodded thoughtfully and looked around her. "Well, my dear. I suppose you shall have to undertake what so many in Sidmouth do to earn extra money. Let out rooms to visitors. I get on tolerably well, I must say, and your house is far larger than mine."

"Really? Do you think we could? We know nothing about managing such an enterprise."

"Come now, your mother was one of the most popular hostesses in the county. How often you entertained out-of-town guests, organizing house parties, Christmas parties, dinners, and the like."

"Yes, but those were with family or friends. I can't imagine boarding strangers here."

"It will take some getting used to, I don't deny. If you'd like, I would be happy to share everything I know." Miss Stirling grinned. "And after those two minutes are spent, I shall help in any other way I can."

Sarah considered Miss Stirling's advice and began forming a plan.

The next day, she called a family meeting, and this time, they all gathered in Mamma's room, where she lay atop the bedclothes, fully dressed in her usual black, a lap rug over her legs. Miss Stirling had returned to lend her voice and support of the scheme.

When everyone was settled, Sarah explained the gap between their income and expenses and how they might fill it—letting out rooms in Sea View.

Viola, with her scarred mouth and tendency to avoid people, was the first to protest. "I don't want strangers here!"

Mamma frowned. "Nor I. A boarding house? Pray do not be offended, Miss Stirling. The term is just so . . . so . . . common." Mamma shuddered.

"What about lodging house?" Sarah suggested.

Ever tolerant, Fran Stirling explained, "Here in Sidmouth, *lodging house* is primarily used when an entire house is available for rent, unoccupied, except perhaps for a servant or two."

"There must be another term we could use," Mamma insisted. "What about . . . guest house? That has a more genteel ring to it."

Fran nodded. "I agree. And most fitting for a lovely home like Sea View."

"What we'd call it is beside the point," Emily said. "Where would we put people? We only have a few spare rooms."

Sarah consulted her list. "There are six good-sized rooms upstairs—seven, if you count my small chamber."

"But we occupy four of those rooms between us."

"We will have to give up our own rooms and share. We might also let out the large dressing room as an adjoining bedchamber, since it faces the sea."

Their mother's brow puckered. "Would you let your father's room as well? To strangers?"

"Yes, Mamma. It has no view, but it is one of the largest. I will clean out the few things he left up there and pack them carefully away. Remember, he slept there for only a few months during our first stay here."

Mamma sighed. "I suppose you are right."

"What about me?" Georgiana asked. "Where would I sleep?"

"Perhaps you might share with me," Sarah offered.

Georgiana's usually sunny expression clouded. "But I adore having a room of my own."

"I am sorry. It cannot be helped."

The fifteen-year-old considered. "Might I at least move into one of the empty rooms in the attic?"

"The attic?" Mamma's brow furrowed. "That is where the servants slept."

Sarah soothed, "I don't see why not. Only Jessie sleeps up there

16

now." Their cook and manservant had rooms belowstairs near the kitchen.

"Oh, very well," Mamma agreed.

Georgie's smile returned.

Sarah added, "And I will have to ask each of you to either help with the guests or earn income some other way, so we can afford to hire someone else."

"I will help," Georgiana agreed. "I can make beds and such."

"Good. Viola?"

She shook her head, freckled face tight. "Absolutely not. Georgie might think it's diverting to act the part of a housemaid, but I do not. I am a gentleman's daughter. It is beneath my dignity."

Secretly, Sarah knew she wasn't wholly wrong.

"You heard Sarah," Emily said. "We all have to do our part."

Mamma frowned in thought. "I could . . . do some mending. Perhaps make some new table linens? I detest this infernal weakness. I wish there was more I could do."

Viola lifted her stubborn chin. "If I must work like a drudge, I will remain in the background. I shan't interact with guests."

Emily snorted. "What—are you going to help Mrs. Besley peel potatoes and wash dishes? Or will you do the laundry?"

Viola shuddered.

Their mother raised a staying palm. "None of my daughters is going to work as a laundress! We can at least send out the laundry."

"Every chore we hire out means spending more of our limited funds," Sarah reminded them. "Funds we'll need for the butcher, greengrocer, and chandler, not to mention wages and taxes."

"But certainly we must draw the line at laundry. We have no mangle. And all those sheets and towels!"

Miss Stirling spoke up. "I send out our laundry. It's quite reasonable. I know the very person."

"Very well. Thank you."

"And what will you do, Emily?" Viola challenged. "Empty chamber pots?"

Sarah hurried to stave off more arguments. "Thankfully, we have the new water closet, and there is still the privy in the back garden, although it could use some work."

"I know the very person for that task too," Miss Stirling said.

Sarah retrieved more paper. "I had better start another list."

Emily said, "I shall write advertisements for the newspapers and take care of correspondence."

"Thank you, Emily," Sarah replied. "Although you may have to help with the guest rooms as well."

She huffed. "If I must."

"Advertisements?" Her mother's brow furrowed once again. "I had not thought of that. Must we alert everyone to our need to supplement our income?"

"I don't think you need to include your surname in the notices," Fran Stirling said. "Using the name of the house and describing its lovely situation and commodious furnishings will suffice."

"Well, that's a relief."

Miss Stirling added, "It's a pity the Sidmouth guidebook was printed a few years ago. A listing in that would help—it's quite popular. But newspaper advertisements can also be effective, although they are more costly."

Mamma changed the subject. "Which meals will we need to provide?"

They all looked at Miss Stirling.

She replied, "Breakfasts certainly, and probably dinner as well—at least several nights a week."

Their mother groaned. "Mrs. Besley won't like that. She is not as young as she once was and threatens to retire once a day as it is."

"I will talk with her," Sarah said. "See if I can smooth the way. And perhaps you might help devise the menus, Mamma? You were always so good at that."

"Happily."

No one asked Sarah what she would do, for they all knew she would do the lion's share.

Leaving Mamma to rest, Sarah and Emily walked with Miss Stirling through the main-floor common rooms—dining and breakfast rooms, drawing room, parlour, and library, and then up the long flight of stairs to the bedroom level, discussing needed repairs, changes, and purchases for the bedrooms, water closet, and bathroom, like new towels and bed linens.

Opening one of the old door latches, Miss Stirling said, "You should have locks installed on the guest rooms. The last thing you want is someone to say their valuables have gone missing and try to hold you accountable."

"Do you know someone who could help us with that?"

"Oh yes. I know the very person. Mr. Farrant is quite handy that way."

Sarah ended up writing a shopping list as well as a list of tasks and projects, which would certainly reduce their already limited funds.

She hoped they would not live to regret the outlay and prayed their efforts would be profitable in the end.

Later that day, Sarah went belowstairs to look through Mrs. Besley's collection of cookery books.

With the elderly cook's blessing and guidance, Sarah was soon preparing her first batch of drop biscuits, about the easiest recipe she could find in *The Art of Cookery Made Plain and Easy* by Mrs. Glasse. The sweet biscuits consisted of only three ingredients: eggs, sugar, and flour, well-combined and dropped onto floured sheets of tin.

While Sarah figured out how to crack eggs without shells ending up in the bowl, their old manservant, Lowen, chipped sugar from the cone for her and grated it fine.

Within the hour, Sarah's arms were sore from stirring and her face hot from looking into the oven to watch the pale biscuits rise and color, trying to gauge when they were done.

Hoping to be efficient, she stepped to the table to stow away the ingredients, but soon a burning smell brought her scurrying back to the oven, too late. The sight of the blackened mounds in their even rows disheartened her. Sarah began to understand why it was difficult for Mrs. Besley to produce flawless baked goods while having to prepare so many other dishes besides, especially with only Jessie to help her in between her cleaning duties.

Sarah was determined not to give up. After being more vigilant with the next tray, she soon scooped a dozen sugary biscuits onto a rack. They were unevenly brown and, after a taste, proved to be a little tough, but certainly edible.

Mrs. Besley and Lowen each ate one with weak murmurs of approval—and great slurps of tea. Despite the imperfect results, Sarah felt inordinately proud of herself.

It was a beginning.

2

Women with a spare room or two—especially at the seafront—saw
an opportunity to make money, and the seaside landlady was born.
Offering accommodation was an ideal business for women: it was
socially acceptable [and] it utilised their domestic knowledge.
—Helena Wojtczak, *Women of Victorian Sussex*

A month later, the first week of May, twenty-six-year-old
Sarah Summers dressed in a simple gown of deep blue
cambric, leaving behind her black bombazine at long
last—not because she no longer grieved, but because she knew
guests would not wish to be greeted by a dour hostess. Standing
before a small mirror, she smoothed her dark hair, pinned back in
a plain chignon, and studied her tired blue eyes. Peter had often
said she had fine eyes. . . .

Sarah blinked away the memory of his gentle gaze and the
shaft of pain that accompanied it. She turned to the open chest
at the foot of her bed and ran a finger over the white linen shirt
she had sewn for him during his absence, and the last letter he'd
sent before going to sea. She knew the short missive by heart, yet
unfolded it anyway and read:

*My dear Sarah, I shall miss you. May our time apart pass
quickly and fruitfully. I pray God keeps you well until*

we are reunited. Please remember to return the book I
borrowed from the vicar. Thank you and God bless you.
Yours, Peter

The mixture of affection, faith, and practicality was so like him, and a bittersweet quiver touched her lips even now. Sarah had prayed for Peter's safe return, yet sadly, those prayers went unanswered.

Shifting her thoughts back to the present, she moved a few more of her belongings into the chest, making room for Emily, and closed the lid with resolve.

Then Sarah stepped into the passage and went from chamber to chamber, inspecting the guest rooms.

Unable to manage more than a few stairs, Mamma had kept her bedchamber on the main level, and Viola moved into its adjoining dressing room.

Emily should have already moved into Sarah's small room on the bedroom level but had yet to transfer her belongings.

Georgie had moved to one of the former servants' rooms in the attic, and relished having not only a room to herself but nearly an entire floor.

Viola still refused to help with preparations, and Mamma was reticent to push her too hard. In part because she empathized with Viola's objections. The situation was, after all, rather humbling for the once-proud daughters and wife of a gentleman. But what else could they do? Sarah desperately wanted to keep what was left of her family together. If the venture failed, she and her sisters would probably have to find far-off situations as companions or, worse yet, governesses as the solicitor had advised. And who would care for their ailing mother then?

Pretty Emily, the writer of the family, had composed advertisements and sent them to newspapers in Bath and London, and to a few publications farther afield. Then they had waited anxiously for a response. Although Sidmouth was becoming increasingly popular with tourists, they expected to host elderly invalids, who frequented the south coast to improve their health.

The first correspondence they received, however, was an angry letter from a Major Hutton, who'd recently moved into the neighboring house called Westmount. He had heard they were opening Sea View to guests and was not happy about an influx of strangers near his *private* residence. He threatened to involve his lawyer if anyone trespassed upon his property. Sarah hoped it would not come to that. Additional legal fees were the last thing they needed. She had tried to pay a friendly call, but the servant who answered the door told her the major was unwell and not receiving callers. Imagining an aged curmudgeon nursing old wounds and old grudges, she made do with sending a polite note of reply, promising to make their guests aware of the property line and to inconvenience him as little as possible.

If they ever had any guests to inform . . .

To their astonishment, the first to write to secure rooms was a Mr. Callum Henshall of Kirkcaldy, Scotland, who would be traveling with his daughter. Emily insisted she had sent no advertisement that far north, so they all wondered how the man had heard of Sea View.

Sarah prayed their inaugural guests would not be difficult to please. She and her sisters had little notion what they were doing! As Miss Stirling had said, they had hosted many guests over the years at their former home, but certainly never paying customers. And in those days, they'd had many more servants to help them.

Despite these shortcomings, Sarah hoped they would succeed in pleasing their guests and gaining the good reputation required to secure more visitors.

God, please grant us favor.

<hr />

Twenty-one-year-old Emily Summers took a deep breath of fresh, invigorating air. This was their last day of leisure before the first guests arrived, and she was determined to enjoy it. She stood atop Salcombe Hill and gazed over the shrubs and wind-bent trees toward Sidmouth below.

Sidmouth, their new permanent residence—whether she liked it or not. They had been there for more than six months, yet it still did not feel like home to her. Would it ever?

She missed their former home—Finderlay, near May Hill, Gloucestershire—but had to admit the views here were lovely. She wondered what Charles would think of the place. Would he change his mind, realize he missed her, and come to visit? Emily might not have minded the move here so much had it not meant leaving him behind, her hope of a future with him seemingly dashed.

Georgiana stood several yards away, throwing a stick to a scraggly terrier, a stray called Chips, who seemed to follow her whenever she left the house. Georgiana planned to spend her free day with a friend, yet had agreed to accompany Emily on a long walk first. Sarah was too busy and Viola refused, saying she would stay in the house with Mamma.

Mamma had tried to persuade her to go out but had given up after a token effort. It was always the same. Viola did what Viola wanted and very little she did not. And because of her . . . condition . . . no one pushed her too hard.

In preparation for their move, Emily had read everything she could about the area, and her frequent walks taught her even more. Sidmouth was situated near the mouth of the River Sid, where it flowed into the English Channel. The town lay in a valley bounded on the west by Peak Hill, its rugged cliff face glowing sandstone-red, and on the east by Salcombe Hill, where she now stood.

Below her, the seaside esplanade ran parallel to the beach, and was lined with businesses: the York Hotel, several lodging houses, medical baths, and there, Wallis's library, her favorite.

Behind these buildings, narrow streets led inland. These held thatched cottages, shops, the market house, and the parish church with its square, battlemented tower.

Past the eastern town lay a grassy field used for lawn bowling and cricket matches.

On the far side of the field, she could just make out their own house—one of a trio of large, detached residences. Their father purchased it two years before as a seasonal retreat, hoping Sidmouth's famous sea air would restore Mamma's poor health. Instead, *he* had died after staying there only once.

A tendril of dark hair blew into Emily's eyes, impeding her view. Reaching up, she found tears there too, and brushed away both with a sigh. It was time to start back.

Emily and Georgie descended Salcombe Hill, stepping to the side of the road to allow a farm wagon to pass. They crossed the river via the wooden bridge near the mill, waved to the miller, then followed the High Street into town.

At the grocer's, where the street divided like two prongs of the letter Y, they veered to the right, onto narrow Back Street, because Emily wanted to stop at the post office. Soon the smells of ale, fried fish, and smoke from the Old Ship Inn assailed them. They continued on, past the lace shop, then the butcher's, where a boy sat on a horse out front, basket on his arm, ready to make a delivery.

Leaving Georgie outside with the playful stray, Emily pushed open the door of the post office, and its bell jingled. "Good day, Mr. Turner." She lowered her voice. "Anything for V.S., care of the Sidmouth post office?"

He looked. "Nothing in the Exeter post, but a letter was hand delivered a short while ago."

Emily's heart rose even as her nerves jangled—the first response to this particular advertisement. "That's for my sister Viola. I'll take it." She held out her hand, and after a moment's hesitation he passed the letter to her.

"Nothing else?" she asked. "For Sea View or Miss Emily Summers?" Emily heard the plea in her voice and hoped Mr. Turner did not.

"No, miss." He gave her an apologetic look. "Sorry, miss."

"No matter." She forced a friendly smile and departed, Georgiana and the dog trailing behind.

Continuing through town to the seafront, Emily could not resist stopping at Wallis's Marine Library, a circulating library and reading room. The veranda out front, with its benches beneath a cheery striped awning and an unimpeded view of the sea, was a popular gathering place for visitors. Georgie remained there, imploring Emily not to tarry too long inside.

Ignoring Georgie's groans, she opened the door with a thrill of pleasure. Ah, the smells of books—ink, paper, leather . . . life.

When Emily entered, she saw two men talking and recognized them as Mr. Wallis himself and the elderly Reverend Edmund Butcher, who had funneled his enthusiasm for the seaside into writing guidebooks about the area. The most well-known was the one Miss Stirling had referred to when first suggesting they open Sea View as a guest house, *The Beauties of Sidmouth Displayed*. Emily had read it cover to cover. It described not only the *Situation, Salubrity, and Picturesque Scenery* of the town, but also a selection of the businesses, lodging houses, hotels, and inns.

Perusing the periodicals and new novels, Emily slowly worked her way closer to the men and overheard part of their conversation.

The two were discussing possible additions and revisions for a new edition of the influential guidebook. Emily held her breath to hear how soon. Oh, Sarah would be thrilled if Sea View were mentioned. Well, thrilled might be an overstatement. This was serious Sarah she was thinking of, after all.

Now, how to go about getting Sea View mentioned, and in a favorable light? If she could manage it, she might be excused from dusting and bed-making for a month!

Should she interject herself into the conversation now? How could she do so without being rude or unforgivably forward?

She had just opened her mouth to address the men when the

door opened and Georgie appeared in the threshold, waving almost frantically.

In reply, Emily shook her head and put a finger to her lips. But her not-so-subtle hint was ignored.

Georgie stuck her head into the library and hissed, "I have to go."

Emily held up the same finger, indicating she should wait a minute.

"I can't wait." Georgie began a side-to-side jig. "Chips just made water on the veranda, and if we don't leave this instant, I may follow suit."

Face burning, Emily hurried to the door, ducking her head in mortification. She hoped the men had not overheard. Either way, now was certainly not the time to try to convince the clergyman and the respected publisher that theirs was a genteel establishment ideal for polite company.

Viola Summers could not imagine anything worse.

Opening their house to guests was the last thing she wanted. How could they expect her of all people to interact with strangers? Nor was she keen to work around the house like a charwoman.

During luncheon that afternoon, Emily had glanced at her, then announced, "If Viola won't help with the guests, then she must earn income another way. Is that not what you said, Sarah?"

Their older sister nodded. "Yes, but what do you suggest?"

"I have taken the liberty of acquiring a paying situation for her."

Shock struck like lightning. "What!" Viola's mouth fell open, tightening her scar.

"Perfectly genteel. Don't worry." Emily lifted a square of newsprint from her lap and read,

"Educated gentlewoman respectfully informs the nobility, gentry, and visitors that she is available for reading to invalids. Letters postpaid and addressed to V.S., Post Office, Sidmouth, will be duly attended."

Viola stared at her. "You did not."

"I did."

Sarah winced. "Emily . . ."

"Why not?" Emily insisted. "She lives a far-too-sheltered life. All she needs is a little encouragement. And her wages will help pay for the extra maid we shall have to engage to do her share of work here."

Viola shook her head. "You know I don't go out among strangers."

"Oh, come. You can call on a few elderly invalids with sight dim enough to need someone to read to them."

"I won't." Viola crossed her arms. "Besides, no one may apply."

"They already have. I picked this up at the post office just now." Emily lifted a letter, unfolded it, and read:

"Dear V.S., There is someone you might greatly help with your services. Perhaps for one hour per afternoon? If that meets with your approval, please apply to Mr. Hutton, this Thursday at three pm."

Emily looked up. "That's tomorrow."

Viola sat there, struck silent. Her irritation with Emily for the moment overshadowed by another thought. She . . . help someone? She, who had always needed help—caused work, summoned shame—help someone?

Sarah frowned. "Hutton? That's the surname of the man who wrote to reprimand us for opening a guest house here. What is the direction?"

Emily scanned the letter's final lines. "Westmount, Glen Lane, Sidmouth."

Their angry neighbor. They all exchanged troubled looks.

Already nervous, Viola was now doubly so.

At least reading to a churlish old man would be better than sweeping floors and making beds.

She hoped.

Their first guests arrived in a donkey cart, driven by local lad Puggy Smith. In his letter, Mr. Henshall had mentioned he and his daughter planned to travel by mail and stage coach as far as possible, and then hire a private conveyance from the nearest inn.

Sarah stood wringing her hands at the window, praying for everything to go smoothly. Mamma, confined to her bed as usual, had promised to pray as well.

The two people who alighted were not at all what Sarah had expected. She'd imagined an octogenarian accompanied by his middle-aged spinster daughter. Instead, a man in his midthirties reached up to assist down an adolescent girl. Then he picked up an instrument case and stout valise, while Puggy followed, carrying a second valise and a pair of bandboxes.

Sarah opened the door to them. "Mr. Henshall and Miss Henshall, I presume?"

"Aye." The man removed his hat, revealing dark blond hair. His side-whiskers and the stubble shadowing his chin were a shade lighter, and his eyebrows fairer yet.

"Welcome. I am Miss Sarah Summers. How was your journey?"

"Long and tedious," the girl replied, before her father could do so.

"No doubt." Sarah held the door wide as the two entered. "I imagine you must be tired and thirsty. Would you like tea?"

"Just our rooms, if ye please," the man replied.

The girl frowned at him. "I want tea."

Sarah looked from sullen adolescent to weary father. The ginger-haired girl might one day be pretty, once she outgrew her spots and bad temper. The man was already handsome—of average height, trim, with broad shoulders. His features were well-formed, but the deep vertical lines between his brows and weary green eyes spoke of concern or perhaps pain. She wondered if he might be ill and had come to Sidmouth for its touted health benefits.

She said brightly, "Then I will show you to your rooms and bring tea to you there. Will that suit?"

"Aye, thank ye." He gave his offspring a pointed look, and the girl begrudgingly echoed his thanks.

Shifting his focus back to Sarah, he asked, "Might there be a room available on this floor? Perhaps . . . with a view of the garden?"

She looked up sharply. Why would he request such a room? Had Emily mentioned it in her advertisement? Unlikely, as their mother occupied it.

"I . . . am afraid not."

"Oh. Nae bother."

She heard his Scottish accent in the way he pronounced *no*.

Sarah swallowed her unease and explained, "Breakfast will be available to take at your leisure from nine till half past ten."

He nodded, and seemed to glance toward the breakfast room before she'd even pointed it out.

She went on. "Dinner is at six. We shan't serve a formal luncheon but will lay out a tray of tea and sandwiches in the afternoon, should you feel hungry. There are also a few places in town that serve meals." Sarah found keys for the newly installed locks and led them up one flight of stairs to their adjoining rooms. On the way, she pointed to a closed door. "We have one water closet, just there."

"That's new," he observed.

Again she looked at him in surprise.

He quickly added, "Newfangled, I mean."

"Y-yes. There is a privy outside, if you prefer. We also have a bath-room." She pointed to the door past theirs. "Or if you would prefer to bathe in your own room, we can bring up a slipper bath.

Either way, please give us a few hours' notice to heat water." She unlocked the door, then, crossing the room, opened the connecting door as well.

"These rooms have a good view of the sea. You may open the windows, if you have come here for our healthful sea air."

"Ha." He gave a derisive snort.

Sarah hesitated, unsure how to react. "Well. Do let us know if you have any questions or need anything while you are here."

The daughter ducked into her room and shut the door none too softly behind her. The man winced, then looked at Sarah from beneath fair lashes. "Sorry."

"That's all right."

"Ye havena daughters, I'm guessin'?"

"No. Though I have a sister not much older."

"Ah. Then ye understand."

She nodded. Standing near him in the confines of the room, she noticed he smelled good—fresh and a little spicy. Surprising, after his many days on the road.

He gestured to the instrument case. "Do ye mind if I play this now and again?"

Curious, she asked, "What is it?"

"A Scottish *guittar.*"

"I don't mind at all. Make yourself at home."

Something sparked in his eyes, but he said nothing further.

She backed toward the door. "Well, I shall return shortly with your tea."

"Bring Effie some, if ye will. All I need is rest and a bit of privacy."

The dismissal stung, though it should not have.

"Of course. Excuse me."

She turned on her heel and quit the room, chastising her foolishness. People did not come to a guest house to strike up a friendship with its proprietors. They came for clean and quiet accommodation.

Sarah told herself she would grow accustomed to her new role in time. This, after all, was as close as she would come to being mistress of a home, or at least its hostess.

She had thought she would have a husband and home of her own before dear Peter died. Now she was resigned to spinsterhood and serving her family.

Even so, a pair of sea-green eyes shimmered in her mind's eye as she walked away.

3

Mrs. Wellard (Late of Manor House, Streatham)
Respectfully informs her friends, the nobility,
gentry, and visitors, that she has resumed
Reading to Invalids.

—*Brighton Herald*, circa 1830

At least it's only a short distance and I am unlikely to encounter anyone on the way.

With a wincing glance at the mirror, Viola tidied her reddish-brown hair and put on her bonnet, preparing to depart.

She had been born with a notched or cleft lip—commonly called a harelip, a term she despised.

Her mother often tried to soothe her, saying the scar—from nostril halfway down her mouth—and the shortening of her upper lip were barely noticeable now. Yet mothers were not objective, she knew, and saw with eyes of maternal affection. When Viola looked into the mirror, the flaws were all she saw. To her, the vertical scar was lasting evidence of her childhood deformity, and the misshapen lip ugly.

During her younger years, people had either stared at her or quickly looked away. So she had taken to wearing a veiled hat or bonnet to cover her face whenever she ventured from home.

She remembered one of the village boys pushing up his own lip and mimicking her formerly lisping speech, and her sister Emily shoving him to the ground with surprising strength. And another time, a woman whose abdomen was mounded with child had screamed and run from her.

Many people still believed the old superstitions, that "harelips" were caused by an expectant mother seeing a person with that defect. Or by a wild hare crossing her path, which would leave the unborn child "hare-shotten." Others thought it was caused by syphilis. Still others called it a curse.

Viola had once asked her parents what had caused her defect. Her mother admitted she had once seen a girl with the condition and had stared fixedly at her, in pity and fascination and a stilling sense of foreboding.

"Then it is your fault I am like this!" Viola had railed at the time.

It had been cruel of her, she knew, but she had wanted someone to blame. Why oh why had she been born like this? Was it Mamma's fault, God's, or her own?

With a final glance in the mirror, Viola pulled the veil over her face and turned to go.

At the front door, Sarah squeezed her shoulder. "Georgie will go with you. If the old curmudgeon treats you rudely or threatens you in any way, leave immediately. Understand? We will find something else for you to do."

Viola nodded and stepped outside, hands perspiring within her gloves.

Their house was angled toward the sea. Behind it and half-shrouded by trees stood their neighbor's house, and farther inland, Woolbrook Cottage, owned by General Baynes.

Together she and Georgiana walked the short distance up narrow Glen Lane and turned at the wooded drive. Reaching a low wrought iron gate, she pushed, and it gave way with a metallic squawk. Emily continued to Westmount's front door, heart hammering in her breast.

What was she doing?

Georgiana hung back with the stray dog that followed her everywhere. "Is this the right place?"

Viola nodded woodenly and forced herself to knock. This was a mistake. They should turn away and retreat before anyone answered.

The door opened.

Too late.

"Yes? May I help you?" A silver-haired man stood in the threshold. He bore the attire and mien of a gentleman and did not seem angry at all.

"I . . . I am here about the advertisement," Viola sputtered. "If it is not convenient, then—"

"Of course it is. Right on time. I have been expecting you."

It would have been one thing to beg off had a servant answered, but the man himself?

"Do come in." He opened the door wider, then glanced at Georgiana. "Would your companion like to come in as well?"

Voice thin, Viola said, "My sister."

"May I wait out here, Vi?" Georgie asked. "It is such a lovely day, and Chips wants to play."

Viola glanced up at the older man. Would she be safe with him? He certainly seemed gentlemanlike.

As if reading her thoughts, the man said, "The windows are open. Your sister shall be within calling distance at all times."

Viola nodded. "Very well."

He gestured her inside. With his trim, upright form and bright eyes, he certainly did not look like an invalid.

She left her veil in place and was rather blinded for a moment, coming from the sunshine into the relative dimness of the vestibule.

Walking at a spry pace, he led the way down the corridor.

She followed him into the nearby sitting room, and, as her vision adjusted, she saw it was rather Spartan in its furnishings. Through an open doorway, she could see into a more formal drawing room, which held a pianoforte.

"Please, be seated." He gestured toward the sitting room sofa.

She sat on the sagging cushion while he settled into an armchair.

Gaze lingering on her veil, he opened his mouth to speak, then seemed to think the better of it.

She said, "Forgive me, sir, but the advertisement specified reading for invalids. You do not seem to qualify."

"Thank you. And you are correct. I don't need you to read to me. My son, Major Hutton, was injured in India and is recovering from wounds to his head and eye, which makes reading difficult."

"Oh." Her mouth felt dry, and her stomach sank. When Emily had announced this scheme, Viola had expected an elderly gentlewoman, or perhaps a mild-mannered grandfather with fading eyesight. Not a wounded officer.

Noticing her hesitation, Mr. Hutton said, "He isn't . . . Well, he's not so bad to look at, if that worries you. One side of his face was burned, but nothing too gruesome. And one eye is still bandaged."

"I . . . was not thinking of that."

"He does have a temper, I'm afraid. Tends to use rather unfortunate language at times."

"Is he in a great deal of pain?"

"Not that he'll admit to. I think he will exercise more restraint in the presence of a lady and not heap the abuse on you he dishes out to the rest of us."

"The rest of you?" Viola asked, having seen no one else in the house.

"There's his, well, orderly or batman, I suppose you'd say, along with a few long-suffering servants. And we expect my younger son—his brother—any day now."

"I see."

"I was thinking an hour a day to start. Not on Sundays, of course." He named an hourly wage. "Will that suit?"

It was more than she'd imagined. She could cover a housemaid's wages with more to spare.

"Yes. Quite well."

"Good, good. You shall earn it, I predict. Well, no use in putting it off any longer. I shall take you to him."

Rising, he led her to a ground-floor room down the passage. When they reached a closed door, Mr. Hutton turned to her, lowering his voice. "I should warn you, he may not react well at first, but he shall come around in time."

Mildly alarmed, she looked at him through the netting of her veil. "He does not know I am here?"

Mr. Hutton shook his head. "I answered your advertisement in his stead. Sometimes those who need help are reticent to ask for it. You do understand."

"But if he—"

Her protest fell away as Mr. Hutton knocked twice and pushed open the door.

Inside, the room was dim, the shutters closed most of the way, although a shaft of sunlight and fresh air leaked in from one partially open window. A cluttered desk stood near the door. Across the room, a figure lay in a couch-bed, somewhat like her mother's, although the bed hangings were less ornate. He wore a banyan, or fine gentleman's robe. As she'd been told, a white bandage covered one eye. She noticed dark hair above, but the details of his face were difficult to make out in the poor light.

"What now?" the prone man growled.

"Good afternoon, Jack. There is someone here to see you, so do behave."

"Whoever it is, send them away."

Mr. Hutton shot her an apologetic look. "Too late. Here she is."

"I told you, no visitors!"

"Miss Summers is not a visitor. She is here to read to you."

"I am not a child."

37

"No, but you have stacks of newspapers gathering dust and correspondence going unanswered."

"Most of it useless twaddle, no doubt."

His father stepped toward the window. "Shall I open the shutters so she might better see . . . ?"

"Leave them closed."

"Right. Well, I shall leave you to it." Mr. Hutton ducked from the room, as though expecting a projectile to be hurled his way.

When he had gone, Viola glanced at the patient, saw him lift a glass of amber liquid and then, casting a look in her direction, set it down again, apparently thinking the better of it.

"Very clever of him to arrange this for a time Armaan would be out."

"Armaan? Is that your valet? Wait, your father mentioned a batman."

He shook his head, wincing at the movement. "Armaan is my friend. We served together in India. He saved my life—pulled me from a burning building."

"Oh. Forgive me."

"It's a common assumption. My own father mistakes the matter. At all events, had Armaan answered the door, he would have sent you marching in retreat. What was your name again?"

She faltered at the abrupt question. "M-Miss Summers." She made a concerted effort to calm down and moderate her speech.

"Summers . . ." He frowned. "That's the name of the wretched people converting the place next door into a common boarding house."

She raised her chin. "We prefer *guest house.*"

He harrumphed. "Do you know, I specifically bought this property due to its secluded situation. The agent assured me the grounds were quiet and the neighboring homes private, and most inhabited only seasonally."

"Things changed."

"What things?"

"Our father died. We . . . um, needed to retrench."

"At my expense."

"I hardly think . . ."

"What is your given name?"

She reared her head back. "Viola. But—"

"No, that was not the name." His brow . . . what she could see of it . . . furrowed.

She said, "You corresponded with my sister Sarah."

"That was it."

An eruption of barking and calling came from outside, and he scowled at the shuttered window. "What the blazes is that racket?"

"My sister Georgiana. She is waiting for me outside with a local stray for company."

"Another sister? Good heavens, how many are you?"

"There are four of us here."

"And your mother . . . ?"

"She is with us as well, though somewhat of an invalid herself."

"Better you should have stayed home and read to her instead."

Viola shook her head. "We must all help, either with the house or financially."

"You chose this?"

"Well, Emily rather thrust it upon me. She placed the advertisement in my stead."

"The fourth sister?"

"Yes."

"I see. I am suddenly thankful I have no sisters."

She managed a wan chuckle and felt his single-eyed gaze on her shadowed profile.

He asked, "Why do you wear a veil?"

She swallowed. "Why do you keep the shutters closed?"

"Ha. Well parried. Actually, the surgeon recommended a dark room while I recover. He recently removed a shard of metal from my eye."

A wave of nausea washed over her at the very word *surgeon*.

Watching her, he said, "If that makes you squeamish, you had better leave now."

Instead of replying, she stepped to the desk heaped with broadsheets and unopened post. "Shall I begin with the newspapers or your correspondence?"

When he didn't reply, she glanced back and discovered his exposed eye glaring at her.

"You are a stranger to me. Why should I trust you to read personal, potentially confidential correspondence?"

She shrugged. "No reason I can think of."

"Have you at least a character reference?"

"No. This is my first situation. I have never been obliged to seek one before."

"A letter from your vicar, perhaps?"

"No."

"Will you not at least reassure me—claim to be a God-fearing, God-honoring young woman?"

She shook her head, throat suddenly tight. God-fearing, yes. God-honoring? No.

His exposed eye lit with interest. "You do not believe in God?"

"I do. I just . . . don't like all His ways."

Again he harrumphed. "I suggest you go home now and take your sister and her cur with you."

"I assure you I am not a gossip, sir. I have no one to gossip to."

"Ha! Except three impertinent sisters, a mother, and a houseful of boarders? With that many females about, details of my personal life would be spread from Peak Hill to Salcombe Hill within the hour."

Feigning bravado, Viola turned to the pile of broadsheets. "Newspapers it is."

She picked up the top few. "*The Exeter Flying Post*? Or do you prefer the London papers?"

"Is there nothing from Derbyshire?"

"There is." She picked up *The Derby Mercury* and scanned

40

its contents. "What shall it be? Grain prices, or marriages and births?"

"If you must read about markets, pray, *not* the marriage market."

She began reading under the heading *Corn Exchange*:

"On the twenty-first of this month, our ports will again shut against the importation of foreign wheat, rye, and beans. On Wednesday, English wheat was one shilling cheaper per quarter, and rye and white pease a full two shillings lower. . . ."

She stopped and looked up. "Why Derbyshire, if I may ask?"

"You may not ask."

"You came here for the sea air, then, as we did?"

He made no reply.

"Shall I go on to the prices of sugar, hops, and leather?"

"No. I was merely gauging your reading skill. You are articulate, I grant you."

Rare pleasure warmed her. "Thank you. I have worked hard to become so." Harder than anyone knew.

"Although you might speak louder," he added. "At least if you insist on remaining way over there."

At that, she crossed the room and sat in an armchair closer to his bed. Nearer now, she glimpsed the scarred skin of his cheek and noticed how dark his hair was against the white pillows. She could not make out the color of his eye. Not brown, she did not think. Green or grey? It was also difficult to determine his age. Perhaps thirty?

She selected an article about the exiled Napoleon and read:

"The health of the Emperor has not been in any degree affected by the indignities and hardships he is made to suffer—nor are his spirits in the least diminished. The island has been visited by contagious fever, from which the town Major and several of the principal inhabitants suffered, but the Emperor remains hale."

Major Hutton frowned again. "Why am I not surprised? The old despot remains in good health while our men guarding him suffer and die."

She read a while longer, then rose to return the broadsheet to the pile. "That concludes our hour, sir."

He nodded curtly. "Remember to keep your guests off my property."

Ignoring that, she took her leave, thinking, *Old despot, indeed.*

They had decided to serve dinners to their guests only five nights a week to avoid overtaxing Mrs. Besley. Miss Stirling had pronounced the plan reasonable, as there were other dining options in town.

They had settled on six in the evening, a compromise between earlier meals in the country and fashionably later dinners in the city.

They had also decided that the sisters would take turns overseeing the serving and assisting Jessie as needed. Viola refused to wait at table, so she ate dinner with Mamma in her room. At least she would keep Mamma company and take care of bringing up trays for Mamma and herself, then carrying the dishes down when they were through. It was something, Sarah thought, although she realized the arrangement was not quite fair to the others.

Sarah was nervous about that first dinner with their guests, Mr. and Miss Henshall. The menu was relatively simple and served *à la française* like a family meal: broiled mackerel, rump-steak pie, and spinach, followed by a baked rice pudding.

She hoped it would meet their expectations, and perhaps even gain their praise.

The father-daughter pair were uncomfortably quiet during the meal. Mr. Henshall tried to engage the girl, Effie, in conversation a few times, but she remained silent and sullen throughout, and he soon gave up trying.

Sarah, helping Jessie refill a glass here or remove an empty platter there, felt self-conscious in her role. She had assumed the guests would prefer to sit alone, rather than having the family join them and be forced to make conversation with the hosts.

Instead there was no conversation at all between the two, which seemed more awkward yet. She told herself things would improve when they had more guests. Hopefully very soon.

A few hours later, after helping to clear the dining room and making sure all was in readiness for the next day's breakfast, Sarah went upstairs to retire for the night. On the way to her room, she heard Mr. Henshall softly playing his guitar. By the time she had prepared for bed, the music had stopped and all was silent.

Sarah fell asleep quickly, exhausted after all the work to prepare for their first guests and all the accompanying anxiety. She felt as though she could sleep for days.

Sadly, something awoke her early the next morning while it was still dark. It was bad enough having to get up earlier than usual to help with breakfast, but to be awoken before sunrise?

Sarah groaned and turned over but heard a door shutting somewhere in the distance. She remembered locking the outer doors before retiring, so it had to be someone leaving. Who would go out at such an hour? At least she hoped it was not someone sneaking inside.

With another groan, she tossed back the bedclothes and rose, crossing to the window.

The night had faded to the faintest grey of approaching dawn. A man in a top hat and greatcoat, collar up against the damp, strode from the house. He turned his head to look for approaching vehicles before crossing the lane, and she glimpsed his profile.

Mr. Henshall. What was he doing up and about at such an hour? Where was he going all alone?

Unease needled her at the thought of his leaving his daughter unattended. And she realized, although he could unlock the door from inside to let himself out, he could not lock it again without a key.

Sidmouth was relatively safe, and it was almost morning. Even so, she didn't like it.

Sarah sighed. So much for sleep. She resisted the lure of the warm bed and began dressing for another busy day.

4

My health is much improved by the sea; Not that I
drank it, or bathed in it, as the common people do:
no! I only walk'd by it, & look'd upon it. . . .

　　　　　—Thomas Gray, poet

Emily had decided Sidmouth was at its best in the mornings, before the crowds took over the beach and the library veranda. Leaving Sea View's lawn, she crossed the road and esplanade, then descended the natural rampart of pebbles to reach the beach.

Because the bay was shallow and Sidmouth had no harbour, large ships rarely came near, except for the flat-bottomed coasting barges that delivered coal and limestone.

Instead many small fishing and pleasure boats dotted the water, their sails picturesque against the deep blue sea. And to her right stood Chit Rock, a tall sea stack that served as a landmark for mariners on foggy days.

Emily loved to *look* at the water—the waves, the boats, the seabirds circling overhead—but the thought of wading into its depths sent shudders of fear through her. She diligently kept her distance from the surf.

At the western end of the beach stood a clutch of houses called Heffer's Row, perched on a rise overlooking the shore, as well as a few other cottages.

Though gaining notoriety as a seaside resort, at its heart Sidmouth was still a fishing village. Fishing was the mainstay of life and primary source of income for many families. Some twenty boats, or "drifters," with names like *Storm Petrel, Osprey,* and *Sprite,* operated from the beach. Many of the fishermen had colorful names too, like Ruder Pike, Banty Hook, and Toot Salter. Each family of fishermen had their own section of beach, and this ancient unwritten right was honored by everyone. The local fishermen had also formed their own cricket team.

Emily had met several of these hardworking people and was acquainted with one family in particular. The Cordey family kept their boats on the far reaches of the beach near their humble cobb-and-stone cottage below Heffer's Row.

Their patch of shingle was the nearest to Sea View, and the sisters often stopped to exchange friendly banter with affable Mr. Cordey, his young daughter, Bibi, and gregarious younger son, Punch.

Emily waved to the men now. "Good morning."

"Mornin', maid'n."

Mr. Cordey's older son, Tom, was quieter and serious. In his midtwenties, he had strong, capable hands, and broad shoulders stretched his wool jersey. Beneath his flat cap, his features were striking, and his eyes a crystalline blue. Her sisters teased her, saying they were all eating a frightful number of fish since they'd made the acquaintance of a dashing fisherman.

Georgiana, her light brown hair billowing around her cheerful round face, ran down to the beach to join her, followed by Chips. She greeted the men as they prepared to launch one of their boats.

"May I go with you?" Georgiana asked them.

"Georgie, the men have work to do," Emily admonished. "As do we. We had better leave them to it and return to our own chores."

Mr. Cordey scratched his temple and repositioned his cap.

"Knows I promised 'ee, maid'n, so why not? Just a short'un afore we head out?"

"Yes, please!"

Perspiration prickled along Emily's hairline. What would Sarah say were she here? Would it be safe? "You are terribly kind," she said tentatively. "But won't it be too much trouble?"

"No trouble a'tall. Not fer me best customers!"

Punch waggled his eyebrows at her. "Will you come too, Miss Emily?"

"No. I . . . don't like the water."

"What's not to like? There's nort better!"

Emily swallowed and admitted, "I don't know how to swim."

"Nor us! But we like the water 'cause it's full o'fish." He gave her a saucy wink.

"Well . . . that is good. For you. I shall . . . follow along on the beach and meet Georgie at the other end—say, in front of the York Hotel?"

Mr. Cordey nodded. "We'll take good care of 'er."

Emily walked slowly along the esplanade—a broad promenade railed and rolled smooth, and nearly a third of a mile long. A crenellated wall bordered its western section—the remains of a small fort, abandoned years before. Behind it was Fort Field, its former training ground. She then passed the library, watching the boat's progress all the while.

As her gaze landed on the bathing machines on the beach, Emily shivered. She would not be venturing into the sea, even in one of those colorful wagons. No. She would remain safe on shore.

A short while later, after Emily collected Georgiana, the two sisters walked back together, Georgie chirping happily about her experience on the water as they went. When they reached Sea View, she continued around the house to the kitchen steps to find a treat for Chips. Emily, meanwhile, quietly let herself in through the veranda door, hoping to avoid Sarah, who would no doubt put her to work. As she tiptoed upstairs, she removed her bonnet and pulled off her gloves. Reaching the refuge of her room moments later, she felt all the relief of a debutante successfully avoiding an odious dance partner.

She opened the door and jerked to a halt, clapping a hand to her mouth to stifle a cry.

A man stood inside, dressed only in pantaloons, arms raised in the act of pulling a white shirt over his head.

She glimpsed leanly muscled arms and masculine physique— lightly haired barrel chest and flat stomach.

Her throat went dry. She lowered her hand and said in a raspy voice, "W-what are you doing?"

The man startled, whirling toward the sound of her voice, his head still cocooned in the shirt.

"Dressing, I believe it is called." He yanked the shirt down, and his head emerged like a mole from its burrow, his arms still trapped within.

His caramel brown hair was tousled in disarray, and his narrow eyes widened as they settled on her.

"Ah, there you are, Emily," Sarah called from behind in a faux-cheerful voice. "You've mistaken your room." Her sister clamped vise-like hands on her shoulders and turned her around. "Pray, forgive us, Mr. Stanley."

Sarah released her hold only long enough to shut the door before firmly leading her away.

"What is th-that man doing in my room?" Emily sputtered.

"It is his room now."

"I have not even moved my things out yet!"

"Though I have asked you repeatedly to do so."

"You might have warned me."

"Mr. Stanley arrived while you were out, expecting a room with a good view. Apparently, he wrote to reserve these dates, yet there was nothing in the guest register, nor could I find his letter."

"Why is that my fault?"

"You are the one who snaps up the post as soon as it arrives."

Emily opened her mouth to argue, then closed it. The name Stanley rang a vague bell in her memory, and her stomach sank. She *had* written back to confirm his stay but had completely forgotten to add it to the register. And she had no idea where his letter had ended up.

"You are right. I forgot to write it down."

"Never mind that now. He was graciousness itself in waiting for us to prepare a room for him, so please don't protest, or at least not so loudly."

"Why not give him your room?"

"Because mine is small and at the back of the house. It's also right under Georgie's, and you know she stomps around like a battalion with a battering ram."

"But my room has an excellent view of the sea."

"Precisely. Just as you described it in your advertisements."

Defensiveness rose. "Oh, so I brought this upon myself. Is that it?"

"Come, my dear. Let us not quarrel again. I am so weary of it."

"What has Mamma to say about you giving my room to a strange man?"

Sarah's bright blue eyes locked on hers, and rare irritation flashed. "Tell me you are not going to run to Mamma with our petty squabbles, which will only strain her nerves."

It was very like something Emily would accuse Viola of doing. The chastisement stung.

Sarah added, "I have moved your belongings into my room. However, if you would prefer an attic room with Georgie . . ."

"Did you gather all my clothes and things?"

"Not everything. I could not make the man wait all day. I packed all I could into your trunk, and Lowen helped me move it."

"My books?"

Sarah huffed. "It would take hours to move all your books! You can live without them for a month."

"Is that how long he plans to be here?"

"Perhaps longer, assuming you don't scare him off sooner. Please don't scowl so. I know you pride yourself on your looks, and that scowl is not flattering."

A month without her books? Thankfully, there were plenty more in the library downstairs. Better yet, this would give her an excuse to visit Wallis's library more often.

Emily asked, "What do we know about this Mr. Stanley?"

"Next to nothing. Although he seems a gentleman."

In her mind's eye, Emily again saw the man's bare chest, and the warm way he had looked at her. He was certainly not one of the elderly invalids they had expected. She felt her irritation fade. While she still hoped Charles would renew his addresses to her, in the meantime, perhaps this guest house business would prove more pleasant than she'd thought.

That night, Emily sat up late reading in the Sea View library by the light of a lamp with a glass shade.

"Miss Summers?"

Emily slowly looked up and saw Mr. Stanley in the threshold. She said, "You had better call me Miss Emily, for there are several Miss Summerses in residence."

"Miss Emily," he said, hands hidden behind his back, his face puckered in apology. "I gather I have been given your room?"

"Oh." She waved away his concern. "Only my former room."

"I do apologize if my presence here is inconvenient."

"Not at all, Mr. Stanley. You are very welcome and have nothing to apologize for." She set aside her book and stood. "It is simply a new situation for us, opening the house to guests. I do hope my—*your*—room is comfortable?"

"Yes. And filled with books, which is just as I like."

Her interest rose. "You are welcome to borrow any that interest you."

"Thank you. Um . . . there is one book I thought you might wish to have returned to you." From behind his back he pulled forth a leather-bound journal.

She recognized it with a jolt.

Her diary.

He ducked his head, embarrassment creasing his features. Her own face heated in response.

"I am afraid I opened the cover—not realizing what it was. And, um, this fell out." He held out the journal and a folded handkerchief, the skillfully embroidered monogram quite visible: *cPs*. Charles's initials.

She thought of all those pages of scrawled entries, detailing her girlish preoccupations, frustrations, romantic fancies, and subsequent heartache.

Stricken, she breathed, "Did you read it?"

He shifted foot to foot. "To be completely truthful, I did read the first page. As soon as I realized it was a personal diary—your diary—I closed it. Upon my honor, that is all I read."

What in the world had she written on the first page? She hoped nothing too mortifying.

"Thank you for explaining, Mr. Stanley. And for returning it to me."

He bowed, swiveled on his heel, and left.

Sitting down once more, Emily pulled the lamp closer. She opened the diary to the first page of writing and read with beating heart.

I will love Charles Parker until the day I die! He found me, crying, after Viola was taken away to meet with yet another surgeon. Charles sat beside me to comfort me and gave me his handkerchief. It smells of bergamot. Of him! I have not yet returned it and never shall. At least, not until we are married! And I will marry him one day, if it is the last thing I do. . . .

Emily's face heated anew. How young she sounded in these few lines. How immature. Had Mr. Stanley looked at the date and realized she had been but a girl of seventeen when she wrote this? Or did he think she was still so . . . so . . . what? Still so desperately in love with Charles Parker? Still determined to marry him at any cost? How forward and desperate he must think her!

Another uncomfortable thought niggled at her. Was there still a lingering kernel of truth to the words, these several years later? If there was, Mr. Stanley needn't know it. Especially now that any future with Charles seemed out of reach.

She rose and started toward the door, glancing at the mantel clock as she did so. It was after ten. She stopped where she was. It was too late for her to knock on his door. Then again, was it appropriate for her to go to a man's bedchamber at any time—her former room or not? Not in their old life, but perhaps now that Sea View was a guest house? Under what pretext could she go to his room? She should wait until morning. Make a point to catch him on his way to breakfast or before he left the house. Emily paced across the library, mind spinning, pulse pounding. No. She would not sleep a wink if she did not talk to him first.

The night air was growing cool, so she retrieved her shawl from the back of the chair, wrapped it around her shoulders, and started up the stairs. She didn't know if Sarah had already gone to bed or not. Emily hoped she would not catch her at Mr. Stanley's door again.

Reaching the landing, she walked swiftly and quietly down the passage. Knowing the way by heart, the darkness posed little hindrance. She reached the door and was relieved to see a sliver of light beneath it. Good. He had not yet gone to sleep.

She knocked softly.

"Yes?" came his low voice.

She did not want to call a reply that might be overheard, so she simply waited.

He tentatively inched open the door, brows rising when he saw who it was. "Miss Emily, I . . . Did you need something?"

He stood there in trousers and white shirt, open at the neck. She had never seen a man in his shirtsleeves before Mr. Stanley's arrival, and now she had seen him twice in partial dress. His hair was rumpled, as were the bedclothes behind him, where a book lay open on the counterpane.

"Forgive the intrusion," she whispered. "I could not sleep until I told you. What you read . . . I wrote that years ago, when I was fresh from the schoolroom. I did not want you to think that I . . . that I am, well, desperate or lovelorn, or some such."

"Are you not?"

"No!"

One corner of his mouth quirked. "I am relieved to hear it. And the handkerchief?"

Fiddle. "I simply never returned it."

"I see. Well. Thank you for telling me." His gaze lingered on her—her eyes, her cheeks, her mouth.

She swallowed. "G-good night, Mr. Stanley."

"Good night, Miss Emily. Sleep well."

Emily doubted she would. Her encounter with Mr. Stanley had not settled her after all. In fact, quite the opposite.

⌒⌒⌒

Early the next morning, Sarah again heard Mr. Henshall leaving the house. Emily, her hair in paper curls, slept on, undisturbed.

Pulling a dressing gown around herself and slipping on shoes, Sarah hurried downstairs and followed Mr. Henshall outside. Which way had he gone? Toward the water or toward town?

The sound of jingling tack caused her to step back. A dairy farmer delivering cans of milk to Westmount or Woolbrook.

He tipped his hat to her. "Mornin'."

"Good morning," she called back. Self-conscious about her attire, Sarah pulled the lapels closer together and added brightly, "Just out for a morning stroll."

Giving up the idea of trying to follow anyone dressed as she was, Sarah returned to her room and began to wash, wondering all the while what Callum Henshall was up to.

Once fully dressed in a printed cotton dress and fichu, Sarah went back downstairs to talk to her mother, planning to ask for advice. Would she be awake yet? Mamma had been sleeping so much more of late, and Sarah was growing increasingly concerned. They had all hoped the move to Sidmouth would be good for Mamma, but so far there seemed little evidence of improvement.

Reaching Mamma's door, Sarah knocked softly. No answer. She must still be asleep. Sarah remembered when she used to be an early riser.

She knocked more loudly, and when there was no response, put her mouth near the wood and called, "Mamma?"

Nothing.

Her concern heightened.

"Mamma?" She knocked again, quite forcefully.

Still no response.

She would have thought her loud knocking would summon Viola from the dressing room, but neither answered.

Please, God, let Mamma be all right. They could not lose their mother too.

She tried the door and found it latched from within. Something Mamma had not done before they began housing strangers.

Although Miss Stirling's friend Mr. Farrant had installed keyed locks for the guest rooms, they had not gone to the same expense for the family rooms, nor the internal connecting doors. These still held only traditional latches.

Sarah knelt to study the door. She pulled it open as far as the catch would allow, until she saw a thin crack of light from within and the metal latch across the space.

Yanking a pin from her hair, she slid it into the crack and, after some fiddling, lifted the inner latch.

"Mamma, I am coming in."

Steeling herself, she opened the door. Light from the unshuttered windows illuminated the room, yet their mother lay unnaturally still. Sarah hurried to the bed, dreading what she might find. She put her hand to her mother's slack mouth, and with relief felt a faint breath, and saw a slight rise and fall of her nightdress-clad chest. Sarah sat on the edge of the narrow bed and even at that rocking movement, her mother did not stir. She picked up her hand, thankfully warm, and felt for her pulse. Slow and steady.

The dressing room door opened, and Viola shuffled into the room, yawning.

Sarah asked, "Did you not hear me calling and knocking?"

Viola stared blankly, then pulled something from each ear. Cotton wool. "I've taken to plugging my ears at night. Mamma has been snoring so loudly, I can hear her through the wall."

"Really? I don't recall her doing that before."

Viola shrugged. "Me either. But I never slept in the next room before. I think it is due to her sleeping draught." Viola nodded to the side table. Sarah looked and saw a bottle and a glass of water beside it.

"Mamma?" Sarah gently shook her mother's shoulder. No response. "Viola, please wet a face cloth and bring it here."

Viola hurried to the wash basin and quickly returned with a damp cloth.

Sarah dabbed it to her mother's cheeks and neck. "Mamma? Time to wake up!"

In an aside to Viola, she said, "How much of that did she take?" Again Viola shrugged.

"Hmm?" Mamma mumbled and slowly opened bleary eyes. "Sarah? What is it? What's wrong?"

"We could not wake you, Mamma. You gave us a fright. How much of that sleeping draught did you take?"

"I don't know."

Sarah lifted the bottle and studied it. "What is in this?" She removed the stopper and sniffed, wrinkling her nose. "Laudanum, if I had to guess. With a high percentage of alcohol and who knows what else. No wonder she has been so groggy."

"Old Dr. Porter prescribed it before we left May Hill, to help her sleep," Viola said.

Together they helped their mother sit up, and after they bathed her face again in the cool water, she seemed to revive.

"Are you sure you need this, Mamma? Something so strong?"

"She might do," Viola said, "with guests clomping around all hours. We all might need some to get any sleep."

"That is not helpful, Viola."

Sarah took her mother's hand. "How about I talk to one of the apothecaries here in Sidmouth about something milder to help you sleep? Or perhaps we ought to ask a local doctor to call and make sure nothing else is wrong?"

Mamma shook her head. "I don't want to be a bother . . . or add to our expenses."

"Your health is far more important. Don't even mention it."

"Very well. I don't wish to worry anyone."

"Too late, Mamma! I was terribly worried when you did not respond to my repeated pounding and calling. In fact, I feared the worst."

"I am sorry, my dear. What a burden I am to you."

"Not at all, Mamma. We love you. And we want you to be well cared for. But please leave off with the sleeping draught."

5

A Lady of a very good Family and Fortune, had frequently been
attacked with a Colic Complaint. She had had the advice of
the best physicians in London, and had often gone to Bath in
the Spring, and drank the Tunbridge Waters in the Autumn.

—Dr. Richard Russell, *A Dissertation Concerning the
Use of Sea Water in Diseases of the Glands*

L ater that morning, Sarah walked into eastern Sidmouth to
visit Fran Stirling. Reaching the marketplace, she knocked
at the door of Broadbridge's Boarding House. Soon she was
warmly welcomed and shown into a cozy parlour that smelled of
furniture polish and freshly laundered linens. Miss Stirling wore
a frilly bib apron, which she quickly removed upon receiving her
and hung behind the door. Apparently even the owner of a well-
established guest house had to do domestic chores from time to
time.

Miss Stirling insisted on serving tea, and when they were both
settled, Sarah asked if she knew of a doctor she might recommend.

Miss Stirling beamed. "I know the very person."

She told Sarah that Sidmouth boasted one physician, Dr. James
Clarke, as well as several surgeons and apothecaries who seemed

to flock to the area to serve the medical needs of the many visiting invalids.

They talked for a few minutes longer until Mr. Farrant stopped by to see if the banister he'd tightened was holding up well.

"Oh yes, perfectly sturdy," she assured him.

It seemed like a flimsy excuse to call, yet based on the gleam in Miss Stirling's eyes, the man's visit was welcome. Sarah knew it was time to take her leave.

After departing Broadbridge's, she stopped by the office of Dr. Clarke and requested he call on Mrs. Summers at Sea View.

He came later that afternoon, and Mamma asked Sarah to stay while the doctor examined her. Sarah sat across the room, twisting her fingers as the older man listened to Mamma's heart and lungs through a tube, felt her pulse, looked into her eyes, and asked a series of questions.

When he was finished, Mamma asked, "Well, Dr. Clarke?"

"You are weak, as you know. You said your previous doctor diagnosed colic, but I also detect glandular issues of a pulmonary nature. No wonder you rarely feel strong enough to venture from bed nor to partake of life's pleasures."

Sarah spoke up. "She is always stoic, though—are you not, Mamma? Even cheerful."

"Thank you, my dear. I do try."

The doctor remained sober. "That shows great strength of character, ma'am, if not of body."

"Well, what do you recommend?" Sarah asked. "Is there no treatment, no medicine that might help her?"

"Indeed there is. Inhaling the salubrious sea breezes frequently suspends the ravages of disease. Also, the use of sea water might be of great service in preventing bilious colics and the most dangerous distempers, and in preserving the lungs. . . ."

Sarah listened closely yet barely understood half of what the man said.

Mamma interjected, "I have been sitting outside in the walled garden, taking the air. Though I am protected there from the worst of the wind."

He nodded. "That is a start. But I believe it is the combination of sea air and sea-bathing that produces the best effect for every disorder of the stomach, lungs, and blood."

Mamma's face fell. "I . . . see."

"You sound skeptical. Are you perhaps acquainted with Mr. Butcher, a dissenting minister here in Sidmouth?"

"I have heard of him."

"He quit London on account of indisposition many years ago, and he never ceases to express how much benefit he has received from residing in Devonshire."

Sarah said, "Yes, we have heard. Or perhaps I should say, have read in his books."

Mamma objected, "Plunging into cold, rough sea water is the last thing I want to do."

"But Mamma, Dr. Clarke says . . ."

She raised her hand. "I will try the medical brine baths first. See if that has any effect before I subject myself to something so drastic."

Dr. Clarke considered. "In that case, let me caution you not to eat or drink either immediately before or after bathing, so the fibers might have no immediate supply to distend them."

"I think there is little risk of that," Sarah said. "Mamma has sadly little appetite at any time."

"Do you truly think it will help?" her mother asked.

"I do." He solemnly nodded. "Beyond doubt, salts found in sea water own a great share in the cures done by medicinal baths. The method might prevent, or even cure, internal glandular complaints."

"Well then," Sarah said, feeling a welcome trickle of hope. "It certainly seems worth a try. Thank you, Doctor."

Leaving Mamma to rest, Sarah walked Dr. Clarke out, then started toward the library they used as an office. Through the drawing room door, she saw Mr. Henshall staring up at the wall.

She walked closer. "Good day, Mr. Henshall. Looking for something?"

"Hm? Oh, just . . . admiring this landscape."

Sarah glanced dubiously at the dark painting. It had come with the house and was not one of her favorites. Ah well. There was no accounting for taste.

"Everything satisfactory with the accommodations so far?" she asked. "Have all you need?"

"Oh, aye."

"And are you enjoying your stay?"

"It's . . . fine. Effie is a bit bored, I'm afraid. I hope ye are not offended."

"Not at all." Sarah thought, then said, "My sister Georgiana is only a year or so older, and when she has time, she loves to go bathing and walking and berry picking and kite flying—all kinds of sport . . . anything out-of-doors, really. If you would allow it, I am sure Georgiana would be happy to include Effie in some of her outings."

"I won't have her going into the water. Understand? Not without me. It wouldna be safe."

Sarah reared her head back at his vehemence. Perhaps he disliked the sea as much as Emily did.

He grimaced. "Sorry. It's just . . . I would worry the whole time."

"I understand."

"But the rest, aye, if your sister wouldna mind."

"I shall ask her. What have you seen of the area so far?"

"Oh, the grounds here, the beach, some of the town. Sadly, Effie is not terribly keen. Prefers to stay in her room with her fashion plates."

"Oh dear. You've come too far to see no more than that."

"So I tell her."

"Have you been to Sidmouth before?"

"Um . . . aye. Though it's years ago now."

Sarah tentatively asked, "And your . . . wife . . . was with you then?"

He nodded. "But I would rather not talk about it."

Sarah blinked in surprise.

Again he grimaced. "Well, if ye'll excuse me, I had better look in on Effie." He turned and strode away.

Sarah watched him go, feeling more bewildered than offended. She guessed his rudeness stemmed from an unhappy past. He was a widower after all, and probably still grieving his lost love. And if so, she could not blame him.

When Viola arrived at Westmount to read to Major Hutton again, two men were arguing outside. The one wearing a stained apron she presumed was the cook. She had no idea who the tattooed man in coarse clothing might be.

The young cook frowned down at the basket the other man held. "Is that the best you could do?"

"It's all they had at the market."

"Leeks and spinach? Never made soup with them before." He held up an aubergine. "And what do I do with this?"

"I dunno. They were out of pease."

"Hang me, it'll be weak soup tonight, mate."

Noticing her approach, the tattooed man greeted her. "Here for the major, miss?"

"Yes. And you are . . . ?"

"Taggart, first and only footman. And this is Chown. He cooks—tries to, at any rate."

Taggart opened the door for her and led her inside to the major's room—probably a study before the addition of the couch-bed that had converted it to sickroom and bedchamber.

In the dim light, the major glanced up and frowned. "You again."

Viola ignored the slight. To protect herself from the man's arrows, she donned her usual armor of indifference. "Good to see you too." Walking to the desk, she observed, "Your staff here are . . . unusual."

"Are they?"

She nodded. "Your cook is a man, not French, nor very experienced, as far as I can tell."

"Why not? He worked in our mess. He sorts the rest as he goes."

"And your footman?"

"Unemployed, as many former soldiers are, unfortunately. He needed a job and I had one to offer."

"I admire your compassion—don't mistake me—but anyone less like a footman, I cannot imagine."

"Why, because he refuses to powder his hair like a fop?"

"Or even to wash it. Or comb it. Or shave. Or press his clothes . . ."

"Is your delicacy so easily offended?"

"Not at all. Though I wonder what your . . . less enlightened guests might think."

He snorted. "I have no guests."

"Little surprise there."

When he said nothing more, she asked, "What shall I read today? The newspapers again?"

When he remained sullenly quiet, she picked up another broadsheet and began reading.

"Sidmouth. This pleasing and fashionable watering-place is now in full beauty, and is every day receiving fresh accessions of visitants, among whom are: Sir John and Lady Kennaway, the Honorable Mr. Bourke, the Rev. J. Trollope, and Colonel Fitzgerald. Our first ball for the season takes place on Wednesday next, at the London Inn."

When she paused for breath, he asked, "Will you attend this ball?"

"No. Shall you?"

"Of course not."

She glanced at his form beneath the loose-fitting, full-length banyan and wondered if something was wrong with his legs. Had they been injured too? She decided not to pry.

"What next?" she asked. "An advertisement for bilious pills? Vegetable tooth-powder, or acidulated essence of anchovies?"

"No, thank you. That is more than enough for today."

"I am supposed to remain an hour."

"Thunder and turf." He wrinkled his long, thin nose. "The correspondence, then."

She stepped to the basket, picked up a letter postmarked *Derby*, and broke the seal. In the dim light, she read:

> *"Dear Major Hutton,*
> *My mother gave us permission to correspond, so I wonder why you have not replied to my letters—"*

"Not that one," he snapped.

She flinched at his grating tone and could not help glancing at the signature: *Miss Lucinda Truman.*

Viola picked up another, its ornate hand more difficult to decipher. She carried it toward the window, to a crack of light between the shutters, and even lifted her veil, although she kept her face averted.

> *"To Major John Hutton,*
> *The honor of your presence is requested—"*

"Not that one either." He raised a frustrated hand. "Look, you might as well pass by any invitations. I am not in a sociable state of mind . . . or body."

She picked up the next. "Another from Miss Truman?"

"No. Set it aside."

She sighed. "You are not making this easy."

"I don't intend to."

"Then, apparently, we are moving back to the safe haven of grain prices."

She read on until she had nearly put them both to sleep. Just as she was about to announce her departure, a dark-complexioned man in gentleman's attire knocked once and entered. His friend Armaan, she guessed.

"Ah, good day. You must be Miss Summers."

"I am."

He bowed, his black wavy hair falling over his brow as he did so. "Armaan Sagar, at your service."

The major scowled. "I thought you swore to protect me. Why did you allow this woman back in?"

"Taggart did, but I would not have prevented her. I agree with your father—the lady is a godsend."

A godsend? Her? Viola could not credit it.

Mr. Sagar gestured with graceful hands. "Please, do not allow me to intrude. Go on with your reading."

The major groaned. "I am numb from listening to her drone on about the markets."

Viola rose. "Our time is up, anyway."

Armaan glanced from her to the major and back again. "Then I shall escort you out."

As they walked to the front door, an awkward silence loomed between them.

To fill it, she said, "Major Hutton told me he has you to thank for saving his life."

"To thank, or to blame?"

She stumbled midstride. "Excuse me?"

"Never mind." He waved a dismissive hand and opened the door for her.

"You pulled him from a burning building, I understand."

He chuckled dryly. "How like him to tell only that part of the story."

64

"There is more?"

"Oh yes. He was only in that place to rescue me." Pausing under the porte cochère, he looked at her, perhaps to make sure she was truly interested.

"Please go on," she urged.

"It was not a . . . how do you say, official battle. Some men I had known in my youth resented that I served with the British. They ambushed me and dragged me into a munitions shed. They tied my hands and began to beat me. Intended to kill me."

He slowly shook his head, eyes distant in memory. "There were four of them. Too many to fight. The major, he started a fire just outside the door as a diversion, contained in a metal drum. The smoke filled the shed and scared most of them off. But one man— Raj—pulled out a piece of burning rubbish and tossed it into a barrel of gunpowder.

"Before Raj fled, he saw the major cut me loose and shot through the smoke, aiming for me and striking the major instead. Then came a great explosion. Fire everywhere. So yes, I dragged him out of there. Shot and burned but alive. Yet he only entered that building to save me. He does not tell that part."

Armaan stared off toward the horizon, where the afternoon sun shone over Peak Hill, gilding it in a golden gleam. "Sometimes I think he wishes I had left him to die."

She said nothing. Simply watched the man's profile, and the emotions crossing his dark, handsome face. In the outdoor light, she realized he was older than the major, perhaps by a few years.

He glanced at her, smiled thinly, then finished his tale. "I received permission to accompany him back to England. To see he gets the care he needs from the English doctors he is used to. We came here because they say the sea air is good for the lungs. I hope so. I feel to blame for his wounds. He says no. He would be dead if not for me. I don't know."

"I am sure he is grateful, even if he does not show it."

Armaan nodded. "He keeps his heart hidden, that one. Yet he is a friend to me, in the place of those who turned against me. I am grateful and don't hesitate to, as you say, show it."

Viola considered pressing for more details about the major's prognosis and decided against it. She was also tempted to ask him who Miss Truman was but held her tongue.

On Monday, Emily hired a sedan chair, a single seat enclosed in a small box carried on two poles. Two strapping young men served as porters. They carried Mamma east along the esplanade, past Fort Field and the library to Mr. Hodges's Medical Baths, near the middle of the beach.

Emily and Georgiana walked alongside. They had agreed to accompany Mamma since Viola and Sarah were busy. Although afraid of the sea, Emily thought she could manage the indoor baths, where the water, she had been assured, did not go over one's head.

Several sedan chairs and donkeys fitted with invalid saddles were there before them, because many people frequented the brine baths—the infirm and the hale alike.

One advantage over a saddled donkey or carriage was that the sedan chair and its bearers could continue right into the establishment, limiting how far the invalid had to walk or be carried.

Inside, the two porters set the chair down and opened its door, one young man reaching in and helping their mother rise and emerge from the small enclosure. Thankfully, Eugenia Summers could still walk short distances on her own.

Meanwhile Emily paid their fees to one of the attendants, who led them into the ladies' dressing room. There, they changed into the supplied brown linen petticoats and jackets with tie waists. Emily noticed that while all the women were clad in the same nondescript clothing, each kept on her own turban or hat, often ornate millinery confections with feathers or artificial fruit and flowers.

When they were ready, the attendant opened a door for them, which opened right onto the sunken bath. Emily and Georgiana each took one of Mamma's arms, and together they descended several steps into the giant communal cistern. All around the perimeter, people sat with heated water up to their necks—women and men both. This surprised Emily, especially when the sexes bathed separately at the beach.

The men wore similar brown linen suits. They sat side by side in a warm, salty mist, several still wearing their hats.

Lightweight bowls of wood and copper floated on the water, carrying scented oils and sweet-smelling pomanders, bobbing perilously each time a bather stirred the surface.

Glancing around at all the perspiring people in their billowing costumes, Emily was reminded of bloated brown mushrooms simmering in a pan.

Among the unfamiliar faces, one came into focus. An older gentleman wearing a tall beaver hat, who nodded in Georgiana's direction.

"Who is that?" Emily whispered.

"Mr. Hutton. He is the man who answered your advertisement and engaged Viola to read to his son."

"Ah. I wondered why he was looking at us."

"Shall I introduce you?"

Their mother spoke up. "I hardly think this is the time or place for introductions."

Emily silently agreed, trying her best to stay calm and keep her chin out of the water.

Georgiana waved to Mr. Hutton but did not approach. It seemed a strange setting for social intercourse, although several women were doing just that, chatting away like chickens in a stew pot.

Then Emily noticed Mr. Stanley across the way. He sat there amid the other men, looking rather miserable and dabbing his sweaty face with a limp handkerchief before tucking it into the brim of his hat. Seeing her, his expression instantly brightened, and he bowed his head in salute. His hat tipped forward and he narrowly snatched it back before it toppled into the water. Emily smiled to ease his embarrassment, and he sent her a sheepish grin in return.

After soaking for the prescribed span, Emily and Georgiana helped Mamma from the bath. They were met by an attendant proffering glasses of warm sea water. Mamma dutifully drank hers. Emily, however, set hers down after one bitter sip.

"Well, Mamma. How do you feel?" she asked.

"Like spent tea leaves after steeping too long."

Emily chuckled, recognizing where she had gotten her way with words.

New guests arrived at Sea View later that afternoon, and Sarah and Emily greeted them in the hall. Sarah was glad to have a married couple staying with them after receiving a single man and a widower. She hoped, however, that a woman would not be more difficult to please. The couple, both dark-haired and well-dressed, were perhaps in their early to midthirties.

"Mr. and Mrs. Elton, you are very welcome."

"Thank you, Mrs. . . . ?"

"Miss Sarah Summers. And this is my sister Miss Emily. You will also meet Viola and Georgiana during your stay."

"I see. Am I the only married woman among us? Ah well." Mrs. Elton lifted her watch pin. "We are rather earlier than we thought. We made excellent time. Our coachman and horses are so extremely expeditious." She looked again at Sarah. "In your letter, you were kind enough to offer stabling here, but that will not be necessary. We have made arrangements with the livery."

"Very good."

Sarah observed the studied elegance of the woman's dress, and her gracious smiles. An affluent couple with a large acquaintance could be good for business.

The newcomers glanced around the hall.

"A very fine house indeed," Mrs. Elton said. "I am extremely pleased with it. You may believe me. I never compliment."

Her husband continued his perusal, saying nothing.

Mrs. Elton walked into the nearby drawing room. "Very like Maple Grove indeed. I am quite struck by the likeness! The drawing room is the very shape and size of the one in my childhood home." She turned to her spouse. "Mr. Elton, is not it astonishingly like? And the staircase . . . You know, as I came in, I observed how alike the staircase was, placed exactly in the same part of the house. I assure you, Miss Summers, it is delightful to be reminded of a place I am so extremely partial to." She sighed. "Whenever you are transplanted, like me, you will understand how very delightful it is to meet with anything like what one has left behind. I always say that leaving one's former home is quite one of the evils of matrimony."

Sarah had some idea what it felt like to be transplanted, but she murmured only a slight sympathetic reply. It must have been sufficient, for Mrs. Elton kept talking.

"My brother and sister will be enchanted with this place. They have promised to visit us. They will have their barouche-landau, of course, which holds four perfectly; and therefore, we should be able to explore the sights extremely well."

She stepped to the large window overlooking the sea. "What an ideal situation. And the view! So much more commodious than staying in a public hotel. I shall write to all my friends back home and tell them they simply must come to Sidmouth and, when they do, they must stay at Sea View."

Hopeful excitement filled Sarah. This was just what they needed. Surely soon now, they would be busy indeed, and their income might meet or even surpass expenses.

After registering the couple, Sarah asked Emily to retrieve the key to the Willow room.

Emily's pretty face furrowed. "Which is that again?"

Sarah selected the key herself and escorted the couple upstairs. Emily followed behind, carrying the woman's bandboxes, although she might have left the baggage for Lowen to handle. She was probably as curious about the Eltons as Sarah was.

Sarah led them to a room at the southwest corner, which had a view of the sea from a modest-sized south window and a view of Peak Hill from the two west-facing windows.

"Lovely . . ." Mrs. Elton breathed, surveying the space, but there was a question in her voice. She walked to the south window.

"You know, we had hoped for an unimpeded view of the sea."

"Oh. Well, you can see the sea from this window. And from these two, you have a fine view of Peak Hill and Mr. Lousada's grand Peak House."

"Yes, yes. Very pleasant."

She did not sound convinced. Lingering in the doorway, Emily rolled her eyes.

"I like it, my dear," her husband said helpfully.

She ignored him.

"I am afraid our other sea-view rooms are occupied at present," Sarah said. "If one becomes available, I could let you know, if you would like."

"Please do."

Sarah nodded and swallowed an awkward lump. She did not like talking about money. "I should mention that those rooms are a bit more expensive. It is standard practice, I understand."

Mrs. Elton turned a knowing smile her way. "But for us, surely, my dear Miss Summers, you might make an exception? After all, one expects a house called Sea View to offer excellent views from every room."

Noticing Emily frown, then open her mouth to speak, Sarah hurried to reply in a friendly manner, "Well, thankfully, all of our guests can enjoy unimpeded views from the drawing room and veranda."

Emily crossed her arms and added tartly, "No extra charge."

While Sarah was all patient forbearance, for Emily, a quarter of an hour quite convinced her that Mrs. Elton was a vain woman, extremely well satisfied with her own importance and overly familiar in her manners.

Emily decided she needed to cleanse the woman from her mind with a walk in the fresh air. Grabbing a cape from its peg, she let herself out the veranda door and hurried down the lawn before Sarah might call her back to some odious chore. Reaching the esplanade, she tilted her face up to the sunshine and breathed deeply of the damp sea spray, letting the clean air wash over her. *Ahh. Much better.*

"Afternoon, miss."

She looked over and spied Tom Cordey sitting on a stool outside their cottage near the end of Heffer's Row. Her mood improved all the more.

She walked closer and saw that he was carving something in his strong, skilled hands. "Good day, Tom. What are you making?"

"Just a little somethin' for Bibi. It's her birthday next week."

"That's kind of you. May I see?"

He opened his hand. In his palm lay a little wooden dog, quite similar to Chips.

"How charming."

He shrugged broad shoulders. "Pa won't let 'er keep a dog, so this is the best I can do."

"Very thoughtful. You make me wish I had an older brother. Any brother, really."

He smiled shyly up at her.

An idea struck. "I don't suppose you would do a little carving for us? Sarah has taken it into her head to name all of our guest rooms after trees, and I can't keep them straight. I suppose she is right, and we can't keep calling them 'Emily's old room' or 'the room where Papa slept.' We'd pay you of course."

He squinted in thought. "Small wooden placards, you mean?"

"Yes, carved with the room names, so we could hang them on each door."

"I could do, yes. Though I'm better at fishin' and carvin' than spellin'."

"I will bring you a list. How's that?"

He nodded his assent. "Though 'twill have to wait till I'm through wi' this, and I can only carve when we're not fishin.' Or the weather keeps us home."

"I understand. No great rush."

"Very well."

"Thank you, Tom. I feel more cheerful already, talking to you." Another shy smile.

Noticing her, Bibi came out to greet her, and Tom slipped the carved toy into his pocket.

Emily talked with the pair a few minutes longer. As she witnessed the warm, teasing fondness between brother and sister, an ache throbbed in her breast. She'd never had a brother, but her oldest sister used to tease her like that. So had Charles. At the thought, her mood lowered once again.

She missed Claire almost as much as she missed Charles. Emily had always looked up to her, and Claire's sudden departure last May had been a blow. She had not even had a chance to say goodbye.

Emily thought back. She had spent a fortnight with a school friend who'd invited her to Cheltenham. When she returned to Finderlay, she'd been stunned to learn that Claire had moved to Scotland. Mamma said Papa's ancient Aunt Mercer was ailing and needed a companion straightaway. Dutiful Claire had gone.

Emily had asked for their direction, but her mother had put her off, saying Claire would still be growing accustomed to her new responsibilities, and fastidious Aunt Mercer would not want her companion to be distracted.

And then, with Papa's declining health and subsequent death, they soon had more pressing matters to worry about.

Emily sighed. How much had changed in the last year. And none of it for the better.

6

To be blind is not miserable;
not to be able to bear blindness,
that is miserable.

—John Milton

The next morning, Sarah arose early and quietly dressed herself in wraparound stays and front-fastening frock before pulling on wool stockings, shoes, and mantle. Still in their shared bed, Emily slept peacefully. Her face in repose, framed in paper curls, looked young and sweet.

As she tiptoed from the room, Sarah reasoned she was duty-bound to make sure Mr. Henshall was not involved in anything clandestine or illegal. But if she were honest with herself, simple curiosity had prodded her awake and into her clothes before the sun had risen.

Tiptoeing down the back stairs to the basement, she walked quietly past the kitchen, where a yawning Jessie was already lighting the stove. She climbed the outside stairs and crept along the house. Peeking around the corner, she waited until Mr. Henshall emerged from the main entrance.

When he did, she followed him at a distance. The cold sea water and warming spring air formed a dense fog—a covering she was glad for, though she feared she might lose sight of her quarry in the smoke-like swirl.

She crossed Glen Lane and started across Fort Field, now and then catching a glimpse of him in the distance, his fair hair visible beneath his black hat and his dark greatcoat flapping behind him like a cape.

Following the sound of his footfalls as they moved from spongy grass to gravel, she turned up the footpath, a back way into the eastern town.

After passing a few houses, he slipped through an opening in a stone wall and disappeared, his footfalls again muffled by grass or perhaps wet leaves.

The parish churchyard.

She didn't know what she had expected. Going for an early morning swim? Trading secrets with a French industrial spy? Meeting a woman at a nearby hotel?

But the church? No, that had never crossed her mind. She wondered if its doors were even open this early.

She slowly tipped her head through the gate, just enough to see inside the churchyard.

The fog was lighter here, and she could see the path leading up to the church's arched porch door, but both the path and porch were empty.

She looked to one side, then the other.

There he was, standing before a grave, bare head bowed, hands clasped over his hat brim.

Her heart twisted at the sight.

She noted the grave's location, then turned and walked silently away, feeling like a rude and brazen interloper.

Later that morning, Emily was sitting in the office drawing up a list of room names when Mrs. Elton popped her head in.

"Ah. Miss Emily, I wonder . . ."

"Yes, Mrs. Elton?"

"Might we have smoked herrings for breakfast in future? The eggs and toast were well and good, but Mr. E has a delicate stomach and sausages make him bilious. Forgive me for speaking indelicately."

Emily bit back a smile. "Not at all. We buy fresh fish locally. Mackerel, herring, whiting . . . I am not sure about kippered, but I will ask."

"One of the local shops could help you, I do not doubt. Also, I would suggest patronizing a different bakery. The bread is of high quality. The muffins . . . less so."

Emily felt her smile falter. They purchased bread loaves from a local baker and Sarah had begun making a few simple desserts, while Mrs. Besley prepared the rest of their food, including muffins.

The woman finger-waved and turned away.

Emily groaned. Reduced to acquiring special muffins and fish for finicky guests. What next?

When Sarah came in a short while later, Emily reported, "Mrs. Elton complained about the muffins and requested smoked herrings for breakfast instead of sausages."

"Did she? She asked me for elderberry jam. Apparently her husband is not fond of strawberry. I explained that elderberries are not yet in season, but she referred me to the greengrocers in town."

"Happy to spend our money, I see."

"Yes. I suppose I could try making muffins. And if I can find some herrings already kippered, I will try to convince Mrs. Besley to serve them. She doesn't like the smell."

"I don't blame her." Emily wrinkled her nose and returned to her list.

"What are you working on?" Sarah asked.

"Copying out a list of our new room names. Tom Cordey has agreed to carve wooden placards for us."

"Excellent notion."

"Although I think we misnamed Mrs. Elton's room. I can think of several names more fitting than willow, like *common* walnut, *wych* elm, purging buckthorn . . ."

"Emily!" Sarah protested on a laugh.

Emily widened innocent eyes. "Only ideas."

That afternoon, Sarah opened the door to another arriving guest. In the threshold, she drew up short, disconcerted to see the man wore dark glasses or "eye shades" and to realize, by his probing use of a walking stick, that he was blind. He'd not mentioned it in his letter when he'd written to reserve a room for two. But then, why should he?

"Mr. Hornbeam?" she asked.

"Yes." He raised a hand in her general direction and walked carefully up the path.

Puggy Smith, behind him, carried his valise. "That's it, sir," the lad directed. "Straight ahead."

As the man of about sixty neared, Sarah greeted him, hoping to guide him with her voice. "Welcome to Sea View. I am Miss Sarah Summers. You will meet my sisters during your stay." Recalling the man's letter, she asked, "Is your son not with you?"

Emotion creased the man's face, but a moment later his expression cleared. "Had to postpone his trip. He will join me in a day or two, I hope."

"I am sorry to hear it."

At the door, he gave Puggy a coin. The lad thanked him and left.

Sarah wished they had another bedchamber on the main level to offer him. She had considered converting the small parlour into an additional guest room and now regretted not following through with that idea.

Sarah said, "Is a flight of stairs going to be a problem? If so, perhaps I might—"

"No problem at all," he assured her, adding on a laugh, "assuming there is a handrail! Just get me started in the right direction."

Sarah hesitated, then asked, "May I . . . take your arm to assist you?" She was not sure if such an offer would be welcome or offensive.

He nodded. "Thank you."

She took his arm and led him first into the office.

Thinking quickly, she said, "I can fill in your details from your letter, but—"

"Need me to sign anything? Just show me where."

She opened the register and pointed to the spot, only to realize he couldn't see her do so.

"Just place the quill where you want me to sign," he said, "and I will take it from there."

On the high back of the library desk, she positioned the book and pen, and he signed quite legibly. After she had given him the necessary details, she led him to the bottom of the stairs. "Here is the handrail. I will let you go first."

He did so. Rail in one hand, idle cane in the other, he moved steadily up the stairs.

"Your room is to the right."

He turned in that direction and, employing his stick again, walked along the corridor.

She said, "The water closet is on the left, just there."

He reached out a hand and felt for the door latch.

"And your room is straight ahead." Nearing it, Sarah reached past him and opened the door. Inside, she led him to the room's pair of armchairs and described the location of the two beds, washstand, and wardrobe.

He said, "Once I get my bearings, I will get about quite well on my own, but I do appreciate your patient help."

"My pleasure. Anything else you need, please do not hesitate to let me or one of my sisters know. We do not serve a formal midday meal, but we do offer tea and sandwiches in the afternoons, if you are hungry."

"Thank you."

Sarah wondered if it was a mistake not to serve luncheon to their guests. An elderly man on his own, and blind in the bargain, might find it difficult to stroll to one of the hotels to dine. Well, it was too late now.

An hour later, her sisters gathered in the dining room for a simple family luncheon.

On her way to join them, Sarah glanced into the parlour to see if the tea or plate of sandwiches needed replenishing. Their new guest sat there alone, sipping a cup of tea. At the sight of the solitary figure in the empty room, her conscience smote her.

"Mr. Hornbeam, why do you not join us? My sisters are just across the corridor in the dining room."

"Thank you, but no," he said pleasantly. "I would not wish to intrude upon your private family time. I am content here with my tea."

Stopping in the threshold, Emily added, "Please, sir. You would be doing us a favor. We grow weary of one another's company. Come and offer us some fresh conversation, if you would be so kind."

"Well, in that case." He rose. "If you are certain . . . ?"

"We are. Here, I shall carry your tea." Emily took his cup, and Sarah put a hand under his elbow.

"Right this way."

Reaching the dining room—they left the door closed this time of day—Emily opened the paneled door and led the way inside. She pulled out a chair, one not occupied in ages, while Sarah gently guided him into it.

Sarah explained, "We have persuaded Mr. Hornbeam to join us."

Viola stilled, glass partway to her mouth. She set it down again.

Georgiana said, "Excellent notion." Without being asked, she leapt up to fetch an extra plate, cutlery, and a linen serviette from the sideboard, and in short order, the man had everything he needed.

"It is only a plain family meal, I'm afraid," Sarah said. "Fried whiting and vegetables."

"A family meal sounds heavenly."

Emily carried over the serving platter. "Fish, Mr. Hornbeam?"

"Just a small piece. I've already had a sandwich."

"Potato pudding?"

"Just a bite."

"Broccoli? I'm afraid there is only a little left."

Georgiana smirked. "He may have mine, if he likes."

Emily scooped the last of the broccoli onto his plate.

Sarah explained, "We serve it with oil and vinegar and a little salt, like they do in France."

"Sounds delicious. Been to France, have you?"

"Viola has."

He waited expectantly, brows raised above his dark glasses, but they all just looked at one another.

Finally Viola said, "That was a few years ago." Then she added wryly, "Some travelers bring back artwork or French wine; we brought back a recipe for broccoli."

He chuckled, and relieved that the awkward moment had passed, the others joined in.

"Tell us about yourself, Mr. Hornbeam," Emily said. "I know from your letter that you come from London but little else."

He nodded. "For many years, I was Clerk Assistant of the House of Commons. However, the gradual loss of my sight put an end to that career. My wife and I have one son, who is now grown. Sadly, my good wife passed on eight years ago."

"I am sorry."

Viola added, "We all are."

"Thank you. And your parents?" he asked in turn.

The sisters looked to Sarah to answer for them.

She said, "Our father died last year. Apoplexy, brought on by . . . stress. He lingered for nearly two months before a second attack took his life." She cleared her throat and then went on. "Our mother lives with us, but her health has not been good in some time. We originally came here for a season hoping the climate would help, and now live here year-round."

"And where was home, originally?"

"May Hill, in Gloucestershire."

"Ah. And what do her doctors advise?"

"Our doctor at home simply prescribed a draught to help her sleep. We have consulted a physician here who prescribes warm and cold sea-bathing. We trust it will help."

"Did the onset of her symptoms date to your father's death?" he asked.

Sarah shook her head. "She was not well before that. She suffered from colic and a fever. The fever left her, yet the weakness has lingered. They assured us it's nothing contagious. But she is still, well, languishing."

He nodded thoughtfully. "I am sorry—for her and for all of you. How good of you to take such excellent care of her and the house. She is blessed with loving offspring." He dabbed the serviette to his lips, then asked, "Does she never join you for meals?"

"Presently, she prefers a tray in her room, although she hopes her strength may yet return. In the meantime, she insists we take luncheon together as a family. She says, 'We may keep a guest house, but you will still dine together like genteel young ladies even if you have to serve yourselves.'"

He smiled. "She sounds delightful. Clearly her mind is still strong, as well as her sense of humor."

"Very true."

"I look forward to meeting her while I am here." He raised his hand. "However, if she prefers solitude, far be it from me to intrude." His mouth quirked. "Although I seem to have intruded already."

They all assured him that he was no imposition, and they were pleased with his company.

And they meant every word.

After luncheon, Sarah began preparing her first trough of muffin dough. Something told her the task would prove to be more complicated than biscuits, but she'd decided she would at least attempt it.

From observing Mrs. Besley, Sarah knew the busy cook often heaped ingredients together by memory and was impatient about waiting for dough to sufficiently rise. Sarah, however, carefully followed the recipe, letting the dough rise for a few hours before forming it into balls, which she rolled in flour, then rolled thin. Lowen helped her stoke the fire and heat an iron plate on the stove. On this, she cooked the muffins, turning them when one side and then the other seemed done. The instructions warned not to let them *discolor*. The first batch became too brown, but on her second try, the muffins were golden perfection.

Sarah told herself she had recently eaten and should wait until breakfast to try one. Lowen showed no such hesitancy, eagerly toasting one on a fork over the fire. When he split it open with his hands, *ew-ow*ing from the heat, the muffin looked like a honeycomb inside. He slathered it with butter and topped it with jam. After a few bites, he pronounced, "Now, that's a good muffin." He finished it off, then added, "You did well, miss. Better than a London muffin-man, and"—he lowered his voice—"better than Martha Besley."

The yeasty smell of fresh bread overcame Sarah's resolve. Following the elderly man's example, she toasted a muffin over the fire, then spread butter and jam on it. She closed her eyes to savor the crunchy outside and soft, warm inside. A good muffin, indeed. Now if only Mrs. Elton would agree.

———

Later, Sarah donned bonnet and gloves, readying to depart for evensong. Viola would stay home with Mamma, and Emily said she had an errand and some correspondence to finish for tomorrow's post, so only Georgiana accompanied her.

On their way to the churchyard, Georgie moved ahead to talk

to her friend Hannah. Sarah lingered behind. She told herself she was doing nothing inappropriate. After all, it would do no harm to stroll through the churchyard before the service. Even so, guilt raised sweat at the back of her neck, and she felt oddly nervous as she walked toward a bendy young elm to look at one particular grave, its granite headstone topped by a Celtic cross. As she neared, she read the inscription, and realization washed over her. *Of course.* . . .

Katrin McKay Henshall
Beloved Wife and Mother
Forever in Our Hearts

Mr. Henshall's wife. Who, according to the dates, had died about three years before.

Their daughter, Effie, must have been ten or eleven years old at the time.

Had Katrin Henshall come to Sidmouth hoping for a cure, and instead, like so many others, died there?

She thought back to her innocent comment, *"If you have come here for our healthful sea air."* And his snort of derision.

No wonder.

Georgie called to her from the church porch, "Sarah, are you coming?"

Sarah hurried to join her, even as she doubted she'd be able to focus on the service.

If nothing else, she would pray for the husband and child left behind.

After finishing the pressing correspondence, Emily walked back to the beach with the room list, figuring the Cordeys would be relaxing at their cottage after a day's work.

Sure enough, Mr. Cordey sat outside with his pipe, Tom with

his carving, and Punch with a mug of ale. She imagined Bibi would be inside, doing the washing up. Tom rose when he saw her, while the other men stayed as they were.

Mr. Cordey pulled the pipe from his mouth. "Evenin', maid'n."

"Good evening. How was your day?"

"Fair to middlin'. Yourn?"

"Good. A new guest arrived today. As nice as can be, though he can't see. I can't imagine being blind—can you?"

"I'd hate it," Punch said. "Then I couldn't see yer purty face." "But you'd catch more fish, 'stead o' gawkin' at foine maid'ns all day."

Mr. Cordey winked at her, and Emily smiled in reply. She then spied lines of split fillets, hanging to dry over a fire. She'd not noticed them before.

"Smoked herrings . . . ?" she murmured.

He glanced over his shoulder. "Aye."

"I don't suppose you would sell us a few? One of our guests requested them particularly."

"Sure us will. Punch, go an' wrap some fer the maid'n."

His son grinned. "Anythin' fer Miss Emily." And he went off to do so.

Mr. Cordey said, "Now, tell yer Mrs. Besley to fry 'em in butter or poach 'em in milk. Not too long, mind."

"Thank you. Please add them to our account."

Tom stepped toward her. "Bring the list?"

"I did, yes." She handed it to him.

He glanced at it. "Trees, ey?"

"Yes."

He silently read the list.

She said, "If *silver birch* is too long, you can just carve *birch*." He nodded.

"And you must let us know how much to pay you. It is awkward to speak of money among friends, I realize, but we want to be fair."

"I'll think on it. What sort o' wood do you want me to use?"

"Heavens, I don't know."

"What are the doors made of? Oak? Pine? Alder?"

"I don't know that either."

"Perhaps I'd better come by and look."

"Of course. You are welcome anytime."

She smiled at him, and he held her gaze with eyes as blue as a summer sky.

Mr. Cordey waved a hand. "Ahoy! There come two o' yer sisters."

Emily turned and saw Sarah and Georgiana walking along the esplanade, no doubt on their way home from evensong.

Punch returned with the wrapped parçel. "Here you go, Miss Sunshine. I wish they was roses, but sadly, these'll have to do."

She chuckled and accepted the grease-stained parcel, holding it away from her dress. "Thank you."

Her sisters came over to greet them. They thanked Mr. Cordey for the herrings, and then Bibi came out to join them and they all chatted amiably for a time.

Eventually, they bid the family farewell and turned to go. As they made their way home, Sarah lowered her voice and said, "Take care there, Emily."

"Whatever do you mean?"

"With Mr. Cordey's son."

"Oh, Punch is a flirt, but he's harmless."

"Not him. I mean Tom."

"Tom? He barely says a word to me!"

"Which is a symptom, I fear. And how he looks at you . . . I think he admires you."

"You are imagining things."

"Perhaps," Sarah allowed without conviction. "But you might wish to be more . . . circumspect in your behavior."

"I don't know how to do that."

"Try not to . . . sparkle . . . so much in his company."

"Sparkle? Really?" Emily huffed. "Very well. I shall endeavor not to *sparkle*. Whatever that means."

"She can't help it," Georgiana defended. "It's her way."

Sarah remained serious. "Just promise me you shall be careful."

Emily picked up a stone and tossed it into the grass. "I shall."

A quiet moment passed, then Georgiana said, "Bibi is a hard worker. I was thinking. . . . Could we not hire her to help us make beds and such? It's a lot for us to do every morning."

"Good idea," Emily said. "We could pay her from Viola's earnings."

"Is she not needed at home?" Sarah asked.

Georgiana shrugged. "I know she cooks supper for the men every night, but she seems to have free time during the day."

"Do you think she'd even want to work for us?"

"She hasn't come out and said so, though I think she'd like having a little money of her own."

"Mr. Cordey might not want his daughter working as a chambermaid."

"It won't hurt to ask," Emily said. "If we ask tactfully."

Georgie wrinkled her nose. "I know I suggested it, but I've had a thought. Might she not bring the smell of fish and damp nets into the house? I should be the last to complain since I often tromp about with wet hems, but the guests might not like their rooms to smell of fish."

Sarah's brow lined with worry. "Good point. I had not thought of that. And we would no doubt insult them if we mentioned it."

Georgie said, "I know! I could say that, as I help make beds too, we'd like her to dress like me—wear one of my frocks, rather like a uniform. I have a few I've—" she coughed—"mysteriously outgrown." Georgie made a funny face, then added, "We could hang it on a peg inside the basement entrance. She could change when she arrives, and then change back into her own clothes when she's finished."

"That might work. As long as she and her father don't think we are being rude."

"I can talk to them," Georgiana said. "I've been told to change out of a stained frock enough times to know how it is done!"

The sisters shared amused looks.

It was certainly true.

7

WARM SEA BATHS
Fitted up in an extremely convenient and comfortable
manner, have been established, both by Mr. Hodge and
Mr. Stocker; they embrace every mode of bathing.

—*The Beauties of Sidmouth Displayed*

Mr. Henshall left the house again early the next morning, and again Sarah went downstairs in her dressing gown to lock the door after him. When he returned about an hour later, a breath of fresh morning air wafted in with him along with his own pleasant scent. His shaving soap, perhaps.

She gently confronted him. "Mr. Henshall, I noticed you leaving the house early these last few mornings. It is none of my affair where you go. But leaving your daughter here, unattended, well, that is my concern. I hope you know I cannot be responsible for her in your absence."

He raised his hands. "Effie can take care of herself. She doesna wish to accompany me. She prefers to sleep in."

"So would I. I would prefer not to have to rise to lock the door after you go. Do you intend to leave so early every morning?"

"Ye mentioned no prohibitions against doing so, or I—"

"No prohibitions, only precautions." She held out a spare key.

"Please lock the door after yourself and return the key before you depart Sidmouth. It is our only spare."

His blinked his round, fair eyes. "I shall. Thank ye for trusting me with it."

Did she trust Callum Henshall? She was not yet sure.

After that, Sarah went belowstairs to help lay out breakfast. During the meal, no one commented on the muffins as they toasted and ate them, but at least no one complained.

Later, emboldened by her modest baking success, Sarah decided to try her hand at making pastry. She had a hankering for jam tarts. She reviewed a few recipes and gathered ingredients. Thankfully, Lowen had grated extra sugar the last time, so she had some ready to use.

Finding butter already on the table, Sarah measured out a quarter peck of flour and sugar, then began mixing in the softened butter. The recipe she'd chosen called for *enough water to make it up in a light paste*. No measurement given, as was often the case in these books. She sloshed in some water from the nearby kettle and dug into the dough with both hands, attempting to work it into a light paste. Instead, she ended up with wet, gooey muck that stuck to her hands and everything else. She frowned at the cookery book in disgust. Then she realized she had missed the phrase *cold water*.

Mrs. Besley walked over to survey her progress. She clucked her tongue and advised her to start all over again.

With their finances as they were, Sarah hated to waste anything, but Mrs. Besley assured her she would find a use for the sticky paste. Dumplings, perhaps.

Retrieving more butter from the larder as well as a beaker of cold water, Sarah began afresh.

Since the butter was hard, she cut it into fine pieces before rubbing it into the flour. Then she added cold water in small increments, working it in until Mrs. Besley pronounced the consistency right. Then Sarah rolled it out as instructed—*as thick as a crown piece.* The recipe suggested doubling it up and rolling it out again seven or eight times. But Sarah's arms were already tired, and she still had work to do outside, so she decided to cut the pastry for tarts as it was and hope for the best. She pressed the rounds of dough into small tins and left them in the cold larder to fill and bake later.

After that, she spent time working in the gardens around the grounds. The white roses had bloomed early this year, and she cut some for the house. Finding a vase in a cupboard, she arranged the stems and carried them into the hall.

There she met Mr. Henshall coming down the stairs, a brown leather book in hand.

Eyeing the flowers, he asked, "From the walled garden?"

She looked up at him in astonishment. "How did you know?"

He hesitated. "Oh, I remembered seeing them . . . from a window upstairs."

Sarah knew perfectly well the rooms she had given the Henshalls overlooked the front lawn, not the walled garden. If he and his wife had visited Sea View's former tenants in the past, why not just say so?

"Well." He lifted the book. "Just off to read on the veranda. I wish you a pleasant day."

"You as well," she murmured, even though uneasiness filled her. If he was lying about the flowers, what else might he be lying about? She told herself not to let something so trivial bother her. But it did.

In the end, Emily decided she should be the one to talk to Mr. Cordey about Bibi helping at Sea View. She didn't want to put her youngest sister in an awkward position, should he refuse, since Bibi and Georgiana were friends.

So after again accompanying Mamma to the medical baths,

Emily walked toward Heffer's Row and found Mr. Cordey near his beached boat.

"Mr. Cordey, we were wondering," she began. "How would you feel about Bibi working for us for a few hours in the mornings? There's a lot for us to do, making beds and tidying rooms for our guests, and it would be a great help to us. We would pay her for her time, of course."

Mr. Cordey frowned, deep lines webbing his sun-weathered forehead and the skin around his eyes. "Like a chambermaid, you mean?"

"Well, yes, though she would be working alongside Georgiana. Me too, at times. We all help out where needed."

"Hmm." He frowned a second time, wincing out at the sea, clearly absorbed in his thoughts.

"If you don't like the idea, it's not a problem," Emily hurried to assure him. "We simply thought she might like coming to Sea View and earning a bit of money."

He slowly nodded. "Her would indeed."

"If you don't approve, we shan't mention it to her."

Another slow nod, and Emily suspected that was exactly what he wished—for her to let the subject drop. She drew herself up, planning to depart, when he finally spoke.

"Be good fer me babber to be 'round womenfolk. Spends too much time with our rough lot." He nodded. "Her may go."

"Thank you, Mr. Cordey."

Dare she address the topic of clothing? Emily swallowed and said, "Georgiana was thinking Bibi might wear one of the dresses she's outgrown while she's at Sea View. We don't have an official uniform, but—"

He raised a calloused hand. "No need. Been meanin' to buy 'er a new frock. Well, new from the second-hand shop. Even Sunday best is shabby now. Leave it wi' me. We shan't shame you and yourn."

"Of course not. I never meant to imply—"

"Don't fuss, maid'n. You mean well, I know. Tomorrow soon enough?"

Emily nodded. "Perfect!"

Punch and Tom came ambling down the beach—Tom with a coil of rope around his shoulder, Punch with an impish grin on his face.

"Well, now it truly is a beautiful day," Punch said. "Miss Sunshine is here."

His older brother nodded. "Miss."

Emily instantly felt self-conscious. What had Sarah advised? To be more guarded in Tom's presence? Not to . . . sparkle?

"Good afternoon, Punch." She glanced at his handsome brother and quickly away again, saying rather stiffly, "And . . . Tom."

Botheration. This was worse! Tom would think her either a schoolgirl with a case of calf-love or suddenly strange and distant.

She mustered another smile and bestowed it on each fisherman in equal measures. "I bid you good day, gentlemen."

"Gentlemen, is it? That's a laugh," Punch teased. "Good day to you too, *gentlewoman*."

She grinned back at him, then dared another look at his brother. Tom was staring at her, steadily, with no hint of a smile.

Fiddle. Perhaps Sarah had been right after all.

On her way home, Emily saw Mr. Stanley, top hat in place, whistling as he strode away from Sea View toward the eastern town. An idea struck. With him out of the house, it would be safe, would it not?

Dare she?

She only wanted to dart in and retrieve something she had left in her room. Something she had hidden.

Going inside, she went up to the bedroom level. At the top of the stairs, she hesitated, looking both ways, then tiptoed toward his room. Reaching it, she gingerly tested the latch, wondering if he had locked it. It gave, and she inched open the door with an anticipatory wince, knowing how it squeaked.

Glancing down the corridor once more, she opened the door just wide enough to slip inside, closing it as far as she could without latching it.

Noticing the unmade bed, she quickly tidied it. That would be her excuse if caught inside. She felt unaccountably warm and giddy as she plumped his pillow and spread the bedclothes into place, her fingers lingering on the counterpane.

On the nearby dressing chest, a small hinged case lay open. Curious, she walked closer to look inside. The plush interior held a cravat pin, a pair of silver sleeve buttons, and a gentleman's ring. The gold ring was engraved with the letter M ringed by tiny tulips. His signet ring, she supposed. She had not seen him wear it and wondered why.

Then she walked to the wardrobe, opened the door, and stood on tiptoes, stretching her arm high, trying to reach the upper shelf.

"Um . . . may I help you?"

At the sound of the masculine voice, she gasped and whirled, cheeks flaming. "Oh! Mr. Stanley. I thought you had gone out. I came in to, um, make your bed." She pointed. "As you see."

"And the wardrobe?"

"I just . . . I left something here."

Brows knitted, he frowned. "So you sneaked in after I left? I came back because I realized I forgot to lock my door. Now I see I should have."

She flinched. "I am sorry. Please don't be angry. I promise I did not come in here to poke through your belongings or take anything of yours."

He remained sober. "You might have simply come and asked me for whatever it is."

"I should have. You are right. Pray forgive me."

His hard expression softened. "What are you after, by the way?"

"Something I cannot reach. I was about to drag over that chair, unless . . . Might you reach it for me?" She liked that he was taller and broader than she. Not as handsome as Charles, but certainly very masculine.

He held her gaze a moment, and then walked closer. In a moment he stood beside her, his shoulder grazing hers as he reached up to the top shelf. "What am I looking for?"

"A box. Small, round, paperboard with a glass top?"

Eyes narrowed in concentration as he searched, he stared blindly over her head. She took the opportunity to study his face. Fair, clear skin. Bushy eyebrows. Fine, straight nose. His mouth . . . thin. His upper lip noticeably thinner than the bottom. His hair a golden brown. His eyes a similar hue.

He glanced down. "Are you staring at me?"

"What? No!"

"Have I something on my face?"

"No." She realized that from a distance he appeared rather ordinary. An average man. Yet the closer one came, the more attractive he became. She dragged her gaze from him and asked, "Have you found it?"

"Here it is." He brought down the small box and studied it. "What is this? A bonbonnière?"

She nodded and reached for it, their fingers touching as they both held the box. He relinquished it, but she held it toward him once more. "Well, go on. You have earned one. They are from my favorite Gloucester confectioner."

She lifted the cover for him, revealing four remaining bonbons. "Just don't tell Sarah you caught me in my . . . your room."

Mischief glinted in his eyes. "Are you attempting to bribe me, Miss Emily?"

"I confess I am."

A corner of his mouth quirked. "Then mum is the word." He picked out a confection, popped it into his mouth, and began chewing. "Mmm . . . delicious."

Emily, however, could not stop staring at his mouth. Thin, yes, but somehow appealing all the same.

She said, "I was surprised to see you at the medical baths the other day. You seem quite . . . healthy to me."

He shrugged. "Supposed to be good for the skin."

Her gaze lingered on his face. "Apparently most effective."

A few minutes later, Emily went back downstairs, a smile lingering on her lips. She saw Mr. and Mrs. Elton entering the house, and her smile faltered. Mrs. Elton's limp curls and listing feather hinted of time spent in the warm baths.

"Gone bathing again, Mrs. Elton?"

The woman looked up at her approach. "Yes. I find it so refreshing. You bathe often here, I suppose, Miss Summers?"

"A few times a week with my mother, yes."

"And you take the waters at Tunbridge Wells, I trust?"

"No. We don't travel a great deal. We mostly remain at home."

Mrs. Elton shook her head. "I am no advocate for seclusion. I think when people shut themselves up from society, it is a very bad thing. I perfectly understand your situation, however. Your mother's state of health must be a great drawback. Why does not she try Bath? Indeed she should. I have no doubt of it doing her good."

"My mother did visit Bath once without receiving any benefit. We hope Sidmouth might do her more good."

"Ah! That's a great pity; for I assure you, where the waters do agree, it is quite wonderful the relief they give. And it is so cheerful a place that it could not fail of being of use to your mother's spirits, which, I understand, are sometimes much depressed."

"Mamma is not—"

"And as to its recommendations to *you*, Miss Emily, well, I fancy the advantages of Bath to the young are pretty generally understood. It would be a charming introduction for you, who have lived so secluded a life, and a line from me would secure you some of the best society in the place. . . ."

It was as much as Emily could bear. Fearing she might explode, she forced a smile and said rather loudly, "Yes, Bath sounds a treat! Do pray excuse me, Mrs. Elton. There is something I must attend to."

"Well!" The woman sniffed, lifted her nose, and started for the stairs. "Come, Mr. Elton!"

Emily retreated into the library.

Happily, as soon as she was surrounded by books instead of Eltons, she began to calm down. Insufferable woman!

Viola walked to Westmount for the day's reading session. Was it ridiculous of her to keep wearing her veil? Probably. But she felt dreadfully self-conscious in a house full of men.

When she arrived, Armaan showed her to the major's room, apology creasing his face. "He is in a mood most foul today. The headache, you understand. I am sorry."

"Thank you for the warning."

She entered his room, determined to be cheerful. "Good day."

The major looked up and scowled. "Again? Must you wear that infernal veil?"

She sucked in a shocked breath, her confidence flagging.

He grimaced. "Forgive me. That was rude." He sighed, then said, "Our mother died many years ago and we had no sisters, so my brothers and I had no one to teach us manners. Ours was— and is—a thoroughly male household."

Viola was struck by something he said. "Your father mentioned a younger son, but I did not realize you have another brother."

His eye flattened. "I did have."

She waited for him to explain, unsure whether to press him. Finally she asked, "What became of him?"

His face contorted with pain of another kind before his expression flattened once more—held stiff and grim with steely control.

"He died on the Continent. I should have protected him, but I failed to do so."

"I am sorry."

"It's one of the reasons I signed on for duty in India. Too many memories of Timothy at home. Too many reminders—in the house and in my father's forlorn face. So I transferred to the East India Company. What is the saying—'out of the frying pan and into the fire'? I will not describe that time, as I have exerted too much effort in trying to forget it. Suffice it to say, I have come to believe we have no business being there. Well, a great deal of business, but little right. It was almost a mercy to be wounded and sent home. For I could no longer fulfill my role in good conscience, even though I was serving as private secretary to the governor by that point."

"Your father is certainly thankful you made it home alive." She remembered Armaan casting doubt on the major's desire to live but did not repeat it.

He snorted and said no more.

After several moments of silence, she said gently, "Tell me about Timothy."

Viola feared he would refuse . . . or rebuke her. Instead, he took a deep breath and began, "We were near in age. Sixteen months apart."

She absorbed that. "I suppose you were close, being so near in age?"

"We were good friends, yes." He glanced at her. "Are you close in age to any of your sisters?"

"Emily."

"What is the age difference between you?"

Viola hesitated. She could think of no way to evade such a direct question. "Sixteen m—"

"Sixteen months?" he interjected with amazement. "The same span?"

"Sixteen minutes, actually."

"Ah. Close indeed. Twins."

Viola inwardly cringed. She normally avoided mentioning it, loath to invite the direct comparison.

"Not that you'd know it," she quickly explained. "We look nothing alike. She surpasses me in every way. In every measure."

"How so?"

"She is far more beautiful, as well as taller. Quick and lively in discourse and repartee. Everyone likes her. She dances well, sings well, and has every advantage."

"And you don't?"

She shook her head.

"Why? What are you hiding beneath that veil?"

She stared through the fine mesh, wanting to stay hidden there. She dreaded his reaction, expecting to see him turn away in disgust. Fearing that very thing.

Yet she did not blame him for thinking her behavior odd. A veil indoors, as though in deep mourning? Or a victim of smallpox?

She licked dry lips. "I am scarred. May we leave it at that?"

For a moment longer he stared at her, then he grumbled cynically, "And I have *no idea* what that is like."

She huffed. "Now, will we waste an entire hour sparring, or shall I read something?"

Yet before she had read more than a few lines, Armaan knocked to tell them the surgeon had arrived.

Viola instantly stiffened, but the man who entered was pleasant and professional and not familiar in the least.

The major made the perfunctory introductions. "Miss Summers, Mr. Bird."

Viola nodded, and the man bowed to her before turning back to his patient.

"Time to remove your bandages and see how your eye is healing," he announced, then frowned around the dim room. "It's too dashed dark in here."

"As I have been telling him." Viola crossed the room and folded back the shutters from one window, then the next, then walked to the door. "I will leave you to it."

"No need. Should only take a few minutes."

"Then I shall wait outside." Although Mr. Bird looked nothing like the surgeon of her nightmares, she was still not keen to spend time in his company.

As she walked away, she overheard Mr. Bird ask, "Your intended?"

Followed by another of the major's characteristic snorts.

It stung, even as she told herself it should not.

A short while later, the surgeon quit the room and tipped his hat to her. "He is all yours."

Hardly.

She tentatively reentered. Major Hutton stood there, both eyes uncovered, bathed in sunlight. She could more clearly see his burn scars now—the mottled web of smooth and raised skin, some light, some deep red on his right cheek and side of his neck. Since this was the first time she had seen him in such good lighting, she also surveyed the rest of his features, his long nose, large, deep-set eyes, and thin, markedly bow-shaped lips. And she decided that, somehow, his unusual features taken together formed a handsome face.

"You look . . . different."

"Any better?" He smirked. "Or do you prefer my face covered in bandages?"

"No, it's . . . I am sure you're glad to be rid of them. And you are standing."

"Very observant. Yes, time to begin regaining my strength."

"And your vision in that eye? Is it any better?"

"Perhaps we ought to test it. Come closer."

She swallowed and slowly crossed the room to him. He was taller than she'd realized, and his shoulders seemed so much broader than they had when he'd been lying in bed.

He said, "Will you take off your veil?"

"I prefer to keep it on."

"I am standing here with my face bared. Can you not do the same?"

When she did not reply, he asked gently, "Are your scars so much worse than mine?"

A moment of silence followed. Then another. With every fiber of her being screaming at her not to, she raised trembling hands and slowly lifted the veil away from her face, draping it over the back of her bonnet.

She forced herself to raise her head. Her chin felt as though it weighed several stones. She waited, stiff and barely breathing.

He looked at her, forehead to mouth, then took one step closer. She narrowly resisted the urge to step back. He took another step nearer, his gaze lingering, probing every exposed inch. Finding his intense scrutiny overwhelming, she lowered her eyes, focusing instead on the striped fabric of his banyan.

Gentle fingers lifted her chin.

She jerked back, startled by his touch. A sharp retort sprang to her tongue and died, unuttered. His eyes were blue. She had thought they were grey or perhaps a dull green. But in this light, they were distinctly blue, the outer ring darker than the rest of the iris.

She blurted, "Your eyes are blue."

"Are they? I always thought they were a plain old grey."

She shook her head.

He said, "And yours are brown. No, wait." He leaned closer. "Green and . . . gold?"

She ran her tongue over dry lips. "Hazel."

Again his gaze swept over her face and rested on her mouth. She stood still, drawing shallow breaths, awaiting his verdict.

Voice low, he said, "For this, you wear a veil? How you must shudder, then, when you look at me."

Mutely, she shook her head once more.

"You are lovely," he said. "Quite . . . lovely."

His hand rose toward her face once more, his fingers coming close before dropping away.

She forced a weak chuckle. "Your vision must still be cloudy."

"Actually, I still can't see a thing from the right eye. And the left is blurry."

"I am sorry. I know you hoped . . ." Suspicion filling her, she tilted her head to one side. "Wait. Did you just trick me into removing my veil?"

"Maybe. I ought to have some consolation after my disappointment." He stepped away.

Armaan knocked a second time and stepped in, and Viola barely resisted the urge to yank down her veil.

"Excuse me, Major. I must ask. I went to exercise the horses, but Taggart stopped me. He said you wished to do so yourself?"

Viola turned to him in surprise. Armaan glanced at her, then looked again, but if he was repulsed by her mouth, it did not show in his expression.

"Surely he cannot ride?" she said.

"Of course I can," Major Hutton insisted, lip curled in disgust. "I have been lying in bed too long as it is."

"What has the doctor said about it?" she pressed.

"I have not asked. I do not answer to him."

"Perhaps you should. Riding seems altogether too risky after a head wound."

"I do not answer to you either."

Armaan intervened. "Miss Summers is wise. Let us wait and ask the good doctor when he returns. And in the meantime, Taggart and I will see to the horses."

"Oh, very well. But if you all insist on mollycoddling me, I shall never regain my strength."

"I disagree," Viola said. "You seem stronger every time I see you."

He glanced at her and away again. Was that a glimmer of hope she'd seen on his face?

"Now you are just being patronizing."

Apparently not.

"No, I am being polite," she retorted. Then she added gently, "You ought to try it sometime."

⸙

That night, having finally finished her work for the day, Sarah slowly made her way up the back stairs, longing for her bed.

In the dim upstairs corridor, she glimpsed a shadowy form ahead of her and paused. Standing at the open door of the linen cupboard, candle lamp in one hand, other arm lifted high, a man scrubbed at the top shelf.

A floorboard beneath her creaked, and he whirled. She recognized the murky outlines of his face with a flare of suspicion. Mr. Henshall. He stood stiff and staring, the picture of a furtive prowler caught in the act.

The act of what? Stealing linens?

"May I help you with something?" she asked, her voice louder than she'd intended. She hoped she had not disturbed those sleeping in nearby rooms.

"Oh, um, I was just looking for an extra blanket."

As she approached, the light of his candle lamp shone onto a lower shelf, where a pile of folded blankets sat in plain view.

She pointed. "They are right there."

He glanced down, his features made almost ghoulish by the flickering play of light and shadow.

"Ah. I see them now. How blind ye must think me."

How blind you must think me, Sarah thought. But she said only, "Anything else, Mr. Henshall?"

"No, that is all I need."

When he made to turn without taking anything, she prompted, "The extra blanket?"

"Oh, right. How daft."

"Shall I walk you back to your room?"

"No need."

"I insist." It was a strange request, Sarah realized, but she knew she wouldn't sleep if she thought him still prowling around the house.

"Then, um, thank ye."

She led the way around the corner to his room.

"Here you are. Good night, Mr. Henshall."

"Good night."

Sarah continued to her room, concern niggling at her. *What was he up to?* For all her exhaustion of moments before, it took her a long time to fall asleep.

8

The Devon coast was becoming a retirement area for invalids,
particularly returned East India Company officials.

—*Sidmouth, A History*

The next day, Emily sat writing at the high-backed library desk. Someone knocked on the doorframe, and she looked up.

Jessie stood there, gesturing someone into the room. "Here she is."

Emily felt slightly disconcerted to see Tom Cordey step forward. As far as she knew, it was the first time he'd been inside Sea View.

His broad shoulders seemed to fill the doorway.

Jessie gazed up at the young man, all dimples and shining eyes, before retreating. Tom had that effect on females, although he seemed utterly unaware of it.

"Morning, Tom."

"Miss." He swiped his flat cap from his head and shifted foot to foot, saying nothing more.

As the silence lengthened, her unease grew. Was he working up his courage to say something? No, surely Sarah was wrong about his admiration. Emily opened her mouth, then shut it. What should she say to divert such a conversation, if that's what he intended?

When she remained quiet, he prompted, "I'm here about the doors?"

"Oh, right!" she exclaimed on a rush of breath, feeling both foolish and relieved. "To decide what kind of wood to use for the signs."

He nodded.

"Well." She rose. "Let's go up and I shall show you."

She led the way upstairs and walked with him to the nearest guest room. Mr. Stanley's room.

Tom ran his hand over the grain of the doorframe. "Oak."

She smiled. "If you say so."

Taking out a carpenter's rule, he held it to the door to demonstrate. "I was thinking eight or nine inches by four, if that suits."

"Yes, perfect."

Footsteps came up the stairs. Emily glanced over and saw Mr. Stanley approaching, mouth quirked.

"Sneaking into my room again, Miss Emily?"

Only belatedly did he notice Tom a few feet away, half-hidden by shadows.

"Oh. Sorry."

Tom stiffened, looking from Mr. Stanley to her. Realizing how the guest's comment might be misconstrued, Emily felt her face heat.

"He is only teasing. Mr. Stanley, this is Tom Cordey, who is helping us with some room signs."

"Good man. Excuse me, but may I 'sneak' past you into my room?"

"Of course. Let me get out of your way." Emily stepped aside.

When the door closed behind him, she glanced again at Tom and saw his jaw clench.

"Do all yer guests treat you so familiar?"

"No. It's just . . . It's my fault, really. He is staying in my old room, and I forgot and let myself in. He means no harm, I assure you."

Tom seemed to measure her words, then his posture eased. "Well, I learned what I come for. I'll get out o' yer way."

When Tom left, Emily went back down to the library. Glancing out the south window, she noticed Mr. Hornbeam on the veranda. Viola was seated near him, head bent over a book, apparently reading to him. That surprised her.

Georgiana stepped outside from the drawing room and spread a lap rug over the man's knees. Through the open door, Emily heard, "There you are, Mr. Hornbeam."

"Thank you, my dear."

Georgie sat on the steps nearby. Viola closed the book, and for a time, the three sat quietly.

Emily studied the man, his head toward the sea, his eyes shielded behind dark spectacles. Curiosity nipped at her.

Going to the door and stepping onto the veranda, Emily began, "Good day, Mr. Hornbeam."

"Ah, Miss Emily." He smiled in her direction.

She sat in a chair on his opposite side. He had been with them two days, and as far as she knew, his son had yet to arrive. "Any word from your son?"

"Not yet. In the meantime, your sisters have been kind enough to keep me company. Very pleasant indeed." He turned back toward the sea.

Watching his contented profile another moment, Emily said, "May I ask you a personal question?"

His mouth quirked. "Let me guess. You want to know why an old blind fool came to the seaside to gaze upon views he cannot see?"

Emily bit her lip, glad he could not see her flush. "Well, I would not have said 'fool.'"

He laughed good-naturedly. "Ha. Only thought it, no doubt, and I would not blame you."

She said, "I suppose you can feel the 'mild, salubrious breezes' Mr. Butcher extols in his guidebook?"

He nodded. "Miss Viola was just reading some of that to me, and it's true I enjoy the air here. Yet it's more than that. I can smell the breeze as well. Salt. Sea. Grass. Flowers."

Emily countered, "Fish. Damp nets and traps. Seaweed."

Again he chuckled. "True but I tend to focus on the pleasanter smells. And the sounds."

Emily glanced at the chimes in the corner, softly tinkling in the breeze. "You mean the wind chimes?"

He nodded. "Not only that—a whole symphony of sounds. Low lapping water, to the rising roar of waves like tympanum, striking rock in a mighty cymbal strike. Then comes the crunching of shoes on pebbles, the flapping of ladies' parasols in the wind, fishermen calling out the day's catch, and the gay laughter of people on holiday." He raised his hands as though conducting an orchestra. "Cue the piccolo trill of curlews and sandpipers, the squeals of children as cold water splashes over their feet, and the warnings of mammas and nursery maids, clucking over their charges."

Emily wished she had pen and paper to write this all down.

"When evening falls," he continued, "the beach empties, the fishermen return to their cottages, the tourists to their hotels, and refreshment sellers to their shops, like birds to their nesting places. Then only the sea remains, tides rising and falling but always there, as constant as their Creator."

A moment of silence followed his speech.

Finally Emily breathed, "You should have been a poet, Mr. Hornbeam."

"Why, thank you, my dear."

Georgie added, "You clearly love music, Mr. Hornbeam. You ought to go to the library with us on Monday evening. There's to be a special concert to raise support for our new town band. It's early days, but it's coming along rather well."

"Perhaps I shall."

"I could walk with you," Georgie said. "Take your arm, if it helps. Though I daresay you get along quite well with your stick." "A very kind offer indeed."

Chips the dog came bounding across the lawn, and Georgie excused herself to go and play with him.

Mr. Hornbeam lowered his voice and said, "It was polite of your sister to offer, but I wouldn't want to impose. I am sure you, Miss Emily, must have many admirers you would rather spend time with."

"Perhaps," Emily allowed. "Yet you are more than welcome to accompany us, just the same. No imposition at all. Maybe your son will be here by then and wish to go along."

His smile dimmed. "Maybe."

Emily saw the flicker of disappointment. "I thought he planned to stay here with you?"

"So did I. It seems his plans have changed. I trust I shall hear from him soon."

"What does he do, if I may ask? Did he follow in your footsteps?"

Disappointment again rippled across the man's face. "No. I had hoped he would pursue the law and a life of service to the Crown. But he has gone his own way."

When he did not explain further, she said, "I am sorry. I do hope he's all right."

Another moment of silence followed.

Emily rose and lightened her voice. "Well, I had better get back to the correspondence. Those letters shan't answer themselves." She touched his shoulder. "And I will keep an eye out for one ad-dressed to you."

Emily felt sorry for the man. She knew what it was like to wait for a letter that never came.

───────

When it was just the two of them, Viola said softly, "I wonder, Mr. Hornbeam, how you knew Emily was the one to have admir-ers? You are right, of course. Are you certain you cannot see?"

He turned toward her. "I cannot see you, Miss Viola, but I can hear you."

Viola stiffened, feeling an immediate stab of mortification. Was her voice more unattractive than she thought? She had worked so hard to overcome her lisp!

He lifted a hand, as though to stay her offense. "Let me explain. When I listen to Miss Emily, I hear confidence. Self-assurance. When she meets someone, it is clear from her manner and tone that she presumes her impression will be a good one—that she will be liked and even admired. It was obvious from our first meeting. However, you, my dear, are all quietness and tentative uncertainty. Your diction, so studied and precise, is beautiful to listen to, yet one must strain to hear the words. In your manner and tone, I hear someone who expects rejection. Or at least indifference. Am I wrong?"

Viola pressed her lips together before replying. "You are not wrong. Did someone mention my . . . defect . . . to you?"

"Defect? No. Have you such a thing?"

Throat tight, she nodded, then realizing he couldn't see the gesture, whispered, "Yes."

"Can you describe it to me? Simply out of curiosity. Blind though I may be now, I was not always so, and like to piece together a picture of those I meet."

Viola ordered her thoughts, then quietly explained, "I was born with a cleft in my lip. You may have heard it called a 'harelip,' but I despise that term. I do not, I assure you, look like a hare, nor is my lip hairy."

He nodded his understanding. "And was your palate cleft as well?"

"No, fortunately. Children born with that rarely survive. They struggle to suckle and are prone to infection. I am told I should be grateful my case was relatively minor."

"But you are not grateful." He stated the words in a matter-of-fact tone, and she neither agreed nor denied them.

"I have suffered through several surgeries in my life. Some that made it worse and necessitated additional procedures to repair the damage."

"And now? Is the cleft closed?"

"Yes, thankfully. I confess I live in fear of it splitting open as it has before. It has been a few years, and the doctors assure me it shan't, barring new injury or accident."

"What does it look like?"

"I have a vertical scar from nostril through my upper lip."

"Which side?"

"Left. The skin above my mouth on that side pulls a little tight too."

Again he nodded.

"It is why I wear a veil."

He reared his head back. "You wear a veil to speak to an old blind man on your own property?"

Her cheeks heated. "It's pushed back now, but if a stranger approached, I could easily pull it down."

He nodded his understanding. "I suppose it's no different from my dark glasses. I wear them to protect myself and to shield others from my defect—in my case, clouded eyes."

She considered that, then asked, "What you said about my speech. Were you being kind?"

He shook his head. "Truthful. Rarely have I heard such fine elocution. Now and then, I hear a faint pause before you pronounce letters like *p* and *b*. Beyond that, your speech is excellent and lovely to listen to."

"That means a great deal to me, as I worked hard to improve it."

"Well done." For a moment they were quiet, then he said, "The others you read to. Are they old blind people like me?"

"Oddly enough, my first client is only about thirty. A major injured during his service with the East India Company."

"Blind, is he?"

"Only in one eye. He was injured in an explosion and suffered a head wound. He can still read with his other eye, but he has blurry vision and headaches, so his family engaged me to read to him."

"Poor man. Perhaps I might meet him one day and assure him a loss of vision is not the end of the world, though for a young man, an officer, I can imagine it might feel that way."

"Yes. He lives as something of a recluse. His face and neck were burned in the blast, and he is scarred on one side. He was also shot in the chest. His lungs were affected, which was why his doctors recommended mild sea air."

"Good heavens. With such injuries, he should be grateful to be alive."

"I am not sure he is."

"Well, no doubt your company is a balm to him as it is to me." He found her hand and patted it. "Thank you for reading to me. If you ever have spare time, I hope you shall do so again. I will happily reimburse you for the pleasure."

After pulling a tray of jam tarts from the oven, Sarah wiped her hands and went upstairs. She proceeded to her mother's room to make sure Mamma was ready for company. Miss Stirling was coming over to take tea and catch up with how things were going, now that their first week as guest-house keepers was drawing to a close.

Finding her mother already dressed, Sarah helped her sit up straighter on the made bed, plumped bolster and pillow behind her back, and spread a lap rug over her legs.

She felt her mother's pensive gaze studying her. Not wanting to add to her worries, Sarah forced a smile and kept on with brisk efficiency, moving a tea table to the center of the room and drawing chairs around it for the visit.

"What's wrong, Sarah? You seem preoccupied."

"Do I? Sorry. All is well."

"Sarah . . ." The single word stretched out and said in that commanding tone told Sarah her mother would brook no further denials.

"I am sure it's nothing. I have just seen one of our guests—a Mr. Henshall—poking about, and I am not sure what to think. I suppose we must grow accustomed to loss of privacy, but I don't like it."

"Henshall . . . ?"

"Yes. A Scotsman."

Her mother's brow furrowed. "That name seems vaguely familiar, although I can't remember why."

"Never mind, Mamma." Sarah kissed her forehead. "May I do anything else for you before I see about the tea?"

"No, my dear. I have all I need."

A short while later, they all sat together in Mamma's room, the sisters gathered around Fran Stirling, their friend and former lady's maid. Miss Stirling was well-dressed as usual with every dark hair precisely in place.

Viola joined them from the dressing room that now served as her bedchamber, comfortable enough with Miss Stirling to leave her face uncovered.

Sarah handed their guest the first cup of tea. "And how are things going for you at Broadbridge's?"

"Oh, well enough. The house isn't half as grand as Sea View, but at least it is conveniently situated in the marketplace. Many guests stay for the location alone, so I am usually quite busy."

As Sarah served the others, Miss Stirling sipped her tea and helped herself to one of the jam tarts Sarah had made. "These are delicious! Are they from the pastry chef in town?"

"No, he's too expensive," Sarah said. "I have begun doing some baking myself to ease Mrs. Besley's load."

"Well done. She was always rather heavy-handed with pastry, as I recall." Miss Stirling took another bite, then looked from face to face. "And how is it going here?"

Sarah sat down. "I believe we are off to a good start. We have six guests staying presently: one married couple, one father-daughter pair, and two men traveling alone."

"Only two females? That seems a disproportionately high number of men." Miss Stirling gave a sly grin. "Unless . . . are these eligible young gentlemen who have heard of the beauty of the Summers sisters?"

Sarah shook her head. "Only Mr. Stanley matches that description. Mr. Hornbeam is a dear but at least sixty."

Emily said, "You forget Mr. Henshall. He is a widower, but he is not *so* old."

Georgiana looked at her aghast. "He must be at least five and thirty!"

Mamma chuckled. "Good heavens. As ancient as that?"

"Well, at least all of our guests seem genteel," Sarah said. "Mr. and Mrs. Elton promise to write to their friends and recommend Sea View. She seems to have a great many respectable friends."

Emily said, "She is certainly impressed with her own self-importance. Let us hope she is a woman of her word."

"In any case," Sarah said, "I think we are doing well, so far. Thank you again for all your help and advice."

Miss Stirling smiled. "My absolute pleasure."

"Oh, and thank you for suggesting locks for the guest-room doors. One person wrote to inquire about that specifically."

Fran nodded. "It is not that I am so wise, my dears, but simply the voice of experience. One of my guests said a valuable watch was stolen and tried to hold me accountable, since initially I had no locks on the doors. Thankfully, we found the watch in a laundry basket. Even so, I engaged Leslie . . . er, Mr. Farrant . . . to install locks that very week. I trust you were pleased with his work?"

"Yes, he was quick and polite."

"Good."

Emily said, "Do you know, Broadbridge's is one of the few boarding and lodging houses listed by name in Mr. Butcher's guide. How did you manage it?"

Miss Stirling shrugged. "I didn't manage anything that I know of. One of my guests attended his church during his stay. This man wrote me a kind letter afterward and mentioned he had praised me to the author. That's my best guess, anyway, as to why the minister mentioned the place."

"So," Emily mused, "we need one of our guests to praise us to Mr. Butcher. Any likely candidates?"

Miss Stirling raised a palm. "Be careful. I understand he doesn't like to be pressured. Prefers to include only those establishments he thinks worthy. So it wouldn't do to be too direct with him. If a guest praised you, it would have to be unstudied and sincere and not a gentleman obviously smitten with one of you." She grinned from girl to girl once more.

"Fiddle," Georgie said. "That disqualifies Mr. Stanley."

Mamma frowned. "Is this man trifling with one of you? Need I be concerned? Had I thought there was risk of that, I would never have agreed to this venture. And here we expected octogenarians and invalids!"

"No, Mamma," Emily assured her. "Mr. Stanley is a perfect gentleman."

Georgie's eyes twinkled. "Though Emily does flirt with him awfully."

"That does not signify," Viola replied. "Emily flirts with everyone."

Emily stuck out her tongue at her twin.

Mamma frowned again. "Take care, Emily," she warned. "Some men can be trusted, while some can't, and it's often difficult to tell which is which."

"I shall be careful, Mamma. Please don't upset yourself. There is nothing to worry about."

Then Emily turned back to their guest, no doubt eager to change the subject. "It's so wonderful, Miss Stirling, how you manage your own business. Very impressive."

"I am not so unusual. I know of a butler and three former

housekeepers who either own a small boarding house or manage one or two lodging houses for absentee owners. Oh, and the pastry chef? He was formerly a cook in Clapham."

"No! But he acts so . . ."

"Arrogant? That's because he is much sought after." She lifted her jam tart. "He shan't like you giving him competition."

Sarah tucked her chin. "I only bake a few biscuits and scones and things. I am still learning."

"I'd say you're a quick learner." Miss Stirling took another bite. "Delicious. By the way, if you ever want to go into business, I know of a certain boarding house that could use a dozen a day."

"I am not ready to open my own shop, but I could manage that." Sarah winked. "At least . . . for a certain special boarding-house keeper."

Jessie appeared in the doorway. "Begging your pardon, ladies. There are two Mr. Huttons come to call, and another man."

Sarah sobered. "That is our new neighbor."

Viola paled and rose. "Pray, excuse me." She retreated into the adjoining dressing room.

"Show them in," Mamma said.

"In here?" Sarah asked.

"Why not? Am I not presentable? I am already dressed for company."

A moment later, Jessie returned and announced, "Mr. Hutton and Mr. Hutton," before scuttling off again.

A tall, silver-haired gentleman stepped in first and said, "Good day, ladies. I hope we don't disturb you."

"Not at all. You are welcome, sir," Mamma replied.

The dignified man glanced around the room. "Is Miss Viola not here?"

"She just stepped out." Mamma glanced toward the dressing room and added pointedly, "She will rejoin us soon, I don't doubt."

"I am Frank Hutton." He bowed, then turned to a second man behind him. "And this is my son Colin. My older son, Major John

Hutton—we call him Jack—lives in Westmount. It is for him that Miss Viola reads."

"Ah. A pleasure to meet you."

The older man gestured his son into the room. "Colin has just arrived for a visit, and when he learned four sisters lived next door, he insisted on being introduced."

A fashionably attired young man with wavy golden hair and a handsome face stepped forward. Overdressed for a seaside guest house, he would have looked right at home in a lord's London drawing room.

His sophisticated appearance was softened by a charming, boyish smile.

"Perfectly true. And who can blame me? I see my father did not exaggerate in the slightest. Four beautiful sisters and their equally lovely mother."

Miss Stirling laughed. "You mistake the matter! I am merely visiting and too old to be a sister."

"Not to my eyes."

"This is our friend Miss Stirling," Sarah explained.

"A pleasure. Then where is the fourth Miss Summers?"

Viola entered rather timidly, veiled bonnet in place.

"Ah, here is Viola," the elder Mr. Hutton said.

Colin bowed. "A pleasure, miss. Everyone at Westmount sings your praises."

Viola curtsied. "I doubt that."

Sarah only belatedly noticed a third man behind the father and son. A man with brown skin and black hair. From India, she guessed. Viola had mentioned him.

She prompted, "And who is your friend?"

"Ah." Mr. Hutton turned. "Almost forgot you back there. This is Armaan Sagar. Friend of Jack's. Served in India together."

Father and son stepped apart, and the third man advanced a short distance into the room and bowed.

"You are welcome, Mr. Sagar," Mamma said.

"Thank you."

Colin looked at Viola in her veil, his expression curious and expectant.

When no one explained, he said, "Going out? We can walk with you, wherever you like."

"Oh, um, no need," Viola said. "But thank you."

"Well." Mr. Hutton drew himself up. "We shan't keep you. Simply wanted to meet you all and introduce Colin."

"And we thank you for calling," Mamma said. "Do come again."

9

Bait the hook well, the fish will bite.
—William Shakespeare,
Much Ado About Nothing

L ate that afternoon, Sarah came up from the kitchen, bills of
lading from butcher and greengrocer in hand. She walked
toward the library to set them with the others before heading back down to help Mrs. Besley.

Entering the room they used as their office, Sarah drew up short,
startled to find Mr. Henshall there. He stood atop the rolling
library ladder, reaching above his head to feel around the top of
the built-in bookshelves, where a few marble busts and other or-
naments were arranged.

Suspicion washed over her anew. "May I ask what you are looking for this time?"

He turned, his fair face reddening, expression sheepish. "Your
sister said I might borrow any book I liked while I was here."

"There are no books up there. Only dust, I am afraid."

He glanced at his hand, which was indeed grey with dust, then
descended the ladder.

He swatted his hands together, pulled a handkerchief from his pocket, and wiped his hands upon it. Then he slowly looked up. "Perhaps I had better explain."

"Yes, I think you should."

He gestured toward two chairs near the fire. "Shall we sit?"

She hesitated. "I do not like being idle, especially when there is much to do, but if you will accompany me belowstairs, you may explain while I shell peas."

His brow puckered in question.

She said, "Our cook is quite busy. I said I would help."

"Very well."

He followed her past the drawing room and dining room and down the back stairs. In the kitchen, they found pots and saucepans bubbling unattended.

It was worse than she'd thought.

Mrs. Besley scurried in, apron stained, expression harried.

"Miss! I'm afraid I've fallen dreadfully behind. Lowen cut his hand with a boning knife and there was blood everywhere. I've set Jessie to cleaning the larder floor and soaking his shirt. . . ."

The old woman noticed Mr. Henshall, and her face sagged in dismay. "Oh, pardon me, sir. I did not see you there."

"I am here to help with the peas, as promised," Sarah reminded her.

Mr. Henshall said, "I will help too, if I may."

"You, sir?"

"Why not?"

Worry lining her face, Martha Besley pointed to a basket of whole fish. "I don't suppose you know how to clean fish?"

His face brightened. "I do indeed. I have caught and cleaned many in my day."

"Then you, sir, are an answer to prayer. Here, let me get you a knife."

Mr. Henshall stripped off his coat, sending Sarah an apologetic look. "Hope ye don't mind?"

"Not at all. I'll find an apron to protect your waistcoat."

They moved into the quiet workroom and stood at opposite ends of the scrubbed table. Sarah started on the peas while he began methodically scaling and filleting the fish.

"Can you talk while you do that?" Sarah asked. "We don't want another kitchen accident today."

"I can."

"You know, we don't expect guests to help. You are a gentleman, and—"

"And ye are a gentleman's daughter," he interjected.

"Yes, but it's my responsibility. It's our house."

"That may be, but I lived here for a summer."

She paused in her task to stare at him. "You did?"

He nodded. "Three years ago."

"So that's how you knew where the walled garden was and where certain rooms were before you'd ever seen them—or so I thought."

"Aye. Though the house has changed a bit since I was last here, with the new water closet and veranda."

"That doesn't explain why you've been poking around the place. Did you leave something behind?"

"Exactly."

She gaped at him. "I was jesting! Surely if you left some personal article, you would have written to the agent to claim it before now."

"It's a long story."

"I'm not going anywhere. Tell me what you were searching for."

With a pointed look toward the adjoining kitchen, he said, "I will, but let's keep it between ourselves."

"Very well."

He lowered his voice. "My wife had her grandmother's jewelry here. A necklace and earrings. I never found them."

Sarah felt her brow furrow. "I don't understand. Why did you not contact the property agent as soon as you realized?"

"I didna know where they were."

"So? He certainly would have searched for you."

Mr. Henshall pressed his lips together. "At the time, I had more important things to worry about. When Katrin died, I didna care about trinkets."

"Of course not."

"Later, I did write to the agent. He wrote back that nothing of a personal nature had been found by himself or the staff—at least nothing that was reported."

"Did you not tell him specifically what you were looking for? Afraid he'd be tempted to take them himself?"

"I don't think they are worth so very much. These are not the crown jewels we are talking about."

"But you want them back?"

"For Effie, aye."

"What makes you think they are still there? Or that you can find them when the property agent failed?"

"Because Katrin hid them."

Sarah stared. "Hid them?"

A pot clanged in the kitchen, and he winced.

"Tell ye what. Why don't ye come walking with me in the morning? To see the sunrise? I will tell ye more then."

Shortly before dinner that night, Mrs. Elton pulled Sarah aside.

"Miss Summers, I wonder. Might Mr. Elton and I be seated at a different table from the . . . blind guest?"

"Why?"

"I don't mean to be rude, but one must put one's own health above mere politeness."

"Your health? Mr. Hornbeam's blindness is not catching."

"How do you know? One reads such horrible accounts of"— she lowered her voice to a theatrical whisper—"Egyptian ophthalmia."

The term had often been in the newspapers a few years ago, when the disease had hospitalized whole regiments of British and French troops, eventually affecting civilians too. Physicians initially believed the condition was not infectious, but in recent years learned better. People were, therefore, justifiably cautious.

Not in this case, however.

"Mrs. Elton, while I understand your concern, Mr. Hornbeam's loss of sight was the result of another condition. I am sure it's nothing contagious."

"That's what they said about"—another dramatic whisper—"Egyptian ophthalmia, and look how many lost their sight."

Sarah had not asked Mr. Hornbeam directly, yet she had gathered his blindness had come on over several years, probably due to glaucoma or cataracts as sometimes afflicted older people, and not because of any communicable illness like smallpox, measles, or heaven forbid, ophthalmia.

"There is only the one table in the dining room," Sarah said. "If you and your husband prefer to dine in your room, that can be arranged, but I do hope that will not be necessary."

"You won't ask *him* to do so?"

"Heavens no. We enjoy Mr. Hornbeam's company. I think you would as well, if you gave him a chance."

"Could you at least ask him about his eyes? Just to reassure me?"

Sarah inwardly sighed. She glanced up and saw the man making his slow but steady way toward the dining room. "There is Mr. Hornbeam now. Perhaps we might ask him together?"

Mrs. Elton blanched and looked ready to bolt. Before she could, Sarah called, "Mr. Hornbeam? Might we have a word?"

"Of course." He directed his steps in their direction.

"Mr. Hornbeam, I believe you have met Mrs. Elton?"

"Yes, at dinner the other night."

"She is wondering . . . That is, she only wants to make sure that your eyes are not . . . That is, that your blindness is not . . . contagious."

"Ah. Rest assured, madame, it is not. I have seen the best doctors in London. They diagnosed an unspecific glaucoma. Age-related,

122

no other cause or illness identified. Nothing to be done for it either. I carried on with my role in the House of Commons until my sight grew too dim. And you know they would never have allowed me anywhere near members of Parliament had anyone suspected contagion."

"Parliament?" Mrs. Elton's eyes widened. "Well. That does reassure me. Thank you. I don't know why Miss Summers insisted on troubling you. I was only curious and making conversation. But she *would* embarrass us both. Ah well, not everyone has refined manners, do they?"

Lip quirked with a slight sarcasm Sarah recognized, Mr. Hornbeam said, "Sadly, they do not."

After that, it was with equal parts relief and trepidation that Sarah watched their guests gather for dinner a few minutes later: the Eltons, the Henshalls, Mr. Hornbeam, and Mr. Stanley.

The menu was simple, and the preparation perhaps not all it should be, due to the delays earlier in the day. Even so, Sarah had tasted the spring soup and thought it delicious. Then there was the fish that Mr. Henshall had cleaned and the peas she had shelled, along with a salad, cold beef, and a boiled lemon pudding.

Sarah thought it best not to mention Mr. Henshall's involvement, unsure whether it would embarrass him or her own family more, at having put a guest to work.

Mr. Henshall, however, showed no such reticence.

"This fish is excellent, if I may say so. After all, I cleaned them myself. A sovereign to anyone who finds a bone."

Mr. Stanley nodded appreciatively, while Mr. Henshall's daughter seemed mortified and lowered her face, picking at her peas.

Mrs. Elton arched one dark brow. "You did? My goodness." She set down her fork.

"Don't look so scandalized," he said. "I begged to be allowed the privilege. Took me back to my boyhood, it did. In those days, we caught and cleaned our own fish, and fried them over an open fire beside the sea. Nothing like it. Though this is deliciously close."

123

"I agree. Well done." Mr. Stanley lifted a forkful in salute and took another eager bite.

Mr. Hornbeam asked, "You grew up in Scotland, is that right?"

"I did. Near Kirkcaldy, north of Edinburgh."

"Do tell us more about life there," prompted the older man. "I find it most interesting."

"Let me see," Mr. Henshall began, his eyes softening in memory. "Ye may know there are many abandoned castles in Scotland, and we lads enjoyed playing in them. One day we stormed Ravenscraig and laid siege to it with our wooden swords. That is, until the baron's land agent set his dogs on us. The vicious beasts chased us, nipping at our heels. We were frightened out of our wits, and shut ourselves in a shepherd's hut, hoping they'd give up the chase. Instead they kept us trapped there for an hour. . . ."

His humorous expressions and accented voice brought the story to life, drawing chuckles from his listeners. Sarah couldn't help but notice how handsome he looked as he enthralled them all with his tale—all except his daughter, Effie, who pushed fish around her plate wearing a pinched expression.

He went on, "Thankfully the shepherd came at last and tossed the dogs some haggis, which tasted far better than we would have, and saved our sorry hides."

Laughter rose at that.

Remaining serious, Mr. Elton asked, "What is haggis?"

Effie snorted. "Ye don't want to know."

A short while later, as Sarah helped Jessie serve the dessert, she noticed Mr. Henshall's silver cravat pin and asked, "Your pin, Mr. Henshall. What is that symbol? A pineapple?"

He looked up at her, eyes glinting. "Bite your tongue, Miss Summers." A crooked grin softened his words. "This is a thistle, the emblem of Scotland."

"A thistle?" Mr. Elton asked. "Is not that prickly plant considered a weed?"

"Perhaps here. But in Scotland they are revered."

"Why?"

Effie groaned, clearly knowing what was coming.

"Because long ago, Vikings landed on the coast to attack under the cover of darkness. Hoping to catch the Scots unaware, they removed their shoes and crept silently through the fields to the Scottish camp. Little did they know that the field was covered in thistles. Stepping on a sharp spine, one of the barefoot Vikings cried out, arousing the sleeping Scots in time, and they went on to rout the invaders."

Lip curled, Effie said, "It's only a legend."

"Perhaps. Yet to this day the thistle remains a symbol of bravery, courage, and loyalty."

Mr. Elton asked a few more questions, while Mrs. Elton remained quiet, leaving Sarah to wonder if she found Scotsmen as unappealing as blind men.

10

Swiftly, swiftly flew the ship, Yet she sailed softly too:
Sweetly, sweetly blew the breeze—On me alone it blew.
—Samuel Taylor Coleridge,
Rime of the Ancient Mariner

The next morning, Sarah rose early, dressed warmly, and met Mr. Henshall downstairs for the proposed sunrise walk. He smiled at her when she descended, yet his eyes remained serious.

Once out of the house, he led the way, walking not east toward the churchyard, but rather southwest up steep Peak Hill Road. When they reached Pilgrim Cottage, he turned left, toward the sea.

Together, they walked out onto the headland near the lime kiln, overlooking the sea and Chit Rock. He walked to the edge of the grassy knoll, his coattails whipping behind him in the wind.

For a few moments, she stood beside him in silence, watching a gannet—a white bird with black wingtips—circling high above the waves before diving into the water for fish.

Then he took a deep breath and began, "My wife and I had not been wed long when I realized she was unwell."

Sarah thought of the headstone in the churchyard. "What ailed her?"

"Physically, she was reasonably hale, but she was laid low by a depression of spirits. She had suffered on and off for years, and her relationship with Effie's father had worsened her condition."

Shock flared. "You are not Effie's father?"

"Not her natural father, no. Though I feel as protective and fond of her as I believe any father would, and perhaps more than her actual father did, as he was a drunken brute who abused his wife and gambled away most of her valuables. Katrin was a widow of less than two years when I began courting her, so taken by her beauty and what I saw as her sweet vulnerability. I suppose I fancied myself something of a white knight, riding in to save her and Effie. Proud fool that I was.

"In the days leading up to our wedding, Katrin cried now and again, which I put down to nerves. I was sure that, once we were married, I could make her happy."

He slowly shook his head. "Not long after our honeymoon period, I realized something was very wrong. I consulted her physician, and he confided her history and his past attempts to treat her. He said there was little more he could do. Katrin and I struggled on for a few years with occasional peaceful periods among the bad. She longed to have another child, but after losing two unborn babes, her spirits sank lower and she distanced herself from me, moving to a separate room."

Sarah searched her mind for something to say and murmured, "At least she had Effie."

He hesitated. "In all honesty, she did not spend much time with Effie. When Katrin looked at her, she saw her cruel husband and sadly could not fully love her. Though I hope Effie did not realize."

She probably did, Sarah thought. Poor Effie.

"And then a few years ago, I saw an advertisement about the health benefits of England's south coast, and I thought, if it's good for the body, perhaps it will be good for the mind and spirit as well. So I convinced Katrin to come here.

"We rented the house for the summer. I wanted to bring Effie with us, but Katrin refused, insisting she stay home with her governess. Sea View was too large for just the two of us and a few servants, yet Katrin seemed so taken with the place that I hoped we'd be happy here."

Sarah studied his profile. "Were you?"

Mr. Henshall slowly shook his head. "We were not."

He stared at the sea for several moments, then roused himself, glancing around. "At first she seemed to improve. Liked to rise early and take long walks. Sometimes she carried an easel up here and painted, and for a time she seemed more peaceful. But it did not last.

"She began behaving more erratically and some days barely left her bed. One night I said to her, 'Why not put on your favorite blue gown and Gran's necklace, and we'll go to the ball? We havena danced in far too long.'

"Katrin was an excellent dancer, very graceful. I am a bit of an ox, truth be told, and woe to anyone who stands too close during a Scottish reel! Yet for her, I would try. I thought it would help her remember happier times, those romantic days of our courtship.

"But she said, 'I canna go. The gown no longer suits me and I have no jewels at hand.'

"I reminded her we had brought her grandmother's jewelry. She had inherited a set of blue sapphires: necklace and earrings, which she had managed to hide from her first husband so he could not gamble them away.

"Katrin said she'd hidden them and it would be too much trouble to bring them back down.

"I was confused and asked her why she had hidden them. Her gamester husband was long gone. Had she some reason to suddenly distrust the servants?

"She replied that she distrusted everyone. Including me."

Pain flashed through his eyes even now. "I was stunned. Did she really think I would do that—steal her jewels and what, sell them? We argued and, needless to say, we did not go to the ball."

Sarah stared at him. "And you think her sapphires might still be in the house?"

"It's possible, aye."

"It's like something out of a fairy story. A hidden treasure!"

"Not a treasure exactly. As I said, I don't think they are extremely valuable. But I would like Effie to have them, if they are still here. I believe Katrin would have wanted that, had she been thinking clearly."

He paused, then went on, "After I was over the worst of my grief, I wrote back to the agent and asked him to search one more time. He informed me the house had been sold to a family as a private home. I thought I'd lost my chance. Imagine my surprise when the same agent wrote with the news that Sea View had become a guest house. I immediately wrote to reserve a room."

"You were the first to do so. We wondered how you had learned about the house, being so far away."

Sarah considered the situation, then asked, "Your wife's jewels. Were they loose, or . . . ?"

"She kept them in a small leather box with brass hinges and a clasp. I realize some servant probably found them long ago, but I felt I must search myself, just in case."

"So that's why you came here."

"Not the only reason. I wanted Effie to see her mother's grave, and personally, to try to gain some peace about her death."

Sarah's thoughts whirled. "Forgive me, but I saw her grave in the churchyard. You said she was reasonably hale, physically. So how . . . ?"

He released a ragged breath. "I'm ashamed to say that after we argued that night, I went into the parlour to pour myself a whiskey and fell asleep on the sofa. I have wondered every day since what might have happened had I stayed with her. If she might not have done what she did. If I might have saved her."

Sarah's heart lurched in pity and dread, guessing what he would say next.

"In the morning, she was gone. The servants and I searched for her, but she wasn't anywhere in the house or grounds. I ran up here in a panic, fearing what I might find. I remember praying as I ran, 'Dear God, please, please, please . . .'

"It took every ounce of courage I had to walk to the edge here and look down. I saw nothing. Rocks and waves, and that was all. I was relieved, but not for long. Fishermen found her later, washed ashore down the beach." He winced then added, "Wearing her favorite blue dress."

"Oh no."

"The constable assumed she'd fallen. I didna say what I suspected. I wanted her to be buried in the churchyard, in consecrated ground."

Another grimace. "The next few days were a blur. Contacting our solicitor. Writing to our families. Making arrangements with the coffin maker and the stonemason for her headstone."

Mr. Henshall ran agitated fingers over his face, digging his fingertips into his forehead. "All the while, fearing—knowing—it was my fault. All . . . my . . . fault."

Sarah gripped his sleeve. "You mustn't say that. You mustn't think that."

He went on as though he'd not heard her. "No kin could arrive in time for the funeral. It was summer after all, and burials are dealt with quickly. Two days later, I found myself standing alone in the churchyard, before a mound of earth—racked with guilt, feeling like the worst man on earth."

A few moments of windy quiet passed before Sarah asked, "Then what?"

"I returned to Scotland, and Effie and I had some good years together. As she grew older, however, she became a changeling. Happy one minute, peevish the next. Nothing I said or did was right. And how often she reminded me that I was not her real father and that he had been superior in every way."

"Heavens!" Sarah said.

He nodded. "I had to bite my tongue not to tell her what he was really like. I pray Effie won't be stricken as her mother was."

"I doubt it. She sounds like a few other moody adolescents I knew."

"Not you, I don't imagine."

"No, though Emily and Viola were certainly difficult at that age. Thankfully, so far Georgiana has not shown a rebellious streak. Let us hope she is a good influence on Effie."

"Hear, hear."

Impulsively, she squeezed his hand. "It is normal, Mr. Henshall. It shall pass."

"Will it? In traditional families perhaps, but a relationship like ours, when my claim on her affection is tenuous?"

"From what I have seen, your relationship is solid and strong. I declare, you make me quite miss my own papa—at least the man he was before hardship embittered him."

He sent her a wry look. "I am not sure I like ye thinking of me as a father figure. Even so, I am sorry yours succumbed to bitterness. Remind me not to do the same."

Would Sarah be in his company long enough to remind him of anything? She doubted it but replied anyway, "I will."

He studied her face, then said, "Your turn."

"Hm?"

He cleared his throat. "I hope ye don't mind, but Georgiana mentioned you were once engaged to be married."

"Oh. Yes, I was." She didn't like to talk about it. She decided, however, that it might help him. And after all he had shared, it seemed right to reciprocate.

"I was engaged to marry a young clergyman—Peter Masterson." Pronouncing his name brought back all the old feelings of love and loss. Peter had been a few years older than she. Serious. Kind. Responsible. She had fallen in love with him and he with her. She should never have agreed to a long engagement.

"He was to receive a family living in Shropshire, but first he agreed to serve as a chaplain on a ship bound for the West Indies. We planned to marry when he returned with his earnings. Instead, he died of yellow fever, as did so many. I did not learn of his death until months later, when his ship made it back to port. There I was, stupidly planning our wedding breakfast and happy future, when Peter was already dead." She shook her head. "A cruel mishap? God's will? Life in a fallen world? I don't know. Either way, I wish I had married him before he left. I am haunted by the thought of him dying alone."

Callum Henshall nodded his understanding. "I am sorry."

Throat tight, she whispered, "So am I."

She'd had one great love in her life, and she did not expect to have another.

⁓

Two ladies they had met briefly at church came to call at Sea View—Mrs. Fulford and Mrs. Robins. Emily chatted with them in the drawing room while Sarah disappeared to put the kettle on. Georgie belatedly joined them, swiping at a grass stain on her dress on her way to the sofa. Viola, as she often did, made herself scarce.

When Sarah had served tea, tall, elegant Mrs. Fulford began. "We are here today on behalf of The Poor's Friend Society, instituted for the purpose of visiting and relieving the sick and distressed poor of Sidmouth."

Birdlike Mrs. Robins spoke up. "My husband is treasurer."

Mrs. Fulford nodded and continued, "We are here to collect subscriptions as well as donations of cast-off clothing, suitable either for men or women, boys or girls. Also, bedding will be thankfully received and appropriated with the greatest care to the most needy and prudent of the poor."

"That is good of you," Emily said. "Very kind."

"We have recently purchased new bedding," Sarah said. "So

we have older bedclothes we could donate. I don't know about apparel."

"I have a dress or two I've outgrown," Georgiana offered, her full lips flecked with biscuit crumbs.

"Nothing too fine or unsuitable for work, if you please," Mrs. Fulford said. "We would not wish the recipient to feel conspicuous."

None of Georgiana's hard-lived-in clothes could be considered fine, but Emily kept that to herself.

Mrs. Robins cupped a small hand to her mouth and said in a diffident whisper, "Donations of monies are also welcome."

The sisters exchanged uneasy glances. That was one thing they didn't have to spare.

"Well, thank you for coming, ladies," Emily said. "I am sure we can find a few things to donate. Bring it to the church, shall we?"

"Actually, the grocer has kindly offered to receive donations on behalf of the society."

"We shall bring what we can to him, then." Emily rose. "And we are already quite active in charitable works. Georgiana feeds strays, and our own Viola reads to invalids. So—"

"Does she indeed?" Mrs. Fulford interjected, eyes alight with interest and one brow arched high. "Excellent. A few residents of our poor house have requested visits. I am sure they would be delighted to have a young lady read to them." She looked expectantly from sister to sister. "And which of you is Viola?"

"Oh, she is . . ."

"Busy," Georgiana blurted.

"Shy," Sarah answered at the same time.

"But we shall pass along your request," Emily said smoothly. "I am sure Viola will help if she can."

"Are you?" Viola walked into the room, chin lifted, eyes sparking. Emily recognized that look. *Uh-oh.* This could end badly. And just when Emily had pacified their visitors with little trouble to herself, and all but ushered them out the door! Did Viola want to test the women, or did she simply enjoy making things difficult for the rest of them?

"Are you sure these ladies will want my help?" Viola sat down directly across from the visitors, her veil noticeably absent. Goodness, what had come over her?

The two women sat there, their placid smiles fading as they studied Viola's face. The birdlike woman's mouth fell open, and Emily longed to drop a worm inside.

Mrs. Robins began to rise, clearly aghast, staring one moment and averting her gaze the next, looking at her colleague, then at her reticule, then at her watch pin.

Mrs. Fulford, obviously the leader of the pair, laid a gloved hand on the other woman's arm and slowly pulled her back down, her focus remaining on Viola's face with an expression of determined pleasantness.

"Miss Viola, is it? We are happy to meet you."

Mrs. Robins turned and said in another of her perfectly audible whispers, "My daughter is expecting a child."

"Yes, I know. Congratulations." Mrs. Fulford slanted her companion a stern look. "But you, Mrs. Robins, are not."

She returned her focus to Viola. "Your sister tells us you read to invalids. We applaud such good deeds. A worthwhile, charitable endeavor."

Viola said coolly, "It is not a charitable endeavor; it is a profitable one. I am paid for my time."

If Viola had hoped to discomfit these ladies with talk of money, she was to be disappointed. They had, after all, come in search of donations.

"And would you consider reading to just one person, perhaps two, gratis?" Mrs. Fulford asked. "It would be so appreciated by some of the elderly poor of Sidmouth, especially those without homes and families of their own."

Viola said nothing, holding Mrs. Fulford's gaze, weighing her expression.

Emily feared a setdown was about to spew forth, so she spoke up. "If Viola agrees, might you in return refer a potential client or two—of the able-to-pay variety? She would be providing a helpful service after all and would appreciate one in turn."

Mrs. Fulford regarded Emily appraisingly. "You are quite canny, my dear. We could use someone like you in the society."

Mrs. Robins whispered, "Really, I don't think—"

Mrs. Fulford rose. "Thank you for your time, ladies. Miss Viola, if you would kindly meet me at the Sidmouth Poor House tomorrow at a time convenient to you, I will introduce you to the resident I have in mind."

Viola blinked, seemingly taken aback by the speed at which arrangements were progressing.

When she remained silent, Mrs. Fulford asked, "Might four in the afternoon suit?"

"Y-yes."

Emily looked at her twin in surprise.

"Excellent." Mrs. Fulford beamed, and the expression took years from her face. "I will see you then."

When the ladies departed, Emily took Viola aside. "That was well done, Vi. I am impressed."

"Are you? You are the one who started all this, but I find . . . Well, I enjoy being useful. And with something unrelated to dusting and privies."

11

A little sea-bathing would set me up forever.

—Jane Austen, *Pride and Prejudice*

Later that day, after helping to clear away the luncheon dishes, Sarah brought the box of broken china pieces into the dining room and laid it on the table. She began trying to fit the pieces back together but after half an hour gave up. It seemed an impossible task.

Returning the pieces to the glove box and setting it aside, she moved into the parlour and sat at her worktable instead. The small portable table contained many compartments for needlework supplies, as well as a pleated silk bag suspended beneath to hold fabric and works in progress. Sarah decided to embroider a new handkerchief for Mamma with sunny yellow primroses in each corner. As she stitched, her thoughts returned to Mr. Henshall, his wife, and his search.

Sometime later, that man himself entered the room and sat in a chair near her.

She offered him a welcoming smile, then said, "I have been thinking about your wife's jewelry. May I ask where you have looked so far?"

136

He grimaced. "Again, I apologize for poking around. I looked only in the public rooms."

"Did your wife sleep in the main-floor garden room? Is that why you requested it when you arrived?"

"Aye."

"That is Mamma's room now. Come with me." Sarah rose. He followed her out. "Are ye certain? I'd hate to disturb her."

"I will go in first and make sure, but I think she'll be glad for the company. She enjoys far too little society in my view."

She knocked softly and let herself in. "Good day, Mamma." Sarah was glad to see her dressed and alert, a book on her lap. "Do you mind if I bring in Mr. Henshall? He and his wife lived here before we came, and this was her room. She left something behind, and he'd like to find it if it is still here."

"Really? How unexpected. Although his surname seemed familiar to me, remember? I believe the property agent mentioned the former tenants. The agent also had the place thoroughly cleaned and some rooms repainted before we bought it, so I doubt anything would have been left lying about. What is it? Perhaps I have seen it."

"A small jewelry case. Leather with brass hinges and clasp."

"Goodness me. I doubt something like that would have gone unnoticed. Probably taken."

"You may be right, but he would still like to have a look, if you don't mind."

"Not at all. I have been longing to meet your Scotsman."

Sarah's neck heated. "He is not mine, Mamma. Please. He is standing just outside."

"Oh. Forgive me. Only teasing you."

Sarah opened the door wider, wondering if he had overheard.

His expression was inscrutable, but something in his grazing glance and the high color in his cheeks made her fear he had.

"Mamma, this is Mr. Henshall. Mr. Henshall, our mother, Mrs. Summers."

He bowed, and Mamma nodded.

"Good day, sir. I understand your daughter is here with you. How is she faring?"

"In truth, ma'am, I hardly know. She is not speaking to me at present. I made the unforgivable error of teasing her in front of strangers." Humble humor glimmered in his eyes.

Mamma nodded. "Ah yes. Parents are the bane of an adolescent's existence. One day admired and respected, and the next reviled. Be grateful you have only the one daughter. Imagine my lot with fi . . . so many."

"I would say I don't envy ye, ma'am, but in truth, I find your family delightful."

"Thank you. For all my jesting, I quite agree."

He said, "I am especially grateful for Miss Georgiana, who has kindly befriended Effie. Your youngest clearly has a heart for untamed creatures."

Mamma chuckled. "Indeed. I trust your stay here will be good for us all. Now, please do make yourself at home and look wherever you like. I will tell you, however, that the writing desk there is my own. Brought from home and filled with private papers."

"Then of course I shan't look there."

Sarah searched inside the window cabinet, while he began searching the built-in bookcase.

Setting aside her book, Mamma watched in idle interest. She asked him, "I understand this was your wife's bedchamber when you lived here?"

"Yes. She enjoyed the view of the walled garden."

"As do I. Has the room changed much?"

"I don't . . . That is, not that I recollect."

Sarah remembered him mentioning his wife's preference for separate bedchambers, so perhaps he had rarely been in this room. It struck her as sad, though she knew separate rooms were fairly common among upper-class couples.

They looked in the wardrobe, bringing over a chair to search its top shelves. Then they searched the adjoining dressing room, where Viola now slept. Nothing.

"Well, thank ye for letting us look."

"You're welcome. Visit any time, Mr. Henshall."

He thanked her again, and together he and Sarah left the room, talking in low voices as they walked back to the hall.

"Where else might she have hidden it?" Sarah asked. "You would think she'd want to have the jewelry near her. Somewhere safe, where she could keep an eye on it. Not in a public room where it would be more likely to be found by a servant or visitor."

"If she were thinking logically, aye."

"What about your bedchamber? Might she have thought it safer in her husband's room?"

"I doubt it. But it might be worth a look. Mine was at the top of the stairs, next to my current room."

"That is Emily's. Or was. A guest is staying there presently. Mr. Stanley."

"Ah well." Callum Henshall waved a dismissive hand.

"As you've probably gathered, Mr. Stanley is an amiable young man. I do not think he would mind if we looked around for a few minutes. We can at least ask him."

"I don't mean to put ye to so much trouble, nor to inconvenience your guests—especially when ye are trying to become established."

"True. And I certainly wouldn't nose around Mr. and Mrs. Elton's room, but I don't think Mr. Stanley is the type to be easily offended." Sarah led the way upstairs and knocked.

Mr. Stanley opened the door, a ready smile on his face, which dampened slightly upon seeing them.

"Good day, Mr. Stanley. I am sorry to disturb you."

"Not at all. What may I do for you?"

"You've met Mr. Henshall, I believe?"

"Yes, at dinner."

"We hate to trouble you, but might we take a peek in your room?

Mr. Henshall and his wife used to live here, you see. He's visiting from Scotland and thinks his wife may have left something."

"Really? How intriguing." He opened the door wider. "I hope it wasn't a bonbonnière."

"A what? No," Sarah said. "Why would you think that?"

"Never mind. Do come in and make yourself at home. After all, it is your home, is it not?"

"Again, if it is inconvenient, we—"

"Not at all. In fact, I will just step out and leave you to it. Is . . . Miss Emily about?"

"I believe she is downstairs in our library. Unless she has already left for her daily pilgrimage to Wallis's."

"Ah. Then perhaps I shall accompany her." He snatched up his hat and hurried from the room.

Sarah and Mr. Henshall exchanged wry glances, then set about their search, again looking on the top shelves of the wardrobe and closet, to no avail.

He scrubbed a hand over his jaw. "Well, we tried. I did not truly think she would hide it in here." He glanced around the room, then gazed out the window with a wistful sigh. "Still, a pleasure to see my old room."

Sarah's thoughts remained on the search. "Remind me. Did she say, 'It would be too much trouble to bring it down again'?"

"Something like that. Which is why I've been looking for high hiding places. Though remember, her mental state was unstable at the time."

"Hmm. Where else might we look? Did she ever venture belowstairs?"

"Not that I know of. She had a bell pull to summon the servants when she needed anything."

"As does my mother."

"What does that leave?"

"Perhaps the attic?" Sarah suggested. "That is certainly the highest place in the house."

"I don't think she ever ventured up there either. I did only to store our valises in the storage room and later to retrieve them."

"Do you think it's worth a look?"

"I suppose we might as well. Perhaps then I will be able to put the nagging thought from my mind. Accept the jewelry is gone forever."

"Very well. Let's go up."

The narrow attic stairs were on the west side of the house, in a passage between the linen cupboard and her father's old bed-chamber, presently unoccupied.

Sarah led the way, explaining, "If you remember, there are several servants' cubicles up here and a sitting room. But these days only one maid, Jessie, sleeps up here, and Georgie has moved up here too."

"Yes, Effie mentioned your sister sleeps in a humble garret like a Gothic heroine."

Sarah chuckled. "Next you will think we banished her up here, but I promise it was her choice. She was willing to do almost anything to have her own room."

Reaching the attic, they walked along the narrow passage, peeking into small servants' rooms, either empty or with a single bedframe and washstand remaining. They saw few places to hide anything, let alone something valuable. They opened the closed door of the storage room where the Summerses had also stored their traveling trunks and valises. Behind these sat an ancient sea chest, a broken coat tree leaning haphazardly against the wall, a three-legged chair, and a wardrobe with a broken mirror. They looked in the mouldering old chest and dusty wardrobe but found nothing of interest.

They knocked next on Georgiana's door and peeked in. The bedclothes were in disarray and stockings lay discarded over the back of a chair. Sarah would have to talk with her about her housekeeping skills. Again, however, they saw few places to hide something and no high cupboards to search. Then they knocked on Jessie's door and gave a cursory glance around, just to make sure there was no obvious hiding place, but Sarah was not keen to poke into the maid's personal belongings.

They stepped into the former servants' sitting room, which held little besides a scarred oak table, a few chairs, and a cabinet filled with old sewing notions and mouse droppings.

"Nothing up here seems promising, I am afraid."

He followed her gaze. "I agree."

They reached the last door and opened it. A discarded cradle, rickety hobbyhorse, and child-sized table and chairs identified it as the former nursery. The cracked and dirty windowpanes overlooked the lawn far below, and beneath them was a long window seat. Sarah raised the hinged top, which revealed a toy box containing a jumble of long-abandoned playthings: a few tin soldiers, a broken draughts board, battledore racquets missing strings, a shuttlecock with one frayed feather, a costume crown and scepter, and a musty purple cape.

Sarah stirred through the remnants like a hungry man searching broth for a morsel of meat. She moved aside the draughts board and stilled.

What was that? Embossed leather and a flash of gilt caught her eye. Had some naughty child tossed a leather-bound book into the toy box? She lifted it out, and her breath hitched. Not a book.

A jewelry case with gilt hinges and clasp.

She turned to Mr. Henshall, mouth agape, and slowly lifted the object toward him.

He stared at it, eyebrows drawn low, then murmured in disbelief, "That's it."

He gingerly took it from her as though it were a wild bird that would fly away if he moved too quickly. He unfastened the clasp and slowly lifted the lid.

Empty.

Sarah sighed. "What a disappointment."

"Aye."

"Why is the case here? Do you think someone found the sapphires while the house was vacant and took them, discarding the case?"

"Probably. Or Katrin might have, who knows, taken them out of the case and tossed them over the cliff. I doubt we shall ever know."

"It is interesting that we'd find the case up here though, is it not? Somewhere high up from which the jewelry would have to be brought down?"

He nodded. "At all events, the empty case tells me our search is at an end. At least finding this proves I was not making up the whole thing as an excuse to sneak around your house."

Sarah looked at him, dismayed for his sake. "I am sorry."

"Why are *you* sorry? I am the one who led ye on this wild-goose chase. You're a busy woman with no doubt far more important things to do."

"That's all right." She managed a small smile. "It was an adventure while it lasted."

They descended the attic stairs to the bedroom level. Mr. Henshall started back to his room while Sarah stopped at the linen cupboard to retrieve a clean towel for herself.

From around the corner, she heard Mr. Henshall's low voice and Effie's higher one, his pleasant while hers held a note of complaint.

"What were ye doing with Miss Sarah?"

"We were just looking for something."

"You like her, don't ye?"

"Aye, I suppose I do."

Effie groaned. "Why? She is so serious—no fun at all!"

The girl's criticism struck a nerve.

The door closed, muffling their voices. But Sarah had heard enough.

She stood there a moment longer, torn between offense and conviction. Was there truth in Effie's words?

12

No major author or poet spent their working life in the town, but there are a surprising number who have stayed or lived here. Fanny Burney . . . Elizabeth Barrett . . . and others.

—Nigel Hyman, *Sidmouth's Literary Connections*

When Viola arrived at Westmount, Armaan greeted her. "Good day, Miss Summers. The major is dressing but will be ready soon."

"That is late for him."

"We went for a swim earlier."

"Swim? Is he . . . able?"

"Yes. He swims well. And the doctor approves, now the bandages are off."

"Good. Though a bit chilly today I would have thought."

"For me, yes. The major does not mind. He swims for strength, not pleasure."

"I see. Well, shall I wait in the sitting room?"

"Please do." He gestured for her to precede him. "Do you mind if I join you?"

"Not at all."

Removing her veil as she went, Viola sat on the sofa while he remained standing. She asked him, "Why did you stay hidden in the back when you came to our house with the Huttons?"

"Perhaps for the same reason you wear a veil. I am never sure how people will react to my appearance, or the color of my skin."

"There is nothing wrong with your appearance or your skin!"

"Nor with yours, Miss Summers."

For a moment she met his gaze, and then shifted. "Well, I hope you know you are always welcome at Sea View."

"Thank you. I would say you are always welcome here, but as you know, the major can be as changeable as the wind."

"Yes, I do know."

Armaan clasped his hands and rocked on his heels. "Shall I ask Chown for coffee? We have some grown in southern India. Very good."

"Is that where you are from?"

He tipped his hand side to side to indicate *close*. "The general region. Come. I will show you."

Viola rose as Armaan retrieved a map of India and spread it on the table before them. "Here is where we were last stationed." He slid his finger to another spot. "And here is where I was born."

She leaned close to make out the tiny print.

"Chik-ma-ga-lur . . ." She tried repeating the foreign word, which tasted like an exotic, spicy morsel on her tongue. "And do you not miss it? Or long to go back?"

He shrugged. "Nothing for me there now. My family are all gone. So no. I was happy to accompany the major here. He has been a good friend to me. A true friend."

Movement caught her eye. Viola looked up and saw Major Hutton in the doorway, fully dressed. He turned and quietly departed, evidently not wishing to interrupt their conversation. Yet she had not missed the quirk of his lips. A smile of amusement, perhaps? Or approval?

After a few more minutes Armaan stowed the map away, and Viola went down the corridor to the major's study.

She found him sitting where she usually sat, and for some reason, possessiveness spurred her to say, "That is my chair."

He glanced up in wry humor. "Is it indeed? I was under the impression this room was mine and all the furniture in it."

"I only meant—"

Rising to his feet, he raised a palm. "I thought I had better begin on my own as you seemed to be helping Armaan read today. *Chikmagalur*, indeed."

Her face heated. "I was only . . . I asked where he was from and he was trying to explain. I am dreadfully ignorant of geography, I'm afraid, so he found it easier to show me."

Again his lips quirked.

"I am teasing you, Miss Viola. Do you not recognize teasing when you meet with it?"

"Not from you." She barely recognized him either, dressed in coat, waistcoat, and trousers rather than a loose-fitting banyan.

"Ah. And no wonder. I am woefully out of practice." He looked away from her and then met her gaze once more. "Actually, it did my cynical heart good to see you showing respectful interest in my friend." He patted the back of the recently vacated chair. "Now, come. Be seated and let us begin. I have tormented you enough for one day."

After she had read to him for a time, Viola looked up and asked, "I was surprised to hear you went swimming earlier."

He nodded. "To strengthen my lungs, and the rest of me. Dr. Clarke suggested it."

"At the main beach?"

He shook his head. "I prefer the western beach. It's more secluded. Perhaps you know it?"

"I have seen it from the headland."

He nodded. "Men primarily bathe there, and men seem to take less notice of my scars."

"I see. Well, very impressive." She had not been jesting when she'd said he appeared stronger, and now all the more. She pulled her gaze from his tall, masculine figure and focused instead on the safer sight of newsprint.

Miss Stirling had suggested they offer a few games for their guests to play, especially on rainy days. They had an old draughts set, dominoes, and a deck of bent cards, but that was about it. Emily, always eager for a chance to visit Wallis's Marine Library, volunteered to purchase one there.

John Wallis Jr. was a member of the renowned Wallis family, prolific publishers of board games, maps, prints, and books of local interest. While his brother carried on their father's work and offices in London, John had moved to Sidmouth and managed the business there.

Now a prosperous man in his forties with two sons, Mr. Wallis was something of a minor celebrity in Sidmouth, known by all and patronized by the highest echelons of society. To Emily, he was more fascinating than any of the famous or titled visitors to Sidmouth.

When she arrived at the library that afternoon, she found him surrounded by an audience of three fashionable females at least a decade older than she was, who hung on his every word, either because they were interested in his work, or because he was an eligible widower past his mourning period.

He was telling them about some of the notable visitors to his establishment. Lords, ladies, actors, and politicians. The women ohhed and ahhed like spectators at a Vauxhall Gardens fireworks exhibition.

When the trio finally departed, Mr. Wallis noticed Emily lingering there.

"And I suppose you, young lady, also wish to hear about all the important people who have come here?"

She shook her head. "No, thank you. Unless . . . have you met any famous authors?"

"Ah! A kindred spirit." His eyes lit. "Have you read *Evelina?*"

"Of course! And *Cecilia* and *Camilla.* Don't tell me you have met the author?"

"I have indeed. Frances Burney. Do you know, Miss Burney actually visited Sidmouth once, though that's nearly twenty years ago, before my time. I met her in London."

Delight rippled through her. "What was she like?"

He thoughtfully tapped his chin. "Ours was only a brief meeting, yet I would say she is intelligent, observant, and tough. Had to be, to be a female writer in those days—and even now."

Emily tucked that away to think about later. "Any other authors?" she asked, all eagerness.

"The poet Robert Southey came here as well." Wallis made a face. "But I could not like him because he disapproved of Sidmouth. Called it a 'nasty watering place, infested with lounging ladies, and full of footmen.'"

She bit back a laugh and shook her head in empathy.

He added, "And naturally, I am well acquainted with Mr. Butcher. You have read *The Beauties of Sidmouth Displayed,* I trust?"

"Indeed," Emily replied, thinking, here was her chance. "In fact, we . . ."

Grasping his lapels proudly, Wallis said, "I commissioned and published the book."

"Yes, I know." And that no doubt explained the fulsome praise of Wallis's Marine Library within its pages.

She took a steadying breath and said, "I understand there is to be a new edition?"

"Yes. We have begun the planning of it."

"And how does one go about having one's guest house mentioned in it?"

His brows rose. "One would need to commission one's own guidebook, I suppose. Or you could appeal to the author, although I believe he prefers to remain objective."

Except in his praise of the publisher's establishment, Emily thought, but only smiled in reply. Miss Stirling had been right.

He rubbed his hands together. "Now, how else may I help you?"

"I have come in hopes of purchasing a game," Emily explained.

"One our guests at Sea View would find diverting. Nothing too expensive, though. What would you recommend?"

He walked over to a display of board games. "The Game of the Monkey. My boys like this one, and so do I. Good for all ages." He handed her the printed game sleeve, which held the folded board.

He explained its premise and reasonable price. "Playing also requires counters and dice or a teetotum. We also have those for sale, if you like."

"Very well. I shall take the game and one teetotum."

"Excellent."

She followed him to the counter to pay for her purchases, consoling herself that at least she had managed to work the name *Sea View* into the conversation, though she doubted it would be enough.

───

Later that afternoon, Sarah carried her portable worktable out onto the veranda and joined the five guests gathered there. Mr. Henshall softly played his guitar while Mr. Hornbeam listened. Effie slouched in her chair, clearly bored. And Mrs. Elton read a ladies' magazine, while her husband looked ready to nod off.

Georgiana ran across the lawn toward them.

"Who will play with me?" she asked, wielding a battledore and holding a feathered shuttlecock in her other hand.

Mr. Elton, startled awake, turned to his wife, who pursed her lips and shook her head.

To Georgiana, he said, "You are extremely obliging—yet you must excuse me. If I were a younger man, but alas, my sporting days are behind me."

Sarah guessed the man was not much over thirty but kept her thoughts to herself.

Mr. Henshall glanced at his stepdaughter and prodded, "Effie?"

She sullenly shook her head.

Setting aside his instrument, Mr. Henshall rose and gave Georgiana a friendly smile. "I shall play if no one else will."

"Excellent." She handed him a racquet and the shuttlecock, then jogged several yards away.

When she was ready, he hit the shuttlecock with a light underarm swing that sent the feathered "birdie" into the air. Georgiana ran to meet it, swung hard, and returned it.

He leapt but missed. "Och! Clearly I don't need to go easy on *you*, Miss Georgiana."

She grinned.

He picked up the shuttlecock and whacked it back, and they kept up a volley of several hits before having to stop and retrieve the bird.

Effie watched them with grudging interest, then finally asked, "May I play?"

Her father nodded and handed her the battledore.

"Let's play doubles," Georgiana suggested. "Less running that way. Who shall be our fourth?" She looked at her older sister. "Sarah, do join us."

"I have too much to do."

"So you always say. Please?"

She glanced over and saw Mr. Henshall watching her. She also remembered Effie's disparaging comment about her being too serious and no fun.

"Oh, very well. For a few minutes." Sarah set down her needlework.

Georgiana found two more racquets, in varying states of repair, and handed them to her and Effie.

The game commenced with much teasing, running, and missed shots.

Sarah was not terribly athletic, but she enjoyed seeing Mr. Henshall smiling and laughing, especially after his earlier disappointment over the jewelry case. She also admired his athleticism and his playful manner with the girls.

He seemed so different from the reserved, somber man who had arrived on their doorstep just over a week before. At the moment, Effie too seemed happier, though the moods of an adolescent girl, Sarah knew, could change in an instant.

Distracted by these thoughts, Sarah raised her racquet too late and . . . missed.

"Sorry," she called, warm with embarrassment.

"That's all right," her sister assured her.

Sarah picked up the fallen shuttlecock and served it back.

It veered wide, but Mr. Henshall ran, stretched out his arm, and returned it.

He hit the shuttlecock in a gentle arc to Sarah, clearly trying to go easy on her.

Sarah swung hard, sending the shuttlecock high. The sea breeze caught it and carried it behind her. "Sorry!"

"I'll get it." Georgiana hurried off to hunt for it among the laurel bushes.

Once she'd retrieved it, she jogged back and prepared to serve. Mr. Henshall adopted a ready stance, feet spread, knees bent.

He returned Georgiana's serve with a light swing, and again, the breeze propelled it with added force.

Sarah leapt to try to get her racquet under it, but the feathers fell to the ground once more.

She served it smartly and the shuttlecock flew. Mr. Henshall ran quickly backward, jumped high, and managed to whack it back.

"Well done," Effie said with rare enthusiasm.

His smile of surprise and paternal pleasure touched Sarah's heart.

"Thank ye, my dear."

Mr. Stanley and Emily came outside and were soon persuaded

to take Sarah's and Mr. Henshall's places. For a few minutes, Sarah sat near Callum Henshall on the veranda, the two catching their breath and cheering on the younger players.

Mr. Stanley proved to be athletic as well, although he curtailed his skill to keep the game friendly, seeming to take delight in hitting the shuttlecock just out of Emily's reach and chuckling when she squealed.

The game probably would have continued longer, but Chips ran up, swiped the feathered birdie in his mouth, and dashed off with it, ending the match.

13

The new and favourite Game of Mother Goose and the
Golden Egg, published and sold by John Wallis.
—Caroline Goodfellow, *How We Played:*
Games from Childhood Past

T he next day, after reading to Major Hutton again, Viola
returned to Sea View only long enough to collect Georgie
and a book before heading to the poor house. Mamma
had insisted Georgiana accompany her, at least the first time, since
they were not exactly sure what Viola might be walking into, and
because a woman like Mrs. Fulford might frown upon a lady crossing town alone.

Viola walked along the esplanade, skirts and veil buffeted by
the wind, the book tucked under her arm. Georgie lagged behind,
playing fetch with Chips, her ever-present shadow. They walked
to the eastern side of Sidmouth, turned inland, and walked up
the byes—the footpath along the river—passing the independent
Marsh Chapel and Mr. Baker's brewery before arriving at the
poor house. Beyond it, the water mill slowly churned and the
wooden bridge crossed the River Sid, leading toward the village
of Salcombe Regis.

Reaching the poor-house door, she discovered Mrs. Fulford there before her. Viola was relieved to see she was not accompanied by Mrs. Robins nor anyone else.

"Ah, Miss Summers. Right on time. And this is your youngest sister, I believe?"

"Yes, Georgiana."

Mrs. Fulford smiled from one to the other. Noticing Chips, she said, "And the stray you feed, I presume?"

Georgie nodded. "Yes, ma'am."

"Well. This is the poor house, and that is the school next door." She pointed. "Built seven or eight years ago, funded by the poor rate and by voluntary subscriptions. If either of you are willing to read to children, that is another need. But first things first." She opened the door.

"May I wait here?" Georgiana asked, either intimidated by the tall, well-dressed woman or simply preferring to remain out of doors.

"Very well," Viola replied. "Don't wander off."

Mrs. Fulford led the way into the neat brick building. Inside, rooms opened off a central corridor with a common dining room overlooking the river.

As they started down the corridor, Mrs. Fulford said, "If you wish to read to other residents in future, I am sure they would be appreciative. I should warn you about Miss Reed, however. . . ." Here, she gestured to the door marked 1. "I have tried again and again to extend Christian charity to her. But she has rebuffed my every attempt, as well as the vicar's. I don't say it to gossip. I simply would not wish you to be rejected and feel she had rejected you personally."

"I understand."

Mrs. Fulford proceeded to the door marked 3. In a low voice, she explained, "Mrs. Denby can still see a little, but her vision has grown increasingly poor." She knocked.

"Come in!" a singsong voice replied from within.

Mrs. Fulford opened the door, and Viola followed her inside.

"Mrs. Denby, good afternoon. May I introduce Miss Viola Summers? She has come to read to you."

A small white-haired woman beamed up at them from her chair. "Has she indeed? What a delightful surprise! Come closer, my dear." She held out a bent hand, and Viola tentatively walked forward and placed her fingers in the woman's frail clasp. "What a pleasure to meet you. How kind of you to come."

Would her warm reception cool once the woman saw her scar? Just how dim was her eyesight?

"Well." Mrs. Fulford drew herself up. "I shall leave the two of you to become acquainted. I believe Miss Viola will be able to read to you, what, once or twice a week, at about this time?" The woman's eyes held Viola's through the veil.

"Yes, I think so."

"Excellent."

Mrs. Fulford nodded to each, turned, and left the room.

Mrs. Denby visibly relaxed when the fine woman departed. She said, "Mrs. Fulford is a kind, managing sort of woman. I am grateful for her."

Viola nodded and looked around the tidy, sparsely furnished room, trying to think of what to say. The only decorations were some pretty pieces of lace on the side table.

She walked closer to inspect them. "Did you make these?"

"Indeed I did, along with my sister and mother. On the side, though, which was rather forbidden at the time. Don't report us!"

She gave her a girlish grin, and Viola automatically returned it.

Mrs. Denby's gaze trailed the pattern of her dotted net veil. She leaned close, squinting, and pronounced, "Machine netting." The old woman shook her head with a regretful twist of her lips. "How things have changed."

"Well. What shall I read for you?" Viola looked around for printed material. "Letters?"

"How I wish! I haven't any. No one's written to me in years."

"The newspaper, then?"

"Haven't one of those either."

Viola lifted the volume from under her arm. "I did bring one book, just in case, though I did not know what you would like, so . . ."

"Oh! What have you brought?" The woman's eyes shone. "A Bible?"

Viola's mouth parted, courage waning. She'd not even thought of that. "Er, no. A book of nature." She read the title, "Gilbert White's *The Natural History and Antiquities of Selborne.*"

The sparkle dulled, but Mrs. Denby said cheerfully, "Well, that sounds rather edifying too. Let's hear it. Do sit down."

Viola sat in the room's other chair and opened the volume. Seeing the opening quotes in Latin and Greek, she turned the page to find heavy lines of introduction and guessed she had made a mistake.

"Why do I not turn ahead to one of the illustrations. You can still see a little, I gather?" She flipped the pages until she came to a line drawing of two birds on a branch, labeled *M & F Goatsuckers*. "Any interest in birds?"

"I adore birds. Love listening to them from my window."

"Birds it is, then." Viola bent her head and read:

> "The *caprimulgus* (or goatsucker) is a wonderful and curious creature. This bird is most punctual in beginning its song exactly at the close of day; so exactly that I have known it to strike more than once just at the report of the Portsmouth evening gun, which we can hear when the weather is still."

"Do those birds really feed from goats?" Mrs. Denby asked. "Or is that a legend?"

"I don't know." Viola admitted.

She turned to another section and read:

> "The language of birds is very ancient and elliptical; little is said, but much is meant and understood. Ravens exert a deep and solemn

note that makes the woods echo; the amorous sound of a crow is strange and ridiculous; rooks, in the breeding season, attempt to sing, but with no great success; the fern-owl, from the dusk till daybreak, serenades his mate with the clattering of castanets. . . ."

Quite a concert, Viola mused, thinking Mr. Hornbeam might enjoy the passage. She glanced up and, finding her listener asleep, sighed and closed the book.

Next time, she resolved, she would bring something more interesting.

They had settled on Saturdays and Sundays as their nights off from serving dinner, giving Mrs. Besley a Sabbath rest of sorts, although she would still cook breakfast on Saturday and prepare a cold collation for Sunday.

Therefore, on that Saturday evening, their guests went elsewhere to dine.

Even so, after their informal family meal, Sarah made coffee and brought up a tray of honey biscuits and fruit tarts. As the guests returned to Sea View after dining out, they gathered in the drawing room over coffee, exchanging experiences and opinions of the quality of food they had eaten at hotel, inn, or public house.

After a time, Georgie asked, "Who wants to play a game? We have The New Game of the Monkey from Wallis's, and I long to try it."

Effie's lip curled. "Sounds childish."

"Not at all," Emily said. "Mr. Wallis assured me it was appropriate for all ages."

Effie shrugged. "Then I will play. At least it's not Mother Goose."

Georgiana cajoled, "It would be *so* much more diverting with more players." She looked around at the others.

"No, thank you," Mrs. Elton replied with a glance at her husband, who had fallen asleep on the sofa beside her, empty teacup balanced precariously in his hand. "We do not enjoy games."

"I wish I could," Mr. Stanley said kindly, "but my sister is expecting me soon. She arrived today and is staying with a friend at the York Hotel. Otherwise I would happily spend the evening here."

With a lingering glance at Emily, he bowed and took his leave.

What a dutiful brother, Sarah thought.

Emily watched him go then said, "I will play. Mr. Henshall, will you join us?"

He hesitated, looked at his stepdaughter, and said, "If Effie doesna mind."

The girl shrugged once more. "Suit yourself."

"Be grateful, Effie," Georgie urged. "We need all the players we can get. Who else? Sarah?"

"One round. Then I must get back to next week's menus."

Mr. Hornbeam spoke up. "I will join you, if you need another player."

Georgiana stared at him, blinking rapidly.

Effie frowned and opened her mouth to object, Sarah guessed, so she said quickly, "That is very kind, Mr. Hornbeam. I'm sure Georgiana could read out the numbers you spin and help you move the appropriate spaces." She sent her sister a pointed look.

"Of course I can," Georgiana dutifully replied. "Come and sit beside me."

Moving to a table in the nearby parlour, Georgiana took the game board from its sleeve and unfolded it, smoothing it flat upon the surface.

"Choose a counter," she instructed, gesturing to a pile of tokens she had gathered from around the house. "I'll use the fish." She picked up a small token made of mother-of-pearl and surveyed the others jumbled there. "Mr. Hornbeam, would you prefer a farthing, thruppence, thimble, or one of the buttons?"

"The farthing."

"And here's a teetotum." On the table, Emily set the new octagonal spinning top with several dots on each side. Once spun, the teetotum would topple onto one of its sides, and the uppermost number indicated how many places the player was to advance. The game board was printed with spaces spiraling in toward the center, numbered from one to sixty-three. The border and several of these spaces were illustrated with mischievous monkeys dressed as humans in fanciful poses: dancing, fishing, fencing, marching in oversized soldier's boots, riding a hobbyhorse, stubbing one's toe, et cetera. Other squares held pictures of various places or objects, like a prison, inn, and well.

Georgiana leaned closer and began reading the rules printed within the board's center square:

"Whoever lands on 5 must pay one for learning to dance. Whoever spins 6 must pay one for a toll. The soldier, number nine, may march on to number thirteen. The Gamester must begin again. The Dandy must pay two for his folly. . . ."

Georgiana read the remaining rules and then sat back. "Thankfully, they are printed right here, in case we forget anything."

The game began, with Georgiana spinning the teetotum for Mr. Hornbeam.

Georgie exclaimed, "It's a five, Mr. Hornbeam, so you must pay the dancing master. That's back one space for you."

They took turns around the table, spinning and moving as indicated.

When his second turn arrived, Mr. Hornbeam held out his hand. "Let me see that teetotum."

With a perplexed look, Georgiana laid it on his open palm.

"But you can't see," Effie said unnecessarily.

He fingered the spinner, carved of animal bone, and asked her, "Are you quite certain?"

He spun the top, and when it toppled, fingered the surface. "One."

Then he spun again. "Three."

Georgiana beamed. "You're right, Mr. Hornbeam!"

Like dice, each side held concave dots carved into it to represent a number.

He said modestly, "You shall still have to help me find the correct spaces."

"I don't mind at all," Georgiana assured him.

The game continued with Mr. Hornbeam spinning another five.

He said, "I ended on four after paying the dancing master, so that puts me at nine. Ah! Which means I land on the soldier and advance to thirteen."

"Good memory, Mr. Hornbeam."

Sarah landed on the courtship space, illustrated with one monkey in lady's dress and bonnet, and a second on bended knee before her.

"You get to move ahead to the inn," Georgie reminded her.

From courtship directly to the inn, Sarah mused. What was the implied meaning there? Whatever it was, Sarah didn't think she liked it. Unbidden, thoughts of her older sister, Claire, intruded. Her courtship had advanced to an inn, and far too quickly. Sarah's stomach twisted, and she hoped her expression did not reveal her unhappy thoughts.

On his turn, Mr. Henshall also landed on courtship, and foolishly, Sarah's cheeks warmed.

"Oh la la," Georgie teased. "You both landed in courtship!"

He moved to join Sarah at the inn, but Effie reminded him, "Two players can't be on the same space. Since ye arrived there last, ye must go back to your former place."

He returned his piece with a melodramatic sigh. "Stuck in courtship."

"Take heart," Mr. Hornbeam said with mischief in his tone. "There are worse places to be."

Later in the game, Sarah fell down the well and had to stay there until another player landed on the same spot.

"See now why we wanted more players?" Georgie said. "You'd be waiting an awfully long time otherwise."

Sure enough, on his next turn, Callum Henshall landed in the well and Sarah was able to go forward.

"Thank you for rescuing me, gallant sir."

"Most welcome, fair—although drenched—lady."

Sarah chuckled.

Effie got lost in the maze and had to begin again, which led to much moaning. Her father then sat in prison for three turns. Mr. Hornbeam landed on the overdressed dandy and had to move back two. He fluffed his cravat, smoothed a prim finger over wiry eyebrows, and said in an affected voice, "How dreadful. My coif shall be spoilt."

The others laughed at his antics, and even Effie spared him a grin.

It appeared Georgiana would reach the end first, but she spun too high a number and overshot the mark, having to return to space fifty. In the end, it was Sarah who won the game, to a chorus of groans and cheers.

She pushed back her chair. "And on that note, I must excuse myself."

More groans sounded. "Come on, Sarah. One more round!"

"I am afraid not." Sarah rose. "Perhaps someone can take my place."

"Who?" Emily asked. "And if you say Mrs. Elton, I shall—"

"Hush."

A cough sounded from the side door, closest to Mamma's room.

Sarah looked over. There her mother stood, leaning on the door-frame, but standing all the same.

"Will I do?" she asked.

"Sorry, Mamma. Did we disturb you?"

"Not at all. Sounds like you are having a good time, and I thought I'd join you. That is, if no one objects."

"Of course not," Emily said. "You are very welcome."

"Here, Mamma. Take my place." Sarah helped her into the chair she had just vacated, her heart buoyed at the sight of her mother dressed and sitting with the others, an expression of pleasure on her face.

She introduced the guests. "You remember Mr. Henshall, and this is his stepdaughter, Effie. And this is Mr. Hornbeam. Mr. Hornbeam, our mother, Mrs. Summers."

The older man rose and bowed. "An honor, ma'am."

"Thank you. Well then." Mamma looked at the others with girlish eagerness. In that moment, Sarah recognized a resemblance to Georgiana she had missed before.

A dimple in her cheek, she picked up the teetotum and grinned around the table. "Shall we play?"

On Sunday morning, the sisters attended the parish church together. All except Viola, who stayed home with Mamma as usual.

Upon entering the nave, Sarah noticed Mr. Henshall there before them, pressed between others in a crowded row. She wished she'd thought to invite him to walk with them and share their pew.

Later that afternoon, Mr. Henshall changed into riding clothes and left Sea View to retrieve two horses he had hired from a local stable.

A short while later, he rode up the lane atop a chestnut horse, leading a smaller grey for Effie. His beaver hat was pulled low, and he held both reins and lead with casual ease.

Sarah went outside to greet him. "Where are you off to?"

"Just a ride around the area. Maybe up to Honiton or down the coast. Want to show Effie more of the countryside. And, truth be told, I miss riding."

With hands encased in fine leather gloves, he angled his hat brim to better see her. "Do ye ride, Miss Summers?"

"Not in ages, no. Though I do like horses."

He nodded. "We keep a few at home. Hopefully my groom is exercising them enough."

Effie came out in a simple green riding habit, looking eager instead of sullen for once. He dismounted to give the girl a leg up into her sidesaddle.

Then he turned to Sarah, his gaze lingering on her face. He seemed to want to say something more, then apparently thought the better of it, and remounted his horse.

"Have a good ride," Sarah called up to him.

Gathering the reins, he glanced down at her once more. "Thank ye."

Sarah watched the two ride off together. She was impressed with Effie, who rode comfortably and competently beside her stepfather. But her gaze quickly returned to Callum Henshall.

She could not help noticing how striking he looked astride his horse, his posture excellent, his shoulders broad, his horsemanship evident.

In his close-fitting riding coat and polished Hessians, he looked every inch the well-to-do English gentleman. She found herself wondering if he ever wore a kilt.

14

Persons who are fond of swimming should be informed that
a little to the west of the beach there is a fine sequestered
bay, in which they may, in calm weather, be safely gratified.
—*The Beauties of Sidmouth Displayed*

On Monday, after the morning chores were finished—
earlier than expected, thanks to Bibi's energetic help—
Viola and Emily went for a walk to stretch their legs,
take the air, and avoid both Augusta Elton and Sarah's endless
to-do list.

Crossing the lawn, they followed Peak Hill Road to the north
and at Pilgrim Cottage turned left, toward the headland and sea.
They reached the summit near the lime kiln and paused to catch
their breath, winded from the uphill climb. Side by side on the
grassy knoll, they peered over the edge at Chit Rock below, project-
ing like a tower from the sun-spangled water. Above them, gulls
circled in a blue sky.

The breeze ruffling her veil, Viola sighed with pleasure. "I never
tire of this view."

Her gaze shifted to the western beach below, on the other side
of Chit Rock. No bathing machines there. No crowds.

A path cut into the side of the hill led from the lime kiln down to the beach. Later in the day, workers would lead donkeys up that path with loads of limestone for the kiln, but for now it was quiet.

As they stood there, two men appeared on the beach below, their heads bare, both with dark hair. Suddenly, and without ceremony, they began stripping off their clothing—coats, waistcoats, shirts, shoes.

Viola turned to go, but Emily gripped her hand. "Who are they?" she whispered. "I have heard that many men swim here."

"Is that why you wanted to come this way?" Viola asked.

"I did not hear you objecting!"

One man had pale skin, and the other's was the color of rich brown coffee. The distance rendered the figures less distinct, yet even so Viola could guess who they were—the major and Armaan.

From this height, the right side of the major's face appeared shadowed, but the scars were not obvious. How broad his shoulders looked, chest tapering to a slender waist. Her mouth went dry.

"We should not just stand here . . . gawking," Viola hissed.

The men moved down to their trousers, and Emily gasped, pressing her eyes closed.

Viola covered hers with her free hand. She had heard men swam without clothes, but had not really believed it. Hearing a splash, she dared a peek between her fingers.

Below, the major dove headfirst under an oncoming wave, while Armaan waded out more slowly. Viola was relieved the water now concealed their bodies.

Emily, eyes suddenly wide, squeezed her hand, grip as tight as her voice. "He's disappeared. Where is he?"

Her sister had always been unnerved by the idea of going into the sea.

Viola pointed with her free hand. "There he is."

The major reappeared, slicing through the water, arms stroking, moving with apparent ease. How strangely thrilling to see him move with such strength and grace, with no sign of the injuries that hindered him on dry ground. Instead, he seemed whole and strong and overwhelmingly masculine.

After swimming the length of the beach, the major stood, waist-deep in water, probably catching his breath. He turned toward a coasting barge on the horizon.

Emily said, "There's something wrong with that man's face. Can you see?"

Viola did not want to admit she knew the men they were watching, so she said only, "How can you tell from this distance?"

Emily narrowed her eyes. "I don't know. Something isn't right."

Viola felt defensive and insulted on the major's behalf.

"Not everyone is as perfect as you, Emily."

"Why thank you, Vi," she dryly replied.

Provoked, Viola said in mock innocence, "Perhaps we ought to try bathing. Oh, that's right, you're afraid of the water."

Emily turned to her with a challenging glare. "I will go into the sea when you walk across Sidmouth without a veil."

She deserved that, Viola knew, but pride kept her from apologizing.

This time, it was Emily who tugged Viola's hand, turning her from the tantalizing sight.

"I never tire of this view" suddenly took on a whole new meaning.

Later that day, as the sisters were setting the table for luncheon, Emily said, "The weather has been so fine lately. We really ought to have a picnic."

Sarah wrinkled her nose. "We have enough work as it is. I cannot ask the servants to do more."

"It need not be an elaborate affair."

"Even a simple outdoor meal would take work and planning. Not only the food and drink, but also tableware and linens, not to mention transporting it all to the site."

"We will all help," Emily insisted. She turned to Viola and Georgie. "Won't we?"

"Happily!" Georgie enthused. "Would we invite our guests or friends?"

"If we invite our guests," Emily pointed out, "then we could count it as that day's dinner rather than adding to Mrs. Besley's work."

"Good point."

"It would certainly be a gesture of goodwill to our guests. Perhaps Mamma might even come."

Sarah countered, "That would depend on where we have it. If you insist on climbing to the top of the Peak Hill, then no."

"How about just partway up the hill, to that lovely grove of trees?"

"Is that still manor land, or Mr. Lousada's property?"

"No one will mind."

Georgie offered, "I will ask him, if you like. I often see him when I am out on my rambles. Oh, may we have a picnic, Sarah, puleeease?"

Sarah turned to Viola, who had been quiet throughout. "What do you say, Vi?"

She expected her taciturn, private sister to reject the notion. Instead Viola lifted her chin and said, "I think it a fine idea and will help with the extra work."

How unexpected.

That seemed to settle it. As the sisters continued their discussion over the meal, the idea took on an appealing aspect. The weather really did continue fine, as Emily had said. Their larder was full with leftover food at the moment, and Sarah had been doing a great deal of baking, so there would be less to purchase and prepare.

Next, to convince their cook.

The sisters went belowstairs together and proposed the plan.

"I have not prepared a picnic in ages, and never for paying guests," Mrs. Besley warned.

"We will all help," the girls assured her.

After they perused the larder shelves and discussed the idea with Mamma, a menu was drawn up and a shopping list written. They decided the picnic meal would resemble the cold collation they served on Sundays, although simpler: cold roast chicken and ham, fish pie, fresh fruit if they could find it, or stewed fruit in glass bottles with biscuits, cheese, rolls, and tarts. Tea and cider to drink.

They would also need sugar lumps and milk for tea, cups, glasses, plates, and utensils.

As the details mounted, Sarah's pulse began to pound.

Later, Mrs. Besley reviewed the list and nodded her head. "We can manage this, I think. And it will make a pleasant change, I own. Might I ask our neighbor's cook to help me?"

Confusion flickered. "Which neighbor?"

"The cook at Westmount. He's as green as they come but eager to learn. He comes by now and again to ask me how to do something."

As if on cue, someone knocked on the basement door, and a moment later, Jessie led an unkempt young man into the kitchen.

Mrs. Besley smiled. "Come in, Mr. Chown, we were just talking about you."

"That don't bode well," the young man said. He wore a stained apron and sheepish expression and was in need of a shave.

"Not at all," Mrs. Besley said. "We were wondering if you might help us prepare a picnic?"

"Never done the like before, but happy to help if I can." He scratched the back of his neck. "Don't suppose I could borrow some suet in the meantime?"

Mrs. Besley beamed like a proud parent of a prodigal. "Well, of course you can."

⌒⌒⌒

Later, Viola walked to Westmount for the day's reading session. It was really becoming quite ridiculous of her to wear her veil on the short walk over, but she did. The desire to shield herself was deeply ingrained.

The footman let her in and gestured down the passage.

"I know the way, Taggart. Thank you."

Before she knocked on the major's door, she untied her bonnet ribbons.

"Come."

Stepping inside, she removed the bonnet, veil and all. As she set it on the nearby side table, she noticed her hands tremble. This was not the first time Viola had removed her veil in his presence, yet she still felt nervous. After all, he did not know how she had come by her scar.

She turned slowly toward him.

He glanced at her, then grunted in satisfaction. "Glad that is dispensed with."

Wanting to shift his focus from her person, she asked, "Good swim?"

"How did you know I went?"

"Oh. I . . . assumed." She blinked, trying to dispel an image of him standing bare-chested in waist-high water.

She stepped to the pile of correspondence and recent newspapers. "What shall I read today?"

"Talk to me first. Armaan has gone riding, and my father and brother aren't much for conversation. How are you keeping— anything new?"

"Yes, actually. I've begun reading to a woman in the poor house."

"Why?"

"I was asked to, and I find I enjoy it. I like being useful."

"Would you like a medal?" He jerked a hand toward the mantel. "Have one of mine. Much good they've done me."

Mortification and anger heated her face. Even her eyes felt hot. "No, I do not want a medal. You asked me for news, so I told you. What would you have me do—sit in the dark doing nothing all day, like you do?"

As soon as she said the harsh words, remorse engulfed her. His doctor had told him the darkness would ease the headaches. How cruel of her. For a moment he said nothing, the tension between them heavy. She expected a rebuke or a dismissal. Instead he gentled his voice.

"I deserved that. I see we are both quite skilled in lashing out when in pain."

"I am not—"

He lifted a hand. "Forgive me. May we start this visit over? Please?"

"Yes. And I am sorry too."

Uncomfortable under his intense gaze, she picked up the post. "There is a letter from your lawyer. Shall we start there?"

"Very well. Though that man's letters usually bear bad news."

Viola unfolded it and began reading, "I regret to inform you that . . ."

She paused. The man's scrawl was difficult to decipher. "I am sorry. I cannot make out this line."

She squinted at it, then glanced up and started, disconcerted to find the major standing close to her. Very close indeed.

"Man's handwriting is atrocious," he said. "What has thwarted you?"

Feeling oddly dizzy at his nearness, his height, she pointed unsteadily to the line.

He bent nearer to study it with his good eye. "The county rate is rising. Thunder and turf. It was high enough as it was."

The words deciphered, she expected him to move away, but he did not. She looked up at him in question.

His gaze swept over her face.

He lifted his hand, and his fingers hesitated inches from her cheek. "May I?"

May he what?

She didn't know but nodded mutely anyway.

His finger touched the side of her mouth, and she flinched.

"Did I hurt you?" he asked, brow furrowed.

She shook her head. "Surprised me."

His fingers neared again, this time lightly, ever so lightly, tracing the outline of her lips. Her skin tingled under his touch. Were her lips really so full, so curvy? Or did his fingers exaggerate their shape?

Then his finger lingered on the thicker, coarser skin of her scar. She knew when he'd reached it; no fine hairs bristled under his feathery touch.

"I still can't believe you wore a veil to cover this," he said, voice low. "You have a beautiful mouth. A beautiful . . . everything. Never doubt it."

No one had ever touched her mouth so . . . sweetly. So admiringly. And her mouth . . . beautiful? Tears pricked her eyes.

Viola didn't want to say it. But the truth fermented and bubbled within. He might as well know all. That would chase that look of admiration from his face in a hurry.

When his hand dropped away, she armored her heart, as she was so accustomed to doing, and drew back her shoulders. "You may as well know the worst. This scar was not due to an injury as are yours. I—"

"You were born with a cleft lip."

The breath left her. "You knew?"

"I assumed as much."

She ducked her head, more self-conscious than ever. "Is it so obvious?"

"No. I might not have guessed, except that I have seen something like it before. In France, during the war. A Frenchwoman I met—who helped us, actually—had such a scar. Apparently, the surgical methods in France are more advanced."

Viola nodded. "Yes, we went there after the war ended. That is where I had my last surgery." *Hopefully* her last.

He narrowed his eyes. "That still doesn't explain why you hide that insignificant scar behind a veil."

"Insignificant? Do you not know people believe it's catching? That, if a woman expecting a child sees someone with a cleft lip, her child will be born that way too?"

"Balderdash."

"Said by a man who has never had someone look at him and run."

"Perhaps not run, but I have certainly seen people cringe and avert their eyes as they pass. My scars are far more extensive than yours."

"Mine run deeper."

"Is this a contest?"

She raised her hands. "Yours were earned while in service to king and country. To save a friend. Yours are a badge of honor."

He gave a derisive snort.

She added, "Whereas mine is a mark of disgrace. Of deformity."

"How you do feel sorry for yourself."

She gaped at him. "That's the pot calling the kettle black if ever I heard it."

"*Pfff.* I suppose you're right. But I hate being like this. Hate people looking at me with pity, or shuddering in revulsion, or both."

She met his gaze, compassion swelling in her breast. "I don't shudder."

He stared at her as if gauging her sincerity, his good eye glowing like a firebrand. She looked away first.

Then, attempting to dispel the heaviness, she teased, "Nor do I see merely your scars. I also see a long, crooked nose. Large, hooded eyes. And thin, bowed lips. Your scars are the least of your problems."

He expelled a wry puff of laughter, and she was relieved when he grinned.

"Thank you. I see I shall have no cause to become vain in your company."

Sarah organized the sideboard that evening, preparing to help serve another dinner to their guests.

The dinners were not as grand as if they were entertaining, but had been good and varied so far, usually beginning with soup and fish, followed by meat and a rotation of side dishes, and finally coffee and dessert.

After the first few nights of guests eating alone, Sarah and Emily had agreed to take turns acting as hostess during the meals. One sat with the guests, keeping the conversation going, while the other oversaw the serving, helping Jessie as needed with refills and clearing away.

Emily was a natural in the role of hostess, asking everyone how they had spent their day, sharing local anecdotes, drawing the quieter guests into the conversation, and often making them laugh. Sarah did her best to emulate her, yet no one could match Emily's charm and repartee.

Mrs. Elton spoke a great deal and tended to dominate the conversation, but Sarah had learned to turn her statements into questions for the others, stemming the flow, at least for a time. This was one thing she did better than Emily, who easily lost patience with the woman and was occasionally brusque with her, cutting her off as she was about to launch into yet another tale of all their impressive new friends in Sidmouth, or how much their neighbors back home were missing them.

Mr. Stanley ate with them only occasionally. With his sister still staying at the York Hotel, he often dined with her instead.

Mr. Hornbeam, always pleasant and polite, was an asset to the company and regularly contributed to the conversation. When asked, he would tell about his experiences in Parliament but seemed to take more interest in others' lives, posing excellent questions. Everyone quickly became accustomed to his dark glasses and his inability to know what food was before him. Those sitting on either side soon learned to offer him dishes without being asked to do so. Even Mrs. Elton grew to accept him.

Viola still refused to sit with the guests or to wait at table and continued to take her meals with Mamma. Sarah understood Viola's hesitance, as one could not easily eat while wearing a veil. And in all honesty, she did not know how Mrs. Elton might react to her defect, considering her response to Mr. Hornbeam. Thankfully, Viola was able to pay Bibi from her reading fees, so Sarah did not protest.

That night, Sarah oversaw the serving, while Emily filled the role of hostess once more.

She asked Mr. Henshall more about his boyhood in Scotland, and after he'd relayed a few tales, Sarah noticed Effie roll her eyes.

"The poet Walter Scott is from Edinburgh," Emily said.

"That's right," Mr. Henshall agreed. "In fact, I met him once."

Emily's jaw dropped. "You never!"

"I did, at a dinner party. He recited a long poem after hearing it only the once. An astounding memory. He then read from one of his own."

"Which one?"

He looked up in thought. "I believe it was 'The Lady of the Lake.'"

Emily's eyes brightened and she recited a few lines. "'Harp of the North! That mouldering long hast hung, on the witch-elm that shades Saint Fillan's spring, and down the fitful breeze thy numbers flung.'"

He nodded. "That's the one. I was surprised to see Scott is lame in one leg."

Emily's expression fell. "Lame?"

"Aye. But it doesna seem to hinder him much. Said he even climbed Edinburgh's Castle Rock."

"Then it must be a fairly minor condition," Emily said, apparently mollified.

"Certainly didna stop him bein' the most popular fellow there." He winked.

Mr. Hornbeam added, "I understand Scott served as clerk to the Court of Session in Edinburgh."

"Aye. And sheriff depute of the county."

Emily remained more interested in what the man wrote. "Do you like his poetry, Mr. Henshall?"

"I own I have not read much of it. Always more interested in music, I'm afraid."

Mr. Hornbeam raised an expressive hand. "Are not songs rather like poetry, set to music? And I for one greatly enjoy Mr. Henshall's music."

Mrs. Elton coughed. "Well, we each have our own levels of taste. I love nothing so much as the opera. Do you not agree, Mr. Elton?"

"Oh. Ah . . . I like that you like it, my dear. Your enjoyment is mine."

He and Mr. Henshall shared a conspiratorial look.

Emily said, "As we have no opera here, perhaps Mr. Henshall might play for us after dinner?"

He glanced at his stepdaughter. "If Effie will sing."

The girl wrinkled her nose. "I'd rather not. Besides, there's to be a concert at Wallis's this evening. Let's go there instead."

He agreed amiably, while Sarah swallowed her disappointment.

So after dinner they all walked down the esplanade to enjoy the special concert given by Sidmouth's amateur band.

When they reached the veranda of the Marine Library, Mrs. Elton pressed her way through the crowd and squeezed onto one of the benches near the front. The others stood at the back, although Georgiana went and found a stool for Mr. Hornbeam and insisted he sit down. Sarah felt a surge of almost maternal pride for her thoughtful sister.

The local band, established by some tradesmen of the town, played several lively martial pieces, but Sarah would have rather listened to Callum Henshall's guitar.

After the concert, applause and donations were duly given, and they all returned to Sea View. Sarah bid the others good-night and returned to the office to do some paperwork.

Later, when Sarah went upstairs to go to bed, she heard soft music and followed the sound to Mr. Henshall's room. For several moments she stood there outside his door to listen. The sweet, mournful tune evoked sad memories and regret. Still, the yearning notes comforted, even as they pierced her heart.

Mr. Hornbeam was not alone in appreciating Callum Henshall's music.

15

I cut and handed the sweet seed-cake—the little sisters had a
bird-like fondness for picking up seeds and pecking at sugar. . . .
—Charles Dickens, *David Copperfield*

The next day, Sarah sat in the library reviewing the upcoming days in the register. They were expecting a Mr. Gwilt from Pontypool—wherever that was. In his letter he'd estimated a late afternoon arrival. He could be there at any time. With the addition of this guest, they would have only one empty room left. Sarah's gratification, however, was dampened by the fact that they had no pending room requests for the near future.

The door knocker sounded, and before Sarah could respond, Georgiana called, "I'll get it."

A few moments later, Georgiana led a guest into the office. "Here is . . . Mr. Gwilt, Sarah."

Her stilted voice and wide eyes signaled . . . something, but Sarah was not sure what it was. The man approached the library desk while her sister lingered in the doorway behind him, pointing at the man with emphatic jerking motions. What was wrong with her? Whatever it was, Sarah would have to deal with it later.

She smiled at their guest, a small, thin-faced man of perhaps fifty. "Welcome."

"Robert Gwilt, arriving as arranged, I am." He spoke in the pleasant, singsong accent of the Welsh. Setting down one of his bags, he removed his hat. "A room for two, if you please."

Sarah glanced at the register again and then looked up uncertainly, searching for a second person behind him. No one. "I am sorry. We have you in a room with a single bed, but—"

"No trouble at all. Parry here can sleep in his cage."

He lifted the burden in his other hand, and Sarah saw with mounting dismay that he carried a birdcage. She gathered a quick impression of colorful plumage and prominent beak. A parrot? Would it talk or squawk and keep everyone up at night?

Mr. Gwilt leaned forward with a conspiratorial air. "Though I like to let him out from time to time. Give him a bet o' freedom, you know. Let him stretch his wings." He winked.

"Oh, Mr. Gwilt, I am afraid we . . ." She rose, about to explain their policy on animals, when she looked more closely at the cage. The parrot inside was unnaturally still. His eyes glassy—glass, in fact. His bird was stuffed.

Sarah didn't know whether to be relieved or yet more disturbed.

She pushed forward the register with unsteady hands. "Well. Never mind. If you will, um, just fill this in. In your letter, you said you would be with us through June. Is that right?"

"Just so." He wrote his name and direction in Wales. Then he extracted a leather purse from his pocket and laid upon the desk several banknotes and an assortment of gold and silver coins. "Here you be. I believe I figured it correctly, but do let me know if I erred."

Sarah hesitated. The money would come in handy. "We do not require payment in advance. However, we certainly appreciate it."

"It's a load off my mind, it is, knowing it's all taken care of."

"Thank you. You must be thirsty from your journey. May I offer you some tea?"

"Very kind of you, but Parry here is tired, he is. Perhaps later?"

"Of course. Then I shall show you to your room." She retrieved the key, led him out of the library, and gestured toward the stairs. "Right this way."

They passed Emily in the hall, and she turned to stare.

"Lovely place, ey, Parry? Such high ceilings. How you would love to fly in here. . . ."

When Sarah returned to the office a short while later, Emily was there waiting for her, eyes flashing.

"That man has a stuffed bird in a cage."

"Yes, I know."

"He talks to it, like it's alive."

Sarah sighed. "I know."

"He's mad."

"Don't say that. We know nothing about him or what he's been through. And other than his . . . pet, he seems an ideal guest. Even paid in advance."

"Good. Otherwise, he'd seem just the sort to abscond without paying, claiming lunacy."

"Hush."

Emily pressed a hand to her forehead. "Oh, how low you have brought us."

Pain and defensiveness flared. "This is all my fault, is it?" Sarah challenged. "Papa's debts? The entail? Our reduced circumstances?"

"No, I . . . I am sorry, Sarah. I know it's not your fault."

Yet Sarah did feel responsible. Not for their father's debts, but for his death, and the calamity that had led to it. For she alone had known what her sister intended to do, and had done nothing to prevent it.

〜

After another call on the major, Viola returned to the poor house, this time with a copy of the New Testament and Psalms.

Mrs. Denby greeted her warmly. "Back so soon? Delightful!"

Viola settled into the chair near her.

"What are we reading today?" the old woman asked, eyes alight.

"I have brought the New Testament and Psalms. Any preference for where I start?"

"Oh! Delightful. How about the Gospel according to John? It's one of my favorites."

After fumbling through the pages to find it, Viola began to read. "In the beginning was the Word, and the Word was with God, and the Word was God. The same was in the beginning with God. All things were made by him; and without him was not anything made that was made. . . ."

Viola read on for a time, until a soft knock rapped the door.

"It's open!" Mrs. Denby called, looking over. The door creaked wide. "Ah, Mr. Butcher. Do come in."

Viola started, glad now she had left her veil in place.

With a glance at Viola, the man hesitated. "I can come back if you are busy."

"Not at all. How kind of you to call. Are you acquainted with my new young friend?"

"I do not believe I have had that pleasure."

"This is Miss Summers. Viola, this is Mr. Butcher. Miss Summers has come to read to me. Is that not most generous?"

"Indeed it is." He bowed to her. "A pleasure to meet you."

Viola sat mute, feeling stunned. This was the author of the Sidmouth guidebook, the man her family wished to impress so he would give Sea View a favorable review. The pressure to say the right thing pressed on her, paralyzing her tongue.

The clergyman was elderly with a long, drooping nose and kind, deep-set eyes. Although dressed in traditional gentleman's attire, he wore a brimless fabric hat that looked rather like a nightcap with a cuff and a tassel on top.

Angling his head, he glanced at the book she held. "And what are you reading, if I may ask?"

Mrs. Denby glanced at her expectantly. When Viola didn't reply, she supplied, "Today it is the book of John. Last time it was . . . oh, I forget." Again she looked at Viola.

Licking dry lips, Viola managed, "*The Natural History and Antiquities of Selborne.*"

He smiled encouragingly. "Excellent choices, the both of them. Gilbert White, the author of *The Natural History*, was a clergyman as well. I do some writing myself, you know."

Viola forced her sluggish tongue to speak. "I . . . yes. My sisters and I have read your book. W-well done."

He nodded. "Thank you. You know, I have a modest library, Miss Summers. You are welcome to borrow any books, should you need more reading material."

"Thank you."

The minister peered at her more closely through the veil. "I don't believe I have seen you at the meeting house?"

"Um . . . no."

"The Summers family attend the parish church," Mrs. Denby explained.

"Of course. Well, I shan't keep you, seeing you are in such good hands. Good day, ladies." He bowed once more, turned, and departed.

When the door closed behind him, Mrs. Denby said, "Mr. Butcher is minister of the Old Dissenting Chapel at the top of the High Street."

Viola nodded, then asked, "You are Church of England too—is that not right?"

"Yes, although here in Devon, we have a long history of dissenting churches: Methodists, Baptists, Congregationalists, and the like."

While not as well-read as Emily, Viola knew dissenters or nonconformists did not hold to the doctrines of the established Anglican Church.

She asked, "Does Mr. Butcher press you to attend his chapel?"

"He has certainly invited me, but he does not press me."

"If you don't want him to call on you, I am sure—"

The old woman's eyes sharpened. "Who said I didn't want him to call? He is a good and kind man."

Viola's neck heated. "Pray forgive me, I did not intend to speak ill of him."

"My girl, if you live to be my age, you will learn to be thankful for anyone who takes the time to visit."

Viola dipped her head, feeling chastised. "Even someone as churlish as me?"

"Especially someone like you."

Viola glanced up, and Mrs. Denby's fond, teasing look eased her discomfort.

The woman's gaze lingered on the veil. "You know, you are welcome to take that off. If you are hiding spots or what have you, they can't be as bad as all my wrinkles and liver spots."

"Very well." Viola slowly lifted the veil away from her face, not nearly as nervous to do so as she had been for the major. And it *would* be easier to read without it.

Mrs. Denby beamed. "Much better. Thank you, my dear."

Her expression grew pensive. "My neighbor, Miss Reed, wears a veil. She used to wear it only when she went outside, but these days she never goes out. She fetches her meals from the dining room and carries them back to her room instead of eating with the rest of us. 'Course, I don't venture far these days either. But I would if I could."

For a moment longer the woman looked wistful, then she smiled, and the wistful expression fled. "Now, do please read some more."

A short while later, as Viola stepped from Mrs. Denby's room, she was surprised to see Mr. Butcher still in the poor house, on the point of leaving another resident's room.

From within came a shrill female voice. "You may strike me off your list, sir. Inflict your good deeds on someone else!"

The door slammed behind him.

He cringed. Apparently hearing Viola's step, he looked over, embarrassment creasing his features.

"Ah, Miss Summers. We meet again." An awkward moment passed. He added, "By the way, I was not simply being polite. You would be welcome to borrow any books you like, especially as it is for such a good cause."

Viola considered. "Now you mention it, Mrs. Denby requested a book we don't have. I don't suppose you have a copy of *The Pilgrim's Progress?*"

He brightened. "I do indeed. A relatively new edition, as a matter of fact. Written by another clergyman, John Bunyan. I would be delighted to lend it to you. I shall deliver it to Mrs. Denby when next I call, and you may leave it with her whenever you are finished. No hurry."

"Excellent. Thank you. That is very kind."

"What you are doing is truly kind." His gaze lingered on her veil. "May I ask . . . was it the smallpox?"

"What? Oh no. Another . . . affliction."

"Ah. I only wondered. So many were taken by it or left scarred." His focus shifted to the door he had just left. "Like Miss Reed there. Have you met her?"

"No, though I have heard her spoken of."

"And none too kindly, I imagine. Miss Reed has tried many a saint, and ordinary mortals like me too."

"It is good of you to try."

He grimaced. "She makes it difficult . . . for herself and those who wish to help. I suppose that is her right. And she has cause to be bitter, I can't deny. She contracted the illness when she was in the first blush of youth and beauty. A 'diamond of the first water,' as they say. She was betrothed to a titled gentleman, and her future seemed secure. But the disease, which killed her parents and brother, left her badly scarred. The lord broke things off, and because of her condition, people did not blame him nor shun him as they might otherwise have done. She and a sister were left with some money and a few loyal retainers, but when the money ran out and the old servants died, they were forced to accept parish charity."

"How sad," Viola breathed, gaze lingering on the closed door, thoughts on the woman within. "And her sister?"

"She died a few years ago. She is the one who told me their story during one of my visits."

"I see."

Mr. Butcher added, "Miss Reed's scars faded over the years, but by then her youth and beauty had faded as well. I believe most people would not be overly troubled by the marks that remain. It is her bitter resentment toward the world and everyone in it that makes people turn away now."

His words itched like woolen stockings. "Well, thank you for telling me."

They talked for a few minutes more, Viola's thoughts once again churning.

Here was the man who, according to Emily, held the future of their guest house in his hands. Emily had asked Mr. Wallis about the new edition of the guidebook and mentioned Sea View, but he'd said it was up to the author to choose the content.

Viola knew she should say something, but her dullard tongue would not obey. Instead, she bid him farewell and walked away, inwardly rebuking herself all the while. How Emily would rail if she knew!

Viola decided she would not tell her.

———

"You what?" Emily scowled, brows drawn thunderously low.

Upon returning to the house, Viola had come upon Sarah and Emily discussing their chances of being listed in the guidebook. Emily had curled her lip and said they would probably have to make a large donation to Mr. Butcher's chapel to secure a mention. Viola had risen to the man's defense without thinking it through. She never could keep a secret from this particular sister.

"I said I met him," Viola repeated. "At the poor house. And he seemed kind and humble."

"Tell me you put in a good word for us."

"I . . . I have not your gift of impromptu speechmaking. Nor of charming gentlemen into doing my bidding. That is your forte, not mine."

Emily put her hands on her waist. "So you said nothing? At a time when he would have been inclined to listen to you?"

"I did say we had all read his book. And that it was . . . well done."

Emily threw up her hands. "Is that all?"

Sarah soothed, "I am sure Viola meant well. She is not accustomed to being out and about in the company of strangers."

Emily was not moved. "Will you see him again?"

"It is possible."

"Then I shall write down something for you to say the next time you meet him. You may commit it to memory, so you won't have the excuse of not knowing what to say."

Viola lifted her chin. "It is not my responsibility."

"We all share the responsibility for our livelihood, whether we wish to or not." Emily snapped her fingers. "That reminds me; I meant to tell you. I wrote to Mr. Butcher a few days ago, inviting him to visit Sea View, to take a meal with us or even spend the night, so he can experience our hospitality for himself."

Worry lines creased Sarah's brow. "What if he comes here unannounced and finds the place in disarray, or Mr. Elton snoring in the parlour?"

"We have to try something. Let's just hope it works and he accepts."

"That reminds me . . ." Viola handed over a few letters. "I picked up the post, since I was passing."

Emily eagerly gathered up the small stack and flipped through them. "No, no, no. Nothing."

"No reply from Mr. Butcher?" Sarah asked.

Viola leaned toward their older sister. "She means nothing from Charles."

Emily wrinkled her nose at her. "None of these have local postmarks, so it doesn't appear Mr. Butcher has replied." She lifted the top one. "Ah! Here is one for Simon Hornbeam."

"From his son?"

"I assume so. Let's take it to him directly."

Mr. Hornbeam had been with them for a week and hoped every day for his son's arrival, or at least a letter. Viola prayed no misfortune had befallen the younger man to prevent him from joining his father as planned.

Sarah remained in the office, but Viola followed Emily as she went in search of Mr. Hornbeam.

They found him on the veranda, his favorite place at Sea View.

"A letter for you, Mr. Hornbeam!" Emily announced in a cheerful, singsong voice.

"Ah, thank you."

Emily extended it toward the man, forgetting he could not see it.

"Shall I read it to you?" Viola offered more softly.

"Yes, please."

Viola sat in the chair nearest him, opened the letter, and read aloud:

"Dear old Pater,

A thousand apologies for not writing sooner. A party of friends has invited me to visit Brighton with them. I know we planned to rendezvous at the seaside, but from all accounts Sidmouth is a sedate watering place—the preserve of the elderly. My friends assure me that Brighton is far more fashionable and diverting.

We went to see the Prince Regent's pleasure palace today. You should see it sometime—forgive me, I sometimes forget you can't. No real loss; I don't know that it is quite your style. You are welcome to join us here, if you like, though it is a devilish long way. There is talk of venturing to Weymouth once we've sampled the entertainments here. So, I may make it to Sidmouth yet.

In the meantime, Brighton is more expensive than I anticipated, so if you would be so good as to advance another twenty, I would be much obliged, Pater-dear.

I know you will understand and find some pleasant way to spend your time.

Yours,
Giles"

Viola glanced over her shoulder at Emily, and the two shared sorrowful looks. Poor man. What to say?

"I am sorry, Mr. Hornbeam," Viola began. "I know how disappointing this must be."

"Hmm. I am afraid Giles disappointing me is nothing new. I had hoped he would mature in time. Sadly . . ." He slowly shook his head. "But a father never stops hoping, and praying, and wishing he had done things differently. Ah well."

Again the sisters shared pained looks. How could they comfort him?

Emily tried, "At least it sounds like he might still come. Eventually."

In reply, the man managed a closed-lip smile, but it was not very convincing.

⁓

The following day, they all bustled about preparing for the picnic on the morrow. They had invited their guests, and everyone accepted. Emily gazed out the window at the sky whenever she passed, hoping the weather would continue fine.

The cook from Westmount came over to assist with preparations, and Bibi stayed longer to help. By noon, Mrs. Besley was huffing and puffing and giving orders to anyone who dared cross her path. Emily was tempted to make herself scarce, but since she had suggested the idea, she resolved not to shirk her duty, even though the book she was currently reading kept calling to her like a siren song. She resisted its call and did whatever was asked of her, chopping, stirring, bottling, and folding linens.

At one point, Sarah asked her to see if the afternoon tea tray needed refilling and to bring down some serving utensils from the dining room. Emily went upstairs to do her bidding.

In the parlour, Emily saw Mr. Gwilt, teacup in hand, a plate of crumbled seed cake on the table beside him, and his parrot in its cage nearby.

Curiosity got the better of her. Joining him, she asked, "Where did you get your parrot, Mr. Gwilt?"

"Oh, now. I know you want me to spin some fabulosity, like I sailed with a great explorer to Africa or South America. That's where most parrots come from, you know."

"And did you?"

"No, lass. Truth is, I bought him in a curiosity shop. He'd been found in some old sailor's lodgings after the man died. Poor creature was scared and starving. They fed him in the shop, but lads used to tease him in there—torment him, more like, the devils. I couldn't abide seeing such a regal creature treated cruelly. So I bought him, which was foolish and impractical, yet it was fate. He needed me, and I needed him, though I did not yet know it."

He glanced fondly at the bird. "Took a long time to gain his trust, after all he'd been through. But he learned to trust me in the end, he did. They say parrots live a long time, and I hoped . . ." Mr. Gwilt shook his head. "He was already an old parrot when he came into my life. Even so, I will never regret bringing him home."

"Did you give him his name?"

Mr. Gwilt nodded. "Parry, short for parrot."

"Could he speak?"

"Oh yes. 'Want more.' And several salty sailor's terms I shan't repeat."

He winked, and she smiled in reply. Despite herself, she found herself liking the man.

Sarah came in. "Oh, here you are, Emily. Find those serving spoons I asked for?"

"Not yet. Just talking to our newest guest for a few minutes."

Her efficient sister began gathering the used plates and cups left by other guests. "Good afternoon, Mr. Gwilt. Have everything you need?"

He beamed up at her. "I do indeed. Excellent seed cake."

Sarah glanced at the dry-looking, caraway-heavy slices but said only, "Pleased to hear it. I will let Mrs. Besley know you enjoyed it."

As far as Emily knew, her sister had not yet attempted a cake.

Sarah reached for his plate, but he raised a palm. "If you don't mind, I will take these seeds upstairs for Parry. Very fond of seeds, he is."

"Oh." Sarah hesitated, clearly taken aback, and she and Emily shared a look. "Well. Of course."

He unfolded a clean handkerchief, tilted the remaining crumbs and seeds onto the cloth, and folded it up again.

"What else did he eat?" Emily asked.

"Mostly vegetables, fruit, nuts, and insects."

Emily hoped the man would not make a habit of collecting perishable food in his room. Then they might have insects indeed!

Sarah bit her lip then said, "Mr. Gwilt, may I ask that you not bring your bird to dinner? Some of our other guests might find that . . . distracting."

"Righty-o, Miss Sarah." He touched the side of his nose. "I understand and shall endeavor to explain."

She blinked. "Explain to whom? Parry or the guests?"

He laughed. "As if Parry would understand such social niceties, raised by sailors as he was."

"Could you not simply leave him in your room?"

"If I must, then of course, I shall."

He appeared crestfallen until Sarah added, "Dinner is a rather formal affair, you understand. But our picnic tomorrow is out of doors and far more casual if you would like to bring Parry then."

His expression brightened. "Thank you. We shall both look forward to it."

16

It was to be done in a quiet, unpretending, elegant way,
infinitely superior to the bustle and preparation, the regular
eating and drinking, and pic-nic parade of the Eltons.

—Jane Austen, *Emma*

At the appointed time, they set out from Sea View together for the picnic. They had hired Puggy and his donkey cart to help them transport the hampers of food, supplies, and a single chair.

Mamma had agreed to come, not wishing anyone to have to stay behind with her. And although they'd hired a sedan chair to deliver her to the baths, so far she had refused to buy an invalid chair to use around the house and grounds. She was not convinced she was a permanent invalid and still held out hope for her strength to return. Instead, she rode in the cart beside Puggy as he drove, a parasol fluttering over her head, while the rest of them went on foot.

Mr. Henshall, carrying his guitar case, accompanied Effie and Georgiana.

Emily walked with Mr. Stanley, and Viola held Mr. Hornbeam's arm.

Mr. Gwilt followed, birdcage in hand, while the Eltons eyed

bird and man askance and gave both a wide berth, keeping to themselves.

And bringing up the rear, Sarah walked alongside those there to help, Jessie and Lowen. In deference to her age, Sarah had insisted Mrs. Besley rest after her labors. She need not scamper about the hillside to serve them.

Sarah had also arranged for Bibi to keep Chips at the house, pacified by a fresh bone. The last thing they needed was for the energetic stray to run amok, stealing their ham.

The old cart lumbered across the lawn, over a dirt track, and partway up Peak Hill, the lower strata ascending gradually. There, on a gentle rise, a grove of trees waited to shelter them.

Mr. Gwilt slowed his pace to walk beside Sarah. With a significant glance at Parry, he lowered his voice and said, "I trust we shall not be having pigeon? Or duck?"

"No . . ." Sarah found herself lowering her voice as well. "Though there will be chicken."

"Oh dear. Can't abide gnawing on a chicken leg." He pointed toward the cage. "Too close, if you take my meaning."

"Well, there will be plenty of other choices."

"Pheasant? Goose?"

Catching on, Sarah shook her head. "No. Nor turkey, never fear."

He pulled a face. "Too bad. I quite adore turkeys. They're delicious."

When they reached the spot, the men helped Lowen, Puggy, and Jessie spread blankets and carry hampers.

Sarah herself positioned the chair on level ground near the blanket's edge, and then she and Mr. Henshall helped Mamma from the cart to her seat.

Soon the platters, bowls, and jars were arranged in the middle of the blanket, and plates and cutlery passed around. Sarah had paid Puggy extra to stay and help, so they left the beverage bottles and jugs in the cart. From there, Puggy poured while Jessie and Lowen handed out glasses.

Within a matter of minutes, they were all seated with overflowing plates and glasses of cool drinks. They were a party of twelve in addition to the servants and driver. Seven guests and the five Summers ladies.

Mrs. Elton sat primly with ankles crossed to one side, and Mamma remained in her chair. Otherwise the company was a happy jumble of cross-legged and sprawled men, and ladies sitting with legs tucked beneath their gowns, now and again rising to their knees to reach a dish or to pass something.

Lowen and Jessie bustled around refilling glasses, until Sarah insisted that they sit and have something to eat as well. Jessie hesitated, but Lowen would not miss such an opportunity. He first spread a lap rug for Jessie on the grass near the cart, and then he and Puggy sat on the rear gate, each with a chicken leg and glass of cider.

Sarah looked around at the contented company, gratification sweeping over her. What was it about eating out of doors? They could not have asked for a better day—a mellow sun overhead, graceful trees lending swaths of shade, and a soft breeze to keep the company cool and any insects at bay. Her heart and her stomach felt pleasantly full.

Sarah leaned near Emily and said, "You were right. This was an excellent idea."

When everyone had eaten their fill, then eaten some more, Lowen and Jessie cleared away all but the desserts. Mr. and Mrs. Elton excused themselves, saying they would walk back alone. And Georgiana and Effie went to pick wildflowers to make flower crowns.

On the freed-up blankets, Sarah, Viola, and Emily clustered near Mamma's chair, talking companionably but softly. Mr. Hornbeam and Mr. Stanley reclined to rest after the meal, eyes closed. Even Mr. Gwilt lay back to close his eyes. Parry kept his open.

Callum Henshall sat alone on the far side of the blankets, apparently lost in thought, plucking gently on his guitar. The music carried a sad, lilting melody, and he gazed off to the horizon, to a pair of silvery-grey terns flying away into the distance.

He glanced over and caught her watching him. Her neck warmed, but she raised her hand in a friendly wave. When he finished the piece, she rose and walked over to join him.

"What was that you were playing? It was lovely."

"Composed by Niel Gow—a famous Scottish fiddler."

"Sounded sad."

He nodded. "A lament over the loss of his beloved wife."

Sarah's full stomach knotted. "Oh."

He regarded her. After a thoughtful moment, he added, "His second wife."

Then he gestured toward the edge of the blanket nearest him, and she sat down.

When she was settled, he explained, "His first wife gave him five children, but after she died, he met the great love of his life. By all accounts, his second marriage was both longer and happier. He composed this lament after her death. Gow wrote it for fiddle, so I no doubt fail to do it justice on this."

She looked at him steadily. "I thought it quite beautiful."

Their gazes held, and the pupils of his soft green eyes seemed to grow. She wondered what he saw in hers.

He lowered his head and cleared his throat. When he glanced at her again, a smile teased his lips. "Do ye play, Miss Summers?"

"No. Well, only the pianoforte—a little. We all learnt, though Viola is our only true proficient."

"Is that who I hear playing now and then, behind the closed parlour door?"

"Yes. She is very self-conscious."

"Does she not realize her talent?"

Sarah lifted one shoulder. "It's only that she does not like anyone watching her."

"Ah."

She looked across the blankets to where Viola sat near Mamma, veil fluttering in the breeze. Nearby, Emily slowly plucked blades of grass and laid them on Mr. Stanley's slumbering head, probably hoping he would wake soon and talk to her.

"Viola was the only one of us willing to practice for such long hours," she explained. "I was too busy and Emily too social and . . ." Sarah almost mentioned her older sister but bit her tongue.

"And Georgiana?" he asked.

"Oh, I don't think you can call what Georgie does 'playing,' exactly. Playing at, perhaps. She has the least patience for sitting still of any of us."

As if to illustrate her point, Georgie came running up from the meadow, flowers sailing from her arms.

Sarah smiled indulgently. "Mamma reminds her that accomplished young females are supposed to play music and draw and sing, but Georgie prefers to play cricket and run and explore."

Although in the present instance, Mamma didn't protest or even seem to notice as she sat in her chair, softly fanning herself, eyes drowsy.

"What about Effie?" Sarah asked. "Is she musical?"

She glanced over and watched Effie plop down cross-legged beside Georgiana and begin making a flower chain.

He followed her gaze. "Aye. She is coming along on both guitar and mandolin, although she prefers dancing."

"Sounds like Emily."

"I want Effie to go to school, but she doesna. When we argue about it, she quotes that book by 'a Lady of Distinction.' What's it called?"

"*Mirror of the Graces?*"

"Right." He called to the girl, "Effie, what is that line you toss back at me, whenever I suggest schooling?"

Effie looked up from her chain and recited, "She possessed no more education than what lay in her guitar and in her dancing master; but in these arts she was admirable."

Sarah chuckled appreciatively, and Effie and Georgiana resumed their handiwork, heads close, sharing whispers and giggles.

Sarah returned her focus to Mr. Henshall. "Well, if a lady of distinction approves of the guitar, who am I to disagree?"

"Would ye like to give it a go?" He lifted the instrument a few inches in her direction.

"Me? I . . ." She glanced at it, the gleaming wood, the taut strings over the well.

When she hesitated, he leaned forward. "Here . . ." He twisted his torso toward her and slid the instrument onto her lap.

"I don't even know how to hold it."

"I'll show ye."

He rose to his knees and shifted slightly behind her, bringing his right arm around her elbow and lifting it to the strings. Then he reached his left hand around her other side, found her hand, and guided it to the instrument's neck.

Sarah's heart beat hard. The close position felt startlingly intimate and strangely thrilling.

"Forefinger here. Middle here. Thumb. Right. Now, with this hand, pluck each string and try to forget they are made of animal gut."

She murmured, "Now you tell me."

"Let's try something fairly simple," he said. "Are you familiar with the old ballad 'Robin Adair'?"

"Yes."

"Good. Then press here, then here, and here, to play the chords. And pluck the melody with your right."

The whisper of his breath tickled her cheek and ear, and the heat of his chest warmed her back.

"I shall never remember all that."

"Very well, then I'll finger the chords and you strum."

He placed his hand on hers and guided her fingers. She found it suddenly difficult to breathe.

Mr. Stanley awoke and raised himself up on his elbows, grass falling from his hair. He glanced over and teased, "I say, if I could teach music lessons like that, I might take up the profession!"

They played a few more measures in their awkward duet until Effie put her hands to her ears. "No, no, no." She rose and came over. "Here, let me."

"Of course," Sarah said, quickly relinquishing the instrument. "Your father was only trying to demonstrate how to play one of these. Do show us how it is done."

As Effie sat and began to play, Sarah glanced over and spied Emily grinning at her. And her mother looked suddenly wide awake and very interested indeed.

<hr />

That evening, Sarah went belowstairs to the workroom, where she now regularly prepared biscuits, scones, and tarts. There, she flipped through her favored book, *The Art of Cookery Made Plain and Easy*, hoping to find a simple cake recipe to try. She stopped when she came to one marked *To make a Pound Cake*. Then she gathered utensils and ingredients and began following the printed instructions.

Some time later, she heard footsteps in the dark adjoining kitchen. Their cook come to investigate?

Sarah called, "It's only me, Mrs. Besley."

Light appeared in the threshold. She glanced up and saw Callum Henshall standing there in trousers, shirt, and waistcoat, candle lamp in hand.

Her heart lifted. "What are you doing down here?"

"Came foraging for more of this." He held up a piece of cold fish pie.

"Can you really be hungry? After today's feast?"

"Aye." His mouth quirked. "It's a rare talent." He looked at the cookbook, bowls, and pans gathered around her. "And what are *you* doing? Ye canna need to bake more. There was plenty left over from the picnic."

"I know. But I wanted to attempt a cake."

"Mind some company?"

She hesitated. Did she? No, she found she did not.

"Not at all. The pot there is still warm if you want tea to go with that."

Setting down his candle, he poured himself a cup and sat on a tall stool. "What sort of cake is it to be, then?"

"A pound cake. The recipe seemed relatively simple compared to the others." Although still tiring, Sarah realized. After beating the butter till it became the consistency of a "fine thick cream," she had beaten together twelve egg yolks and six egg whites. Already her arms were throbbing from the effort.

She glanced at him sitting there across the table. A foot propped on the stool rung, he balanced a teacup on raised knee with one hand, while the other popped the remaining morsel of pie into his mouth with a smack of satisfaction.

Sarah pulled her gaze from his puckered lips as he chewed, back to the printed page.

Following the directions, she added a pound of flour, a pound of grated sugar, and a few caraways.

Setting aside his cup and swatting the crumbs from his hands, he rose and came around the table. He stood beside her and peered down at the recipe. "What's next?" he asked.

She was instantly aware of his nearness, the warmth of him close to her.

"Um . . ." She had no idea. Collecting herself, she read the next line. "'Beat it all well together for an hour with your hand or a great wooden spoon.'"

She glanced over in time to see his fair eyebrows shoot high.

"An hour? Och."

She nodded. "Exactly."

"No wonder cooks have arms like caber tossers." He sent her a quick sideways glance. "Present company excepted, of course.

Yours, Miss Sarah, are slender and feminine. What I've seen of them at any rate."

Her cheeks flushed hot. Another glance. If he noticed, she would blame the heat of the oven. Thankfully, he made no comment.

He washed his hands in the nearby basin and dried them on a towel. "How about I give it a go? And ye supervise to make sure I do it correctly."

"Really? Thank you."

He rolled up his shirtsleeves, exposing masculine forearms sprinkled with golden hairs. Suppressing the desire to touch them, she handed him a large wooden spoon.

He set to stirring. The longer he beat the mixture, the more the ropey muscles of his forearms protruded.

Forcing her attention elsewhere, Sarah busied herself for a time, putting away ingredients and sweeping up spilled flour. Then she buttered a pan and added more fuel to the fire before coming back to view his progress.

"You are much stronger and faster than I am. I don't think we'll need an hour at all. That looks good already."

He held the bowl for her, and she scraped the batter into the pan, smoothing out the top. Carrying the pan over to the oven, she slid it inside.

Then she returned to the table to finish cleaning up.

His gaze rested on her cheek. "May I? You've got something just . . . there." He gestured vaguely to her face.

She stilled, wary and eager at once. He gently lifted her chin with one hand while he swiped something from her skin with the other.

"Just a wee dab of batter." Showing her the creamy dollop on his index finger, he then raised it to his mouth. He didn't lick it, but rather pressed his lips to the spot like a kiss.

Throat dry, she swallowed. "Well?"

He nodded thoughtfully, his focus returning to her cheek before lowering to her mouth. "Wants a wee bit of sugar, if ye ask me."

And Sarah was no longer certain they were talking about the cake.

⌒ ⌒ ⌒

The next morning, Viola carried over a plate of Sarah's biscuits and scones to their neighbors at Westmount to unload some of the extra bounty of Sarah's new baking endeavors. They had a lot left over after the picnic.

She knocked on the kitchen door, meaning to simply drop off the covered plate and go, but instead of Mr. Chown coming to the door, Mr. Hutton senior answered it himself, dressed except for a cravat, hair slightly rumpled from sleep.

"Ah, Miss Viola. Come in, come in. You've caught me helping myself to coffee."

"You are up early," she said.

"Can't sleep after sunrise. Can't sleep much period, these days. Don't get old, Miss Summers."

She smirked. "I shan't if you shan't."

He grinned and lifted his cup. "Chown has not even finished laying breakfast yet, but one must have his coffee first thing."

"Indeed."

"Jack and Armaan have gone for a swim, and Colin . . . well, most days we are lucky to see him by noon."

"Another swim?" At the memory of watching the major and Armaan in the water, Viola's cheeks heated anew.

"Yes, they go most days. Jack is determined to regain his strength."

"Impressive. Well." Viola lifted the plate. "I will just leave these, then."

"Please, join me for breakfast. And bring those."

"Very well."

He poured a cup of coffee for her, and then Viola followed him into the breakfast parlour, where Chown was arranging platters

200

of bread rolls and cold ham and said he would return as soon as he could with boiled eggs.

Viola took the seat Mr. Hutton pulled out for her. After a moment's hesitation, she untied her bonnet and removed it, setting it on the empty chair beside her. One could not drink coffee through a veil.

He took his own seat, glanced up at her, and stilled.

Drawing a shaky breath, Viola told herself it didn't matter. If the patriarch was going to be disappointed or find her revolting, better to know before she became attached to this family. In truth, more attached than she already was.

Had the major told his father of her defect, described her scar and how she'd come by it? Or was Mr. Hutton shocked? She lifted her chin, forcing herself not to look away.

His eyes turned downward at the corners. He appeared not repulsed, but simply sad.

"Well, my dear. It is good to see your face clearly at last."

"Did the major explain?"

"He did. He was afraid I might blurt out the wrong thing. And I confess, in the past I might well have done. But these last few years, with so many of our lads coming home broken and battered, and now my own son so cruelly injured . . ." He shook his head. "No. I have learned I was wrong to put so much value in surface things. A woman's perfection. A man's prowess with horses or hunting . . ."

Mr. Hutton rose, crossed the room to the sideboard, and opened a drawer. From it, he withdrew a small, oval frame. He carried it over and laid it on the table before her. The frame held a miniature portrait of a handsome soldier in uniform—a proud, fine head upon broad shoulders.

Jack Hutton. Before gunpowder and fire had changed him. Scarred him. Stolen some of his swagger. How young he looked. How confident.

"He doesn't like me to leave that lying about. Doesn't want the reminder of what he used to look like. But I thought you might like to see it."

Mr. Hutton peered down at the image. "He thought himself invincible. Immortal. Young men often do. He was only a lieutenant then, out to rise in the ranks and conquer the world."

Viola studied the face. The posture. The bearing. There was no denying this had been a striking, attractive man, despite his long nose and thin upper lip. Yet there was a certain haughtiness she didn't like. Perhaps hardship had beaten it from him, even as it left him scarred. She would not wish it back for all the good looks in the world.

Mr. Hutton returned the miniature to the drawer and sat back down with a sigh. "Now I just want my son to heal, inside and out, and to embrace life again."

"So do I." She passed him the plate. "In the meantime, try these."

He picked up a biscuit and took a bite. His eyes widened, and he quickly took another. "Your sister made these, you say? Delicious. Too bad I am too old for her. I would marry her myself!"

Viola chuckled and helped herself to a ginger biscuit. Delicious indeed.

The two were sitting there companionably, chatting and laughing, when the major entered, hair still damp, towel in hand, and a slight frown on his face. He wore a dressing gown thrown over trousers, a wide V of neck and chest showing.

He drew up short upon noticing her there. "I wondered what all the jabbering was about. What are you two up to? Thick as thieves the pair of you, plotting my demise, no doubt. I shall have to watch my back!"

In contrast to his words, Viola saw the humor and affection in his expression, and her heart warmed at the sight.

His father said, "Very true. Now go and finish dressing, my boy. You'll embarrass Viola."

"Not at all," Viola mumbled even as her face heated once more.

She wondered what they would say if they knew she'd seen him dressed in far less.

Inspired by Mr. Henshall's playing, Sarah sat at the pianoforte that morning. Laying her list of tasks on the bench beside her, she selected a piece of music and tentatively began to play.

Her fingers felt dull and slow at first, but soon the familiarity began to return, and with it, the pleasure.

She would have to practice more often.

All too quickly, the list of waiting tasks prevailed and claimed her attention. Sarah rose and walked from the room.

Mr. Henshall, hat in hand, was leaning against the doorframe of the nearby drawing room. When he saw her emerge, he straightened in surprise.

"Miss Summers. I thought it must be Miss Viola playing. Ye denied being skilled, but that was quite good."

"Thank you. Your playing inspired me to practice again."

"I'm glad."

He smiled, and she grinned back foolishly for several ticks of the hall clock. With effort, she recalled herself to the present.

"Well, have a pleasant day." She glanced at his hat. "Going out?"

He nodded. "Effie and I have hired a carriage and are driving into Branscombe for the day."

"Excellent. I have never been, but I hear it's a pleasant village."

He held her gaze. "You are welcome to join us, if ye like."

"Sadly, I have several projects to attend to."

"Anything I could help with?"

Sarah blinked, taken aback by the question and oddly tempted.

Effie came trotting down the stairs, dressed to go out. She looked from adult to adult and frowned.

Sarah replied, "No need—thank you."

He nodded. "Then don't let me keep ye."

But what if I want you to? came the unexpected thought. Startled by it, Sarah turned and walked away, feeling his gaze following her all the way into the office.

Later that morning, Sarah sat at the desk, bent over an invoice, while Emily stood in the far corner on the library ladder, searching for a new book to read.

Mrs. Elton appeared in the doorway. "Miss Summers, you are so kind and accommodating. I wonder . . ."

Sarah stiffened and braced herself for another special request.

"I do hate to complain," Mrs. Elton went on. "In fact, I have said nothing before now because the last thing we want is to cause disunity among your guests, but . . ."

Sarah suppressed a groan. "Yes, Mrs. Elton?"

"Mr. E and I came here for peace and quiet. Lately music is being played with alarming regularity. The pianoforte was one thing. But now the . . . what is it, a lute?" She wrinkled her nose in distaste.

"A guitar."

"Well, whatever it is, it is jarring to Mr. E's rather delicate nerves."

"Really?" Sarah feigned casual concern. "I find it most soothing. Quite lovely. Mr. Henshall is a fine musician as well as a thoughtful gentleman. He plays softly and not overly late."

"A gentleman? I thought he was a Scot?" The woman chuckled as though at an amusing joke, but Sarah did not join her.

"I could ask him not to play after posted quiet hours, although I don't believe I've ever heard him playing after ten."

"Heavens! We retire by eight most nights. Mr. E requires a great deal of sleep."

"I understand. Yet surely you realize that in many houses, dinner is not even served until seven or eight?"

Mrs. Elton sent her a quelling look. "We are not in London, Miss Summers. We are here and paying handsomely for the privilege."

"I am certain a compromise is possible," Sarah said evenly. "But I cannot ask the whole house to remain silent at such an early hour of the evening."

The woman's expression became brittle. "That is disappointing, when you have hitherto been so accommodating. Perhaps I shall not pass along my glowing compliments to Lady Kennaway after all. I know that good woman likes an early night as well."

From atop the library ladder, Emily offered in feigned sweetness, "Would you like some cotton wool to stop your ears, Mrs. Elton? I hear Lady Kennaway swears by it."

"Emily . . ." Sarah softly chastised, though she could hardly blame her. She faced Mrs. Elton and said, "Perhaps we might move up quiet hours to nine and keep them in place a bit longer in the morning?"

"Excellent. Thank you." Triumph glinting in her eyes, Mrs. Elton finger-waved and walked away.

When she was out of earshot, Sarah turned toward her sister and said in a low voice, "Take care. We cannot afford to offend the Eltons. They are very well connected."

Emily harrumphed and descended the ladder. "Hard to believe that woman has any friends. Or keeps them any length of time. She may have seemed charming at first, but that has worn thin, like cheap gilt from a bracelet."

Approaching the desk, Emily narrowed her eyes. "Where are they from again? I know we have it in the register, but I can't recall."

"From Surrey, I believe. I forget the specific town."

Emily held her gaze. "You do know the more you give in to her, the more she will demand."

Sarah released a long, pent-up sigh. "Yes. Yet I hope our efforts will be worth it in the end."

Emily harrumphed again and began flipping through the register.

17

Though oft I have been
In a Bathing Machine
I never discovere'd till now
The wonderful art
Of this little go-cart,
'Tis vastly convenient, I vow.

—*The Merry Guide to Margate,*
Ramsgate and Broadstairs

L ater that day, Sarah stood in the hall, straining, arms trembling with the effort of keeping the framed painting aloft. On the ladder above her, Georgie attempted to guide the hanging wire onto the waiting hook.

"Please hurry," Sarah said through gritted teeth, feeling the heavy frame begin to slip. "I can't hold it much longer."

Nearby, a door opened and footsteps approached.

"Och. Here, allow me." Mr. Henshall was at her side in an instant, bracing the frame easily.

Georgie attached the wire. "Much easier to do when the frame isn't shaking. Thank you, Mr. Henshall."

He released the frame and angled it until it hung straight.

"Yes," Sarah agreed. "Thank you for rescuing me."

"My pleasure." Then he took Georgiana's place atop the ladder to make sure the painting was secure.

Nearly bouncing with eagerness, Georgie asked, "May I go now, Sarah? Hannah is waiting for me."

"Very well."

When Georgiana had hurried away, Mr. Henshall lingered. Sarah's gaze moved from his expressive eyes to his slightly up-turned nose to the prominent dimple in his chin.

She said, "I am surprised you are back so soon. How was Branscombe?"

"Charming. But Effie wasna feelin' well, so we came back early."

"I hope it's nothing serious?"

"Just the collywobbles, I think. Too many sweets in the carriage is my guess. She went to lie down."

Sarah prayed that was all it was.

He looked up at the large painting in its gilded frame. "I like it."

Sarah nodded. "So do I. It's one of the few we brought with us. It was not included in the entail because Mamma commissioned it using her own money. That is Finderlay. Our former home."

The grand house was set among lime trees, with a lovely garden and parkland rolling away into the distance.

"A bonnie place," he said. "I gather ye miss it?"

"I do. I have many happy memories there . . . and a few sad ones too. Despite them, it's a comfort to have this here."

"It looks well where you've placed it."

"Thank you."

Studying the image, he said, "It is grander than our home, although the estate is entailed through the male line as well. I had hoped to have a son to leave it to, but sadly, no."

"Maybe one day, you might . . ." She broke off, feeling her neck heat.

He regarded her with interest. "Might what?"

"Never mind. I almost said something foolish. Something I would not like said to me."

He cocked his head to the side. "You intrigue me. What has ye blushing like that?"

"I only meant . . . It's not my place. I just thought . . . well, you might marry again and have a son."

His gaze bored into hers. "And why is a suggestion of marriage and children something you would not like said to you?"

The heat rose to her face. She forced herself to keep her chin up and explained, "When Peter died, I was grief-stricken, of course. And some well-intentioned people tried to comfort me. Within a matter of weeks, if not days, they began saying, 'You are young. You will find someone else. You will fall in love again and marry.' I hated it. He is not so easily replaced."

"I agree those sentiments were premature, but there was truth in them. Ye might yet marry and have a family of your own."

She shook her head, throat tightening. "I have had one great love in my life. I don't expect to have another."

He stilled, taking that in. "How long ago did he die?"

"Just over two years."

"And you still feel that way?"

Sarah hesitated. Did she?

Instead of answering, she huffed and said, "As a man, you might remarry and have children at any age. But as a woman . . ."

"Come, you are not so ancient. Ye canna be more than thirty."

Sarah's mouth dropped open. "Do I look thirty? I am only six and twenty!"

"There, you see?" One corner of his mouth quirked. "Very young. Though ye are quite serious and responsible, and perhaps that makes ye seem more . . . mature."

She shook her head, lips pursed. "Good try."

For another few moments, they gazed up at the painting in companionable silence, then he turned to her with a boyish grin. "Now, what else can I help ye with? Leaking roof? Loose tile? I have become rather handy. Comes with living in an old house. Always something needing repair."

Sarah looked at him speculatively. "Actually, if you are serious . . ."

She led him to the hall closet. "There are many little annoyances. For example, this door refuses to stay closed."

He examined it. "Floor slopes rather sharply here. And the frame has warped, see? That's why the latch doesn't catch. I can rehang the door, if you like. Perhaps install a better latch?"

"Really? Could you? Yes, please. That is . . . assuming it won't require costly parts."

"Don't think so. The work shed in the back has drawers full of old tools, as well as discarded fittings and hardware. At least it used to. If ye don't mind, I could have a sort through and find something to suit."

She had briefly forgotten he had once lived there himself. He seemed to know the house and outbuildings better than she did.

"That is a remarkably generous offer, and I accept. Gratefully!"

Sarah thought, then added, "We could compensate you somehow, perhaps with a discounted rate for your room?"

"Let's wait and see. I havena managed to repair it yet."

A few hours later, Mr. Henshall had planed and rehung the door and adjusted the old latch so that it now closed securely.

Best of all, it had not cost them a farthing.

Sarah latched the door once more with a satisfying click.

"Excellent. Thank you." She repeated her offer to make it up to him somehow.

He thought, then said, "There is one thing I would like in return."

"Oh? And what is that?"

"A few hours in your company. Away from your duties here. We might . . . hire a horse and carriage and go for a drive, or even go sailing."

Mind reeling, she blurted out the first excuse that came to her. "We have no boat."

"Not a problem. According to the guidebook, several people keep pleasure boats here, 'attended by expert and careful seamen.'"

True. She had forgotten. She regarded him with interest. "Like sailing, do you?"

He nodded. "I grew up near the sea. Spent a lot of time on the water. It's easier to travel to Edinburgh by boat, crossing the firth, than to drive around to the nearest bridge."

"How large of a boat would you hire?"

"A modest sailboat is all we would need."

"Not too small, if you please. I'd be afraid of tipping over. And not in bad weather."

"Of course not. You may choose the time and even the boat, if ye like."

Sarah thought. Was she really agreeing to this? Should she?

He retrieved a copy of *The Beauties of Sidmouth Displayed* from the library and flipped toward the back of the slim volume until he reached the listing for Pleasure Boats.

Sarah scanned the names. "I am some acquainted with Mr. Puddicombe and Mr. Heffer. They both seem pleasant, trustworthy fellows."

"I'll start with them." Eagerness lit his face. "Where shall we go? Exmouth? Or Dawlish?"

"So far? That would probably take several hours. It would be difficult for me to get away for too long."

"Then we might simply sail along the coast as we please. Perhaps take another small picnic?"

Sarah stared vaguely into the distance, imagining it. Riding the gentle waves, a fresh breeze on her face, sea birds soaring above them, sitting close to Callum Henshall. It sounded peaceful and relaxing and . . . romantic.

Doubts pressed in. Would he think this meant they were courting? By agreeing, would she be guilty of giving him false hope? She was the eldest daughter living at home. She had responsibilities to her mother and sisters. Forming an attachment with any man, especially one who lived so far away, would be irresponsible.

But to vocalize any of that seemed far too presumptuous. He

was only asking for a few hours of her company, not a lifetime. She instead expressed a more practical concern. "I have little experience with boats. What if I become seasick?"

He smiled gently. "Then I would remind ye to look out at a fixed point on the horizon. And if that failed, I would hold your hat as ye fed the fishes and lend ye my handkerchief afterward."

She chuckled. Oddly, his words put her at ease. He could not have romance in mind with talk of feeding fishes.

In the morning, Mr. Henshall appeared in the office doorway, features tight. Quite different from his warm, pleasant manner of the day before.

"Miss Summers. I don't know what to do. I don't wish to break down one of your doors, but something is wrong with Effie. I hear her crying in her room, and she refuses to let me in."

Sarah rose instantly. "Did the two of you argue?"

"Not this time."

"Is her stomach still troubling her?"

"Ah dinnae ken." In his anxiety, his accent thickened.

Together they hurried upstairs. Outside the adjoining rooms, Sarah asked him, "Do you mind if I try talking to her through the inner door, instead of out here in the corridor? I don't wish to embarrass her."

"Of course." He opened the door to his room for her.

Sarah laid a hand on his arm. "Wait here a moment. I will see what I can do."

Sarah entered Mr. Henshall's room alone, noticing his fresh, lingering scent yet unable to identify it. Heather? Scots pine?

She stepped to the connecting door and knocked softly. "Effie? It's Miss Sarah."

"Go away."

"Is something wrong? Might I help in any way?"

"There's nothing ye can do. Nothing anyone can do."

"Now, now. I am sure that's not so. Are you not feeling well?"

"I feel awful. I am dying, I know it. Just leave me to die in peace."

The girl could certainly be dramatic. No wonder her poor father was worried.

Sarah considered. While she had paid Mr. Farrant to install keyed locks on the external doors to guest rooms, she had not gone to the same expense for the internal doors. These held only traditional latches, like the one on her mother's door.

Sarah said, "Please open the door. Your father is understandably concerned and so am I."

An indecipherable moan was the only reply.

Pulling a pin from her hair, Sarah knelt and employed the same method she had used when her mother had not responded. Opening the door a crack as the latch allowed, she inserted her pin and lifted the latch.

"Effie, I am coming in." She rose and opened the door.

Lying on her side in bed, the girl whipped her head around, revealing a tear-stained face. "I told ye not to come in."

"My dear," Sarah said gently. "You cannot say you are dying and expect a responsible adult to do nothing."

Effie moaned again and buried her face in her pillow.

A moment later, the girl lifted her splotched cheek once more. "I've ruined your towel. I will pay for it from my spending money."

"Never mind that." Glancing around, Sarah saw no sign of a spoilt towel. A suspicion began to form.

"Effie, how old are you? Thirteen, almost fourteen?"

The girl nodded into her pillow.

Sarah hesitated. How to phrase the question in a way that did not embarrass the girl or insult her?

She asked, "Are you having your . . . courses?"

"My what?"

Sarah lowered her voice. "Are you . . . bleeding . . . down there?"

Eyes widening, Effie nodded emphatically. "How'd ye know? A hemorrhage, I think it's called. I am dyin'."

Although relieved, Sarah kept her expression even, not wishing to add to the girl's vexation. "No, you are not."

Sarah sat in a clothes-strewn chair near the bed and faced her. "I have good news and bad news for you, my dear. The good news is that you are not dying. You have begun to menstruate as females do at about your age. It's perfectly normal."

Effie stared. "Georgie too?"

"Georgie too."

She sat up. "And the bad news?"

"It will happen every month for the next, oh, thirty years."

Effie's mouth parted in shock. "Ye must be jokin'. There's nothing normal about that!"

Sarah barely restrained a chuckle. "Did your mother not warn you? I realize you were rather young when she passed away."

The girl shook her head. "We rarely spoke. I spent more time with a nurse and then governess."

Sarah patted her arm and rose. "Well. I will bring you some cloths more suitable for the purpose. However, first let me go and reassure your father you are well. Would you like to explain the situation, or shall I?"

Again, Effie shook her head, this time emphatically. "I could never tell him that! Ye tell him, please. I would die of mortification."

Sarah feared she might as well.

She didn't see Mr. Henshall in the corridor, so she hurried to her room for a few things and then to the cleaning closet for a basin before returning to Effie's room. She left a short while later, with a stained towel soaking in the basin of water. As she carried it carefully down the stairs, she found Mr. Henshall pacing the hall.

"There ye are." He ran an agitated hand through his hair. "I was just about to go charging off for a doctor."

"Dr. Clarke will be calling on Mamma soon, but Effie does not need a doctor, she—"

His gaze strayed to the bloody water. "Losh! Is she . . . ?"

"She is well. Do not be uneasy. Give me one moment." Sarah hurried belowstairs to leave the basin and towel in one of the workrooms to scrub later. Then she washed her hands and returned to calm the concerned man.

Leading him into the parlour, she gestured for him to sit and explained gingerly, "Effie is not hurt nor ill. She is . . . becoming a woman."

"A woman . . . ? Ah . . ." His mouth O-ed, and he stared off into the distance, his neck reddening above his collar.

After a moment, he shook his head. "That thought never crossed my mind. What a fool you must think me. She seems such a wee girl yet. Though come to think on it, as moody and pettish as an adolescent, to be sure."

Sarah clasped her hands. "She asked me to tell you. She is too embarrassed to discuss it with you."

"And no wonder. I'd no doubt make a muddle of such a talk."

"Well, this is usually left to a female relative, so do not be too severe with yourself."

He slowly nodded, still looking distracted. "What do I need to do?"

Sarah twisted her fingers together, wondering if a talk of such a nature would make things awkward between them. Well, it couldn't be helped.

"I have given her what she needs for now. I doubt I can go into details without becoming mortified myself. I will . . . write a few things down for her, and you may read the note first, if you like."

"Good idea. More discreet." He rose and exhaled with evident relief. "I cannot tell ye how much I appreciate your help. I thank God this happened while we were here. I dread to think how clumsily I might have managed it on my own. Effie would no doubt have stopped speaking to me forever."

"I doubt that." Sarah grinned. "Though . . . maybe for a year."

He reached for her hand, and finding them joined, wrapped both of his around them.

"I am forever in your debt."

About two weeks had passed since Dr. Clarke first called, and that morning he returned to see how Mrs. Summers was progressing. Again Mamma asked Sarah to be present during the physician's visit.

"And have you been making use of the medical baths?" Dr. Clarke asked.

Mamma held up two fingers. "Yes. Twice a week."

"Any improvement?"

"A . . . little."

Sarah shot her a look. "A very little, Mamma. If any."

He stroked his chin, considering. "If the warm baths have not proved efficacious, then it is time to try the cold."

Mamma groaned. "Must I really go into the sea?"

"I think it our best recourse. Sea-bathing is good for one reason, because the sea *is* a cold bath."

"Will it truly help?"

He nodded. "Allow me to describe a case from the writings of Dr. Richard Russell. He had a patient who labored under a disease in spite of all the efforts of physic. She was confined to her bed for almost a year together, in an unhappy, languishing condition. There appeared no hope of her recovery. There remained yet one, and only one remedy untried, which was sea water. The patient therefore was removed to the Isle of Wight, in this very channel. She began to bathe in the sea; first twice in the week, then three times, and afterwards every day. Her appetite improved, she grew stronger daily, and gained fresh spirits. After four weeks of bathing, the lady recovered. Upon the restitution of her health, she went abroad every day, mixed in company, and enjoyed the pleasures of life. Her bloom returned, and, if I may be pardoned the expression, she arose like a second Venus from the sea, completely fair and graceful."

Sarah shifted uneasily. "Good heavens."

Mamma sighed. "Oh, very well. I will do it."

"Now, before you begin, I have a few precautions for you. Bathing ought to be postponed till past noon, or at least a few hours after breakfast, to allow for digestion. And some degree of exercise should always be taken prior to entering the water, to produce a sensation of warmth over the whole body. By no means go into the water chilly."

Sarah frowned. "Mamma can barely walk. I don't see how she is to take sufficient exercise to warm herself."

"Even walking up and down the beach first will help, I assure you. And after bathing, you will gain an additional advantage by drinking a glass of sea water as soon as you come out of the sea."

Mamma smirked. "I shall no doubt swallow plenty as I try not to drown."

"Now, now, madame. You need not be anxious. The bathing machine operators will take good care of you."

He added, "If nausea or thirst trouble you after taking the sea water, drinking ass's milk will help. But these inconveniences will pass after two or three days." After a few more instructions, Dr. Clarke rose, donned his hat, and took his leave.

When they were alone, Mamma said, "When we first visited Sidmouth, I saw a notice from a local man who supplies donkeys with proper saddles for invalids and ass's milk, yet I never thought I would be so poorly as to need either one."

"I know, Mamma. But if it will help, please try."

Mamma sighed once more and patted Sarah's hand. "I shall."

———

When Emily joined her sisters for luncheon that day, Sarah shared the doctor's advice and asked for volunteers to go seabathing with Mamma.

Emily immediately asked to be excused. It had been one

thing to accompany her into the controlled environment of the medical baths. The open sea was an altogether different—and frightening—prospect.

Sarah and Viola were both too busy to go. Thankfully Georgiana, who liked the water, declared she would be happy to seabathe with Mamma.

They began that very afternoon.

Recalling the doctor's admonition to take exercise before entering the sea, they did not hire a donkey or sedan chair to carry Mamma to the beach. Instead, Emily and Georgiana each took an arm and helped her walk the modest distance. Once they reached the bathing machines and helped Mamma inside, Georgie remained with her. Emily waited on shore with an extra towel and warm shawl, ready to help Mamma home again, worrying all the while.

A short while later, the pair emerged from the bathing machine. Mamma appeared winded and weak, wet hair fallen from its pins and hanging around her shoulders in uncharacteristic disarray.

She was so limp and tired that they regretted their decision not to hire a chair. The two girls struggled to help Mamma across the beach and were relieved when sturdy Tom Cordey offered his strong arm to assist her home.

18

Mrs. Elton was growing impatient to name the day, and settle with Mr. Weston as to pigeon-pies and cold lamb.

—Jane Austen, *Emma*

T hat same afternoon, Viola made her way to the poor house to call on Mrs. Denby again.

As she walked along the esplanade, she glanced ahead and saw a man step out of the York Hotel. He tipped his hat to two ladies, and then turned up Fore Street. As he turned, Viola glimpsed his profile, and a prickling familiarity crawled over her like a millipede. A moment later he passed out of sight.

It couldn't be him, she told herself. It was only her imagination. She had allowed herself to think of the surgeon recently, and those memories were now haunting her.

And really, she had barely seen this man's face. Would she even recognize him after seven or eight years? Most likely it was not him. He lived far from Sidmouth.

Despite these inner assurances, the shivery feeling persisted. So instead of turning up Fore Street, Viola passed by the hotel and took the footpath along the river, just in case.

Reaching the poor house a short while later, she gave Mrs. Denby a brown paper parcel of biscuits Sarah had sent along for her, and then read from *The Pilgrim's Progress* for a time. The old woman sat listening, back hunched and head bent.

"As I walked through the wilderness of this world, I lighted on a certain place, where was a Den, and laid me down in that place to sleep; and, as I slept, I dreamed a dream. . . ."

When Viola noticed the woman's eyes begin to close, she paused, laying the book on her lap.

Gaze straying to the lace pieces on the table, she said, "Will you tell me about your time as a lace maker?"

"Oh." Mrs. Denby lifted her head, instantly alert. "If you like, of course. Let's see. My family and I made Honiton lace. Are you familiar with it? Very popular in these parts."

"I have seen some in the shops. Beautiful."

The old woman nodded. "My mother, sister, and I made sprigs like these." She gestured to the pieces. "And my aunt did sewing on, joining the sprigs or sewing them onto netting."

"How did you learn? Did your mother teach you?"

Mrs. Denby shook her head. "I was put to lace making at a local school at just six years of age." She looked past Viola, eyes cloudy with memory.

"I remained there until I was fifteen. At first for a few hours a day. Then we'd read for an hour and learn our sums. After three years, I was working ten to twelve hours a day. Oh, but it was cold in winter. We could have no fire, for fear the soot would stain the lace. I can still remember how my little fingers ached with cold. . . ."

Mrs. Denby lifted her hands and stared at the knobby, enlarged knuckles as though they belonged to a stranger.

"Sometimes I dream I am still making lace, weaving the bobbins over and under. Though in my dreams, my fingers don't look like this. . . ."

Viola guessed that years bent over a lace pillow had contributed to the woman's hunched back as well as gnarled hands and failing sight.

Mrs. Denby returned her gaze to Viola and continued her story. "The lace mistress was firm but fair. The lace dealer she worked for, however, was a hard man. If our day's work was not done, we had to stay and finish. If work was wanted, we sometimes had to sit up all night, earning only a few pence. The dealer and the shops made most of the money, not us.

"When I left school, I worked alongside my mother and sister at home. In those days, the dealer mostly paid us in goods. Sometimes goods we did not want or need!" She shook her head once more, lips pursed in rare disapproval.

"Why?" Viola asked.

"I think it was to keep us from buying supplies and making our own lace to sell. Some of us did a little work on the side, but that fine thread was expensive. And most completed pieces are the work of several lace makers. Still, we managed to make these. They are all I have left of my family, and I treasure them."

Viola leaned close to inspect the intricate sprigs once more.

Mrs. Denby went on, "How well I remember our entire family sitting together, pillows on our laps, working through the night to finish in time for trading the next morning in return for breakfast."

"Heavens."

"Those were hard times. But I would go back if I could. Oh, to spend even another hour with my family. How I miss them."

Viola felt unexpected tears prick her eyes.

The woman took a deep breath and said more cheerfully, "Be glad you still have your mother and sisters, my girl. What a blessing! I hope you appreciate every moment."

Guilt niggled. Viola knew she did not always appreciate the family she had. "You are perfectly right. I will try to remember that."

Mrs. Denby grinned and helped herself to another of Sarah's biscuits. "Delicious! Would you help me write a note of thanks to your sister?"

"Indeed I will. Happily."

"Fiddle!" Sarah muttered, frustration pulsing through her. This should not be this difficult.

"What is it? What's wrong?" Mr. Henshall asked, stepping into the library-office, concern lining his brow.

"Oh, forgive me. I did not realize I had complained so loudly. I am only trying to balance this ledger, without success."

"Perhaps I could help. A fresh pair of eyes might find what ye missed."

"Really? I would appreciate that. Although I am embarrassed for you to see the state of our finances."

"Not at all. And I shall keep it to myself, whatever it is—ye have my word."

"Very well." She gestured to the chair beside hers.

He sat down and leaned over the ledger, his broad shoulder brushing hers. She could feel the warmth of it through her dress, and smell his fresh, masculine scent.

"Walk me through each column."

She pointed to each in turn. "This is the seller, what goods or services we purchased, the date, and the amount owed. And this is the date I paid the bill."

He studied the numbers, his fingers slowly tracing each entry. "What do these tick marks mean?"

Her neck heated. "That I have asked for an extension."

"Ah." He continued scanning the numbers. "What about the fuel expense here? Did you order for the entire year?"

"Yes, we received a lower price that way."

He nodded and turned back the pages. "And ye pay . . . quarterly?"

"Yes." She thought, then realization dawned. "Oh . . . that's it!"

She turned back to the current month. "I've accounted for it this month as well, when it's not yet due. How silly of me."

"Not at all."

"And you saw my error in no time."

He shrugged one shoulder, and she felt the movement like a caress through her sleeve.

He said, "I have a man of business at home. We review each other's work. Find each other's mistakes. Two sets of eyes are better than one."

She nodded. "Like that verse: 'Two are better than one; because they have a good reward for their labour.'"

He turned toward her, bringing their faces surprisingly, intimately close. Searching her expression as if for hidden meaning, he said softly, "I agree."

Suddenly light-headed, Sarah looked away. The words had just popped out. Would he think her forward? After all, she was happy in her single state. Or at least resigned to it.

"I hope you don't think I was . . ." She swallowed. "Hinting at anything."

"No? Ah well." His eyes crinkled at the corners and shone with an odd mixture of sadness and humble humor.

"I am . . . content as I am," Sarah said. "As I am sure you are."

"I am not."

"No?"

He slowly shook his head, gaze lowering to her mouth.

Sarah drew a shaky breath, then nervously pressed her lips together.

His eyes followed her every movement and seemed to darken with . . . what? Attraction? Desire?

"Miss Summers." Mrs. Elton drew up short in the doorway. "Oh. I do beg your pardon. Am I . . . interrupting anything?"

Sarah drew back from Mr. Henshall and stood. "Not at all. Mr. Henshall was just helping me with something."

The woman's gaze shifted from one to the other. "So I see."

Mr. Henshall rose, bowed, and took his leave. "Excuse me, ladies."

When he had gone, Mrs. Elton began, "Well. Mr. E and I have

been thinking. We have made so many new friends here in Sidmouth, like *dear* Lady Kennaway, and we would enjoy inviting them over for an evening party. As we're staying here in Sea View instead of a private lodging house, we find ourselves at a disadvantage. I don't see that you offer private dinners on your printed list of services, but I was wondering if we might host a dinner here, assuming you—and your cook, of course—would be willing to oblige us?"

Sarah hesitated. "I don't know. Perhaps. How many people were you thinking of inviting?"

"Oh, we have *so* many friends here, it will be difficult to narrow down the guest list. How many does your dining room accommodate?"

"Twelve, comfortably."

Her brow puckered. "Only twelve?"

"We could bring in extra chairs and squeeze in a few more, if you don't mind being snug."

"Well, we are all becoming *quite* the bosom friends, so I don't think anyone will mind being cozy."

"We would need a fair amount of time to prepare. And, as you know, we serve dinner to our guests five nights a week, but Saturday and Sunday evenings are a possibility."

"So many limitations!" Mrs. Elton sighed. "I told Mr. E we should let a lodging house of our own, but he argued that an entire house for just two people did not make sense. I assured him we would make many friends to entertain, yet would he listen? We are popular wherever we go."

"I am sure. What are your thoughts on the menu?"

"Oh, whatever you think best—or perhaps ask your mother, who probably entertained often. She was a gentlewoman, I understand."

Sarah stiffened. "Yes, she is." Had Mrs. Elton intended it as an insult, or was she simply verbalizing a fact none of them wished to face? Did running a guest house put them in "trade"? Were they gentlewomen no longer? Either way, Sarah told herself to overlook the slight.

Instead, she thought back to all the lovely dinners they had hosted at Finderlay. Flowers on the table, pristine white cloth, every piece of silver polished, every dish and goblet positioned just so. And the food! Mrs. Besley did wonders with the few loaves and fishes they gave her here, but the lavish meals at home, prepared by a host of kitchen staff . . .

"Would you prefer several dishes set on the table at once, so your guests might help themselves as they like? That is how we often served meals at home, at least among family and friends." She could still see her mother presiding over an impressive array of serving dishes overflowing with roast game, veal olives, duck ragout, pigeon pie, sweet breads, fricassee of chicken, salads, calves' feet jelly, and more, served à la française. People helping themselves, or gentlemen serving the ladies, servants there to refill glasses. Everyone talking with their tablemates to the right and to the left, jovial conversation mingling. Laughter, ease, pleasure, warmth . . .

"Something more formal, I think," Mrs. Elton said, breaking the nostalgic spell. "With several courses."

"Several. I see. And have you any specific dishes in mind?"

"What would you suggest?"

"Well, fresh seafood is plentiful here. Crab, lobster, prawns . . ."

She wrinkled her nose. "I don't like shellfish. Mild fish is un-objectionable, I suppose—as long as it does not taste like fish."

"Ah. Well. Salmon is mild. Sole? Turbot?"

"Whatever you think."

"Soup?"

"Yes, we must have soup."

"Pease soup?"

"Too ordinary."

"Julienne? I would have to ask our cook what she can manage with what's in season."

Mrs. Elton raised exasperated hands. "More limitations."

Sarah chose to ignore that. "Any preference for meat? Chicken, lamb, beef . . . ?"

"Which would you advise?"

"Fricassee chicken is delicious. Spare ribs are tender but expensive. Pork cutlets would be a good moderate choice."

Mrs. Elton waggled a finger. "No. No pork. I intend to invite Emanuel Lousada." She stepped closer and said sotto voce, "Jewish, you know. Does not eat pork."

Sarah reared her head back. "Mr. Lousada is coming to your dinner party?"

The highly respected man had played a major role in developing Sidmouth into the resort town it was, building several properties, including a fine residence for his family.

"Why does that astound you? He is a gracious man and known to be quite hospitable. He shall no doubt reciprocate with an invitation to Peak House."

"Goodness."

Mrs. Elton raised her long face till she was looking down her nose at Sarah. "You do not keep company with Mr. Lousada?"

"We have not yet had that pleasure," Sarah replied evenly. "And as far as vegetables and salads?"

"Yes, several of each."

"Very well. I will need to talk to Mrs. Besley. Again, it will depend on what is in season locally or available from the greengrocer. She serves a dish of tomatoes with balsamic on sea kale that is delicious."

"Sea kale?" Mrs. Elton wrinkled her nose a second time. "I don't think so. What about beetroot? Mr. E is partial to beetroot."

"As am I. But I don't believe they are in season yet."

"Asparagus?"

"A bit past season."

"How trying are these limitations!"

"Now, don't worry. I shall talk with Mrs. Besley—"

"And your mother."

"And my mother, and plan a delicious menu. I shall also prepare an estimate for how much such a dinner would cost. It will be expensive, I fear."

Mrs. Elton raised a dismissive hand. "Ah well. The price of having friends. And still less costly than letting a lodging house of our own. Yes, yes. Quite worth it. I shall finalize our guest list."

With a triumphant lift of her chin, the woman turned and eagerly departed the room.

On Sunday, Sarah helped lay out the cold collation Mrs. Besley had prepared: sliced meats, bread, and cheeses. Potted shrimps. Meat and egg pie. Fruit and jellies. These she arranged on the mahogany buffet in the breakfast room for guests who wished to eat either before or after church.

A short while later, a small contingent from Sea View set out together to attend divine services. Effie, Georgiana, and Mr. Henshall strolled together, followed by Viola, her hand on Mr. Hornbeam's arm, and Sarah and Emily, walking side by side.

They had invited Mr. Gwilt to join them, but he'd politely declined, saying he and Parry would sing a few hymns together in their room.

Mrs. Elton insisted on attending the Old Dissenting Chapel in hopes of meeting the Reverend Edmund Butcher. Sarah had overheard Mr. Elton mutter that he prayed none of their home congregation learned of it.

When they reached the churchyard, Sarah and Emily happened to walk up the path with Lady Kennaway, whom they had met in passing and occasionally exchanged greetings with before or after services.

Sarah greeted her. "Lady Kennaway, good morning."

"Good morning, Miss Summers. Miss Emily. How is your mother? I trust her health has improved?"

"She has begun sea-bathing, on Dr. Clarke's advice," Sarah said. "And we all have high hopes."

"Good. I shall pray for her."

"Thank you. We appreciate that."

Emily spoke up. "By the way, we have one of your friends staying with us."

The woman's eyebrows rose. "Oh? May I ask whom?"

"A Mr. and Mrs. Elton." When no flash of recognition dawned, Emily added, "From Surrey."

"Elton? I am afraid I don't recall that name." Lady Kennaway added in conspiratorial tones, "Please don't mention I forgot them, however. Dreadful to get old."

The lady appeared perfectly sharp and well-informed to Emily. She smiled and assured her, "Not at all, my lady. You seem quite young to me."

When the woman continued on toward her pew near the front, Emily leaned close to Sarah and hissed, "The Eltons are nothing but preening name-droppers!"

"We don't know that," Sarah whispered back. "Perhaps Lady Kennaway forgot, as she said. A lady like her no doubt meets a great many people."

"*Dear* Lady Kennaway . . ." Emily mimicked Mrs. Elton's fawning tones.

"Hush," Sarah admonished with a glance around the church. "Now is not the time nor place."

19

Fishing and pleasure boats are frequently seen
spotting the deep blue of the ocean with their white
sails, and affording, as they tack and shift their
positions, a pleasing and interesting spectacle.
—*The Beauties of Sidmouth Displayed*

The next day, Callum Henshall and Sarah set out from Sea View for their sailing trip. Mr. Henshall offered to carry her small basket, and together they walked down to the beach to meet Mr. Puddicombe.

In the distance, Sarah saw a modest-sized boat beached on the pebbles, bow out, ready to depart.

Mr. Puddicombe, a successful fisherman who owned several boats, stood waiting for them dressed in coat, boots, and wool cap.

Mr. Henshall offered his hand. "Thank ye for taking us out yourself."

"Only the best fer one of the Miss Summerses." He grinned, showing a missing front tooth.

Sarah smiled into the man's weathered face. "You are very kind."

"Now, miss, you step in and move forward. You too, sir, if 'ee don't want to ruin yer foine boots."

"Not at all. These have waded into the North Sea plenty of times."

Puddicombe nodded his approval. "Good man."

Mr. Henshall helped Sarah inside and handed her the basket. Together the men pushed the boat farther into the surf, and then Mr. Henshall leapt nimbly in, while the older man climbed inside with wet boots and heaving effort.

They rowed into deeper water, and then Mr. Puddicombe hoisted the sail. The light cloth unfurled and flapped until the wind filled it and drew it tight. The wind tugged at Sarah's bonnet as well, but the ribbons tied under her chin held it in place.

With gentle waves lapping against the hull and lines snapping against the mast, they sailed farther from shore.

As Sarah surveyed Sidmouth from this new vantage, the Sid Vale reminded her of a large center stage, ringed by a rising amphitheater of hills. Looking up, she saw Mr. Lousada's house atop Peak Hill and, there between lofty elms, the Lodge, where one of the county magistrates lived. These, along with charming Witheby Cottage, overlooked the town.

Mr. Puddicombe gestured to the tiller. "Want to give it a go, Miss Sarah?"

"No, thank you."

He turned to Mr. Henshall. "You, sir?"

"I would indeed." Shifting closer, Mr. Henshall maneuvered the tiller and adjusted the sail, his arms strong and his hands deft.

Soon they had passed Chit Rock and were sailing along the western beach.

The older man watched Mr. Henshall for a time, then again nodded in approval.

As they sailed west, Sarah admired the red face of Peak Hill with green foliage cascading over its edges like a leafy lace shawl. She also admired Callum Henshall, his coppery blond hair ruffled by the breeze, his golden eyebrows over sun-narrowed eyes, his handsome profile and lean torso.

To her relief, the wind was mild and steady and the sea calm. She closed her eyes and inhaled the fresh salty spray, ears filled with the sounds of splashing sea, flapping sail, and distant cries of gulls.

When she opened them again, she found Mr. Henshall watching her, lips quirked.

"Enjoying yourself?"

"I am, thank you."

"Ready to feed the fishes?"

She grinned. "Not yet."

They soon approached lofty High Peak. Sarah marveled at the landmark, which she had only seen from a distance before.

After they passed the second peak, the coastland changed, now fluted with inlets, small waterfalls, and beaches.

At one point, Mr. Henshall pointed out a few spiky plants poking out from a rocky cliff wall. "Look there. Thistle. Seems it grows here as well."

Sarah squinted to better see the feathery purple flowers, each set atop a spiny ball.

She realized she'd seen them before, along the verges of roads and fields. The local people called them dashels. Sarah had never given the plant much thought, for as Mr. Elton had said, they looked rather like weeds. Now she regarded the purple crowns with new appreciation. What had he said they symbolized? Courage and loyalty? She glanced at the Scotsman. Yes, it seemed appropriate.

Eventually Mr. Puddicombe relieved Callum at the tiller.

"Where are we?" Sarah called to their pilot over the wind.

"Near Otterton."

They rounded a massive rock outcropping, and a hidden bay came into view. Mr. Puddicombe nodded toward it. "That's Ladram Bay."

In the bay stood large sea-stack formations, like huge statues in a fountain, one as large as a ship.

"Beautiful . . ." Sarah breathed.

230

They beached the boat in the scenic spot, and Mr. Henshall took the picnic basket from her and helped her alight. After exploring a bit, they spread a cloth on a large, flat rock, as the sandy beach was studded with pebbles.

Mr. Puddicombe accepted a sandwich with a grunt of thanks and wolfed it down before returning to the beach with a pole to fish from shore.

Sarah and Mr. Henshall sat together, talking, eating, and soaking in the gorgeous scenery.

She said, "This was an excellent idea. Thank you for inviting me."

"My pleasure. I hope it shan't be the last time."

She regarded him curiously. "The last time I relax and enjoy myself?"

He held her gaze. "The last time you spend with me."

For a few sun-streaked seconds, Sarah allowed herself to daydream about what it would be like to be courted by Callum Henshall. The two continued to look into one another's eyes, until the moment grew heavy and awkward.

He cleared his throat and said, "I've been thinking of what ye said about the loss of your betrothed—the great love of your life. And I rather envy ye. You possess the romantic ideal, a courtship never sullied by reality or disappointment."

She frowned at him, illogically irritated. "You don't know that my marriage to Peter would have been a disappointment. He was a good, kind man."

"You're right, of course. I suppose I was recalling my own marriage." He slanted her a tentative glance. "I know his loss was painful, but I would think you'd be eager to try again, since your first experience with love was so positive."

"And you are not? Eager to try again, that is?"

He shook his head. "A few acquaintances have shown interest since Katrin's death, and I have kept my distance. I had thought Katrin was a certain person, that she and I would be happy together. I was wrong. In any case, I told myself not to be hasty in forming another attachment. To be cautious." Another sidelong glance. "Although at present, I am finding that rather difficult." His gaze lingered on her face. "To me, ye seem all that is admirable. A kind, bonnie lass who cares deeply for her family. I wonder if my impression is too good to be true?"

His flattering words warmed her, but also disconcerted her. It seemed far too soon to be having such a conversation.

"I could ask the same of you," she said. "Are you truly as you seem?"

He harrumphed. "If I seem to be a frustrated father and disenchanted widower, then aye, right ye are."

She shook her head. "That is not how I see you. Perhaps you are a poor judge of character—especially your own. I see a responsible man who does his best to make things right. I see a father who is patient and gentle with a stepdaughter who is often sour and snappish."

Sarah thought of her own faults and added, "And please do not saint me or overestimate me. I am far from perfect. I try too hard to manage things and people, to wrest control from God because my faith is not all it should be. I try to hold my family together—what is left of it." She lifted a cupped palm. "But it's like . . . trying to hold water in my hand. And it's difficult for me to ask God for help. To accept His will, when He allows things I don't like to happen."

"Like the loss of your betrothed?"

"Yes. Among other losses."

"So." He drew a long breath and then exhaled. "You are reticent to love again because ye fear ye could never be as happy. And I, because I fear to repeat the unhappiness."

She attempted to lighten the moment. "So you see? We are both hopeless cases."

Once again, he held her gaze, sunlight shimmering in his eyes. "Speak for yourself. I, for one, am still hopeful."

After the trip, Sarah returned to Sea View and returned to work. A glow of relaxed happiness lingered, even as she warned herself it was only temporary. Mr. Henshall would leave soon, while her responsibilities would remain.

Mrs. Fulford proved to be true to her word and had recommended Viola to others of her acquaintance. Soon Viola was also reading to a Mrs. Gage, who'd rented number five in Fortfield Terrace, an elegant row of tall, adjoining houses at the back of Fort Field. Mrs. Gage was neighbor to Mrs. Fulford, a full-time resident, while the other ten homes were let as seasonal lodgings. The lord of the manor had long ago commissioned an architect to build a seafront crescent to provide accommodation for fashionable visitors. The scheme was never fully realized, however, leaving the field open in front, formerly used for military exercises and now for sport and recreation.

While indoors and out, Mrs. Gage used a wheeled Bath chair—an open, upholstered chair with a steering mechanism in front and push handles in back—which could be pulled like a wagon or pushed from the rear.

The wealthy widow asked Viola to read aloud from the social column in the newspaper—the notices of births, marriages, appointments, and deaths. She asked which names mentioned were known to Viola and what additional details she might share about the people involved.

Some days, instead of reading, she asked Viola to push her along the esplanade to take the air. She confided that she could ask her maid, but she preferred Viola's company, as Viola offered livelier conversation.

As Viola strolled and Mrs. Gage rolled, often with her little dog, Nero, on her lap, the plump older woman asked her to identify every person they passed. Viola knew some but not enough to satisfy her curious new client.

Once or twice, Georgiana or Emily happened upon them during one of their walks, and Mrs. Gage insisted the sisters walk beside her in entourage and join in the conversation because Georgiana and Emily were acquainted with more people.

As far as Viola could tell, there was nothing wrong with the woman's eyesight or her ability to read, but she was happy to pay Viola for her time, so Viola did as she requested. She planned to save the extra money—after Bibi's wages were paid—to buy a gift for Mrs. Denby.

Viola realized that, in reality, she was performing the role of lady's companion for Mrs. Gage—although for only a few hours a week.

The thought of a lady's companion reminded her of Claire.

Viola still sometimes wondered why her eldest sister left home to fill the role of companion to ailing Great-Aunt Mercer. Had Papa insisted?

Viola had always spent a great deal of time alone and never attended social events, so she was often the last to know when something happened. Claire's departure had taken her by surprise, nearly as much as it had Emily, who was away at the time with a school friend.

They had all known Papa wanted Claire to marry the son of an old friend of his, and that she had refused. Had Claire gone to Scotland to escape the pressure to marry a man she did not like? Or had Papa sent her to live with his demanding aunt as a sort of punishment? He had been a benevolent, if distant, father until the last two months of his life. Yet he'd often lost his temper when crossed.

Viola had secretly hoped her sister might return after Papa's death and once their disagreement had been forgotten. Sadly, no. Claire never even corresponded with them.

Oh, Claire. Would they ever see her again?

After that day's appointment with Mrs. Gage, Viola went to Westmount to read to the major as usual. When she arrived, she walked in on a flurry of activity.

Chown was bellowing orders, Taggart wielding a broom, Mr. Hutton clearing ashes and crumbs from the table beside his favorite chair, and Colin . . . still in his dressing gown, yawning.

He smiled when he saw her. "Ah, Miss Vi. Please forgive the chaos. Visitors are expected tomorrow, and we have all been conscripted to get everything shipshape." He shook his head. "House full of bachelors. What does one expect?"

"May I ask who is visiting to cause such a flutter?"

He stepped closer and said in conspiratorial tones, "It is a lady, you see. The beautiful Lucinda Truman." He added with a theatrical shudder, "And her mother."

Recalling the name from the major's correspondence, Viola's stomach knotted. "Are they . . . friends of the family?"

"I suppose you could say that. She is Jack's betrothed."

Viola's throat closed as if someone had gripped it tight. The major was engaged?

She drew in a shaky breath and endeavored to keep her expression neutral. "And . . . what is Miss Truman like?"

"Oh, beautiful, as I said. A golden-haired angel. Family's decent. Father passed on and mother a bit of a . . ." He cleared his throat. "Well. You will meet them during their stay and may judge for yourself."

Would she meet Miss Truman? Did she want to? Viola was curious even as she dreaded it. "Are they to stay long?"

"Ten days, I believe. You must have read about it in Miss Truman's latest letter?"

"No, he . . . must have kept that one back to read himself."

"Love letters, you know." Colin gave her a winking grin. She could not return it.

When she remained sober, his grin faded. "Surely Jack mentioned her to you?"

No, he had not. She had begun reading one of Miss Truman's letters, but he'd told her to set it aside without explanation. Aloud, Viola said, "Only in passing."

"They have not seen each other since Jack's return," Colin explained. "His decision. Hoping to heal up first. Can't blame him for that."

Viola swallowed and looked around the adjoining sitting and drawing rooms. "And where is the major? Preparing for the visit as well?"

Colin nodded. "Having a shave and haircut as we speak."

"Ah, well, in that case, I shall take my leave. No wish to be underfoot. Please do tell him I called."

Emily saw Mr. Gwilt sitting on the veranda that day, his birdcage on the chair beside him.

"Good afternoon."

"Ah, Miss Emily. Greetings. Will you join us?"

He lifted the cage from the chair and set it on the floor. "Parry won't mind giving up his chair for a lady."

"Thank you . . . both."

She sat beside him, and for a time the two gazed down the lawn and across the esplanade to the sea.

"Are you enjoying your stay?" she asked politely.

"I am. A pleasure it is to be somewhere so lovely with such friendly hosts."

"Have you traveled a great deal?"

"Hardly at all. I've spent the last decade rarely straying farther than my own back door."

He must have noticed her concerned look, for he patted her hand and said, "And I wouldn't have been anywhere else for the world."

He inhaled and released a satisfied sigh. "Coming here now though . . . Yes. I appreciate the good company most of all. Parry is good company as well, don't mistake me. But rather more quiet than he used to be."

She was relieved when he winked at her, and she smiled in reply.

"You may wonder why I keep him when he can longer talk to me."

"No, I . . ." Emily started to demur, then admitted, "I own I am curious."

"Sometimes I wonder it myself—why I was content to leave my wife of many years in a country churchyard yet determined to bring him with me."

Emily stared at him. "You had a wife, Mr. Gwilt?"

"You may well be surprised, the likes of me being so blessed."

"I did not mean . . ."

He raised his palm. "It's all right, my dear. I am not easily offended. Cannot afford to be, considering my traveling companion."

His gaze returned to the sea. "Yes, Mrs. Gwilt and I were married for five and twenty years, and I loved her with all my heart. Yet I prefer to remember her as she was, before a long illness ravaged her, body and mind."

"I am so sorry."

He nodded, expression pained. "It stole her speech and memory. I felt so dashed helpless. I cared for her, I did, as best I could, although she could not speak to me and barely seemed to know who I was. Oh, the years of silence."

His eyes glistened with unshed tears. He blinked them back and worked his lip in an effort to maintain control.

"That's when I realized I needed Parry as much as he needed me." He laid his hand on the cage between their chairs. "He talked in those days. Filled those silent rooms with pleasant chatter."

"I am glad you found each other."

Again Mr. Gwilt nodded, his gaze lingering on the parrot. "When my wife passed, Parry was there beside me. All too soon, he was silenced too, and the house became unbearably quiet. Unbearably empty." He took a deep, steadying breath. "Yet he still looks well, and his bright colors cheer me." He moved the cage forward, so they might both view the parrot.

"And of course, for all that I loved him, and sometimes forget the truth of it, deep down I know he is—*was*—only a bird."

After a moment passed, he sniffed and added, "After I had him
. . . preserved, a local tavern keeper offered me a crown for him.
Wanted to set him on a shelf behind the bar." Mr. Gwilt somberly
shook his head. "Now, if he'd offered a guinea, I woulda left this
wee *dutty* there in a trice."

Emily started at that, and a bubble of mirth threatened. She
glanced at him, unsure if he was jesting or how she should react.

He sent her a mischievous grin, and she burst out laughing.

Mr. Gwilt joined in, and Emily thought she had rarely heard
such a beautiful sound.

20

After I got back to the machine, I presently felt myself in
a Glow that was delightful—it is the finest feeling in the
World, and will induce me to Bathe as often as will be safe.

—Frances Burney, diary

Thankfully, Mamma's second bathing experience went
better, and she returned to Sea View shaky but smiling.
And, after a few days, she released Emily from the task of
accompanying her, saying that between Georgiana and a walking
stick, she could manage the distance herself. They were all relieved
at this evidence of Mamma's improving strength—perhaps Emily
most of all.

During those days, Sarah, Mamma, and Mrs. Besley also discussed options, consulted shopkeepers, and planned a menu for
the Eltons' dinner party. Together they calculated a fair price to
charge—enough to cover their costs, reward staff for extra effort,
and hire a waiter for the evening.

Sarah presented the proposed menu in written form and self-
consciously quoted the price. She held her breath, waiting for Mrs.
Elton to faint away in shock or at least to protest.

When Mrs. Elton said nothing, Sarah added, "Mrs. Besley and
my mother both feel the price is fair for the menu and number of

guests. But if it exceeds what you expected, we could exchange the beef in favor of chicken. Or mutton is also less expensive, and haricot mutton is very tasty."

Mrs. Elton studied the page. "No, I like the menu as it is. And it shall be worth it, for us and for you. For when such renowned personages come here as our guests, Sea View's reputation will be assured."

Renowned personages? Sarah licked dry lips. "You mentioned Mr. Lousada. Who else are you planning to invite?"

"Dear Lady Kennaway and Sir John, of course. General and Mrs. Baynes. Mr. Wallis of the Marine Library. He may be a publisher, but he is so well-known. I don't think anyone looks down on him as a tradesman, even if he"—another of her theatrical whispers—"*sells* books and prints."

She returned the menu to Sarah and continued, "Then there's Mr. Butcher. We attended services at his chapel specifically to make his acquaintance, although we are Church of England. And I suppose we must have his wife as well."

Sarah's ears began to buzz. Mr. Butcher? This could be the opportunity they'd been hoping for. Emily had still received no reply to her letter. But if he accepted an invitation from the Eltons, that would still give them an opportunity to impress the man. Emily would be so pleased!

Mrs. Elton went on to list a few other names, most of whom were visitors to Sidmouth and unknown to Sarah. Then they settled on a date—the Saturday a little more than two weeks hence.

Twisting her lips to the side in thought, the woman added, "I believe I shall deliver the invitations in person. It will give me a chance to pay calls and further our acquaintance, which will ease the flow of conversation around the table. Unless you think sending them by post would be more correct?"

Sarah considered. In her experience, people did not like to be pressed for an immediate answer. She said, "Writing would give people a chance to review their schedules and respond by letter."

"Is there sufficient time for that?"

"Yes, unless you plan to have the invitations printed."

"I had not thought of that. . . ."

"No need. A handwritten invitation is perfectly acceptable."

"So many details to consider."

"Yes." Sarah agreed completely. Her heart beat hard, and perspiration dampened the back of her neck. She hoped they could make a success of this dinner.

⌒⌒⌒

Viola's mood remained rather more somber than usual, even for her. She missed going to Westmount, chatting with Mr. Hutton and Armaan, and being teased by Colin. If she were honest with herself, she missed the major most of all. More than once, she reviewed their various conversations and interactions. No, he had not mentioned his engagement, but why should he divulge such personal information to a stranger paid to read to him? And he'd not really encouraged her—in fact he'd barely been civil toward her, at least initially. She could not claim he had deceived her. Yet their last few encounters had taken on a more personal aspect. And he had touched her mouth. She had thought it meant something—or might. She had clearly been wrong and foolish. Yet he had been wrong too. An engaged man should not go around touching women's lips, and she would tell him so. If and when she saw him again.

Would she?

Because Viola had curtailed her visits to Westmount, she found herself with unexpected free time and began visiting Mrs. Denby more often.

When Viola entered her room at the poor house that day, the old woman slapped her hand down as though swatting an insect. Viola heard the distinct sound of crinkling paper.

Suspicion rose. "What do you have there, Mrs. Denby?"

She looked up, as guilty as a child hiding candy. "Ah, well. Didn't want you to catch me reading. I can still see a little, you know, but I don't want you to stop visiting me."

"I won't. Now, what are you hiding?"

The old woman extracted a piece of paper she'd stuffed between herself and the arm of the chair and held it aloft. "I received a letter. Me! A rare treat at my age. Oh, and did I enjoy showing it to Mr. Banks. He often receives letters, and does he lord it over me!" She giggled, then extended the letter to Viola.

"Would you read it to me, my dear? I'd like to hear it again in your lovely voice, and you might find it interesting as well."

"Oh?"

Mrs. Denby nodded, lips pursed in a suppressed smile.

Curious, Viola accepted the letter, recognized the handwriting, and read aloud:

"Dear Mrs. Denby,

Thank you for your kind note about my small offerings of baked goods I've sent with Viola. You were exceedingly generous in your compliments, and since I am now baking for our guests, your encouragement is timely and appreciated.

Thank you, too, for befriending our Viola. She speaks very highly of you, praising your amiability and excellent spirits. Sometimes I think our dear sister undervalues her worth, and it is heartening when someone outside of our family recognizes her for the jewel she is.

Yours sincerely,
Miss Sarah Summers"

An uncomfortable knot lodged itself under Viola's ribs. Did Sarah really see her as valuable, or was she merely being polite? Disbelief and longing wrestled within her. Her, a jewel? It was a compliment she was not quite able to believe.

During dinner that night, Sarah helped Jessie serve the meal while Emily acted as hostess. Mr. Stanley dined with them, a rare occurrence since his sister's arrival in Sidmouth. Sarah noticed him gaze often at Emily from across the table, his every look betraying admiration.

A shadow appeared in the doorway, and Sarah glanced over, surprised to see Lowen. He rarely ventured into the dining room.

He cleared his throat. "There's a Giles Hornbeam to see Mr. Hornbeam."

Mr. Hornbeam's head snapped up, and his mouth fell slack before rising in pleasure, a crinkling web of smile lines fanning out beneath his dark glasses.

Sarah replied, "Please show him in."

A handsome man of about thirty, dressed in the height of fashion, appeared in the threshold, hat in hand.

"Good evening."

Mr. Hornbeam rose. "Giles, my boy. I knew you'd come."

The younger man gave a general bow to the room. "A thousand apologies for intruding. I did not realize you would be dining so early."

Sarah quickly reassured him, "Not at all, sir. You are very welcome." She gestured to the table. "Please join us. I shall set another place. We have plenty."

He raised a staying palm. "Don't go to any trouble on my account. I will dine at the hotel later."

"The hotel?" his father said. "I have a bed for you in my room here."

"And I am sure it's perfectly comfortable, but . . ." He shifted foot to foot. "May I have a private word, Pater?"

Mr. Hornbeam hesitated. "Won't you sit for a few minutes while I finish this excellent meal? If you are not hungry, I am sure Jessie would bring you a cup of tea while you wait."

Jessie nodded. "Of course, sir."

Again, the gloved palm rose. "No, thank you. I am sorry to interrupt your meal, but it won't take more than a few minutes, I promise."

For a moment, Mr. Hornbeam stood still, his expression, his whole form, tensing as if steeling himself.

"Very well." He laid down his serviette. "Pray excuse us, everyone. Do go on without me." He made his way effortlessly around the table, not even using his stick.

Sarah watched the two leave, and as soon as the door closed behind them, she sent Emily a look, signaling her to start up the conversation and break the awkward silence.

Emily took her cue and asked Mr. Henshall about the book he was reading, and the two discussed the Waverly novels for a time.

A few minutes later, Mr. Hornbeam reentered and everyone turned expectantly. The disappointment creasing his face was painful to see.

Pausing in the threshold, he said, "My son will not be joining me here after all."

"I am sorry, Mr. Hornbeam," Sarah said.

"Thank you."

He walked slowly and more gingerly around the table, reclaimed his seat, and settled the serviette on his lap. He said, "I am not truly shocked. An old man like me cannot compete with a party of amiable young friends."

Mr. Henshall said, "I'd say you have a party of amiable friends right here, Mr. Hornbeam, though perhaps not as fashionable as your son's."

"Nor as young," Mr. Gwilt added, with a self-abasing grin.

Mrs. Elton asked, "In which hotel is he staying?"

"The London Inn, but only for tonight. He returns to Weymouth tomorrow to rejoin his companions."

"Perhaps we ought to have gone to Weymouth," Mrs. Elton said. "Or even to Brighton."

Emily's eyes flashed and she opened her mouth to reply. "Then—"
Sarah could almost guess her tart retort. *"Then don't let us
stop you."* She sent Emily a warning look and said quickly, "Then
we would not have met you two, which would indeed be a pity."

Mr. Elton nodded in acknowledgment, then glanced again at
his wife. "I am enjoying Sidmouth, my dear. Though, of course,
we could go somewhere else next time, if you prefer."

Mr. Hornbeam admitted, "My son found Brighton quite diverting."

Emily smiled sweetly and added, "And a long, long way from
here."

After dinner, Sarah spoke to Mr. Hornbeam privately in the hall.

"I am surprised your son traveled all this way if he did not
mean to stay longer."

Mr. Hornbeam nodded vaguely. "Yes."

"May I ask why he did so?"

"Well, he did not come this far for advice, I assure you. He left
here with his purse heavier and mine far lighter."

"Ah."

He grimaced. "Yes, 'Ah.'"

"I am sorry."

"Do please stop apologizing, my dear."

"Am I making you feel worse? It was not my intention."

"Not at all. You have nothing to apologize for. Your kindness—
yours and your sisters'—eases the sting of his callous disregard."

"I am glad."

He patted her shoulder. "And I am glad I came here."

"We are too."

Mr. Henshall stuck his head out of the parlour. "How about a
game of chess, Mr. Hornbeam? I shall call out the moves."

The older man hesitated. "Chess, ey? I should warn you, I was
pretty good in my day."

"And still are, I have no doubt."

Mr. Hornbeam managed a smile. "Thank you, Mr. Henshall. I would enjoy that."

Sarah admired the Scotsman in that moment even more than she had before. She met his gaze across the distance and hoped he could see all the warmth and gratitude she felt.

21

Often it's only when you see other folks minding a thing,
that you begin to mind it for yourself. I make no doubt, if
Eve had been so unlucky as to have a hare-lip, she'd not have
minded it till Adam came by, looking doubtfully upon her.

—Mary Webb, *Precious Bane*

T he next day, Viola again avoided Westmount. But half
an hour after her usual time with the major, Armaan
walked over to Sea View, letter in hand.

Viola answered the door. "Good day, Mr. Sagar. Everything
all right?"

"No, miss. The major is not happy. He is most irritated you
do not come."

"Oh."

"Are you ill?"

"No. I simply assumed that with houseguests . . ."

He shook his head. "The major wishes you to come."

Armaan handed her a note, written in a scrawled hand.

Miss V.S.,

*I was under the impression you agreed to come to West-
mount for one hour a day. Was that not our arrangement?*

An arrangement for which I am paying you? Please do your duty or have the goodness to explain your absence.

Sincerely,
J.H.

Irritated is right.

When she looked up, she saw Armaan's dark eyes watching her with speculative interest. "I think he misses you."

"Misses me?" With the beautiful Miss Truman in residence? Viola barely resisted an unladylike snort. Even so, she took a deep breath and said, "Very well. I shall come directly, if that suits. Just give me a minute to gather my things."

After collecting her veiled bonnet and gloves, she joined him outside.

On the walk over, she asked, "How is the visit going? Are Miss Truman and her mother enjoying their stay?"

Unease lined his face. "I am not certain. Things are improving, I believe, but were rather strained at first."

"Why?"

He opened his mouth to reply, glanced at her, then seemed to think the better of what he'd been about to say. Instead, he said, "The first day, they found the food intolerable. Then Chown sought much help from your Mrs. Besley, and now meals are more edible. Almost good."

"That's a relief."

He sent her a sidelong glance. "Hosting guests can be awkward, yes? You know this."

She nodded. "Better than ever." But Viola wondered what he'd meant to say.

When they reached Westmount a short while later, Armaan led her first to the drawing room.

Viola's nerves were taut with anticipation at the thought of meeting the major's betrothed. She left her veil in place, feeling the need to shield herself. She didn't know what she expected. No, that was not true. She did know. She expected a vain, spoiled beauty. Had Miss Truman been repulsed by the sight of her scarred intended? Had she reacted by doing something melodramatic, like fainting? And when she recovered, had she lifted her haughty nose in the air and declared she would not be shackled to a marred man when she herself was so perfect? Part of Viola hoped so. Then, imagining the major's reaction to such a spectacle, she banished the petty thought.

Crossing the threshold, Viola braced herself, but the young blond woman who came forward to greet her was all warmth and sincerity. Pretty, yes, although not overly affected.

"Miss Summers, I am happy to meet you at last. I have heard so much about you."

She curtsied, and Viola automatically returned the gesture.

"I understand you have been reading newspapers and correspondence for Major Hutton."

"Y-yes."

"Then you have read my letters?"

"Um, no. The major managed those more . . . personal missives himself."

"Oh good! That is a relief." Miss Truman pressed a hand to her chest. "I am sure you would have judged my writing girlish and silly. And I am told my spelling is atrocious!" She grinned, and Viola found herself beginning to relax.

"Are you enjoying your visit to Sidmouth?"

Miss Truman glanced behind her as though to make sure they would not be overheard. "I would not say *enjoy*, exactly, as we have hardly ventured out."

Viola asked, "And how are things going . . . here?"

"In all honesty, seeing him again, as he is, was something of a shock. I cannot deny it. He had written—I believe he dictated that letter to his, um . . . friend. That was before you joined his little troop here." Another grin, although it soon wobbled away. "I had been forewarned to expect scars, a damaged eye, and his poor ear . . . mangled. Yet I confess it was worse than my inexperienced imagination could conjure. I have lived a terribly sheltered life, I am afraid."

Viola nodded her understanding. "I am sure it must have been difficult at first. But you will grow accustomed to the marks in time. Soon, you will hardly notice them."

Miss Truman stared at her, pink lips parted in wonder and eyes alight with, perhaps, hope. "Do you really think so? Are *you* used to them?"

"Oh yes. I don't say I am blind to them, but they certainly no longer shock or disturb me."

"But then . . . you bear scars yourself, I am told, which might inure you to the sight." Miss Truman's gaze lingered on her veil.

Viola's chest constricted as betrayal burned through her veins. The major had described her as a scarred woman? As an unfortunate creature with a harelip? Was that the sum total of her person?

The childhood taunts and jeers she had suffered had left her with emotional scars, and although she would bear them forever, they had, for the most part, healed. And lately, she had grown rather calloused to the snubs of those she did not care about. But this?

"The major told you?" she asked.

"I believe his father first mentioned it, and then the major warned me to be kind." Miss Truman's limpid eyes sought hers behind the filmy veil. Viola knew her features were shadowed by lace—blurred—though not completely hidden.

Did it require *such* effort not to react negatively to her appearance? To be kind to someone like her?

When Viola made no reply, Miss Truman said, "Forgive me. Perhaps I should not have mentioned it. I only wanted you to know that I knew. To give you leave to remove your veil if you wished to."

"Not especially," Viola murmured. *Not now.*

The young woman blinked and forced a cheerful smile. "That's all right. Well, I gather you are here to read to the major? I did offer to read to him myself, but he said you were already employed to do so. Shall we?" Miss Truman gestured down the passage and walked with her to the study.

Reaching the open doorway, Viola saw Major Hutton standing at the window, shutters again open, looking outside.

Hesitating on the threshold, Miss Truman began shyly, "Pardon me, Major, but—"

"I have asked you to call me by my given name," he said evenly, without turning.

"Oh yes. I keep forgetting." She dipped her head. "Here is Miss Summers."

"Ah." He turned, yet his gaze remained on Miss Truman. "Would you like to join us?"

"Oh. Thank you, no. I shall wait with Mamma." Lashes fluttering, she nodded vaguely from him to Viola and hurried away.

When she had gone, Major Hutton faced Viola, expression stern.

"Look who has finally come. Has your unexcused leave ended, and you decided to return to active duty at last?"

"I only missed four days."

"Days for which I am paying you."

"You may subtract it from my fee."

"No need. You shall make up the time."

"Shall I?" she challenged.

His voice gentled. "I hope so."

She removed her bonnet and sat down. "Why are you angry? I simply assumed you would be too occupied with your houseguests to want me to read the news."

"Assumptions are dangerous things." He studied her profile. "Is that the only reason you have stayed away?"

"Of course," she coolly replied. She wanted to ask him . . . so many questions. But she had the right to ask only one. "Shall we begin?"

After picking up the day's mail at the post office, Emily walked back along the esplanade toward the Marine Library, eager to find a new novel to read.

When she neared Wallis's veranda, she saw Mr. Stanley leaning an elbow on the railing, talking with a young woman seated on the bench nearby. Emily's stomach cramped in disappointment until she realized this must be his sister.

Noticing her approach, Mr. Stanley jerked upright and seemed all at once unsure what to do with the pastry in his hand.

"Miss Summers."

"Mr. Stanley." A fleck of icing glazed his lip, and she bit back a smile—and the urge to wipe it away.

Emily turned instead to his companion, a pleasant-looking, genteel young lady in a simple day dress, spencer, and chip bonnet.

Following the direction of her gaze, Mr. Stanley said, "Ah. Miss Summers. Allow me to introduce my sister, Miss Stanley."

The young woman rose, and the two curtsied to each other. Then she glanced at her brother and scratched a gloved finger to her lip with a significant, raised-brow look. He colored and wiped his mouth.

She said, "Summers? Ah . . . the family who owns the boarding house you chose."

Emily steeled herself and was relieved to see no derision in the girl's expression.

"That's right," he began, "but—"

Emily spoke up. "We have only recently opened the house to guests, and my sisters and I are muddling along as best we can. Your brother has been most patient and obliging."

Miss Stanley's dimples appeared. "I am not surprised. I have provided him many opportunities to learn patience over the years."

"Very true," he said.

She gave him a playful elbow in the side.

The young woman's friendly demeanor and caramel-brown hair were similar to her brother's, and Emily quickly decided she liked her.

Miss Stanley glanced from Emily to her brother with a mischievous sparkle in her eyes. "And now I understand why we see so little of him lately."

"So little!" he protested on a laugh. "I call on you and your friend almost every evening."

Emily looked past them toward the library window. "Is your friend not with you?"

Miss Stanley shook her head. "Poor thing has a megrim and decided to stay in bed."

"What a pity."

"Therefore I have been on my own for hours." Miss Stanley sighed. "Pray do not be offended, Miss Summers, but I cannot help wishing my brother had chosen to stay in the same hotel. It would be much more convenient."

"For you, perhaps," he replied. "Yet I prefer Sea View with all its homelike comforts."

His sister sent him a sly glance. "And you know, if you resided in our hotel, Miss Marchant and I would pester you all day to fetch our shawls, bring us ice creams, and escort us shopping."

"There is that as well," he agreed. "I enjoy my freedom."

Emily observed the way brother and sister fondly teased each other, and felt a wistful pang. When they were younger, she and Viola had often wished for a brother—and not only because of that awful entail.

She smiled at his sister. "Well. A pleasure to meet you, Miss Stanley." Another round of curtsies and a bow followed, and then Emily continued into the library alone.

Once inside, the lure of book covers and printed pages did not instantly draw her as usual. Seeing the clerk busy with another customer, Emily paused at the window and watched Mr. and Miss Stanley leave the veranda and stroll away.

Their familiar affection reminded her of how Charles had once treated her and her sisters. In their younger years, he had filled the role of brother in many ways: teasing them, joining them for lawn games and dancing lessons, walking with them into the village, and occasionally bringing gifts of game from his hunting expeditions.

He had been unfailingly kind to Claire, Sarah, and Georgiana. He had been kind to *her* too, although he sometimes admonished her for boisterous behavior or unladylike outbursts of laughter.

In hindsight, his manner had been more reserved with Viola. Her surgeries and recoveries had isolated her for long periods, so perhaps he simply did not know her as well. Or perhaps because of her condition, he deemed her too sensitive to tease.

As Emily grew older, Charles's attentions toward her had changed. He had corrected her less and admired her more, or so she'd thought. They began spending a great deal of time together—riding, walking, talking—and Mamma began to cluck like a proud mother hen in expectation of one of her brood marrying.

They had danced together several times the final night of the house party given in honor of his friend Lord Bertram. Was it already a year ago? Charles had held her close as they danced, smiled into her eyes, and once, when they were alone, seemed about to kiss her. . . . In fact, he was so attentive that Emily had almost wished she had not accepted the invitation to spend a fortnight with a school friend right after the party.

Shortly after that, Papa had suffered an apoplexy, and thoughts of romance had, for a time, receded. He had lived for another two months, bedridden, frustrated, and angry, until a second attack ended his life.

Charles had absented himself from the neighborhood during those weeks, choosing to spend time in his family's London house. He returned for Papa's funeral but kept his distance from Finderlay. At first, Emily had supposed his absence was out of respect for their mourning period. But when she happened to see him in passing—at church or in the village—she quickly became aware of his new aloofness toward her. Yes, he politely acknowledged her and asked after her mother's health, but then took his leave of her as quickly as possible.

Mamma had advised her not to press him. Said that gentlemen like Charles did not like to be chased. Pressured. Emily had tried to heed her mother's advice . . . for a while. But it had not brought about the desired result. And she still didn't understand why.

With a heavy sigh, Emily turned to a nearby display of new novels, determined to lose herself in the comfort of books.

Sarah was sitting at the desk, flipping through the blank pages in the register, when Emily returned from the post office.

"Any new room inquiries?" she asked.

"Only one from an elderly couple requesting a ground-floor room." Emily raised the three letters she had collected. "And unfortunately, Mr. Butcher has declined my invitation to visit Sea View."

Sarah was about to tell her Mrs. Elton had invited the man to her dinner party, so perhaps all was not lost, but Emily went on before she could.

"I did receive one interesting letter, however."

"Oh?"

"Do you remember Mrs. Jane Lewis?"

"Yes. I did not realize you were still in contact with her. I thought you lost touch after she moved away."

"I had. But I remembered she moved to Surrey. To Hinchley Wood, which, as it happens, is quite near Esher."

Sarah looked up and stilled. "You wrote to ask her about the Eltons."

Emily nodded, a gleam of satisfaction in her eyes.

"Let me guess, she does not remember them either?"

"She does, actually. She owns she is acquainted with them and also admits she does not like them—that no one likes them."

"Poor Mr. and Mrs. Elton . . ."

"Poor Mr. and Mrs. Elton!"

"Well, if no one likes them. How sad they must be."

Emily rolled her eyes. "*Sad* is not the word Jane Lewis used, nor the word I would use for them either." She lifted the letter and read an excerpt:

> "*I trust I am not insulting a new friend of yours, if friend you consider her. Her husband is all right, I suppose, but Mrs. Elton! I do not like to speak ill of anyone, yet I have come to believe her a manipulative, rude, selfish person who insinuates herself abominably. There it is. I hope you don't think the worst of me, but you did ask for my honest opinion.*"

"Good heavens," Sarah said. "It is worse than I thought."

Emily's eyes flashed. "It's exactly as I thought."

"Well, what are we supposed to do about it now? I can't turn them out for being unlikeable. And their dinner is already planned."

Emily slowly shook her head. "We shall live to regret it."

Feeling agitated after her talk with Emily, Sarah walked from room to room with a feather duster, taking out her angst on any dust that dared gather.

Seeing Mr. Gwilt and his parrot sitting alone together in the parlour, she went in to talk to him.

"Good day, Mr. Gwilt. I do hope you are enjoying your stay?"

"I am indeed. Parry is too."

"I am glad to hear it. And where will you go after Sidmouth? Back home?"

"Heavens. Trying to get rid of us already?"

"Of course not!" she assured him on a laugh. "You have paid for six weeks, and six weeks you shall have." She added more softly, "Longer, if you wish. I am only making conversation."

"Ah. No, not home. To be honest-like, there is no home any

longer. I sold it. Didn't like rattling around that old place, just Parry and me."

"I see. Then, are you thinking of settling down in Sidmouth?"

"I don't know about settling, but I may stay on a bet longer. What I've seen of the place so far I like, I do."

"Which seems precious little to me, if you don't mind my saying. You've hardly left the house."

"True, true. It's just that, well, I don't like to leave Parry alone too long. He gets lonely."

Sarah suspected it was the man who grew lonely, and said, "I have an idea. I will be walking into town in a little while. Perhaps you would like to accompany me? All I have planned is a visit to the greengrocer—you like fruit, I know—and perhaps we could stop at the library afterward?"

"Oh, that does sound pleasant. I like to read, I do."

"Wallis's is a circulating library as well as a shop. You can borrow a book for a reasonable fee. In fact, I have a subscription and have been too busy to use it. You would do me a favor by selecting a book. Emily will scold me otherwise for letting my account languish. She is a great reader."

"So I have gathered. Yes, I'd like that, I would. And if it will help you, all the better. But . . . Parry."

She winced apologetically. "I don't think they allow pets in shops like that. I know! We can leave him in the office here. Emily will be there for the next hour or so, finishing up some correspondence. She and Parry can keep each other company."

"Excellent notion! Thank you, Miss Sarah. You are extremely obliging. Just give me a few minutes to prepare. We shall both be down shortly."

He hurried happily up the stairs, while Sarah returned to the library.

"You are going to keep Parry company for the next hour or two. Please don't make a fuss."

"Parry?" Emily groaned. "You must be joking!"

"Shh . . . It's the only way I could convince Mr. Gwilt to venture into town."

"Why do you care?"

"I just do."

"Oh, very well. I've certainly spent time with less pleasant males. And at least Parry shan't talk about himself incessantly." She smirked. "I hope."

Mr. Gwilt came back downstairs, hat on head and birdcage in hand.

"Here we are." He set the cage on the desk. "Thank you, Miss Emily, for watching over him. I trust he shall not be too much trouble."

Shedding her pique, Emily gave the man a friendly smile. "We will keep each other in line, never fear. Have a good walk."

22

I have not wasted the little wealth I formerly
possessed in self-indulgence, and am not ashamed
to confess, that in this my old age I am poor.
—Captain Thomas Coram,
Foundling Hospital founder

On her way to the poor house the next day, Viola stopped at the post office for Emily, then continued up Back Street. She was surprised to see Major Hutton standing in front of one of the shops, talking to a smaller man. The major wore a bandage over his ear and a patch over his right eye. Otherwise, he was dressed in fine gentlemen's attire, with a beaver hat brushed to perfection. As far as she knew, it was the first time he had braved the busy shopping street. Miss Truman's doing, she suspected. What else would prompt him to overcome his reticence?

She began to approach, but hearing the combative tenor of the conversation, she stopped at the window of Kingwill's Repository, feigning interest in the local fossils and Devonshire marble displayed there.

The small, balding man said, "We do not serve just anyone, sir.

As I told him yesterday, I am a tailor to English gentlemen. It says so right on my sign."

"And what makes you think he is not a gentleman?"

The tailor gestured toward the shop window. Armaan stood stiffly inside, staring down at rolls of fabric, hands clenched. "Well . . . he does not *look* like one."

"But he is. I can vouch for that. I can also vouch for the fact that you will have no more business from me, my father, nor my modish brother if you do not serve Mr. Sagar with every sign of respect you would show any other man. Do I make myself clear?"

"Yes, sir. Major, sir. I understand. And you will be pleased."

"It's Mr. Sagar you need to please. And I will hear of it if he is not, or if you overcharge him."

"Never, sir. I am most respectable. Ask anyone."

The tailor fled into his shop, and the major turned to go. Seeing Viola there, he redirected his steps in her direction.

As he neared, she said, "It is good to see you out and about."

Pulling a face, he said, "Only came because that man refused Armaan service yesterday."

"I am sorry to hear it."

He shrugged. "Think it bothers me more than it does him. He is used to it."

He glanced down at the brown paper parcel in her hands. "Out on another mission of mercy?"

"Just taking these to Mrs. Denby."

"May I walk with you?"

Her heart lightened. "Of course." They turned north, toward the poor house. After a few steps, she asked, "Did you leave Miss Truman and her mother at Westmount?"

"No, they are taking tea at the York Hotel."

"Ah."

Together Viola and the major walked past the shops and onto Mill Lane. Viola was conscious of his nearness as they strolled side by side. His arm brushed hers, and her own tingled in reply.

A carriage careened around the corner and sped toward them. In response, he threw an arm around her and pulled her close, away from the street.

Her pulse thumped in reply. "Th-thank you."

For a moment longer, his arm remained around her waist. She felt the warmth of it through her muslin day dress and barely resisted the urge to lean closer. Until she recalled Miss Truman. Then she straightened and walked on.

When they reached the poor house, he opened the door and held it for her.

"Will Mrs. Denby mind another visitor, do you think?"

"Not at all. She will be delighted." Viola led the way inside and down the corridor to Mrs. Denby's room.

And she was right.

They were welcomed with warm greetings and effusive thanks for the visit and the gift. Viola made the introductions, and the woman beamed up at Major Hutton.

"You are very welcome, sir. Viola reads to you as well, does she?"

"She does indeed." He sent her a teasing glance. "When she can spare the time."

Mrs. Denby squinted up at his face. "Would it be terribly rude to ask what happened to you?"

"Injured in an explosion, ma'am. But thankfully I lost sight in only the one eye. And how did you lose yours?"

"By years of lace making. How dull my story is by comparison!"

"Not at all."

"And I can still see . . . a little." She added in a mock whisper, "But don't tell Viola, or she will stop visiting me."

He laughed. "No chance of that. I have it on good authority that she quite dotes on you. And I can understand why."

"You are too kind, sir. Too kind!" She winked at Viola. "And handsome too, if you don't mind my saying."

He grinned. "Now, what man would mind that?"

Mrs. Denby insisted they share her biscuits, and while they ate, she regaled them with a story she promised was true.

"Many years ago, a wealthy dowager wearing a fine lace collar was traveling across town in a sedan chair—not a carriage, mind— when she was accosted by a highwayman. Can you imagine? When he demanded, 'Yer money or yer life,' she thought he said, 'Yer money or yer lace,' and fainted dead away. When she came to, she gave him all her money, a considerable sum, rather than part with her French lace!"

Her listeners chuckled until Mrs. Denby sobered. "Not that stealin' is funny. 'Course not."

Which, for some reason, made Viola and the major chuckle once more.

He said, "Then that story is an exception to the rule."

Mrs. Denby smiled again, but it was a weak effort, and Viola wondered what had saddened her.

When they left the poor house half an hour later, Major Hutton said, "I believe I am smitten. I can see why you come here. She is a delight."

"I am glad you think so. I completely agree."

Together they began the walk back. He said nothing further about Miss Truman and neither did she. She did not want to spoil the pleasant spell.

They were halfway down the esplanade when she realized she had walked back across town and along the seafront with her veil pushed back from her face.

Eager to get her chores done quickly so she could return to her writing, Emily stopped at the next guest room and knocked.

From within a cheery voice answered, "Come in!"

She pushed open the door. "Good day, Mr. Gwilt. Just here to see if you have any rubbish I can remove for you."

He looked up from the book he was reading, half-moon spectacles perched on his thin nose. "That is kind. The bin is just over by there."

She walked toward it, nodding to Parry in his cage as she crossed the room. Eyeing the book in Mr. Gwilt's hands, she asked, "May I ask what you are reading?"

"*Tom Jones* by Fielding. Mr. Wallis recommended it."

"What do you think so far?"

"Truth be told, it's rather . . . well, scandalous for my tastes. I like a swashbuckling adventure where good triumphs over evil, and nothing to make one blush. I suppose that makes me namby-pamby?"

"Not at all. Have you read *Gulliver's Travels*?"

"Not in ages."

"We have a copy, and you would be welcome to borrow it."

"Thank you. I would enjoy that, I would."

She dumped his bin into her larger one, reached to gather up crumbs on the table near the parrot, then stopped. "I almost took his seeds." She raised her voice and said in affected tones, "I will leave them for you, Parry, in case you get . . . peckish." She chuckled at her little joke, proud of herself for her tolerant condescension.

Mr. Gwilt looked at her askance. "He does not actually eat anything, my dear. You feeling all right?" He gazed at her in mild concern, as though she were the mad one for talking to a stuffed bird.

And perhaps she was.

Her tasks finished, Emily returned to the library. For several minutes she sat motionless at the desk, resting her cheek in her hand. She was supposed to be writing back to the elderly couple who'd requested a ground-floor room, which, sadly, they could not offer. But she had gotten no further than the salutation. Instead, she stared blankly ahead, lost in thought.

She had so hoped Charles would come around in time and realize how much he missed her. Loved her.

Briefly, she had been distracted from her disappointment by her flirtation with Mr. Stanley. But with him spending more time with his sister, Emily's thoughts returned to Charles.

Emily had not been alone in thinking she would marry their neighbor. Everyone had thought so. She had long been in love with him, and the attraction had seemed mutual.

She still felt the pain of his sudden detachment, when his teasing, affectionate manner had become cool and distant.

Emily pressed her eyes closed, trying to block the memory of the last time she spoke to Charles, but the mortifying scene surfaced anyway.

He and his mother had come to bid them farewell three or four months after Papa's death, as they were packing and preparing to depart Finderlay. While their mothers talked in the drawing room, Emily had taken Charles aside. They were on the cusp of leaving, after all. Surely she had given him enough time. She kept her tone casual and asked how soon he might be able to visit them in Sidmouth.

His expression had turned stony. "I am afraid I shall not have that pleasure. Though I do wish you a safe journey."

She had frowned up at him, perplexed. "What is it, Charles? Why are you behaving this way? Have I done something wrong?"

Emotions rippled over his face, but he quickly mastered his composure. "Not at all, Miss Summers."

"Miss Summers? When I have been Emily and you Charles for years?"

"We are children no longer."

"I know. I thought we were, well . . . more." She'd gripped his arm, and it stiffened into a lifeless branch under her touch. "Has something happened? Tell me, Charles, for heaven's sake. What is the matter?"

The muscle in his jaw pulsed. "Everyone knows I am fond of you and your sisters, Miss Summers. If I have led you to believe my intentions were more than they are, I apologize. We are friends—that is all."

Stunned, Emily sputtered, "W-why? Because of our . . . distressed circumstances?"

"Not primarily, no. Your sis—" He broke off and ran a hand over his face.

"My what?"

"It is not my place to say."

"My sister? Is that what you meant to say?" Incredulity flared into anger. She knew other people thought ill of Viola but had not thought Charles one of them.

He grimaced. "I have said too much already. Please know I am deeply sorry for your family's . . . grief. I feel it keenly."

He bowed curtly, turned on his heel, and strode from the house.

Recalling the scene now, Emily felt sick all over again.

She had not attempted to speak to him a second time before they left May Hill, and recalling Mamma's advice, she had resisted the urge to write to him. Yet since then, he had neither written nor come to visit them.

Why? Might he be courting someone else? Is that why he remained estranged? Her heart ached at the very thought.

While Emily sat there, lost in reverie, Viola returned from her visit to the poor house. She walked in from outside, still wearing her mantle, bonnet, and gloves.

Emily stared at her, arrested by her bare face. "Where is your veil?"

Viola shrugged and reached up as if to assure herself it was still on the back of her head. "I did not wear it."

Before Emily could react, Viola set a few letters on the library desk. "I picked up the post, since I was passing."

Emily eagerly searched through the day's collection. That longed-for letter had still not come. She slapped her palm against the desk. "Nothing. Again. He truly has cut our acquaintance."

Sensing her sister studying her, she glanced up and saw Viola frown.

"You still blame me, don't you."

Emily's focus shifted to her mouth, lingering on the scar. Then she looked away. "I don't know. My heart hurts, and I . . . I want to blame someone."

Viola huffed. "That is not fair."

Emily threw wide her arms. "None of this is fair!"

When Viola had stalked off, Emily sighed. She decided that if Charles would not write to her, she would write to him. She was tired of waiting. She wanted to know why he had changed toward her. Toward them. Was it honestly because of Viola—when he had known her and *about* her all their lives? Or had he simply realized he did not care for *her*? Did not esteem her, love her, enough to marry her? The not knowing was worse, surely, than learning the truth would be. At least, she hoped so.

Finding she was out of paper, Emily went to her mother's bedchamber. The room was empty, as it rarely was. She glanced from the window and saw Mamma sitting in the garden with some needlework, a lap rug covering her knees. The sea-bathing appeared to be helping her, at least to a degree. The sight of her mother out of this bed and this room, sitting in the sunshine, cheered her.

Taking advantage of the quiet, she sat down at Mamma's writing desk, pulled forth a sheet of paper, dipped a quill into the ink pot, and began to write.

Dear Charles,

I hope you will forgive the intrusion, if intrusion a letter from a lifelong acquaintance and former neighbor could be. I do not mean to seem forward. But we were all good friends once, or so we believed. Only now you are so changed. What have I done to deserve your cold indifference? Or is it not me, exactly, but because of my sister?

She paused and stared blindly at the wall, thinking. If the latter were the reason, what could she say to refute it? What could any of them say, really?

A floorboard creaked in the passage, and her heart lurched. She did not want any of her sisters to catch her writing to Charles. They would deem it inappropriate. Demeaning. Desperate.

She quickly slid the page under the leather desk pad and pulled forth a blank sheet in its place.

Georgiana appeared in the threshold. "Oh, it's you. What are you doing in here?"

"Writing a letter. I ran out of paper."

"That's a regular habit with you. Perhaps you ought to become a jobbing writer and get paid by the word. Our money problems would be over."

"Ha ha. I wish."

Georgiana looked past her. "Where is Mamma?"

"In the garden." Emily nodded toward the window.

Georgiana crossed the room, and Emily laid a hand over a corner of the letter sticking out.

Her sister stood near her and peered out the window. "So she is. Perhaps I shall join her."

"Have you and Bibi made all the beds? Is the parlour dusted?"

Georgiana huffed. "You are getting worse than Sarah!" And she stomped from the room.

Emily inwardly groaned. She had succeeded in angering two sisters in a matter of minutes.

When Georgie's footfalls faded, Emily lifted the desk pad. She stilled, taken aback to find not one letter hidden there, but two.

The second was folded and bore surprising postal markings. *Edinburgh.*

Glancing out the window to assure herself Mamma was still in the garden, she unfolded the letter and read the signature. It was from their Great-Aunt Mercer. Here, then, was Claire's direction at last. Emily had asked for it several times. Her requests had clearly displeased her mother, who always had some reason the timing was not right. But now? Finding this letter felt like a sign.

Thinking better of the letter she had begun to Charles, she wadded it up and tossed it into the nearby fireplace. The dying embers obliged by rousing themselves to flaming life, destroying the evidence of her foolishness.

She would write to Claire instead.

23

I was terribly frightened, and really thought I should never
have recovered from the Plunge—I had not breath enough to
speak for a minute or two, the shock was beyond expression.
—Frances Burney, diary

That day at luncheon, the family began gathering in the
dining room at the usual time. Even Mamma joined
them, managing to cross the house with the help of her
stick. Emily hurried to lay a place for her, pleasure and hope warming her heart. It was almost like old times.

Georgiana burst into the room, mischief dancing in her light
blue eyes. "Viola walked across town without a veil. That means
Emily has to go sea-bathing!"

Emily suddenly wished she had never confided the challenge
to their younger sister.

"What's this?" Sarah asked.

"A silly wager—that's all."

Viola spread a serviette over her lap. "If Emily truly is scared,
she does not have to."

Emily's spine stiffened in resolve. "Of course I will. I am a
woman of my word, after all. Let us go."

"It does not have to be now," Viola said.

"Why wait?"

Viola glanced out the window. "The weather is grey and blustery today."

"Perhaps if she does not go directly, she will lose her courage," Georgiana said.

"Wait and go later," Mamma said. "Dr. Clarke advises no bathing immediately after eating or drinking."

Emily laid aside her serviette. "I am not hungry."

Mamma shook her head. "Don't do anything rash, Emily. Besides, you can't go alone, and Georgie has already been bathing with me. I don't want her to overdo or risk a chill."

Sarah said, "And I am meeting with the wine merchant for the Eltons' dinner."

"Well, she can't go bathing alone," their mother insisted. "It is not safe."

"She would not be alone," Georgie said. "One of the bathing machine attendants will assist her in and out of the water. Mrs. Heffer or Mrs. Barrett, most likely."

"I shall go in with her," Viola announced, with a little jut of her chin.

Emily glared at her. "Why? You don't like sea-bathing either. Afraid I will back out?"

Viola held her gaze. "The lady doth protest too much."

"Oh, very well." Emily rose. "Come if you're coming."

They retrieved towels, put on their bonnets, and left the house, walking across Peak Hill Road and past Heffer's Row to the esplanade, and onto the pebbles.

The beach was all but deserted today, thanks to the gusty wind and choppy waves. Out in the water, Emily glimpsed the figure of a lone swimmer. At least the man was a fair distance away. She had heard that, at some seaside resorts, men tried to sneak near bathing machines in hopes of catching sight of scantily clad women.

As they passed, Mr. Cordey looked up from the nets he was mending. "Not goin' in today, are 'ee maid'ns? Storm's a brewin'."

"We shan't be long." Emily waved and continued on.

"You really are determined to get this over with, I see," Viola said in a low voice. "Pride goeth before a fall, remember."

"Better than having you hold it over my head for the foreseeable future. And why *did* you cross town without a veil? The wind probably blew it back and you did not even realize. Now you are simply taking advantage of your chance to torment me."

"I said you did not have to."

"Right. And never hear the end of it?"

They stopped at the first bathing machine they came to.

The vehicles looked like four-wheeled enclosed carts with doors on either end. They were normally rolled into the sea and back out again by horse or, in a pinch, by a few strong men.

"Afternoon, ladies," a sturdy older woman greeted them, tucking a flask into her apron pocket. She wore a dark dress, kerchief, and close-fitting bonnet cinched under her chin. "'Bout gave up on more customers today."

"Is it too rough, do you think?" Viola asked.

"Naw. Not if 'ee don't wander too far. You ladies want to be dipped or go in yerselves?"

Emily had heard that inexperienced swimmers often used the services of a "dipper," a strong person of the same sex who guided the bather out of the cart, dunked them in the water, and yanked them out again. Emily shivered at the thought of anyone pushing her into the water.

"We will, um, go in on our own. Although perhaps you might help us back into this, uh, machine, when we are through?"

"'Course miss. Strong swimmers, are 'ee?"

Was that whiskey on the woman's breath?

"I would not say that," Emily allowed. "But we shall manage without being . . . dipped."

They paid their shilling and six pence, climbed the few steps, and entered through the rear door.

Inside, they found themselves in a small wooden chamber with two little windows high on the walls for light, and benches below. They began to undress, helping each other with their fastenings.

Outside, the jingle of tack let them know the attendant was yoking a horse to the end nearest the sea, ready to draw the carriage forward. Later the horse would be moved back to the other end to draw them out while they redressed in perfect privacy.

Frequent bathers might own their own bathing costumes, and some were even attractive, but Emily had never had the need nor the desire. Instead, she and Viola gingerly donned the provided dun-colored bathing dresses left hanging on pegs.

The bathing machine lurched into motion, jostling them. Emily reached for a wall peg for support, while Viola sat down hard on the bench with a little squeal of surprise.

Once deep enough, the vehicle came to a halt. Even so, a gust of wind shook the small hut on wheels.

"Ready?" Viola asked, pulling on the matching gathered toque over her hair.

Emily wrinkled her nose as she adjusted her own cap. "How many others have worn these?"

"Don't think about it. Perhaps the salt water keeps them clean."

Emily tied a cord around the waist of the shapeless sack covering her body, neck to ankle. "We shall turn no heads in these horrid things."

"Good." Viola gestured toward the seaward door.

Emily bit the inside of her cheek and pushed it open.

The view framed in the wooden threshold was of sea, nothing but open sea.

Her stomach lurched and she swallowed, hard.

"The wager was your idea, remember," Viola reminded her, not sounding very happy about the prospect herself.

Emily stepped out onto the small platform, and Viola squeezed beside her. In the silvery distance, Emily again spied a dark head moving across the water, this time toward shore. The swimmer she had seen earlier, she hoped. Not a rare shark.

The attendant appeared, lowered the ladderlike stairs, and offered them a hand down.

Emily forced herself to go first, gripping the woman's hand tightly, and gasping as the cold water enveloped her body and stole her breath.

The water wasn't too deep here, and her toes sank into soft, wet sand, free of the pebbles that studded the shore.

Next, the woman reached behind her and helped Viola down into the water as well.

"Ho! It's cold!" A wave slapped Viola in the mouth, and she sputtered.

"Stay close," the woman warned. "I'm gonna move the horse."

Viola dipped herself experimentally in the water, paddling about, the skirt of the bathing dress billowing around her. Not to be outdone, Emily did the same and ventured a little deeper. Emily splashed Viola, and her twin splashed back.

"See? Nothing to be afraid of!"

From the corner of her eye Emily glimpsed a looming grey wall, but there was no time to react. The rogue wave broke over her, knocking her down. Emily found herself underwater, the undertow churning wildly, spinning her dizzy. Her worst nightmares had become a reality—water up her nose, lungs burning, unable to see, to breathe. She forced open her eyes in panicked desperation to find the surface. To find air. Her involuntary somersault slowed, her toes touched sand, and she instinctively pushed upward and shot to the surface, sucking in a desperate breath and coughing on salt water.

Emily looked around, disoriented. Where was the bathing machine?

She pivoted, half expecting to see Vi smirking at her, amused by her sputtering, bedraggled state. But Viola was nowhere to be seen.

Her heart pounded like a mallet.

"Vi?" She turned a complete circle, searching for her sister. Nothing. *God, no. Please!* If anything happened to Vi . . . her peevish, annoying, beloved twin sister, she couldn't bear it. Why had she been so unkind to her over the years? Why?

Then she saw it, the bathing machine on its side. It had been knocked over as she had been. Where was the stout bathing woman? Had she, in her inebriated state, been knocked into the water?

And was Vi trapped beneath the vehicle even now? Or had the current swept her away?

She looked around once more in mounting desperation. *Please, God, no, please.* Their family had suffered too many losses.

A man wearing nothing but pantaloons came running across the beach, hair wet, a bundle under one arm. He threw down the pile of clothing, ran into the surf, and dove under. Emily took a startled step back, lost her footing, and nearly went under again. A moment later, the man reemerged with a mighty splash, tossing his head back, dark hair flying from his face.

In his muscled arms, he held a slight female—Triton stealing away with a sea nymph. If Emily had not seen him run a moment before, she might believe he had the tail of a fish.

Clearly air deprivation had addled her brain.

Emily wiped the water from her eyes. It was her sister he held in his arms. Was she alive, or . . . ? The latter did not bear thinking of.

The merman walked slowly toward her.

Emily called, "Is she hurt?"

As he neared, she heard Viola coughing and gasping to catch her breath. Emily sloshed through the water to meet them, concern for her sister overpowering her fear of the sea.

At that moment, the attendant reappeared from around the capsized vehicle, drenched bonnet dripping.

"Lawks! That ain't 'appened since aught eight. You'm all right?"

But Emily had eyes only for her sister as Triton carried her toward safety.

One minute, Viola was standing in the water near Emily, and the next, a wave broke over her with vindictive force. Suddenly submerged, Viola struggled to right herself, clawing at the water. The undertow seemed to snag her bathing dress like an anchor and refused to let go.

Help me! she inwardly cried.

Viola wanted to live. For all life's trials, she wanted to live.

Almighty God, please . . .

Suddenly something or someone grabbed her and hauled her forcibly up from the sea. Meeting with longed-for air, she sucked in a breath only to choke on salt water and begin to cough. She was lying in someone's arms. Would her rescuer be repulsed to see the face of the woman he had plucked from the waves? She drew another gasping breath and looked up, blinking water from her eyes. But this was not a stranger, nor Mr. Cordey or another fisherman.

It was Major Hutton.

He held her in his arms, against his bare chest.

"Thank God," he muttered. "I had just got out when I saw the wave knock you over. When you didn't surface, I feared the worst."

"M-Major . . ."

"Let's get you out of here."

He gritted his teeth and forced his way through the heavy swell.

Viola tried lifting her head on a neck made of pudding. "My sister . . . ?"

"I am here." Emily's voice. She came trudging through the rough water toward them. "Are you well?"

"I hardly know."

The major set Viola on her feet in shallow water but held on to her from behind, both hands firmly grasping her waist. He said near her ear, "Are you able to stand?"

"I think so."

Emily closed the distance and wrapped her arms around her.

"Oh, Vi! I am so sorry."

Viola coughed again and said hoarsely, "For what? You didn't send that wave."

"For everything. When I thought you were gone, my heart nearly stopped."

Viola stared at her, her stunned gaze clearing. "I am sorry too."

Emily turned to her rescuer. "Thank you, Mr. . . . ?"

The major grimaced, perhaps conscious of his state of dress. "Let us leave formal introductions for another time."

Emily blinked, mouth ajar. Viola wondered if she had noticed his scars. "Very well." Emily took Viola's arm in a protective grip. "I can help her from here."

He hesitated. "If you are certain."

Up the shore, Mr. Cordey and a few other fishermen hurried into the surf to help the struggling horse still attached to the tipped bathing machine, and to drag the cart back to shore.

Tom Cordey waded into the water toward them, concern etched on his tanned face. "Are you all right?"

"I think so."

Major Hutton said, "Well, you are in good hands, so I will take my leave with what remains of my dignity."

Viola turned to him. "Thank you, Major. With all my heart."

〜〜〜

After their family dinner that evening, the girls all gathered in Mamma's room with their tea and pudding. Emily glanced at Viola, and by silent agreement began relaying a softened version of the accident, minimizing the situation to avoid upsetting Mamma's nerves and spurring Sarah's remonstrances.

"The machine overturned?" Mamma sat upright in alarm, perching on the edge of the bed. "You might have been drowned."

"We are perfectly well," Emily hurried to assure her. "Don't upset yourself. We were not in any great danger."

Excitement flashed in Georgiana's eyes. "That's not what Bibi told me. She said Tom and some other men had to rescue you."

"Bibi exaggerates," Emily said. Then added dryly, "Perhaps she will be a novelist one day."

"Oh, Emily," Mamma said, eyes downturned. "I told you not to do anything rash. Did we not warn you to wait for better weather? You endangered not only yourself but Viola as well."

The old defensiveness flared. The words *Why is it always my fault? Why not Viola's?* rose to her tongue, although she managed not to say them.

Viola discreetly reached over and took her hand. "I am just as much to blame as Emily, if not more. And no one could have foreseen that wave and the bathing machine going over. We just wanted you to hear what happened from us, before the rumor mill begins spinning its wheel, but evidently we are too late."

Mamma patted the bed beside her. "Come here, the both of you."

Sharing an uncertain glance, Emily and Viola rose to obey. Thankfully Mamma's pique faded, and as the two sat on either side of her, she wrapped an arm around each of them, drawing them close. "Oh, my dears. I thank the Lord you were not injured or worse. I don't know what I would have done if the sea had taken you."

"We are right here, Mamma. We are not going anywhere."

Emily braved a glance at Sarah, expecting to see anger, and was taken aback to see tears in her eyes and her usually stoic expression contorted with emotion.

Voice hoarse, Sarah said, "I am just so glad you are both safe."

Later that night, Emily decided to make use of the bath-room between the Henshalls' rooms and the Eltons' to indulge in a hot bath after her cold dip in the sea.

She helped Lowen carry the pails of heated water, since he began huffing and puffing after a single trip up the stairs.

Now, after a long, luxurious soak, she emerged, wearing a warm dressing gown and a towel around her shoulders. Her newly washed hair, towel-dried as best she could, hung around her like a cool, velvety curtain. She longed for nothing more than to sit by the fire with a cup of rich, steaming chocolate and a book.

As she walked toward the room she shared with Sarah, Mr. Stanley came up the stairs, likely having spent the evening with his sister.

He did not smile when he saw her. Instead his brown-eyed gaze swept over her with unusual intensity, his thin mouth drawn tight.

"What's this I hear about you nearly drowning today? I hope it isn't true."

Emily paused on the landing, the light from the lamp at the top of the stairs illuminating his approach.

"Not quite. Although it was certainly frightening. I have read accounts of bathing machines overturning in other seaside towns, but not here."

His mouth parted and his eyes slanted downward. "The bathing machine overturned?"

"Yes."

"Thunder and turf. You might have been killed! Are you truly all right?"

Emily was touched to see him so concerned. "You are kind to worry, Mr. Stanley. But as you see, I am perfectly well. And so, thank God, is Viola."

"You do indeed look well. Then again, you always do."

In the flickering light, his gaze lingered on her face, then shifted to her hair, loose around her shoulders. She felt suddenly self-conscious standing there in such a state.

He cleared his throat. "Well. I am relieved. Georgiana said some man rescued you? I wish it had been me." He gave her a crooked grin, signaling a return to lighthearted teasing, yet it did not quite reach his eyes.

"He rescued Viola," Emily clarified. "Whereas I walked from the water on my own two feet."

"Of course you did." He held her gaze. "As you will no doubt face every challenge this life throws at you. I fully expect to read about you in print one day—accounts of the brave, bright, and accomplished Emily Summers."

For a moment longer they stared at each other, then he looked down at his little finger.

Following his gaze, she recognized the ring she had seen in his room. "I have not seen you wear that before. Is it your signet ring?"

His eyes flashed to hers, then away again. "Um . . . no. Not exactly. It was a gift." He shifted and said, "Well, I have kept you standing here long enough. Good night, Miss Summers." He bowed and started toward his room.

Emily watched him go, an odd ache in her chest. "Good night, Mr. Stanley."

24

The Bathing was so delightful this morning
. . . that I staid in rather too long.

—Jane Austen, letter

On Sunday afternoon, Viola returned to the poor house and told Mrs. Denby about her misadventure of the previous afternoon.

"Good heavens! Thank the Lord you are safe," the woman exclaimed. Then she added, "Mr. Butcher was here earlier and mentioned that a fishing boat capsized near Otterton yesterday at about that same time. A fisherman's son drowned."

"Oh no. I am sorry to hear that." Viola thought for a few moments before asking, "Why does that happen?"

"I don't know. The sea is unpredictable."

"No, I mean, why does God protect some people and not others?"

"I don't know that either, my dear. I wish He promised us all peace and safety, but He does not."

Viola looked at the woman with interest and a shiver of foreboding. Jane Denby had lost her parents, sister, and husband. Was there more to her story?

"Your mother must have been so relieved," Mrs. Denby said. "Or did she box your ears for going bathing on such a day?"

"Both!" Viola chuckled, then sobered, noticing the woman's expression take on that wistful sadness she had seen once or twice before.

Viola hesitated, then said gently, "May I ask, did you and your husband have any children?"

"We did, yes. A son." Her face contorted. "But he went bad."

"Oh no. I am sorry. You don't have to tell me if you don't want to."

"I don't mind you knowing. No one has asked me about Robbie in years, yet he is never far from my thoughts."

She looked into the vague distance, regret lining her face. "We did not raise him to behave like that. My own son, a thief. How the shame and grief bowed us down. His crime, his name reported in the newspapers."

She slowly shook her head. "Worse yet was what he stole. Lace, from Mrs. Nicholls's shop. Lace was even more valuable then— before machine lace came about. He was caught when he tried to sell it. Said he did it because the dealer paid us so poorly. And I think he resented the Nicholls family, because they were more successful than we were. I told him to stop blaming others. To accept responsibility for his own actions."

She sighed. "I don't know if he ever repented, though he tried to convince the judge he'd never do the like again. They transported him anyway, to New South Wales, wherever that is. If he'd been a woman, he might have got off with a few months of hard labor. But he was a man, though still young and foolish." Her thin lips trembled.

"My husband, God rest him, tried to comfort me, saying it was not our fault—or at least, not entirely. But we must have done something terribly wrong. We tried our best, though no doubt we could have been better parents. I suppose we spoiled him, being our only child. Whatever the reason, nothing in this life has made me feel more of a failure. Not my sorry education, or poverty, or being reduced to living in a poor house."

Viola's heart squeezed. She thought of Mrs. Denby's happy nature. How did a woman who'd suffered so much remain cheerful?

Mrs. Denby went on, "The proverb says to 'train up a child in the way he should go: and when he is old, he will not depart from it.' I have held to that hope—that although on the other side of the world, Robbie would one day return to what he learned in our home." Her mouth puckered. "If he lived that long. I know it is possible, nay, probable, he is long dead."

"Is there no way to find out?"

"Not that I know of. If he did die, I pray he repented before his final breath and asked the Lord to have mercy on his soul."

Throat tight and eyes burning, Viola whispered, "So do I."

Mrs. Denby laid a hand on hers. "For years, I struggled to go on with my life and faith," she confided. "Then I made it my goal to give thanks in everything, and hold tight to joy, even when it wants to slip from my grasp."

"How?" Viola asked. "After everything you've been through?"

The old woman nodded. "Many days, I failed. Yet as with anything, it gets easier with long practice." She patted Viola's hand, her weak smile fading. "Now, I am tired, my dear. Do you mind if we don't read today?"

"Not at all, Mrs. Denby. You rest. I will come and see you again soon."

"How gracious you are, my dear. I give thanks for you too."

On her way back to Sea View, Viola walked a different way, strolling past the stalls in the marketplace before emerging onto the esplanade. Finding herself near the York Hotel once more, she glanced over, stopped, and stared. There he was again, the same man she'd glimpsed before, sitting on one of the benches out front.

A second man approached, hailing, "Mr. Cleeves!" The men shook hands, and the newcomer sat down to talk.

Viola's stomach cramped. This time, she could not explain

away the flicker of recognition or blame her imagination. This time, there could be no mistake. Abner Cleeves. Here, in Sidmouth.

The blood began pounding in her brain. *Calm down*, she told herself. *He doesn't even know you're here.*

Conversing animatedly with the other man, he did not look her way, and Viola's wild heart rate began to slow. She pressed a steadying hand to her chest and exhaled. When her trembling eased, she forced herself to turn like a rusty gate and walk away, ears alert for any sound of footsteps following her.

How foolish, she reprimanded herself. *He has done his worst to you and got his money. He wants nothing more to do with the unfortunate Miss Summers.*

She wondered if he was having a holiday in Sidmouth or had come to set up practice there, as did so many surgeons. She prayed not the latter. She didn't know what she would do if she had to encounter the man regularly.

As she walked home, she prayed she would never see him again.

That evening, several people gathered in the parlour again, talking, laughing, and playing games in the snug room lit by candlelight. For a moment, Sarah felt as though she'd been transported back to former days at Finderlay, when the house had often been full of family, friends, and happy occasions.

Sarah sat at her worktable, embroidering more primroses on Mamma's handkerchief and keeping Mr. Henshall and Mr. Hornbeam company as they played another game of chess. As Mr. Henshall described the moves, the older man kept track of the positions in his mind and seemed to be winning.

Nearby, Emily and Mr. Stanley faced each other over the draughts board. Emily laughed and teased her opponent, playfully refusing to crown one of his pieces. Mr. Stanley was more reserved but smiled softly at her antics, his expression wistful.

Had she and Peter ever behaved that way? Not that she recalled. Peter had certainly been kind and attentive, although not given to teasing or flirtation. He was a quiet, serious man, and she had liked that about him.

Mr. Hornbeam directed his opponent to move his queen to a certain square. "Checkmate, I believe, Mr. Henshall."

Callum studied the board for a way of escape, then sighed. "Right ye are, sir. You win again."

Mr. Hornbeam tilted his head to one side. "I do hope you are not going easy on me because I am blind."

"I wish I could claim it! No, sir. Ye beat me fair and square."

Mr. Hornbeam nodded with satisfaction and rose. "Rematch tomorrow night?"

"I shall look forward to it."

When the older man had taken himself to bed, Mr. Henshall remained.

"What have you and Effie been doing?" Sarah asked. "We have not seen much of you lately."

"We took a trip into Lyme. Walked out onto the Cobb and took a meal in a public house there. Effie did some shopping."

"Sounds lovely. Did Effie enjoy herself?"

"Aye. I believe she did."

"Good."

He glanced at her sewing. "No baking tonight?"

"Had not planned to." She glanced up from her needle. "Unless . . . have you a special request?"

He sent her a knowing glance. "I think ye have enough guests making special requests."

"I won't mind." To herself, Sarah added, *Not for you.*

"Well then. I am partial to shortbread, should you want to try something new. The thin and crisp variety, favored by Mary, Queen of Scots." He grinned. "And yours truly."

Sarah made no promises but knew she would not be able to resist making some for him.

When next Viola walked over to Westmount, she was confused to see a post chaise waiting. Miss Truman, attired in carriage dress, hat, and gloves, set a stack of bandboxes on the front step under the porte cochère. Her mother, meanwhile, handed a valise to the postilion, who carried it to the chaise.

Pulling her veil over her face, Viola walked up the path. "Miss Truman, are you leaving? I thought you and your mother planned to stay a few more days at least?"

Miss Truman's eyes glistened with tears. Her mother's expression, however, was tight with resolve.

"Oh no." Viola asked, "What happened?"

Miss Truman pressed her lips together, then said, "I am afraid I . . . ended our engagement."

Breath escaped Viola like a punctured balloon. "Ohh . . ."

Her mother lifted her pointy nose in the very picture of hauteur. "And can you blame her? No. No one who has seen that man would blame my beautiful daughter for crying off. That my angel should have thrown herself away, consigned herself to be a recluse's constant companion and helpmeet—his nurse! And her, in the bloom of youth? No. It would be too cruel. If anyone dares call her a jilt, they shall feel my wrath!"

"Mamma, don't go on so." Miss Truman sent Viola an apologetic glance, then gently urged her mother down the path. "Do give me a few minutes to say good-bye to Miss Summers in private. I shall join you directly."

"Very well, but don't tarry. The sooner we leave here the better!"

When the older woman had entered the chaise, Miss Truman turned back to Viola. "Please forgive my mother. She can be rather vulgar when roused to my defense. Like a lioness with a threatened cub." Miss Truman shyly met Viola's gaze through the veil, then looked away again.

"I hope you don't think too badly of me. Some will, I know.

Abandoning one of our own wounded heroes in his hour of need. I did try. I came here resolved to remain faithful to my promise. I stifled my revulsion and determined to make the best of it. The scars I might have grown accustomed to in time, as you said. But his dour manner? His reclusive nature? No. I would have chafed under the isolation."

Viola was torn by conflicting desires: to upbraid the girl, or to embrace her. "H-how did the major take the news?"

"Oh, he is . . . Well, he puts a brave face on it. One never knows how the man is truly feeling, does one? I would not be surprised if he appears to you completely unaffected, even relieved." Again the young woman's eyes filled, but she managed a smile and pressed Viola's hand.

"Good-bye, Miss Summers. Take good care of him."

Her? "I . . . will do what I can."

Viola watched as Miss Truman walked away and joined her mother inside the vehicle. As soon as the door closed and the horses moved off, Viola let herself into the house and walked directly to the major's room. She supposed she should have stopped to ask Mr. Hutton or Armaan how the major fared, and if he was in any state for company. But she was too worried to wait. What if his self-worth had been shattered by the vain chit? What if he believed himself unworthy of love? Believed no gentlewoman would ever have him?

She knocked on the partially open door, expecting either a curse or, worse—no answer at all.

"Come."

She tentatively inched open the door, fearing to find him back in bed or sprawled in an armchair and drowning his sorrows in a bottle of brandy.

Instead, she found him at the desk, writing a letter. Writing to his lawyer, perhaps, to pursue a breach of promise suit? Or already writing to Lucinda Truman, pleading with her to change her mind?

He glanced up. "Ah, Miss Summers."

"How are you bearing up? Miss Truman is young and foolish and too much under the sway of her mamma. Please don't break your heart over it. You will recover in time. I promise." Impulsively, she took his hand and lowered herself, sitting on her heels beside his chair and looking into his face, willing him to value himself as she did.

"Miss Summers, I . . . am touched. Apparently you met with Miss Truman as she departed?"

"I did, yes. And she told me. Don't be vexed. I am glad to know. I want to help."

"Good." He rose, and she was struck anew by his height. "You can help by boxing up these newspapers. I have let this pile gather dust too long as it is."

Viola got unsteadily to her feet. "I don't understand. Are you honestly all right? About Miss Truman leaving?"

"I am. It did not take me long to realize how she felt. I could see it in her face. Her unease whenever she forced herself to meet my gaze. The subtle curl of her lip when confronted with my scars. Nor did she like my home here. The lack of society and formal dinners and parties. Do you really think she would have been happy here? With me? No."

"She would have gone through with it, if you had exerted yourself. Taken her out somewhere. Entertained her. Tried a little harder."

"Very likely. And do you think I wanted that? To be united with a woman who could barely stand to look at me or remain in my company? Who shrank back whenever I came too close, though she tried to hide it under a guise of shyness, behind fluttering lashes and coy smiles? I was not fooled. I waited for her to say something, and when she did not, I hinted to her mother that I would agree to a quiet and amicable parting of ways. She took me up on it."

"Miss Truman had tears in her eyes when I saw her."

"That surprises me. So do you. Do you want me to go after her and beg her to change her mind?"

"What I want is of no account."

"There you are wrong."

For a moment, she stared at him, then anger flared. "I want no part of this. I have enough to feel guilty about in my life as it is."

"You have nothing to feel guilty about. Miss Truman did not love me, and I certainly did not love her. I had been regretting my rash offer of marriage even before India. I believe it is half the reason I decided to go."

"Oh." Viola studied him warily, wanting to believe him. "Well . . . good. I was worried you would be devastated."

He took her hand, pressing it warmly before releasing it. "I appreciate your concern more than you know. But I am well. And she will be happier in the long run, I am convinced."

"I hope you are right."

One corner of his mouth quirked. "Am I not always?"

"Definitely not," she retorted. "Hardly ever."

Colin joined them at the tail end of their conversation, leaning a casual shoulder on the doorframe. "I would not worry about Lucy Truman if I were you, Miss Vi. She will be right as rain in no time. And she'll be engaged to some other eldest son in a fortnight, mark my words."

But it wasn't Miss Truman she was worried about.

Colin went on to tell his brother that Taggart wanted to hire someone to chop up a tree that had fallen in the recent gale.

"No need. I shall it do it myself, and you will help. You could do with some exercise too."

"No doubt." Colin straightened. "Very well. I'll tell Taggart not to call in the cavalry, for the cavalry is already here." He winked at Viola, pivoted in an impressive about-face, and departed the room.

For a long moment, Viola remained where she was, gazing at Major Hutton, the man who had come to her aid, lifting her from the sea.

"By the way," she said, "what were you doing on the main beach the other day? I thought you preferred the western one?"

"I decided to swim nearer home, since no one was about. And thank God I did."

Gratitude washed over her anew. "Thank you again for coming to my rescue."

He slowly nodded. "Would that I could always do so."

What did that mean? Conflicted, Viola turned to the desk, and her gaze fell to the letter the major had been writing when she arrived.

Mr. Bird,

I would like to meet with the surgeon you mentioned and learn more about his new methods. Please call at a date and time convenient to you both.

Sincerely,
Maj. J. Hutton

Surgeon? Immediately her stomach roiled. Tapping the letter, she asked, "What is this about? Some new method of restoring hearing in that ear?"

He smirked. "What ear?"

"You know what I mean."

"I don't believe there is any hope for my right ear, but with the remaining one, I want to hear what the man has to say. He specializes in scar reduction and other facial surgeries."

Bile climbed her throat. "Is this because of Miss Truman?"

"In a way. Her disgust certainly solidified my resolve to do something about this gore." He circled a finger around the right side of his face.

"You want to win her back?"

"Never. I am not grieving her loss, Miss Summers, if that is what you are tempted to think. Yet if there is a way to become less revolting, I believe I owe it to myself, and to the seeing public at large, to pursue it. Who knows? Perhaps one day I might ask another woman to share my life and bed, and I don't want her to pull away in disgust."

He stepped near and held her gaze. Once again Viola recalled the sensation of being held against his naked chest and could barely breathe.

She won't pull away, Viola wanted to say, thinking he might be referring to her. But if he was not? Viola could make no such assurances for any woman besides herself.

"What is this surgeon's name?" she asked instead, feeling queasy just posing the question.

"Mr. Bird's colleague? I don't recall."

It surely wouldn't be Abner Cleeves, she thought, reminding herself of the many surgeons who came to Sidmouth. Even so, bile soured her throat once more at the memory of the man she'd seen outside the York Hotel.

She swallowed and said, "If it's Cleeves, run the other way."

25

All who would win joy,
must share it;
Happiness was born a twin.
—Lord Byron, *Don Juan*

Later that afternoon, Emily and Viola sat together in the library, curled up in the two armchairs near the fire, knitted blankets over their legs, empty teacups on the little table between them. Outside, a cold rain fell, but inside they were warm and peaceful, enjoying each other's company and conversation—just the two of them, which they had not done much of in far too long.

They talked about their ill-fated bathing experience with more abandon now that there was no one about to hear them. They teased each other as they recalled the details: the tipsy attendant, the awful costumes, Viola goading her, saying there was nothing to be afraid of, only for them both to be knocked down by a fierce wave and Viola having to be rescued.

Emily said, "When I saw that wild, half-naked creature emerge from the sea holding a woman in his arms, I thought the undertow had addled my brain! It was like one of those old mythology prints come to life—Triton and the nymph. I wondered if he had the legs of a man or the tail of a fish!"

Viola laughed, and Emily noticed her blush as well. "You really can tell a story, Em," she said. "Perhaps you ought to write it all down—changing the names of course."

"Hmm . . . maybe. I still can't believe Triton turned out to be your major." Emily slowly shook her head. "Certainly not the invalid I had in mind when I wrote that advertisement."

They talked about the mishap a few minutes longer, how the fishermen had rallied to help, and Tom running into the water to make sure they were all right and then seeing them home.

After that they were quiet for a time, content to watch the glowing, crackling fire.

Then Viola said, "When I returned from France to recover from that last surgery, you came into my room and read to me from a story you were writing, remember? So you read to an invalid long before I did." The two shared a fond look, then Viola asked, "Whatever became of that story? I remember liking what I heard."

"Heavens, I don't know. I have written the beginnings of many stories and have yet to finish one."

"Perhaps you should. I would be first in line to read it."

Emily smiled at her sister, thankful for the renewed warmth between them.

Jessie knocked on the library door and showed in Tom Cordey.

Emily had not heard the front door knocker. Coming to the main entrance would have been quicker, and Emily wondered if Tom chose the back door—used by servants and tradesmen—because he saw himself that way, or because he believed it a neighbor's privilege to stop by casually.

Then again, seeing Jessie's blushing cheeks and shining eyes, maybe there was another reason he began his visits belowstairs.

"Good day, Tom," she said, rising.

He nodded. "Miss Emily, Miss Viola."

"Thank you again for coming to our aid the other day."

"No bother."

She gestured him inside. "Come in, come in."

He stepped into the room with a few small pieces of wood in his hands.

"Thought I ought to show you two signs before I make the others. See which you like better."

Viola sent her a questioning look that Emily interpreted as, *Shall I go?* But Emily wanted her to stay.

"Viola, come and give your opinion too."

Tom set the four-by-eight pieces of polished wood on the top of the desk, and the sisters gathered around to study them. One was rectangular with beveled edges, while the other had rounded corners.

Both examples were carved with the name of one of their rooms, the letters darkened with stain for legibility.

And both were spelled wrong.

Emily stood there, awkwardness turning her stomach. She did not want to offend this good man, this neighbor, but nor could they hang a misspelled sign on their door.

Viola sent her another nervous glance, waiting for her to respond first, to take the lead.

Emily pressed her lips together, then began, "I really like the beveled edges, don't you, Vi?"

"I do, yes."

"Well done, Tom. This is even finer than I imagined."

"Glad you like it."

"One . . . minor thing." She pointed to the word, *Berch*.

He said, "You said I could leave off the silver, if it was too long."

"Yes, that's not a problem. But just so you know, birch is spelled with an *i*."

His face stiffened and his tanned neck grew red.

"Everyone spells things differently," she hurried to reassure him. "It was no doubt my fault. You were working from the list I wrote, and my handwriting is not all it should be."

Viola added helpfully, "That's true. It's abominable."

She wrinkled her nose at her sister. "Thank you for noticing." Actually, Emily's hand was as good as her spelling, but she would say almost anything to remove the mortified look from his face.

Tom rubbed the back of his neck. "Told you I were better at fishin' and carvin' than spellin'."

"You are certainly skilled, Tom. These are wonderful, truly. I look forward to seeing the others."

He glanced at her tentatively, as if gauging her sincerity. Then he nodded with apparent satisfaction and turned to go.

When he had departed, Emily sighed and slumped back into her chair.

Viola resumed her seat as well. "You managed that beautifully, Emily."

"Thank you. I am glad you were here with me."

The stormy weather continued into June, keeping the family and their guests subdued and somewhat housebound. Georgiana and Effie decided to put on a play to give themselves something to do. They spent hours in the attic, writing a script, pulling together costumes and props, and clomping about on the bare floorboards as they rehearsed.

Mr. Elton read by the fire, content, while his wife paced the public rooms like a caged animal, longing to be out paying calls.

Meanwhile, Mr. Henshall continued to play chess with Mr. Hornbeam, and the older man often won. Viola had grown rather fond of Mr. Hornbeam, who was so much warmer to her than her own father had been.

Mr. Stanley played draughts with Emily rather less often lately. Braving the weather, he seemed to spend even more time with his sister. Viola could tell that Emily felt his absence keenly.

When the rain slackened somewhat, Viola decided to dart over to Westmount. Georgie no longer accompanied her on most outings, now that she was comfortable with her clients, but her younger sister had grown bored with playacting and asked to go along.

Together they ran to their neighbors' house, Georgie in a hooded mantle, and Viola under a sheltering umbrella.

When they arrived, Taggart showed them into the drawing room, where Mr. Hutton sat with a newspaper and Colin slouched on the sofa. Mr. Hutton informed them that Jack was sequestered with his lawyer, who had arrived with some papers needing attention, but he insisted the ladies stay for a while.

Colin straightened. "Yes, please have mercy on us. We are drowning in boredom."

Armaan came in and invited Georgiana to play a game of draughts, while Mr. Hutton returned to his newspaper. Viola sat on the other end of the sofa, and Colin jumped to his feet as though bounced.

"I am so bored," he lamented. He crossed the room and ran a hand through the faint dust atop the pianoforte. "I wish we might at least have some music."

Without glancing up from her game, Georgiana said, "Viola plays, and uncommonly well."

Viola demurred, "My sister exaggerates."

"I do not."

Mr. Hutton looked up from the newsprint. "Perhaps you should allow us to judge for ourselves."

Viola shook her head. "No, thank you. I play only in private."

Colin groaned. "And deprive the rest of us of the pleasure of hearing you?"

"She is awfully shy," Georgie allowed.

"Come, Miss Summers. Take pity," Colin wheedled. "We are starved for diversion here—and can we convince Jack to venture to the assembly rooms to play cards, or even to the billiard room? No. We must have some entertainment or go mad."

"I . . . don't like anyone watching me."

"Who wants to watch? We only want to listen. Tell you what. You play the pianoforte, and we shall go into the next room. How's that?"

"If you really want me to."

"I do."

"Very well."

Georgie rose from her game. "Must you be so dramatic?" Heaving a sigh, she followed the men into the adjoining sitting room.

Viola sat on the bench and paged through the few sheets of music on the shelf before her. She waited until the others had vacated the room, then, foregoing any of the available scores, began playing one of her old favorites. As she struck the first notes, they seemed to jar the silence, calling attention to her and making her feel terribly self-conscious. But she forced herself to continue on, and as she did, her awareness of self faded, and the memory of the music and the satisfaction of smooth ivory beneath her fingers superseded her discomfort.

Soon, she was playing with passion, letting the music wash over her. What peace. What pleasure.

She reached the end. And when the resounding chords filled the room, then faded, she drifted into another piece, forgetting time and place in the majesty of the music.

Eventually she became aware of someone nearby. She should have been instantly uncomfortable. But glancing over, she saw it was the major, standing in the doorway, arms crossed, head bowed, concentrating, listening without staring.

As the final notes of that second piece danced across the air between them, he looked up, met her gaze, and said only one word. "Beautiful."

He must be referring to the music. Yet, in the way his gaze stroked her face, her shoulders, her hands, it felt like a praise of her whole person.

And perhaps it was.

Later that day, the weather cleared at last, and Viola went to pay a belated call on Mrs. Gage, the newer client Mrs. Fulford had referred to her. The woman, eager for a change of scenery after the recent stretch of poor weather, asked Viola to take her out for a walk.

A short while later, Mrs. Gage's footman and sturdy maid lowered the wheeled chair down Fortfield Terrace's few steps. Then Viola began rolling her along the esplanade, the little Pomeranian on her lap. Together they walked along, nodding to passersby, exchanging greetings, and enjoying the freshened air. It was really rather pleasant.

An idea struck.

"Mrs. Gage, may I ask . . . is this your own personal chair, or—"

"No, mine was too bulky to bring in the carriage. This one was hired from someone here in Sidmouth."

"From whom?"

"I don't know. My footman arranged it. Ask him."

"I shall."

Later, she returned Mrs. Gage to Fortfield Terrace in time for the older woman to have a lie-down before friends arrived for a game of whist.

The footman opened the door for Viola on the way out and was happy to tell her where to acquire a Bath chair. "Yes, miss. Several fellows here in town rent both sedan and Bath chairs. I hired this one from Radford and Silley."

"Thank you." Mrs. Denby, who struggled to walk more than a few steps and rarely left the poor house, might enjoy a little outing. And Viola would certainly enjoy giving her one.

She decided against a sedan chair, not only because it would be difficult to have a pleasant outing with two strange men accompanying them all the while, but also because paying two porters would prove expensive.

Yet she could competently maneuver a Bath chair herself, thanks to her experience with Mrs. Gage. She was eager to give it a try.

⌒⌒

Viola showed up at the poor house the next day, pushing a simple wicker Bath chair—the least expensive model, without a folding hood. Thankfully, the day was fine, so neither of them would need protection from the elements besides a bonnet—and Viola wore hers with her veil pushed back.

"Good day, Mrs. Denby. Do you fancy a ride?"

The older woman eyed the chair, curious but wary. "Did you rent that for me?"

"I did."

"Where would we go?" Tentative eagerness sparked in her expression.

"You pick. The High Street? The promenade? Somewhere else?"

Jane Denby's eyes took on a distant, thoughtful look. "The High Street. I have not been there in years."

Viola smiled. "Then let us go."

"Are you sure it is all right? That chair . . . I can't repay you."

"Already paid for. It is ours for the next hour." She gestured to the door. "Shall we?"

"Yes!" Mrs. Denby clapped, but then her eager expression clouded. "I should warn you. You may not wish to be seen with me. Some people may remember me, and what my son did."

"My dear friend. If anyone snubs us, I shall give them double. But in all honesty, if anyone stares, they are most likely staring at me."

The woman's downcast mouth hitched up at one corner. "We make quite a team, don't we?"

Viola's heart warmed. "We do indeed."

A short while later, they rolled down the High Street together. Mrs. Denby called out, "Not so fast! I want to take it all in!"

And when they sloshed through a lingering puddle, she giggled like a girl.

Reaching the Y of Fore Street and Back Street, Viola asked, "Which way?"

Mrs. Denby hesitated, then replied, "Let's go left."

They rolled past the London Inn and shops on Fore Street, pausing to look at a few window displays.

Passing a secondhand shop, Viola stopped at the window, her attention arrested by a display of cast-off spectacles.

"Look," she said. "Have you ever worn spectacles?"

"Never had the money."

"Let's go in. Just to try them on. It will be diverting, if nothing else."

"If you like."

Thankfully the door to the secondhand shop was just wide enough to permit the Bath chair to pass through. Inside, they maneuvered their way past cluttered shelves to the window display.

Viola picked up a quizzing glass, a single lens held by hand. She parroted the affected voice of a London dandy. "I say, what exquisite company. Have you ever seen such well-turned-out ladies?"

Mrs. Denby chuckled and picked up a lorgnette, a pair of hand-held spectacles on a stick. She positioned it to her eyes and said in tones of grandeur, "Shall we go to the opera, my lady?"

Viola clapped her hands. "Well done." She attempted a pair of nose spectacles that pinched rather sharply, while Mrs. Denby tried on a frame with oval lenses, sliding the arm pieces over her ears.

"These are rather good, actually." The old woman peered through them at the price tag on the lorgnette. "I can read better. And well enough to see I shan't afford these."

"Those you are wearing are not so expensive." Viola glanced again at the handwritten price tag. "And if they will help you see . . . ?"

"Sadly, my girl, I haven't even that much."

"Well then, I shall just have to find another client to read to."

Mrs. Denby shook her head. "Don't do that. I won't have you thinking I want your money. It's your company I treasure."

Viola pressed her hand. "And I yours."

They moved on.

Soon they reached a short cross street, which ended at the brick market house, topped by a ball and weathercock. There they looked at some of the stalls. They bought two iced buns, with a promise not to tell Sarah, along with several ripe plums, which they ate there and then, the sweet juice dribbling down their chins. After wiping away the evidence with a handkerchief, they continued on their way.

As they left the marketplace, Viola pointed out Broadbridge's Boarding House, explaining it was owned and managed by a friend.

When they reached the end of the street, Viola again asked, "Which way?"

The old woman hesitated, then said, "Let's brave Back Street."

"Bravo."

They turned up the narrower street, where stood the post office and Mrs. Tremlett, wine merchant, opposite. Shops and tradesmen lined both sides, with lodgings above and the Old Ship Inn at its end.

A few doors ahead, Viola knew, was the Nicholls lace shop. A young woman sat on a little stool out front, bent over the plump pillow on her lap, bobbins moving in her hands, making lace. Glancing up and seeing them, the woman rose and disappeared into the shop. To avoid them, or just a coincidence?

"That's her daughter, Caroline," Miss Denby said in an awed voice. "How grown she is."

"Shall we continue on, or . . . ?"

"I'd just like to look in at the window."

Viola rolled her in front of the shop, turned the chair to face the bow window, then came around to stand beside her.

Above the window, the word *NICHOLLS* was painted in large, no-nonsense lettering.

Beside the door, a modest trade card announced,

M. & C. Nicholls
Honiton Lace Manufacturer
A choice selection on hand. Prices moderate.
Laces cleaned, repaired, and restored.
Patterns always in stock.

From cords strung behind the glass hung various finished articles of lace for sale. Table centres, dinner mats, collars, fichus, and handkerchiefs edged in queen shell lace and lover's knots. On the ledge below were arranged smaller articles and dress trimmings, lace borders and ruffles, as well as supplies of thread, pins, bobbins, and patterns.

Viola's gaze was drawn to an intricate black lace mourning veil with a honeysuckle border, until she reminded herself she was trying to grow accustomed to going without.

Mrs. Denby, on the other hand, stared longingly at a shawl displayed prominently in the center of the window, in pride of place. The antique shawl had an intricate pattern of flowers, leaves, and birds.

Following her gaze, Viola leaned closer to admire the fine details. "It's beautiful." She glanced back at Mrs. Denby and saw the woman nod.

"My sister, mother, and I helped to make it. The sprigs, you see? The flowers and leaves and birds?"

"How wonderful to see your work on display."

She nodded. "Does my heart good, I admit. Takes me back too. I told you how it was. All of us sitting in our cottage, or outside for the light if the weather was fine, working away. Sometimes we chatted, but even if we were silent, their company was pleasure enough, though I didn't always appreciate it at the time."

The shop door opened, and a white-haired woman stepped out, pristine apron over black dress, mouth a thin, downturned line.

Mary Nicholls. Although the two women were of similar age, she appeared far straighter and stronger.

Mrs. Denby stiffened, then said, "Good day, Mrs. Nicholls."

"Jane."

"I was just showing my young friend here your excellent collection. You always did have the best patterns."

The woman in black gave a curt nod of acknowledgment. "Thank you. We have not seen you in an age."

"I don't get out much these days."

Viola was tempted to say, *"She lives just up the road. You could visit her anytime."* But she held her tongue.

Mrs. Nicholls said, "It's good to see you."

Mrs. Denby blinked in apparent surprise. "And you."

"There are not many of us left from the old days."

"True." Mrs. Denby managed a weak smile. "Well. Good-bye."

Hearing her cue, Viola heaved to turn the chair and started down the street.

Mrs. Nicholls called after them. "Jane?"

Viola paused and turned the chair back around.

Mrs. Nicholls looked at its occupant and said, "You are always welcome here. I hope you know that. I hold nothing against you. What happened is . . . in the past."

Mrs. Denby slowly nodded and raised a hand in farewell.

They were quiet on the way back, saying little as they passed the Old Ship Inn and returned to Mill Lane, which would take them to the poor house.

"Are you all right?" Viola asked softly.

"I think so. When I saw her, all the shame came flooding back, but it's not her fault."

"Nor yours."

"How I wish I could believe that. Well. I am glad that is out of the way—that first meeting after all these years. Should I see her again, it shan't be so awkward."

"She was quite kind."

"Yes, surprisingly so."

As their hour came to an end, Viola delivered Mrs. Denby to her room and helped her out of the wheeled chair and into her own. The woman beamed. "Thank you, my dear. I can't remember when I've enjoyed myself more. I shall sleep for a week!"

Viola smiled back. "You know, I was thinking. This worked rather well. Would you like to go to church with us? I could come by and pick you up, and we could go together."

"Really? I would like that above all things. What a dear you are. The daughter I never had!"

Viola returned the chair, thanked Mr. Radford, and started for home in a haze of happy satisfaction.

On the street, she stopped abruptly, almost tripping, her limbs suddenly paralyzed. She stood frozen outside a shop she didn't see, and stared.

Closer now, she saw Abner Cleeves looked older, with more silver in his side-whiskers, but that wiry, close-cropped hair, those smooth patrician features, those dead pond-water eyes were the same.

Strolling with another man, he walked in her direction. As he was about to pass by, he sent her a vague glance, then looked again, eyes narrowed. She prayed he had not recognized her. An instant later he nodded politely and continued past.

A few doors down, Mr. Radford stepped out and called, "Miss Summers, you forgot your receipt."

Viola accepted it with a silent nod of thanks, trying not to draw more attention to herself.

"Miss Summers?" a voice echoed. A familiar, languid voice that seemed to hiss on the letter S. The man she desperately hoped to avoid had turned back, retracing his steps. He stopped a few feet from her, and only the solid shop wall at her back kept Viola from retreating.

His gaze dropped from a general survey of her face to her mouth, lingering there.

Half to himself, he murmured, "Ah yes."

His companion returned as well to see what had captured his attention. He looked from one to the other, brows raised in expectation, evidently waiting to be introduced.

"Miss Summers, a pleasure to see you again," Cleeves began. "Allow me to present Dr. Davis."

His colleague lifted his hat and bowed.

Abner Cleeves circled gloved fingers near her lips, and Viola recoiled, leaning her head back.

"See here, Davis? When this girl first came to me, she had a gaping cleft in her mouth. I repaired it."

Viola wanted to refute his claim, furious at him for taking the credit, for causing her so much needless pain, but her throat closed and her mouth felt as though stuffed with cotton wool, rendering her mute.

Apparently taking her silence as permission to expand, to point her out as evidence of his skill, Cleeves went on. "After scarifying the margins of the cleft with scissors, I applied a pinching clamp, and then sutured the margins together with waxed stitches. . . ."

An image flashed in her mind. A surgical tray laid with gleaming instruments: a curled needle, scissors, knife, pincers . . .

Someone held her head from behind, keeping her from moving, while this man grasped a portion of her upper lip, his other hand holding the gleaming scissors, their blades open like bared teeth. Then the cut-cut-cutting, the blood, the pain, the stifled screams.

Viola broke into a cold sweat and began to tremble.

"As a child she cried incessantly," Mr. Cleeves was saying. "Therefore the wound refused to heal and the sutures tore. After a second attempt with similar results, we waited until she was an adolescent and had developed more self-control. Then I pressed pins through the lip to reinforce the closure. Those we left in place for about eight or nine days—by then, the two sides are usually united. Then I drew out the pins, applying a piece of plaster and dry lint. And . . . voila." He gestured to her mouth, and Viola thought she might be sick.

The second man nodded. "Most impressive."

Viola shook her head. She longed to correct him. To tell him that his final procedure had not worked either. To describe the tearing and infection that left the cleft larger than before, due to all his cutting and *scarifying*.

Glancing at her uncertainly, the second man asked, "Was she rendered speechless?"

"No. Just modest. Right, Miss Summers?"

Viola opened her mouth, but still the words would not come.

"Many struck with harelip struggle to speak, or at least clearly," Cleeves explained in an aside to his companion, as though she were some exhibit on display. "The procedure repairs a patient's ability to communicate as well. If the palate is only partially cleft, it can be plugged with cotton, otherwise a plate of silver, gold, or lead can be inserted as a palatal obturator, which can be kept in place with a sponge. Either will restore speech."

"Astounding. Quite astounding."

"Thank you. I pride myself in pioneering new methods."

She wanted to shout at him. To call him a liar. A charlatan. A fraudulent pretender to medical skill. Her hands tightened into claws, and her brain pounded in silent rage.

How the French surgeons had exclaimed over the condition of her mouth, using words like *sauvage* and *barbare*. They had told her parents that whoever had done this had utilized techniques two hundred years out of date.

"Perhaps she might appear before our next society meeting," Dr. Davis said. "Our members would be most impressed." He turned to Viola and said slowly and loudly as though she were hard of hearing, "You would not mind, I trust?"

And all Viola could do was stand there and shake her head.

26

Blest with soft airs from health restoring skies,
Sidmouth! to thee, the drooping patient flies;
Ah! not unfailing is thy port to save
To her thou gav'st no refuge but a grave . . .
—Memorial, Church of St. Giles and St. Nicholas

On the first Sunday in June, a group from Sea View again set out for church together. They walked along the footpath in pairs: Sarah and Emily, Georgiana and Mr. Hornbeam, Mr. Henshall and Effie. They had asked Mamma to join them, but she decided she was not equal to it, which seemed a setback after recent improvements to her strength and stamina.

Viola had left earlier to fetch Mrs. Denby, and there the two came, Viola pushing the Bath chair from behind, the elderly woman sitting inside with her knobby hands on the steering handle. Her back might be hunched, yet her face was wreathed in smiles.

Sarah had not yet met the woman but felt as though she knew her, both from her sister's descriptions and from the friendly letter Viola had helped her write.

Converging on the churchyard path, Viola made the introductions.

Mrs. Denby nodded to each in turn, her eyes sparkling. "I am delighted to meet all of you." Then she held out her hand to Sarah, who stepped forward to take it. "And, Miss Sarah, how I have appreciated the delicious gifts you've sent along with Viola."

Another woman in a wheeled chair arrived, pushed by a liveried footman and attended by a maid in black. This woman was somewhat younger, plumper, and more elegantly attired than Mrs. Denby. Still, the two women nodded to each other as their "chariots" passed, like equally regal queens.

"Good morning, Mrs. Gage," Viola called, and Emily and Georgiana greeted the woman as well.

Mr. Hutton senior came strolling up the path, and since he was alone, Viola insisted he sit with them.

Together they all processed into the church and down the long nave. Mrs. Denby returned the greetings of a few elderly people who were clearly astonished and happy to see her, which served to brighten Mrs. Denby's already cheerful smile. Viola positioned her chair at the end of their customary pew and sat beside her, and the two shared a prayer book throughout the service.

After the benediction, Sarah and Viola lingered in the back of the church, waiting for Emily, Georgiana, and Mrs. Denby to finish chatting with their many friends.

Looking around at the numerous memorials on the walls and floor, Viola asked, "Do you think Mamma will end up being buried here? So far from Papa?"

"Hopefully, we shan't face that dilemma for a long time. Who knows, Mamma may yet rally."

"Do you really think so?"

"It's possible. Consider Mr. Butcher."

"Yes, though not everyone who comes here is cured." Viola gestured around her. "You need look no further than these memorials for evidence of that."

Sarah could not disagree, and found her gaze drawn to two memorials near them:

MARY, WIFE OF ROBERT LISLE, OF ACTON HOUSE,
in the County of Northumberland Esq.
died 21 February, 1791, aged 39 years,
and by her own desire lies buried here.

And another:

O Lord receive my soul.
Close to, and underneath this stone are deposited
the remains of
Charlotte Temperance,
eldest surviving daughter of
Thomas and Elizabeth Alston,
of Odell Castle, Bedfordshire.
She died at Sidmouth, on the 10th of November, 1810,
aged nineteen.

Viola, following her gaze, said, "So many deaths. And consider Mrs. Denby, who has lived here all her life, and is still frail."

"Yes, but perhaps if she had spent her youth toiling in some dark northern mill instead of making lace in temperate Sidmouth, she might have died long before now."

"I suppose that's true. Thank heavens she is still with us."

Sarah studied her formerly isolated, taciturn sister. "You are very good with her and generous with your time."

Viola shrugged. "I enjoy her company."

Sarah slowly shook her head at Viola's modesty, and a warm fondness spread through her. "I know I'm not your parent, Vi, yet I am proud of you."

Viola looked at her in surprise, and tears sprang to her eyes. "Thank you, Sarah. That means more than you know."

Later that afternoon, Sarah sat on one of the cushioned chairs on the veranda. She took a deep breath of sea air and sweet peace, enjoying a few minutes of leisure.

The door from the drawing room opened, and Callum Henshall stepped outside, carrying his guitar. "Ah, Miss Summers. May I join ye?"

"Of course."

He sat in a nearby chair. "Except for our brief time at sea, I have rarely seen ye sitting still, let alone relaxing."

"A Sabbath rest seemed in order."

"And well deserved, in your case. Ye work hard."

"There is always more to do, it seems." She studied his profile, noticing he appeared preoccupied. "Is something the matter?"

He twisted his mouth to one side. "Not really. Effie is more irritable than usual, if ye can believe it. She now insists we visit the Bath shops on our way home to make up for the 'intolerable stay in sleepy Sidmouth and endless days of torture in spine-rattling coaches.'"

Sarah said, "I am sorry your stay has proved a disappointment."

"Only for her. My stay has exceeded all expectations." He held her gaze, and Sarah's heart tripped.

"And I don't think she truly hates it here," he said. "She has grown rather fond of your family. It's me who disappoints her, limiting her freedom and spending money, not taking her to a ball or dressmaker. She did enjoy our ride, and sailing to Ladram Bay, much as you and I did. Even so, I shan't propose another long journey anytime soon. I doubt she'd ever forgive me."

He gave her a wry grin, and Sarah returned it but felt her chin tremble.

"I am sorry to hear that . . ." It was on the tip of her tongue to call him Callum, but she resisted.

He looked at her, then away again, squinting toward the sun-streaked bay. Gulls wheeled in the sky, and someone on the beach flew a kite, scattering the seabirds and spurring a squawking protest.

He said, "I know ye have many responsibilities here, with everything being new and so much to learn and oversee. Perhaps in time, though, ye might get away for a wee while. Travel. Miss Emily mentioned a great-aunt in Scotland?"

"Oh . . . yes. But we are not close." She thought of Claire in Scotland too, but did not mention her. It would require explanations she was not quite ready to give.

Several moments of silence passed, broken only by the call of seabirds and the tinkling of the wind chimes in the corner.

Then he asked softly, "Do ye plan to stay here indefinitely? Postpone your own life?"

She stared at him, feeling defensive. "This *is* my life. My family. Our mother needs me."

"Perhaps one of your sisters might take on your role?"

Sarah paused to consider. "I suppose Georgiana might . . . one day. When she grows up a bit and spends less time caring for strays."

"Seems to me you have taken in several strays as well, myself included."

Seeing his self-abasing expression, her irritation faded.

"But you're right," he added. "She is still quite young. What about Miss Viola?"

"Viola refused to work among the guests. That's why she began reading to invalids, to bring in income another way. So no, I don't see her stepping into the role. She has become more involved lately, less reclusive, yet I still think it unlikely."

"And Miss Emily?"

"Oh, Emily lives with her head in books . . . both those she's reading and those she hopes to write. She is so creative and talented, I would hate to ask it of her."

"Then, ye are trapped here."

"For the time being, yes. Though I don't see myself as trapped. I enjoy it, for the most part. I like to be useful, to organize."

"Ye might do that in another capacity. As mistress of your own home."

She looked at him, and he held up his palm. "Dinnae say it. You've had one great love in your life and don't expect another."

She pulled a face at him, and he smiled, then quickly sobered. "I have a man of business and tenants to keep the estate going for a month or two, but I canna stay away much longer. I, too, have responsibilities."

"I understand," she replied, hoping she did not appear as bewildered as she felt. Was he intimating that if things were different, he might stay? Or was she reading too much into his words?

"I want to be a good steward," he continued. "A cousin will inherit instead of a son, yet I am duty bound to manage the land well and keep the house in good order."

"I am sure you do so admirably."

He inhaled deeply. "So ye see . . ."

He let his sentence fade away, unfinished, but she filled in the words, at least in her imagination. *We are at an impasse.*

Emily was crossing the hall when Mr. Stanley came jogging down the stairs, book in hand.

"Good afternoon, Mr. Stanley. We missed you this morning."

"How was church? Edifying service?"

"Yes, the vicar gave a sermon of his own composition. I thought it well written, convicting, and blessedly brief."

He shifted uneasily. "I hope you don't think too badly of me. I am not always such a slugabed. I attend regularly at home."

Emily raised a palm. "No criticism intended." She gestured to the book in his hand. "What have you there?"

"The first volume of *Emma*. I found it on the bedside table and guessed it might be one of your favorites."

Emily had begun to reread it before Mr. Stanley's arrival but had since moved on to other novels. "And are you enjoying it so far?"

"I have read only the first chapter." He lifted the volume. "And it has already solved a mystery—one concerning me."

"What are you talking about?"

"The mystery of my missing letter." He opened the book and withdrew a folded rectangle. "Now we know how you managed to misplace it before writing down my room request."

"Oh!" Belatedly she remembered. She had laid aside *Emma* to write a reply to his letter, using it *temporarily* to mark her place in the book. Instead, she had forgotten all about it.

He gave a long-suffering sigh. "I suppose it's better than being relegated to the rubbish bin."

She looked up into his face, unsure if he was offended or jesting.

His quick grin reassured her. "At least it was put to an important literary use."

She held out her palm.

His dark brows rose in question. "Why do you want it back?"

"It's a matter of record keeping."

"Yes, we have all seen how fastidious you are about that."

The warm light in his eyes softened his teasing.

She joggled her palm up and down. She wasn't exactly sure why she wanted the letter, but she did.

He handed it over. "Then what shall I use to mark my place?"

Emily thought, then reached up and tugged from her head the length of ribbon she wore as a simple bandeau.

"There you are." She extended the ribbon.

He stared at it yet made no move to take it.

The mischief faded from his eyes. "I . . . should not accept it."

"Why not? It is only to mark your place in *my* book. I don't expect you to wear it." She grinned again, but he remained serious. Did he think she'd meant it as a love token?

Had she?

It was not as though she'd given him a lock of her hair. Did he believe accepting it signaled some attachment or obligation on his part?

After a long moment, he slowly, almost reverently, took the ribbon from her, smoothing it flat between the pages.

"Thank you, Miss Summers. I shall leave it behind when I go."

How strangely formal he suddenly seemed. Had she been too forward? She had not meant to be.

"As you wish, Mr. Stanley."

He bowed, turned, and started back upstairs, with none of the vigor he'd displayed on his way down.

Emily watched him go, feeling perplexed and almost . . . chastised. Charles had corrected her on various matters of etiquette over the years, and she had not liked it then either.

She carried his letter into the library and unfolded it on the desk. When it had arrived, she'd read it perfunctorily—scanning for the dates requested in order to dash off a quick reply to a stranger.

Now she studied the fine handwriting. The formal structure and excellent spelling. She looked at the closing: *Mark Stanley, Esq.* and his direction.

Esquire. The term could mean he was a son of a knight or younger son of a peer. Then again, it could mean he was a barrister or some appointed official, although he seemed too young for that. In any case, he was certainly a gentleman.

Mark. A straightforward, masculine name. It suited him.

Remembering his hesitation to accept the ribbon, Emily's heart sank. Perhaps she had misread his flirtation as she had misread Charles's. Yet Mr. Stanley *had* accepted it, she consoled herself, only to recall that he intended to leave it behind when he departed.

At Westmount the next day, Viola was in the midst of reading aloud the London news when the major blurted, "Does it bother you?"

Viola looked up, startled. "Which part?"

"Having to let out rooms in what was meant to be your private home."

She huffed. "What is the point of discussing that? What is done is done."

"Is your family in such dire financial straits?"

"Unfortunately, we are. Although Sarah would box my ears if she heard me admit it. We are excessively proud, for all of that."

"I thought you had several guests already?"

"Presently, yes, but no further room requests for the future. However, we hope things will improve. A new edition of Mr. Butcher's guidebook is planned—*The Beauties of Sidmouth Displayed*. And we are endeavoring to get Sea View mentioned in it. A good write-up would certainly bring in more guests."

"What has been done to that end?"

Viola thought. "Emily has introduced herself to Mr. Wallis, the publisher, who wields great influence over the author. And she wrote to invite the minister to visit Sea View, to experience its commodious qualities for himself."

"Did she? Do you know, Mr. Butcher called here once, but I sent him away with a flea in his ear. I am staunch Church of England."

"I did not realize you attended."

"I don't. Not since . . . all this." He circled a hand around his right side. "And has the minister responded to your sister's letter?"

"Eventually, he wrote back to say that he prefers to remain objective, and that he has a *commodious* home of his own in Sidmouth and therefore need not avail himself of ours."

"Hm." The major pulled a face. "I have no right to call anyone rude, but . . . rude."

"Emily thought so. But I met the man at the poor house, and he seems thoroughly kind to me."

"Did you mention Sea View to him?"

Viola shook her head. "I am afraid my courage failed me. And who knows—if he did visit us, he might not be impressed. We still don't know precisely what we are doing, and half the time are at sixes and sevens."

"Correspondence," he said abruptly.

Viola blinked, taken aback by his sudden shift from the personal to the professional.

"As you wish," she coolly replied. She began flipping through the stack. "Any preference?"

"You know what? Never mind. I have been reminded of something I must do. Let's adjourn until tomorrow. I will, of course, pay you for the full hour."

Viola felt chastised and humiliated to be reminded that she was a paid subordinate. Talk of money always embarrassed her.

She wanted to protest, but her pride was provoked, so she turned and stalked from the room without even a good-bye.

She had gotten no farther than the entry hall when she realized she had forgotten her manners . . . and her bonnet.

With a sigh, she turned back.

She found him squatting near the room's rubbish bin, digging through its contents, and extracting something from it.

"Pardon me. I forgot my . . . What are you doing?"

He straightened to his full height. "Our talk reminded me of two letters I've received and neglected to answer."

"Oh. Shall I read them to you?"

"I can manage."

"I am sorry to hear it. Very soon, you will not need my visits."

"Perhaps," he replied, holding her gaze. "But I shall still want them."

***

Later that day, Sarah sat alone in the office, again trying to balance their accounts. Recent outlays for the Eltons' dinner had consumed most of the money they'd received from Mr. Gwilt's advance payment. Perhaps they should have required at least a deposit from all their guests upon arrival.

Sarah rose and went to talk to her mother. When she reached her room, she was surprised to find it empty. That had been happening more often of late. She glanced out the window into the

315

walled garden—empty as well. Had Mamma gone sea-bathing with Georgiana again? That was probably it, she told herself. There was no need to worry.

But she did. She certainly hoped her mother was all right, wherever she was.

Sarah returned to the library and reviewed their ledger once more, looking for any additional cost-saving measures she might find. She wondered what Mr. Henshall might advise. For a moment, she wished she could share the problem with him. Share much more besides . . . Imagining it filled her with longing, quickly dampened by fear. What would become of her family if she left them?

No.

Sarah rested her head in her hands. She rubbed her throbbing temples, willing away the alluring daydream. Her duty was to her family, and Callum Henshall's duty was to his.

Closing the book, she instead picked up the latest edition of *The Exeter Flying Post* and began perusing the Help Wanted column. She ran her finger down the listings, bypassing ads for apprentices and cooks and searching the notices for governesses or companions.

One post was offered in Brighton, many hours from there by coach. Would she really ask one of her sisters to take such a situation? And so far from home? Or should she apply herself, leaving the others to muddle along without her?

No.

Sarah laid down the paper with a heavy sigh.

A familiar Scripture whispered through her mind. The verse about casting all your cares upon God.

Sarah pressed her palms together, closed her eyes, and began to pray.

Sometime later, Sarah heard a floorboard squeak and glanced up. Mr. Gwilt hovered in the doorway.

"Sorry. I did not mean to interrupt."

"That's all right. Do come in."

He approached the desk. "I have been, um, thinking of the future."

"Oh? Then we have that in common. Do go on."

"You once said I could stay on longer, if I liked. Perhaps you were simply being polite."

"Not at all. You are perfectly welcome."

"Thank you. I have so enjoyed my time here with your family, and the truth is I . . . have nowhere else to go."

Her heart twisted for the lonely man, and emotion heated her eyes.

Seeing her expression, he hurried to reassure her. "Now, now, it's not as dire as all that. I am not destitute. I have my savings from selling our home. Not a grand place, mind—brick terrace, two up, two down. Got a fair price, though. Money won't last forever, but I can afford to stay a mite longer before I find work. That is *if* anyone will have me. I'm not a young man, I realize, yet I'm still able-bodied and able-minded . . . mostly." He chuckled weakly.

Sarah asked, "What kind of situation would you take up?"

He shrugged. "Some sort of clerk, perhaps. I was employed as a bank clerk for years. When the missus took ill, I started doing bookkeeping for nearby shops, primarily from home, so I wouldn't have to leave her for long."

For a moment he looked away, expression forlorn, then he managed a small smile. "In any case, I will pay in advance, as before. Perhaps an extra week to begin with? After that, I would need to cash a bank draught."

"The bank in Exeter could help you with that." Sarah hesitated to repeat what she'd said when he first arrived, until her conscience needled her.

She swallowed a reluctant lump and began, "Again, we do not require payment in advance, but—"

Mr. Gwilt raised his hand. "No, no. I like to pay as I go. Never one to run up debts, not I."

Relief swept through her. "I confess, payment would be much appreciated."

In fact, it might just be an answer to prayer.

27

The place is very full—and there is so much quadrilling
& cricketing, that nobody can doubt its intellectuality.
—Elizabeth Barrett (Browning),
letter from Sidmouth

When Viola knocked on Westmount's front door the next morning, Taggart answered, but for once no welcoming smile lit his face, nor did he fling wide the door and invite her inside.

Instead, he gave her an apologetic wince. "Not today, miss."

"Why? Is everything all right? Is Major Hutton well?"

"Yes, miss. He's just . . . meeting with someone and won't have time today."

"May I ask whom?"

He shook his head. "Sorry, miss. I've been told to keep my mouth shut." And he slowly closed the door.

Wondering what was going on, and hoping the major truly was all right, Viola slowly walked away. She had some time before Mrs. Gage expected her, so she took the long way, walking to the esplanade for a view of the beach before strolling eastward along the remains of the old fort.

Through an arched gateway in the stone wall, she saw Colin

Hutton on the grassy field within, dressed for cricket, stretching, jogging in place, and experimentally swinging a flat wooden bat.

She walked through the archway to greet him.

Seeing her approach, he beamed. "Good day, Miss Vi."

"All ready for today's match?"

"Not a bit of it. Yet I am looking forward to it all the same. What about you?"

"I would like to come, but I am supposed to read to Mrs. Gage soon. I hope to persuade her."

"You do that. We need a good cheering section. Oh, by the way, I would not bother going to Westmount today."

"I already tried. Taggart turned me away. Said the major was meeting someone?"

Colin nodded. "Mr. Bird is introducing him to another surgeon he knows."

"Which surgeon?" Viola's heart pounded, again recalling her dreadful encounter with Mr. Cleeves on the street.

"Someone who might be able to do something about his scars, apparently. New technique or some such." He grimaced. "I decided to leave the gruesome talk to them."

There were several surgeons in Sidmouth, Viola reminded herself, so the chances of it being the same man were small. Regardless, she asked, "What sort of a man is he?"

Colin screwed up his face. "What sort?"

"Old? Young? Tall?"

"Looking for a husband, Vi?" he teased.

"No. Just . . . tell me."

"I don't know. Not young, though younger than Papa. Rather slight. Well-dressed, I noticed, for a blood-and-bone man."

Viola shivered, then asked, "Hair?"

"Yes, he had some."

"Colin, you are rubbish at descriptions. What is his name?"

"I did not really pay attention."

Viola licked dry lips. "It was not . . . Cleeves, was it?"

Colin frowned in thought, then shook his head. "That does not ring a bell."

She released a long, relieved breath then asked, "If a meeting was all it was, why did Taggart not tell me?"

Colin lifted a shoulder. "I don't think Jack wants to say anything until he knows more—doesn't want to get anyone's hopes up. Perhaps I shouldn't have said anything either, but you are practically one of the family."

Her heart warmed. "Thank you, Colin."

Nevertheless, Viola was tempted to return to Westmount and wait to see who emerged—and might have, if Mrs. Gage was not expecting her.

The entire town was looking forward to the cricket match between Sidmouth visitors and local fishermen. Everyone, it seemed, except Major Hutton, who had declined to attend. Viola hoped Mrs. Gage would want to watch, but when she arrived at the woman's home and the footman showed her into the parlour, Mrs. Gage seemed unaware of the event soon to begin outside her own front door. Fortfield Terrace was tantalizingly close to the playing field that lay between the fashionable row of lodging houses and the esplanade.

"Oh, good. You're here," Mrs. Gage said. "I have been wondering what will happen next." The woman nodded to the chair Viola usually sat in, where the novel *Belinda* waited to be read.

Seated on the sofa, Mrs. Gage picked up her embroidery, liking to work while she listened. "Lady Delacour is such an interesting character, is she not?"

"Y-yes," Viola replied, her gaze drawn to the window, wishing again she could attend the big event. "Are you not interested in the match?"

"Hm? What match?"

"The cricket match between Sidmouth fishermen and visitors."

"Ah yes, I heard something about that." The older woman flopped a dismissive hand. "Not something we ladies would be interested in."

Viola tried to ignore the disappointment sinking in her stomach.

"Well, shall we begin?" She picked up the book and started to read where they'd left off.

"Lady Delacour's history, and the manner in which it was related, excited in Belinda's mind astonishment, pity, admiration, and contempt: astonishment at her inconsistency, pity for her misfortunes, admiration for her talents, and contempt for her conduct."

She turned the page and took a breath before continuing.

From outside came a rising wave of voices and the sound of musicians tuning their instruments.

Mrs. Gage frowned. "What's all that racket?"

Viola rose and stepped to the window. A moment later, Mrs. Gage joined her, leaning on a gold-tipped ebony cane. The woman could walk short distances, rather quickly when she wanted to, and evidently she wanted to now.

The front windows overlooked the field. The match had not yet started, but a great deal of activity was going on.

Open-sided tents had been set up around the perimeter by some of the inns and other businesses. The brewer and one of the bakers were sharing a marquee, taking advantage of the opportunity to sell refreshments. And nearby, the Sidmouth band began playing a rousing martial piece.

"What's all this?" Mrs. Gage breathed.

"It's as I told you. A cricket match is being played between visitors and our fishermen. Several of the local men are reputed to be quite good."

"Bah. Better than gentlemen who played at Eton, Oxford, and Cambridge? I doubt it."

Viola made do with a shrug.

Mrs. Gage looked at her knowingly. "Shall we lay aside our reading for today, and go outside and watch?"

Mood lifting, Viola eagerly nodded. Her wish had been granted.

Viola retrieved the woman's bonnet while the footman helped his mistress into her cloak and into the chair.

Mrs. Gage accepted the bonnet and tied it under her chin. "We must take Nero with us." She patted her knee, and the fluffy little orange-and-cream Pomeranian leapt into her lap.

Viola put on her own bonnet. Had she the courage to forgo a veil amid such a large crowd? She hesitated, then positioned it over her face.

Again, the footman and maid lowered the wheeled chair down the terrace steps. Then Viola rolled it the short distance across the drive to the field.

Spectators had already gathered. Some Fortfield Terrace residents had dragged out chairs to sit and watch in comfort. Other ladies sat on blankets with fluttering parasols over their heads, while groups of men and lads stood clustered here and there, jesting and placing wagers.

Across the field, another open-sided tent shielded from the sun wealthy Emanuel Lousada and his guests.

And on the western side of the field, her own sisters and some of their guests sat on blankets spread on the grass, like a second picnic. Seeing her, Sarah, Emily, and Mr. Gwilt raised hands in greeting. Meanwhile Georgie and Effie sat near each other talking and giggling and petting a pile of fur she assumed to be Chips.

Seeing Mr. Hutton and Armaan nearby, Viola waved to them, then returned both hands to the chair handles to position Mrs. Gage to have a good view of the game and company.

The visiting gentlemen removed their outer coats and played in shirtsleeves and light waistcoats over fawn-colored trousers. They wore narrow black cravats and their top hats. Among them were a few men she recognized, Colin Hutton and two of their own guests: Mr. Henshall and Mr. Stanley.

The fishermen also wore shirts, waistcoats, and trousers of varying shades. Their hats ranged from wide-brimmed felt hats with low crowns to old tricornes to flat wool caps. Their number included Punch and Tom Cordey.

The fishermen's team won the coin toss and batted first. Around the field, some of the visiting spectators grumbled that the game was fixed.

Colin took his place as wicket keeper while the other gentlemen spread across the field—Mr. Stanley, Mr. Henshall, and others Viola did not know.

Toot Salter stood before the wicket, bat ready, while Mr. Henshall bowled the ball toward him.

Thwack. He hit the ball, and the visitors scrambled after it. Toot ran toward the opposite wicket, while Punch, the other batsman, ran to swap places with him, becoming the next to bat.

Colin stood not far behind the striker's wicket, awaiting the next delivery. Punch gave it a whack, but Mr. Henshall caught it after a single bounce. He threw it hard and hit the wicket before Punch and Toot could again swap places, and Toot was declared out by Mr. Wallis, who was acting as umpire.

Then Tom stepped up to bat. Holding the bat low, he tapped the ground in preparation.

On the pitch, Mr. Henshall took his running start and bowled the ball. It bounced once in line with the stumps.

Thwack! Tom hit it dead-on.

The ball flew past the visitors' team, all the way to the fence, their boundary.

An instant four runs.

Tom raised his bat high in triumph, and his teammates and the locals cheered.

Eventually, when everyone had been called out, they switched sides.

The fishermen spread across the field—Toot Salter, Ruder Pike, and others whose more common names Viola could not recall. Punch took over as wicket keeper, and Tom took to the pitch.

A young gentleman she didn't know swaggered up to bat. He wore his side-whiskers trimmed to a precise point and a flower in his waistcoat button.

"Let me have your best delivery," the dandy said with a sneer. "Pretend I am a fish."

One of the Oxford or Cambridge players Mrs. Gage had predicted, if she had to guess. She hoped Tom bowled him out.

Viola was distracted from the game when Georgiana, trailed by Chips, came striding in her direction to greet them. Seeing the stray, Mrs. Gage's Pomeranian leapt down and started across the field.

"Nero, no! Come back," Mrs. Gage shouted, her voice rising in panic, "Please stop him before he's trampled!"

Viola darted after the dog, just as Tom ran and bowled the ball overhand. She vaguely heard the crack of wood on the hard ball. From the corner of her eye, she glimpsed a flash of movement shooting straight toward her and tried to duck, too late. The ball slammed into her face.

She cried out in both pain and alarm. *No, no, no.* She threw her veil back and cradled her mouth with both hands.

The crowd's cheer erupted, then faded.

The umpire shouted something. The game ceased. All around her, people turned to see what or who had disturbed the match.

"Viola! Vi!" Sarah's voice, calling from a distance.

A man shouted, "Delay of game! Interference! That would have been a run!"

Emily's angry voice. "Is that all you care about? Can't you see she is hurt?"

"She should not have wandered onto the playing field," the man defended, their voices drawing closer.

Emily retorted, "You, sir, are no gentleman."

Viola stood there, hunched over, face in her hands, pain throbbing through her mouth.

Had her lip broken open again? The scar split? She tasted blood and salty tears.

Colin Hutton stood at her side. "Miss Vi? Are you injured?"

Sarah touched her arm. "Is it your mouth?"

Viola nodded and Sarah drew in a sharp breath. "Oh no."

Mr. Hutton senior said, "Come, let's get her to Westmount. Mr. Bird is there with Jack. Perhaps he might help."

Sarah gave her a handkerchief, and Viola wiped her nose, slowly raising her head. All around her, eyes stared. She pressed the cloth to her mouth.

Mr. Hutton waved to two youths perched on the seat of a farm wagon. "Take these ladies to Westmount. It isn't far."

"Aw, sir. The cricket."

Mr. Hutton offered the youth a gold coin, and he snapped to attention. "In that case, sir, right away." He elbowed his mate from the bench.

Colin and Armaan helped Viola and Sarah into the back of the wagon, and Mr. Hutton gave Emily a hand onto the bench with the driver.

Georgiana appeared, Nero in her arms, and restored him to his mistress.

Vi called to her, "Please take Mrs. Gage home for me, after the match."

"I will," Georgie called back. "Don't worry."

The wagon lurched into motion, and Colin, Armaan, and Mr. Hutton started across the field on foot to meet them at Westmount.

Gesturing to the retreating Colin, Toot Salter addressed the opposing team. "If 'ee don't have another player to replace him, that means we win."

"I will play," Georgie offered.

The dandy with the flower in his waistcoat button scoffed. "You are but a girl."

Mr. Wallis apologetically shook his head. "This is a gentleman's game, miss."

"Let her play," Viola heard Mr. Henshall call as the wagon pulled away. "I've seen her bat. She is better than most of you lot. . . ."

Arriving at Westmount a few minutes later, Viola saw the surgeon, Mr. Bird, just leaving. The major came out of his room to see what all the hubbub was about.

"What's going on?"

"Miss Summers is here. And her sisters."

"I told you. I don't want to see anyone. I am in no mood for a social call."

"Viola's hurt."

"What?" His head snapped up. "How? Is she all right?"

His father delayed the surgeon's departure. "Mr. Bird, could you please take a look?"

Not another surgeon, Viola thought. *And please, God, not another surgery.*

Tears blurred her vision as she looked at her sisters. "I'm th-thcared." In her distress, she lisped the word.

Sarah squeezed her hand. "All will be well."

The surgeon approached.

"Come, come, why all this commotion over a bloodied lip? Compared to the major's wounds, this is trivial. Unless . . . have you lost a tooth? I am not a dentist, you know."

"No, I d-don't think so." Viola ran a tentative tongue over her teeth, then sent Sarah a subtle nod of permission.

Sarah nodded back and explained, "My sister was born with a cleft lip, so . . ."

"A harelip?"

"A cleft," Sarah corrected. "She has undergone several surgeries and fears it may have split back open."

"Ah, forgive me. Now I see the reason for concern. Let me take a closer look."

Reluctantly, Viola lowered the handkerchief.

Dr. Bird frowned at the loitering men. "The rest of you, except her sisters, please wait in another room."

When they had gone, he palpated her lip, then carefully lifted it to peer underneath.

"Your teeth cut the inside of your mouth. That is what's bleeding. The scar is intact."

Viola let out a ragged breath, and Emily squeezed her hand.

"Thank God," Sarah murmured.

"I don't think stitches will be necessary. It will heal on its own in time."

"That's a relief," Viola murmured.

"What would really help is getting some ice on it to keep the swelling down and reduce the strain on the scar."

Sarah stepped to the adjoining room and asked the men, "Have you any ice?"

"No, dash it," the major replied. "Perhaps one of the hotels?"

Emily stood. "We have some in our cellar. I'll go." She hurried toward the door. Mrs. Besley planned to make ice cream with it, but this was more important.

Colin followed her. "Let me. I am an excellent runner."

"Thank you, but you don't know your way around the house. I will be as fast as I can." The truth was, Emily couldn't just stand there and do nothing.

She ran across the drive and started up the sloped lawn toward Sea View. Running headlong was not exactly ladylike, but she did not care.

She hurried down the basement stairs and pushed through the back door, running past the kitchen toward the cellar door.

Mrs. Besley emerged. "And just what are you doing, young lady, running through here like a wild animal?"

"Getting ice."

"No, you are not!" she thundered. "That is to make ices for the guests!"

"It's for Viola. She was hit in the mouth at the cricket."

"Oh." The woman's eyes widened. "Then of course. Let's hurry."

Mrs. Besley flew into action, and soon a quantity of ice had been chipped from the block and secured in a tin.

Emily ran back down the hill and up the drive, heart pounding hard from anxiety as well as exertion.

Reaching Westmount, she handed over the precious burden and bent low, resting hands on knees to catch her breath. Her mother would scold her for such an ungainly position—especially with men present.

"Are you all right?" Sarah asked.

She nodded, panted, and replied, "Just winded."

Sarah pressed her shoulder. "Thank you, Emily."

When Emily straightened, she found Viola holding her gaze, brow creased in astonishment or perhaps pain. "Yes, thank you."

"Shh. Try not to talk."

The surgeon wrapped the ice in a cloth and handed it to Viola. "Hold it gently to your mouth. That's it. That should help."

A few minutes later, Mr. Bird took his leave. When he had gone, the elder Mr. Hutton reappeared in the threshold. "My son asks that you stay here for a time, Miss Viola. Mr. Bird will be returning this evening and could make sure all is well with you at the same time. You've suffered a shock, after all, as well as an injury, and it would ease his mind."

"That is excessively kind," Sarah began. "But I think Viola would be more comfortable at home."

"Actually, I would like to stay," Viola said.

Sarah glanced at her in surprise. "If you are sure . . . ?"

"I am."

Sarah took the bloody handkerchief from her. "I will take this home to soak." She turned back to Mr. Hutton. "What time will Mr. Bird return?"

"Eight or so. Assuming no other emergencies."

"If I can't get away then, I'll send Georgiana to walk you home."

"Or Emily," Viola suggested.

Emily turned to her, and the twins' gazes locked and held.

Sarah looked from one to the other, eyebrows raised, and repeated, "Or Emily."

Viola had mostly wanted to stay to assure herself Major Hutton was well and to hear what he had learned from the visiting surgeon. After her sisters had gone, the major appeared in the doorway.

"Are you truly all right?"

She turned toward him. "Yes, so your Mr. Bird says."

He peered at her. "Your lip looks like a mangosteen."

"A what?"

"A purple fruit. From India."

"Thank you very little, sir!" Despite herself, Viola felt a smile tremble on her lips. Her exceedingly sore lips. "Don't make me laugh. It hurts."

She thought a moment, then asked, "Why did you refuse to see me earlier today?"

"I needed to think. I didn't want anyone to influence my decision."

"About surgery?"

"Yes."

"Are you—" She stopped and started again. "I know it is your decision. But you are doing so well. The blurry vision in your left eye has improved, and your chest has healed. You're gaining strength, you're swimming, and saving drowning damsels." Another little smile. "Are you sure you want to undergo an experimental surgery?"

"I don't want people to look away in revulsion for the rest of my sorry life."

She held his gaze. "I won't look away." For a moment, tension buzzed between them, then she flushed and modified, "That is, if I . . . happen to see you . . . in the future."

Did she really think her opinion counted? When people turned away from her too?

To cover her embarrassment, she attempted casual humor. "Then again, I doubt the word of someone with mangosteen lips counts for much."

He remained oddly somber. "Yes. The future is sadly uncertain, after all."

Georgie, Effie, Mr. Henshall, and Mr. Stanley returned from the cricket match, talking animatedly as they trooped up the lawn to Sea View. Emily and Sarah, assisting Mamma, went out onto the veranda to meet them.

Emily noticed that Georgie wore a flower tucked behind her ear, in sharp contrast to her untidy hair and grass-stained skirts.

"I take it your team won?" Emily called.

Mr. Stanley shook his head. "No, but your little sister won the hearts of everyone—visitors and locals alike."

"He exaggerates," Georgie said, clearly self-conscious. "How is Viola?"

After assuring her all was well and Viola would be home soon, Emily asked for more details about the match.

Effie spoke up on her friend's behalf. "Georgie was amazin'! She had a long batting run, and everyone cheered for her."

"Well done," Sarah said.

Georgie wrinkled her sweat-streaked face. "Could have done better. I should have known to back up farther when fielding. Can't believe I missed that ball."

"Never ye mind, lass," Mr. Henshall said. "You played well. None of us guessed that skinny *chiel* would hit it so far."

Mr. Stanley nodded. "When Henshall insisted your sister be allowed to play, I admit I had my qualms. But he was right. She was very brave to step in as she did, especially with so many opposing the idea, yet she proved the naysayers wrong and did us all proud."

"I am proud of you too, Georgiana," Mrs. Summers said, giving her shoulder an affectionate squeeze. "But then, I am proud of all my girls." She put her other arm around Effie, drawing her close to her side. "You too, my dear."

Effie twisted her neck to look up at Mrs. Summers. She did not pull away, but leaned in closer, eyes bright with wonder.

28

The assembly rooms at the London Inn are large
and well fitted up, and generally well attended. The
rooms are open for cards every night, and, during
the season, there is a ball every Wednesday.
—*The Beauties of Sidmouth Displayed*

Emily and Viola sat together on the veranda late the next
morning. Mamma, with the aid of her walking stick, came
out to join them. Sarah moved from one corner to the next,
knocking down spider webs, which sent the wind chimes to clang-
ing. Then she crossed the lawn to a flower border and began cutting
a bouquet for the table. Only Georgie was absent, having gone
sailing with Effie and Mr. Henshall. Emily had offered to help Bibi
with the morning bed making so she could go.

Eventually, Viola rose and excused herself, saying it was time
she visited Mrs. Denby.

"Are you sure you feel up to it, my dear?" Mamma asked, eyeing her still-swollen lip.

"I do, thank you." Viola pressed Mamma's shoulder. Then,
after a moment's hesitation, pressed Emily's as well.

Emily felt the warmth of it through her soul.

After she had gone, Emily asked, "Mamma, may I attend the ball tonight?"

"I don't know, my dear. It depends on whether Sarah can spare you."

They looked over as Sarah returned with a handful of long-stemmed flowers.

"She'll have to do more than spare me," Emily said. "She'll have to accompany me. I cannot go alone. Georgie is too young for balls. And you know Vi won't go."

"I am not going to a ball," Sarah said flatly. "I have far too much to do."

"You always say that!"

"Because it is always true. Especially with the Eltons' dinner coming up."

"Pardon me," a male voice interrupted. They all turned to see Mr. Stanley in the doorway.

"I did not intend to eavesdrop. But my sister plans to attend the ball and has conscripted me as escort. I would be honored to escort you too, Miss Emily, if your mother does not object."

Emily looked eagerly at her parent. "May I, Mamma?"

"I suppose that would be all right. Thank you, Mr. Stanley."

"My pleasure."

Emily rose and walked into the house with the young man.

He said, "I shall even dance with you, if you'll allow me, and endeavor not to step on your toes."

She laughed. "I cannot promise the same. I am out of practice after our mourning period."

He nodded, holding her gaze. "Then we shall muddle through together."

That evening, Emily took great pleasure in donning a favorite ball gown and dancing slippers. She wished she had help with her hair but resigned herself to doing the best she could on her own.

A soft knock sounded.

"Come in. It's open." She expected Sarah. But when she saw the person reflected in the looking glass, she gasped happily and whirled on the dressing stool. "Stirling! Sorry. Miss Stirling. Old habits die hard."

"I know." The former lady's maid smiled. "Never mind. I hear you are going to the ball?"

"Who told you that?"

"A little bird," she coyly replied. "I thought I would see if you wanted a hand with your hair. My old habits die hard too."

"Yes, please. You are so kind, and I am all thumbs. I was just wishing a fairy godmother would make an appearance, and here you are."

Later, when she was ready, Emily went down and met Mr. Stanley in the hall. He looked handsome and broad shouldered in formal evening clothes. Even so, with his square build and ordinary features, he could not compare to her memory of Charles Parker in evening attire. She told herself to stop comparing and enjoy herself.

"You look lovely." His eyes shone with admiration. Then abruptly his expression sobered and his manner became formal. He bowed and said, "Shall we go and collect my sister?" He frowned. "Perhaps I ought to have done so first so we three might walk together."

Why did he suddenly want a chaperone? He hadn't seemed to mind being alone with her before. She hoped it was a sign of his respect and nothing more.

"I will walk with you into town," Miss Stirling offered as she came down the stairs. "I am going that way, as it happens."

"Ah. Good." He opened the door for the ladies and then tucked his hands behind his back, not offering either of them his arm. He kept his distance, staying to the far side of the esplanade, while Miss Stirling remained between them.

Was there something about her that made men wary? Emily thought again of Charles's change toward her, from open warmth to cold reserve.

Miss Stirling walked with them as far as the York Hotel, which faced the beach. There she bid them farewell and turned inland toward her boarding house.

Emily and Mr. Stanley went into the hotel together.

In the vestibule, Emily greeted his sister and was introduced to her friend, Miss Marchant, who was pretty and—judging by her elaborate gown—wealthy, and clearly aware of both.

"Are we ready?" Mr. Stanley asked.

His sister rested a hand on her abdomen and confided, "I hope I shall be able to dance. Our dinner is not agreeing with me. Rather greasy."

"I am sorry to hear it," Emily said. "Perhaps you two might come to Sea View some evening and dine with us. Tomorrow we are having Mrs. Besley's famous roast with Yorkshire pudding. It's delicious."

"Sounds lovely," Miss Stanley agreed, giving her a warm smile.

Her friend wrinkled her nose. "I have already arranged to dine here in the hotel, but thank you all the same."

"Oh well. More for me," Mr. Stanley teased as he led them outside.

On this second meeting, Miss Stanley still seemed warm and winsome like her brother. A friendly, unaffected girl. Her friend, however, struck Emily as proud and aloof. She did not really care, though. She was not going to the ball to make friends with haughty incomers. She had come to dance and to forget her disappointments for a while.

Saying little more, the four of them walked the short distance up Fore Street to the assembly rooms at the London Inn.

Leaving their hats and cloaks with an attendant, they entered the spacious rooms lit by candelabra and filled with well-dressed people and lively music. Emily's body hummed with anticipation, as well as nerves. She had once been the belle of the ball back home. But now? Here?

Mr. Stanley danced first with Miss Marchant, then with his

sister, extracting a promise from Emily to dance the next set. While she waited, Emily stood in the candlelit background with a cup of punch and plastered a pleasant expression on her face, pretending not to feel self-conscious standing there alone.

Mrs. Elton swept in on her husband's arm, as though making a grand entrance. No one took any notice. Seeing Emily, she walked over to greet her. "Ah, Miss Emily, you are here before us. I did not realize you had leisure to attend social gatherings."

"On occasion."

Mrs. Elton turned side to side, so that her skirt and flounced petticoat swirled to pretty effect. She glanced up expectantly, evidently waiting to be complimented.

Before Emily could oblige her, the woman asked, "How do you like my gown? Do you like my trimming? I fear my hair is not as I like, as I traveled without my maid. Your hair looks well, I must say. Perhaps I should have asked you to help with mine."

Emily smiled politely. At least someone was speaking to her, even if it was Mrs. Elton.

The woman said, "Nobody can think less of dress in general than I do—but upon such an occasion as this, when everybody's eyes are so much upon me, I would not wish to be inferior to others."

"Not at all, Mrs. Elton. You look very well indeed."

"Thank you. Well, ta-ta!" She and her husband went in search of more important people to meet.

Emily remained where she was, surreptitiously studying the assembled company. Most were strangers to her. Visitors. Incomers. But she recognized a few residents.

Among the musicians, she recognized Mr. Farrant, who had installed their locks. And Mr. and Mrs. Mason, local dancing masters, were serving as unofficial masters of ceremonies.

A party of four entered, and Emily's idle gaze sharpened as she recognized Lord Bertram, a friend of Charles Parker's. She had last seen the man at a house party hosted by the Parker family.

Tonight, he was accompanied by the flower-wearing dandy from the cricket match and two striking young women in fine gowns, feathers sprouting from their curled coiffures.

Would this man know that Charles had broken things off with her? Know the reason why?

The old ache sliced through her chest, and she turned away, hoping he would not see her, or at least, not see the expression on her face.

Mr. Stanley appeared before her. "Are you ready for our dance, Miss Summers? My sister survived, so I have high hopes for you."

"I . . ." Emily licked dry lips, heart beating hard. If she had to be seen by one of Charles's friends, better to be dancing with a gentleman than standing alone like a wallflower.

"Yes, thank you."

He held out his gloved hand, and she placed her white kid–gloved fingers in his.

The dancing master called for a country dance, men in one line facing the ladies in the other. The musicians played the introduction, bows and curtsies were exchanged, and then the couples began the first pattern.

She stepped on Mr. Stanley's toes twice. And once, glancing over and seeing Lord Bertram and the dandy look in her direction and laugh, Emily turned the wrong way and felt her cheeks burn. Were they laughing at her?

"Sorry," she murmured.

Mr. Stanley sent her a reassuring smile. "No matter."

He followed her gaze, and finally his brave expression faltered. "Do you know that fellow?"

She blinked up at her partner. "Hm?"

"That man you keep looking at."

"Sorry. I did not realize."

Their turn at the top of the set came, and all eyes fell on them as head couple. Emily concentrated on the patterns to avoid humiliating herself with more missteps.

Mr. Stanley said, "He watches you too, I notice."

"Does he? I don't know the man well, but we have a mutual acquaintance. A friend from back home."

He studied her face. "A . . . special friend?"

She swallowed. "I once thought so."

"Did he . . . disappoint you?"

She nodded.

"I am sorry." He nodded his understanding and glanced at the foursome. "And his companions?"

"I don't know them."

"Very handsome."

Lord Bertram or the women? Emily wondered but didn't ask for clarification. The truth was, the four were the most elegant people in the room, and many admiring glances lingered on them.

When the dance ended, everyone clapped for the musicians, then Mr. Stanley escorted her from the floor. Too late, she realized they were headed rather close to the quartet she wished to avoid.

Lord Bertram's gaze locked on hers. "One of the Miss Summerses, I believe." He bowed.

Midstride, she jerked to a halt and dipped a graceless curtsy. "Lord Bertram. G-good evening."

Before she could move on, the man's dandy friend spoke up, his face alight with interest. "Ah, the pretty little shrew who shouted at me at the cricket. Do introduce us, Bertram. There's a good fellow."

Lord Bertram glanced coolly at his friend, then said, "Miss Summers, allow me to introduce Mr. Sidney Craven."

Mr. Craven bowed over her hand. "A pleasure, Miss Summers. And these are my sisters, Caroline and Persephone."

Emily managed another curtsy, this one slightly more graceful. The younger sister replied in kind, while the elder made do with a dip of her head.

"Summers . . . Was that not the name of—"

Lord Bertram interjected, "Miss Summers and her family are friends of Charles Parker's."

"Oh . . ."

They eyed her with interest.

Emily slowly turned to include Mr. Stanley, reluctant to introduce him should he blurt out he was a paying guest in their house, and was relieved to see him a few feet away, talking to his sister.

Lord Bertram looked past her. "Are your sisters not with you tonight?"

"No. Busy at home."

"Are you here alone?"

"Of course not. I came with Mr. Stanley and his sister."

Hearing his name, Mr. Stanley returned to her side. Meanwhile, his sister and Miss Marchant joined the next dance with new partners.

Emily said, "Lord Bertram, allow me to introduce Mr. Stanley. Mr. Stanley, Lord Bertram, Mr. Craven, and the Miss Cravens."

Mr. Stanley bowed.

Bertram looked from one to the other. "And have you two been acquainted long?"

"No, not long," Mr. Stanley began. "I am—"

Emily spoke over him. "Mr. Stanley is staying with us. He is a . . . family friend. Is that not right, Mr. Stanley?"

"Oh, er, yes. And fortunate I am to be on such good terms with the Summerses. Delightful family. And the house. What a prospect! An unrivaled view of the sea."

That's going it a bit brown, Emily thought, but kept her expression serene.

"Let it for the season, have you?" Mr. Craven asked her.

"Actually, my father bought it a few years ago, hoping the sea air would improve my mother's health."

The music started up.

"Come, my lord. You promised me the next dance," Persephone urged.

"Indeed, I did. Pray, excuse us. A pleasure to see you again, Miss Summers."

Mr. Craven turned to Emily. "May I have this dance?"

"But, Sidney, you promised to dance with me!" his sister Caroline pouted.

"I can dance with you anytime, Caro. What say you, Stanley? Step in for me—there's a good chap."

"With pleasure." Mr. Stanley offered the young woman his hand.

The dance commenced, another lively country dance with much skipping and whirling. Her partner gazed into her eyes at every opportunity, his look more wolfish than friendly. His every touch of her hand or waist lingered overlong. When they reached the bottom of the dance and waited their turn to rejoin, he leaned near and whispered in her ear, "I have heard of the beauty of the Summers sisters, and you exceed my imaginings."

Emily managed a half smile and shifted away from him, uncomfortable with his intense stares, his proprietorial touches, and his unexpected words. Had she and her sisters some reputation among strangers? Even if for something positive, like beauty, the thought made her strangely uneasy.

She decided to remove the smug leer from his face. "You do know it was my sister you struck with a cricket ball the other day, and you were terribly rude about it afterward."

"Oh, I . . . I do beg your pardon. Which sister was it? Not *the* sister . . . ?"

"What do you mean? It was Viola. My twin."

"Your twin? You jest. She looked nothing like you. I would have noticed that!"

Emily rolled her eyes. What a prig.

After the dance, Emily returned to the refreshment table, feeling uncomfortably warm, both from the dance and from her partner's unwelcome flirtation.

Lord Bertram asked her for the next. He proved to be a skilled

341

dancer, and watched her with keen interest, even speculation, as they moved through the patterns. Otherwise, he behaved with perfect decorum, unlike his friend. When they stood out for a turn at the bottom of the dance, he cleared his throat and asked, "Are your sisters . . . all in good health?"

She looked at him in surprise. "Yes, as far as I know."

"Good, good."

They rejoined the line, and Emily's mind spun faster than the turns of the dance. Was he asking about Claire? She certainly recalled the man showering her eldest sister with attention during the Parkers' house party. But that was more than a year ago.

After the dance, the elder Miss Craven appeared at her side and said in a low voice, "Do take care where Lord Bertram is concerned."

Her aloof expression and patronizing tone vexed Emily. Was she jealous of Lord Bertram's attentions to her?

"Why?" she asked tartly.

"I would rather not go into particulars. He is, after all, a friend of my brother's. However, I advise you not to trust him implicitly. He flirts with many women he has no intention of marrying."

Did she assume the Summerses were beneath the respectable notice of such a man? *Insolent girl*, Emily inwardly seethed. She said, "I can take care of myself."

"So others have thought before you."

Emily glared at her but said nothing more.

Miss Craven lifted her nose in the air. "I beg your pardon," she said, turning away stiffly. "My interference was kindly meant."

Was it? Emily wondered. She thought back. Yes, there had been a budding attraction between Claire and Lord Bertram, who had come to stay with the Parker family for a few weeks. He and Claire had danced with each other and flirted throughout the various entertainments hosted on his behalf. Emily remembered Claire was obviously smitten with the handsome young man. But he had paid no call to them at Finderlay, nor sought their father's blessing, nor planned to return, as far as she knew. Perhaps she had not known the whole.

Mr. Stanley returned to her side once more. "Miss Summers, what is it? You seem upset."

"I . . . I am afraid I am not feeling well."

His brows knitted in concern. "Then I shall walk you home directly."

His sister and Miss Marchant wanted to stay longer, so promising to return for them soon, Mr. Stanley escorted Emily to Sea View.

Both were quiet on the walk back.

When they reached the veranda, Mr. Stanley began, "Miss Summers, there is something I should tell you. Perhaps I should have confided it earlier, but—"

Viola opened the door, appearing startled to find the two of them there. "Sorry. I was just going out to take the air. Don't let me interrupt."

"No interruption at all," he said. "I only walked your sister home and now must return for mine."

"Oh. I see." Viola looked from one to the other, uncertainty scoring a line between her brows.

After Mr. Stanley had bowed and taken his leave, Viola turned to her. "You are home earlier than I expected. Is everything all right?"

Emily sighed. "May I tell you tomorrow? I need to think."

"Of course."

Leaving Viola on the veranda, Emily retreated into the house.

"You saw what?" Emily glowered at her sister as the two of them stood in the hall together the next morning.

Viola winced at her sharp tone and repeated softly, "I saw Mr. Stanley kissing someone."

"It wasn't me."

"I did not say it was."

Emily propped a hand on her hip. "When was this, supposedly?"

"Last night."

"Mr. Stanley walked me home, but he did not kiss me."

"This was later. I just thought you should know."

"Where did you see this? Not here in the house."

Viola shook her head. "On the esplanade."

"Are you even sure it was him? From such a distance?"

"Yes. I went outside to take the air, remember? I sat on the bench not far from there."

"It was probably just his sister. She attended the ball with us, and he planned to walk her back to the hotel after he brought me home." Though why he would bring her to the western end of the esplanade when the York Hotel was on the opposite end, Emily did not know. Perhaps she had simply wanted a stroll.

Even so, Emily insisted, "Most likely, he was simply embracing his sister."

"There was nothing brotherly about the embrace I saw."

Might it have been the sister's friend, the haughty Miss Marchant? Emily wondered, then asked, "What did she look like?"

"I did not see her well, as she was turned away from me most of the time. But tall with dark hair. Does his sister have dark hair?"

"No, light brown and she's quite petite." Again Emily frowned at Viola and challenged, "Are you quite certain about what you saw?"

"Do you think I would make it up? That I enjoy seeing you disappointed and unhappy?"

"Sometimes I think you do."

Viola pressed her bruised lips together and said nothing more.

Emily looked away, troubled. She liked Mr. Stanley and enjoyed his company. His attention. She knew she had no claim on him, but the thought of him kissing someone else made her feel rather betrayed.

As if hearing his name, Mr. Stanley came somberly down the stairs.

"Pardon me, ladies. May I have a private word, Miss Emily?"

"About what?" Emily challenged. "About the tall, dark-haired woman you were seen kissing last night?"

"Ah." He paled, his Adam's apple rising and falling. He clasped his hands, looking as guilty as a schoolboy before a headmaster. "Shall we step into the next room, and I shall endeavor to explain?"

"Whatever you have to say to me, you may say in front of Viola." Emily took her sister's hand, led Mr. Stanley into the small parlour, and closed the door.

There, he exhaled deeply. "Her name is Maria Pritchard."

Emily lifted her chin. "And you kissed her there on the esplanade?"

He pressed his eyes shut. "She kissed me, but . . . yes, I did. I am sorry you saw that."

"I did not, but Viola saw you and told me. I did not believe her. My own sister. How stupid of me."

"You are shocked, I realize. Does it make it better or worse if I tell you we are engaged?"

Emily's mouth gaped. "I hardly know!"

He flinched at her harsh tone and looked down, rocking back on his heels.

"Shall I go?" Viola whispered.

"No, please stay." Emily gripped her hand tightly, then glanced again at Mr. Stanley. "Did you honestly escort me to a ball and then ask another woman to marry you in the same night?"

"Of course not. Our engagement is of long duration." He added hastily, "Though not in the usual sense. It was a secret engagement, formed in our youth."

"Why secret?"

"We were young and knew our families would not approve. I realized it was wrong almost immediately. But as a gentleman, I could not break it off."

"Why did you not tell me?"

"As I said, it was secret—no one knew of it."

"Very convenient for you, these last several weeks."

"I never meant . . ." He grimaced and changed tack. "I came to Sidmouth for a holiday. Yes, to spend time with my sister, but mostly to enjoy my freedom while I could. Then you burst into my room and into my life . . . quite literally." He ran an agitated hand through his hair. "I know I flirted back. Allowed you to believe I was as free and spirited as you. I didn't flatter myself I might hurt you. You were too pretty, too confident to give any serious thought to a man like me. Still, I should have been more circumspect in my behavior toward you, more reserved."

Throat tight, Emily said, "She gave you that ring, didn't she?" The tulip design should have alerted her, Emily realized. Tulips symbolized perfect love.

He nodded. "I recently began wearing it, hoping it would remind me of my obligation—and to keep a proper distance from you. Yet every time I was in your company, you were so . . . clever and witty and beautiful. . . . I couldn't resist. I told myself you knew I would be leaving in a few weeks. No harm would be done."

He inhaled and lowered his voice. "Then last night I saw how you reacted to seeing that man. How you paled in his presence and held on to my arm for support."

"What man, Em?" Viola whispered.

"I will tell you later."

Mr. Stanley continued, "You told me his friend had disappointed you, and I glimpsed the vulnerable woman behind the cheerful mask. I knew then how wrong I had been to think I could not injure you. And I feared it was already too late, that you would be hurt no matter what I did next."

"That's why you were quiet on the walk back."

He nodded. "I was torn between my feelings and duty. I started to tell you, but when we were interrupted, I decided maybe that was for the best, as you were already upset. I resolved to tell you this morning no matter what.

"After I left you last night, I collected my sister and her friend and walked the two back to their hotel. As soon as I entered, I saw them—Miss Pritchard and her mother, baggage around them, apparently just arrived.

"My sister and Miss Marchant proceeded upstairs while I stood there, dumbfounded, waiting for my cue. Not sure if I was even supposed to acknowledge our acquaintance, let alone anything else."

"But when Miss Pritchard saw me, she rushed forward and presented her hand to be kissed in front of her mamma and everyone else. I did so, rather woodenly, unsure what she intended.

"She presented me to her mother, saying, 'This is the Mr. Stanley I have told you so much about.'

"Then she asked if she and I might take a walk along the mall, saying she had been sitting too long in that cramped chaise, and a moonlight stroll was just what she needed.

"I was sure her parent would object, as it was late by then, though, yes, there was plenty of moonlight to see by. Instead her mother said, 'Oh, very well. You are engaged, after all.'

"I stood there, mouth wide, no doubt looking like a trout stunned to find a hook in his mouth. Miss Pritchard handed over her bandbox, grasped my arm almost fiercely, and all but dragged me outside."

"You did not know she was coming?"

He shook his head. "I asked her why she had not written to inform me and to let me know that our private arrangement had become public. She didn't say it in so many words, but I gather she sensed me pulling away and came to settle her claim.

"We walked along the promenade, my mind spinning, filled with dread. She chatted happily, seemingly unaware of my befuddled state. As we neared the end of the esplanade, I glanced toward Sea View, to the light in the library window, where I imagined you were.

"She seemed to realize my attention had drifted, for she whirled on me, eyes blazing. I thought I was in for a reprimand, which I surely deserved, but she took my face in her hands and kissed me.

"There were still a few people about, and I feared we'd be seen." He frowned. "I am sorry you learned about it this way. Truly sorry. More than you know."

Unexpected tears heated Emily's eyes, and she blinked them back, reminding herself it was Charles Parker she loved, not this man.

"I will pack my things and take a room at the hotel," he said. "You are no doubt eager to see the back of me, and I don't blame you."

"I did not say you had to leave."

He twisted the ring on his little finger. "I think it best. For everyone."

Emily raised her chin. "And add insult to injury by departing early with me to blame for the loss of income?"

"I will pay in full before I go."

Perhaps Emily should have been too proud to accept his money, but her pride had taken too many blows recently to regard such a trivial thing.

She nodded. "Very well."

"Give me ten minutes."

Emily and Viola went into the office to wait. Emily retrieved his tally form and totaled his bill but asked Viola to be the one to take his money. Viola somberly agreed and sat behind the desk while Emily stood to one side.

A few moments later, Mark Stanley entered, valise in one hand, hat in the other.

After paying his bill, he tucked his small purse into his pocket and said, "Once again, I apologize. I also regret not being able to take a proper leave of the rest of your family. Do please assure them of my gratitude and best wishes."

"We shall, of course."

With a regretful parting look, he bowed and took his leave.

When he had gone, Viola said, "I am sorry, Emily. Truly. I know you probably don't believe me, but I am."

"Thank you." She pressed her sister's hand. "It's foolish of me to take it to heart. It was only a harmless flirtation, or so I told myself. Even so . . ."

Georgiana came in with the post.

"I saw Mr. Stanley leaving just now. I thought he meant to stay longer?"

Viola glanced at Emily, then said evenly, "His plans changed. I believe his sister wanted him to join her at the hotel."

"Oh. That's a shame. I liked him."

So did I, Emily thought.

When Georgiana had handed over the letters and gone upstairs, Viola gave Emily's hand a final squeeze, and went to see if Mamma needed anything.

Emily sat at the desk with the day's post, hoping for some good news to distract her from the unhappy scene with Mr. Stanley. Flipping through the few letters, she stopped at one postmarked from Edinburgh.

She eagerly lifted the seal and unfolded the letter. Noticing how unexpectedly brief it was, she read:

Dear Emily,

Thank you for inquiring into my well-being. I continue in good health, which is an undeserved blessing.

I was surprised to receive your letter. I understood from Aunt Mercer that Papa had forbidden any contact with me. So while I appreciate the gesture, please respect our father's wishes in future and refrain from writing again. Postage rates to and from Scotland are terribly expensive.

Sincerely,
Clarice

Emily's stomach knotted as she reread the stolid, stilted words. Claire, her Claire, had not written this. Yet she could not deny the handwriting was familiar.

And she had signed it *Clarice*. A nickname Emily had sometimes called her in jest when Claire had been too serious or mother hen–like. Was there a hidden message there?

Emily thought again of seeing Lord Bertram last night, his questions about her sisters, and Miss Craven's warning.

She rose swiftly and went to find Sarah.

29

[A] false step in one daughter will be injurious
to the fortunes of all the others.

—Jane Austen, *Pride and Prejudice*

Viola walked upstairs to see how Emily was doing after the upsetting encounter with Mr. Stanley. Approaching the small room she and Sarah shared, Viola heard her sisters talking within.

Emily said, "Do you really think that's why Charles withdrew from me?"

"I think it very likely," Sarah soberly replied.

"Because of one sister? That hardly seems fair."

"Like it or not, it reflects poorly on the rest of us. The humiliation and disgrace extend to us all. Some would see it as a proof of family weakness."

Viola pressed a hand to her mouth to cover a gasp. Betrayal snaked through her veins and twisted her stomach until she thought she would retch. She had known or at least suspected that Emily blamed her for Charles disassociating himself from their family, but that Sarah should lay the blame at her door as well? Categorize her flaw as a disgraceful family weakness?

Sarah went on, "What else besides this wretched business could have caused his withdrawal? When such terms of cordiality had marked the whole of our acquaintance?"

"I suppose you are right. . . . This must be the reason."

"I love her," Sarah said. "Yet I cannot deny how materially the credit of the rest of us must be hurt by her false step."

Emily groaned. "If this becomes generally known, who will willingly connect themselves with our family?"

The two continued to talk, but their words faded to a dizzying buzz like swarming bees. A false step? That struck her as unjust. But the rest of it? The humiliation, the proof of family weakness, the disgrace? Oh yes, Viola felt all of that and more deep in her soul.

When Viola entered the major's room a short while later, she found him flipping through the *Gentleman's Magazine*—the etchings and brief captions had proven easier to read than heavy columns of newspaper print. He glanced up at her once, then again, quickly setting aside the magazine.

"What is it? What's wrong? You look very ill indeed."

Viola made a face. "Thank you," she dryly replied, and then walked to the desk. "Where shall we begin today?"

"With you sitting down and telling me what has happened."

Viola hesitated. Should she confide in a man she'd been acquainted with for little more than a month? Yet the desire to unburden herself weighed heavily on her heart. She sat in the chair and turned to face him. "It's only . . . I overheard Emily and Sarah talking. I knew Emily resented me, but it's even worse than I thought. When I think of what they said . . ."

"Tell me."

"I can hardly bear to remember it, let alone repeat it."

"I begin to lose my patience. Just tell me. Confession is good for the soul and all that."

"Very well." She sighed. "I've long known Emily blames me, at least in part, for her hopes being dashed with a certain young man—a neighbor from May Hill. And when Emily is hurt, she can lash out, and often speaks without thinking. But Sarah . . ." Viola shook her head, feeling miserable all over again. "Sarah never says an unkind word about anyone unless it is true. And barely then."

"Go on."

"She said I reflect poorly on all of us. That my humiliation and disgrace extend to us all. She called it a proof of family weakness. Said she could not deny how materially the credit of the rest of them must be hurt by me. She also said something about impropriety—a false step—although I may have misheard that part. My heart was beating so loudly!"

His eyebrows lowered thunderously. "You must have misheard."

"Perhaps. But one thing I know Emily said—'Who will willingly connect themselves with our family?'"

Viola stared blindly across the room, shame washing over her anew.

She mastered her emotions by degrees and took a deep breath. "Do forgive me. I should not have told you all that. It was just so . . . shocking, though I suppose it should not have been." She rose and returned to the desk. "Well. You are not paying me to pour out my familial woes, but to read to you. Correspondence or newspapers first?"

Ignoring that, he asked, "What brought on this . . . talk of theirs? Has something happened?"

"I am not sure. Emily did receive a letter today, though I am not sure who sent it. Oh, and last night she attended a ball at the assembly rooms. Evidently she encountered someone—some friend of the neighbor who disappointed her. I suppose that may have set her off." She did not mention Emily's flirtation with a guest and the upsetting discovery that he was already engaged.

The major's forehead creased. "Had your sister a realistic expectation of this neighbor making her an offer of marriage?"

Viola nodded. "We all thought so."

"Why does she blame you?"

She gestured to her mouth. "For being like this. It casts a shadow over our entire family. Impacts all of our prospects."

"The devil it does."

She nodded emphatically. "Consider. So many sisters and none of us married. Well, Georgiana is only fifteen, but still. One cannot deny it has had an effect.

"Sarah's intended died. That, at least, was not my fault. Yet we all thought Emily would marry Charles. Until last year when he suddenly detached himself with barely a word of explanation."

"Why is that your fault? As a neighbor, had this young man not known all of you a long time?"

She nodded, considering. "I suppose it was one thing to befriend us. To flirt with Emily. But marriage and the prospect of children? No."

He shook his head, a bitter twist to his lips. "I cannot believe that your own sister . . . You know, you once told me your twin surpasses you in every way, but I beg to differ."

"It's true. She does. You saw her the day you rescued me, and again when I was injured."

He frowned. "I barely noticed her." He looked into her face. "Has she eyes that change color, from amber to green to the color of golden topaz, depending on her mood?"

Mouth ajar, she blinked at him. "No. Hers are brown."

"Has she charming freckles as you do?"

"N-no."

"And is her voice as clear and lovely as yours?"

"Well, she has not had to work on her enunciation for years as I have." In fact, Emily spoke rather rapidly, using many, many words. Father had called her a chatterbox.

Viola hoped the major would not ask to meet Emily formally, when not distracted by some emergency. For if he spent much time in her sister's company, he would never again look at her as he was looking at her now. His good eye shone with intense light, difficult to meet, yet drawing her like a winged thing to a flame.

He asked, "And how did your sister react to seeing my scars? Did she shrink away, repulsed? I would not blame her."

"Perhaps at first. But she will grow accustomed to them as she has to mine."

He snorted. "Evidence to the contrary."

"Please don't think badly of her. Emily has a passionate nature and says whatever comes into her head. But I still love her and always will. Although I sometimes wonder if she loves me."

"She seemed genuinely concerned about you the day of the accident. Are the two of you not close?"

Viola shrugged. "We might have been closer, except that I was a delicate child. Struggled to feed. Always thin. She was rumbustious, as children should be."

"Why was that a problem?"

"My parents and nurse worried Emily would accidentally knock me over and hurt my mouth. So they kept her away a great deal, which was difficult for us both, being twins. And then there were the horrendous surgeries and painful recoveries. No one wanted to see that." A hazy memory returned. "Though Emily did sneak into the sickroom once and held my hand and cried with me. How I miss her." Viola lifted both hands. "Is that not stupid? We live in the same house and I still miss her."

"Not stupid in the least."

She sniffed and wiped her eyes. "Forgive me. What a soppy bore I've been."

"Not at all." He hesitated, then in a voice low and husky said, "Come here. Please."

She stared at him, then walked slowly, warily forward.

He thrust out his hand toward her. His large, masculine hand.

Viola looked from it to his face and found his arresting, uneven gaze fixed on hers.

She swallowed and laid her hand in his.

He said nothing, only clasped her hand, rubbing his thumb over her knuckles, and continued to regard her in solemn silence.

Tears heated her eyes and began to flow, and she was powerless to stop them.

⌒⌒⌒⌒⌒

While Viola relished the comfort she had received from her visit with the major, it did not erase the feelings of betrayal and resentment that rankled her.

After reading to Mrs. Denby the next day, Viola retrieved the post on her way home. When she reached Sea View, she marched into the library, tossed the bills onto the desk, and turned without a word.

Emily called after her, "What's wrong? You are stomping around here like Georgiana on a mission. What is the problem?"

Viola turned back. "I am, apparently."

"What do you mean? I thought things were better between us."

"So did I, briefly."

"Did I say something to upset you? You are so terribly easy to offend, it's difficult to know. I admit I have said hurtful things in the past, but I sincerely don't know what I have done wrong now."

Viola walked closer. "I overheard you and Sarah talking. Blaming me for not only Charles breaking things off, but also for injuring all of my sisters' reputations and prospects."

Emily stared, mouth ajar, looking sincerely flummoxed. "What are you talking about?"

"Don't bother denying it. I heard you!"

"When was this?"

"Yesterday. I came to Sarah's room and heard you from outside the door."

"Oh!" Emily breathed. "I had just received a letter. Oh, Vi. We were not talking about you."

"Come, I heard you. Sarah called me a 'disgrace,' a 'proof of family weakness.' And you said, 'Who will willingly connect themselves with our family?'"

"We were not talking about you, I promise."

"How can you expect me to believe that? You have long resented me, and made it quite clear you thought I was at least part of the reason Charles distanced himself from our family."

"I know I did. And I was wrong. Completely wrong. It wasn't because of you, it was because of Claire."

"Claire?" Viola felt incredulity pucker her face. "Because she decided to move to Scotland and become a lady's companion? I know it reflects poorly—if accurately—on our financial situation, but it is still an acceptable role for a gentleman's daughter. Surely nothing to deserve criticisms like 'disgrace,' or 'a false step.'"

"I didn't know either, but Claire didn't go to Scotland to become a companion, at least not entirely. She went because she thought she had no other choice." Emily went on to explain the few particulars she knew. "Lord Bertram convinced her to elope with him after that house party. But somewhere along the way he changed his mind and deserted her, leaving her reputation—should it become known—in tatters."

"Lord Bertram?" Viola repeated, thinking back.

Anger darkened Emily's face. "I still can't believe I danced with that man! Had I known . . ."

"And you think Charles learned of it? And that's why he withdrew?"

"Sarah thinks so. It certainly aligns with the timing of his change toward us."

"Who all knows she left with him?"

"Sarah shared a room with Claire, so she knew. Claire begged her not to say anything until she was safely away."

"Even knowing it would break our parents' hearts?"

Emily nodded.

"Poor Sarah."

"Yes, she feels it keenly. Apparently Papa learned of it the next day and went after them, but by then it was too late."

Viola searched her memory. "I remember how angry he was. And how he refused to speak her name. I thought him so unjust! Why didn't they tell us?"

"They reasoned the fewer people who knew, the less chance it would become generally known and ruin the rest of us by association."

"Is that why Papa had an apoplexy?"

"Sarah believes so. It's only conjecture, but again, the timing aligns."

"And Mamma? Is this why she almost never mentions Claire?"

Emily nodded once more. "Papa said Claire was dead to him. Forbade Mamma from speaking her name. She has chosen to honor that request, even after his death."

"Good heavens."

"So now do you believe me? I am sorry you had to hear about it like this. Sarah only told me because I stumbled upon Claire's direction and wrote to her. The reply I received . . . well, it raised more questions than it answered."

"How so?"

"I will show it to you later. But it did not really seem as though Claire had written it. It was so stilted and impersonal. I think Aunt Mercer told her what to write. She was Papa's aunt, after all, and quite likely to enforce his edict."

"No wonder Mamma never liked that woman." Viola was quiet for several moments, taking it all in. Then she asked, "What are we going to do?"

"About Claire? What can we do?"

"Must be something. Also, now I feel awful. For I told the major what I overheard. He was quite furious with you."

Emily huffed. "No doubt in the past I would have deserved his censure, but not this time! You will make it right, won't you? Explain the misunderstanding when next you see him?"

Viola nodded, relieved for herself although concerned about Claire. "I will."

Viola walked over to Westmount later that day to explain. When she arrived, Taggart told her the major's father was with him, talking over some news from home, as he had received a letter from an old friend.

Viola decided not to interrupt them. Instead, she wandered into the drawing room, sat at the pianoforte, and began to softly play.

Some time later, the major came in and asked, "May I join you, Miss Summers?"

"You know I don't like to be watched."

"I know, and I promise not to stare."

Viola stopped playing. "You were right, by the way."

"Ah, my favorite words. What was I right about this time?"

"I did misunderstand what Emily and Sarah were discussing. They were not talking about me."

"I am glad to hear it. Do you . . . wish to tell me what or whom they were discussing?"

"Perhaps another time? I don't know all the particulars myself."

"Very well. You must be relieved. I know I am, for your sake."

"Yes." She exhaled a long breath, deciding not to share her concerns about Claire, not until she had learned more details.

Major Hutton stepped closer and handed her a few pages of sheet music. "In that case, might you play this piece? I purchased it at Wallis's a few days ago. Are you familiar with it?"

She turned the pages, studying the complicated score. "No. It seems rather difficult."

"I ask you only to try it. I shan't critique your performance. Music proficient I am not."

"Very well. Though I shall probably make many mistakes in my first attempt."

"Isn't that true for most things in life? Perhaps I might sit beside you and turn the pages, if that would help?"

"Can you read music?"

"I am out of practice, but I should be able to decipher the notes."

"In that case, please." She slid over to make room for him on the bench, pulse quickening in anticipation.

He glanced at the space she made for him but walked to her other side. "Do you mind if I sit here instead?"

"Of course not." She slid the other way, her heart hitching to realize he wanted to sit with his "good side" toward her. He sat beside her on the bench, flipping his coattails behind him.

She inhaled the fresh, masculine scent of his shaving tonic, his nearness filling her senses.

He leaned toward the music, his broad shoulder brushing hers. She glanced over, and saw his good ear and well-trimmed side-whiskers very close indeed.

He squinted. "My sight-reading is not what it once was—in more ways than one. If I miss my cue, nudge me."

Viola nodded. Side by side as they were, she would barely have to move to accomplish it.

She began to play, tentatively at first, faltering over a complicated measure, then gaining more confidence as her fingers became familiar with the melody and repeating refrain.

When she neared the bottom of the page, he leaned closer, following along, and his leg rested against hers. She could feel the firm muscle, the warmth of him through her muslin day dress and shift.

She nodded, and he turned the page, settling it into place.

After a slight pause, she continued on, finding her way through the measures like a winding path through a garden maze.

The music filled her, pleased her. She reveled in the rhythm of the lower notes rumbling through the instrument, the melody climbing from the depths, rising higher, then soaring.

"Lovely . . ." he murmured.

She glanced over and found his gaze on her, not on the music. Her heart thumped. She fumbled a fingering before soldiering on to the end of the page.

Again she nodded, but he didn't notice. The note lingering in the air, she nudged him, harder than she'd intended.

With a little grunt, he straightened and turned the page.

Nearing the crescendo, she closed her eyes, allowing the music its sway, the reverberating chords pulsating through her as though the strings extended from the instrument through her fingers and into her soul.

As the final notes faded, she slowly became aware of the silence, the stillness of the man beside her. He did not applaud nor praise her.

She turned and saw that he had turned not only his head but his upper body toward her as well, to better see her. His knee brushed hers and rested there. Was it a conscious action, or was he unaware of the contact . . . and the effect it was having on her?

Their faces, formerly a shoulder-width apart, were now even closer as he angled toward her. She drew in a shaky breath as the space between them dwindled.

He was so close. Achingly, temptingly close. Her fingers tingled, longing to reach out and stroke his cheek.

His mouth parted slightly and his eye burned bright.

He spoke in a low voice that rumbled through her as the music had done. "There is . . . so much I want to say, but words seem inadequate."

She ran a nervous tongue over her lips. His focus snapped to her mouth, lingering there.

He leaned closer, gaze lifting to hers, measuring, waiting. She held her breath, not moving, and certainly not moving away.

When she did not retreat or object, he leaned closer yet, his face, his mouth, nearing hers. Her eyelids fluttered closed as his lips touched hers, softly, warmly, deliciously.

A moment later, he lifted his head, breaking the contact too soon.

His gaze again met hers, and a soft smile teased a corner of his mouth. "Thank you. That was . . . perfect."

Leaving her to wonder if he had meant the music, or the kiss.

"Don't stop now," a voice called.

For a moment, confusion muddled Viola's kiss-addled brain. Don't stop kissing? She was ready to agree with that.

Then she realized the voice belonged not to the major but to his father.

"Play another. Oh . . ." His gaze fastened on his son seated close to Viola, and his eyes widened in surprise. "I say . . ." Awkwardness tinged his tone. "Pray excuse me."

"Not at all," Viola said, even as her cheeks heated.

The major rose from the bench. "I was only helping Miss Summers turn the music."

"Is that what young people are calling it these days? Well, I shall leave you to it." He turned and strode from the room.

The awkwardness spread to the two of them.

She rose as well. "I had better go."

He nodded. "Thank you for obliging me. By playing, that is." With a wince, he bowed and gestured for her to precede him out.

He walked her to the front door. There, he said, "I hope I did not overstep. The moment seemed to call for more than words."

She nodded, cheeks burning all the more. "I understand."

He studied her face with a look of concern. "Are you upset?"

She shook her head. "Embarrassed."

He ran a light finger over the hot skin of her cheek. "You, my dear Miss Summers, have nothing to be embarrassed about. Trust me."

30

Sews up Hare Lips. Fixes Gold Roofs and Palates.

—Josiah Flagg, Jr., broadside advertisement

Later that afternoon, Sarah and Emily sat in the library together, quietly discussing Claire's letter and the final preparations for the Eltons' dinner party the following evening.

Mrs. Elton entered the room, wearing a frown. "I can't understand it, but the response to our invitations has been most disappointing. I cannot help but think it must have something to do with this house or your family. Miss Viola, perhaps. Or maybe the weather. There must be some reason so few have written to accept, and not the ones we most wanted. Is there some village fête you forgot to warn us about?"

Emily shook her head. "Not that I know of."

Sarah took a steadying breath and said, "I am sorry you are disappointed with the response, but everything is arranged for tomorrow—the food is in the larder and Mrs. Besley has already begun preparing it. There's no going back now."

"Of course there is. There will be no dinner party. None we shall host, at any rate. I am canceling. Do what you like with the food. Serve it to your guests."

"But . . . you will pay for it, as agreed, won't you?" From the desk drawer, Sarah pulled the tally form itemizing the couple's expenses so far, including the cost of the dinner.

"Why on earth would we? My friends shan't be eating it."

Sarah expelled a huff. "We have gone to great expense on your behalf."

Mrs. Elton shrugged. "A risk of business, I suppose. One should not enter trade if one cannot bear the risks. Well. You are less disappointed than we are, I assure you."

"I highly doubt that."

Her husband wandered in, looking from Sarah to his wife and back again. "And what are we discussing?"

"We are discussing exorbitant fees." Mrs. Elton turned back to Sarah. "And I would like to remind you, Miss Summers, that we asked very politely for the music to stop, and it has not. Nor have you accommodated all of our special requests for breakfast. You will, I trust, compensate us for the many little troubles and disappointments by reducing our bill?"

Sarah stared, stomach twisting. "I am afraid we cannot do that."

Mrs. Elton's false smile faded and with it all semblance of civility. "That is a pity, for now we shall be forced to tell Mr. Butcher and Mr. Wallis about our thoroughly unsatisfactory experience with Sea View."

Her husband spoke up. "Now, my dear, I thought it rather pleasant."

"Do shut up, Philip."

Sarah swallowed. "I am sorry you feel you must do that. But I must still charge you the agreed-to amount."

"Wait until our friends hear about this!" Mrs. Elton glared at her in disgust.

Sarah managed to hold her gaze. "We must each act according to our own conscience."

Emily was less circumspect. "Go ahead and tell them, Mrs.

Elton. And why not begin with your bosom friend Mr. Lousada, or *dear* Lady Kennaway?"

"Perhaps I shall." Mrs. Elton raised her hands. "I have never been treated with such disrespect in my life!"

"Really?" Emily began. "That is not what I—"

Sarah cut her off. "Don't."

Mr. Elton silently held out his palm, and Sarah laid the bill into it.

"Do not pay that," his wife seethed.

"I am a man who pays my debts, Augusta, and keeps his vows, even when it tries one's patience to do so." He sent Sarah a significant look and pulled out his purse.

Someone rapped the front door knocker. Emily hurried to answer it, and soon returned with a surprising visitor.

Sarah glanced up and her mouth fell ajar. "Lady Kennaway. What an . . . unexpected pleasure."

At the name, Mrs. Elton whirled to face the newcomer, and her countenance took on a greenish hue.

"I have come to pay an overdue call." Lady Kennaway looked from stunned face to stunned face. "Have I come at an inconvenient time?"

"Not at all." Emily beamed. "You are just in time to greet your dear old friend, Mrs. Elton."

Mrs. Elton sputtered, "L-Lady Kennaway, I . . . I am . . ."

Lady Kennaway frowned at her, then turned to Emily. "I am not the least acquainted with this person."

"That is all right," Emily soothed, taking her arm companionably. "She will be departing soon. But you, I trust, can stay and take tea with us? Mamma has been longing to meet you."

"With pleasure."

Mr. Elton handed over banknotes and gold coins to make up the total.

Sarah accepted them with relief. "Thank you, Mr. Elton."

He gave her an apologetic nod and left the room.

When Viola returned to Westmount the next day, Taggart opened the door to her as usual. Inside the house, however, she was immediately met by Major Hutton, dressed in a dark blue frock coat, light pantaloons, and a fine waistcoat striped in tan and ivory.

"Miss Summers, might I have a word?" His manner seemed as formal as his attire.

"Of course."

She supposed he now regretted that kiss and intended to renew distance between them and restore their relative positions as employer and paid staff.

She followed him into the drawing room, which again seemed so formal after all the hours they had spent in his private room.

Once there, he began, "I have thought a great deal about our . . . last meeting. I realized that you might, very justifiably, assume that my behavior would, or at least should, lead to a declaration. You are a gentleman's daughter, a lady, and have every right to expect a gentleman to behave honorably toward you. I acted without thinking and allowed my emotions to . . ."

Defenses rising, Viola held up a hand. "Please stop. I don't expect anything from you. You are under no obligation whatever. You no doubt regret our . . . what took place, so let us say no more about it. Forget it ever happened."

He looked at her earnestly, appearing almost hurt. "Can you forget it? I cannot."

She blinked up at him. What did he expect her to say? She tried again. "I simply want to assure you, you are under no obligation. I expect, nay, want, nothing from you."

His brow furrowed. "You injure me."

She huffed. "What do you want from me? I am releasing you. Is that not what you hoped for? You are clearly regretting our"—she lowered her voice—"kiss."

"No. Not exactly. In all honesty, I am torn. As you are no doubt well aware, I am not a whole man. Making you an offer of marriage, while perhaps on the surface the honorable thing, would be incredibly selfish. If I were truly honorable, I would let you go."

"Nonsense. There is nothing wrong with you. Nothing that disqualifies you from the marital state."

"Blind in one eye, deaf in one ear, and half a scarred face do not disqualify me?"

"Far from it. Your injuries do not bother me. You are still a man, with much to offer a woman. But that woman is not me. I have no intention of marrying. In fact, I have long been resigned to being unmarriageable."

"Have you? Why?"

"Don't be stupid. It's obvious I should not have children. Marrying you . . . marrying anyone would be irresponsible."

"Has a physician told you that? Or is this your own conclusion?"

"I don't think physicians know a great deal about it, but most people blame the mother, assuming she must have had impure thoughts or seen a hare or someone with a cleft lip. But I don't know that it is *not* inheritable, as much as red hair or freckles or any other trait passed from parent to child."

"Is it not God who knits children together in their mother's womb? If He allows it, must there not be a reason?"

"What reason? What possible reason . . . what possible good, can result from this?" She jerked a hand toward her mouth.

His gaze lingered there. "I can think of something."

Looking away, he cleared his throat and asked, "What is your minor scar to mine? In your economy, I am far less worthy than you are."

"Not at all. You were not born this way. Your flaws are not transmissible to passersby or your offspring."

"I might have prevented mine. Acted differently. Defended myself. You had no choice. If either of us is at fault, it is certainly not you."

"I . . . want to believe you. However—"

"And I want to believe *you* when you say my injuries do not bother you." He shook his head. "But I don't."

Someone knocked on the partially open door.

Annoyed at the interruption, the major frowned and called, "Yes?"

Taggart opened it and announced, "Mr. Cleeves, sir."

Viola stilled. It *was* him. No. Why had the major not heeded her earlier warning?

Abner Cleeves stepped in, all smiles. "I know you are not expecting me. I only wanted to drop off the surgery estimate you requested." He handed a folded piece of paper to the major.

Viola stood there, paralyzed again by all the fear and powerlessness she'd always experienced in this man's presence.

Noticing her, Mr. Cleeves said, "Ah. Miss Summers. Major Hutton and I recently discussed your case. How . . . fortuitous that you two are acquainted."

The major had talked about her with *this* man? She was stunned. Sickened.

Taking advantage of her silence once more, Cleeves said, "Another of my triumphs. As I explained, her early procedures were not successful because her incessant crying strained and tore the sutures. But as you can see, she looks rather well now. Her appearance has exceeded even my high expectations."

The man smiled at her, and Viola felt as though she were frozen within a block of ice, her angry cries trapped within, unable to strike back, or even to move.

"Well, that's all for the present. I will see you soon." Cleeves bowed and took his leave.

Only when the man had left the house did Viola find her voice.

"Major, tell me you are not planning to let that man operate on you."

"'That man' is a renowned surgeon. A pioneer of new surgical methods, according to Mr. Bird."

"How does he know?"

"His colleague, Dr. Davis, introduced him. Apparently he spoke at a meeting of their medical society about advances in epidermic transplant. Everyone was very impressed."

She paused, taking it all in. Oh yes, Abner Cleeves had always been quite the showman—good at making himself sound qualified and his planned procedures all but guaranteed. But his skills did not back up his boasts.

Before she could begin a rebuttal, the major continued, "And he himself told me about many of his cases. A laudable success rate. You heard him just now. He admitted your initial procedures did not have the desired results because of crying, which I will not succumb to. You cannot blame him for that."

"Of course I cried! They gave me nothing for the pain save watered wine. Anyone would have cried."

"I won't. Besides, he assures me the pain will be manageable and the recovery brief."

She shook her head. "He has you fooled, just as he fooled my parents."

"You were young. And your memory is clouded by years and pain. Your recollection of details is not reliable."

Viola gestured out the window. "Then go and ask my mother. She was there and is certainly reliable."

"A mother cannot abide her child's cries. I doubt she can give an objective account either. In fact, I understand your mother became hysterical, so Mr. Cleeves refused to continue overseeing your case."

"Rubbish. Naturally my mother was upset. His attempts had left me worse off than before. My parents refused to let him try again. We had to wait because of the war, but when it was over, they took me to France to have his hack job repaired."

"I am sorry you had to go through all of that. But there is no point in arguing about your specific surgery, as what I require is quite different. He explained his process, and his experience with

369

other wounded soldiers. He even offered letters of recommendation."

"Works of fiction, I do not doubt."

He slowly shook his head, eyes downturned, almost pained. "I do not doubt you suffered. And I understand this rakes up difficult memories. Yet you sound so vindictive. Are you out to ruin this man? Perhaps he did not succeed with you, but does that disqualify him completely? Void his every ability, every technique he's learned and experience he's gained in the intervening years?"

Blood roared in her ears. "I don't trust him. And I don't want to see you hurt. Disappointed. Worse off."

"Worse off than I am now, you mean?"

"I did not mean you are in a bad state now."

"But I am. And I don't want to look like this for the rest of my life. Not if there's a solution."

"It's not worth the risk!" she cried, then took a deep breath, trying to calm down. "If you really must undergo a dangerous, unproven procedure, then find a different surgeon."

"Mr. Cleeves has pioneered this new technique. It is not as though any old barber surgeon or apothecary could do it. He is a specialist and has every confidence in his ability to reduce these scars."

She shook her head. "And when my parents consulted him, he called himself a surgeon dentist, skilled in repairing cleft lips and palates. You would trust a dentist to cut skin from other parts of your body and plant it on your face like the merest sod?" She felt nauseous at the thought.

"Mr. Bird and Dr. Davis both speak highly of him."

"And I have personal and negative experience with the man."

"From years ago, yes. Which means you cannot be impartial. Nor are you a physician or trained surgeon."

"So my word counts for nothing?"

He sighed. "I did not say that. But I have made my decision based on the best medical advice available to me—advice you,

Miss Summers, are not qualified to give. The procedure is scheduled for Monday. Dr. Davis has arranged the use of an operating theatre in Exeter."

Tears stung her eyes and clogged her throat. Might there be any truth to his words? Was she unfairly biased? At the moment, rejection and offense overruled everything else.

She stepped to the door. "It's your choice, of course, though I cannot in good conscience continue to come here if you put yourself in that man's power. I won't be a party to it." Grasping the door handle, she turned back. "Good-bye, Major. For your sake, I hope I am wrong. But I doubt it."

Tears blurring her vision, Viola hurried back to Sea View, ran past Emily straight to Mamma's room, and threw herself into her mother's arms.

31

I should be obliged to work weekdays and Sundays to earn
enough money to put straight what a silly hare had put crooked.
I knew it would take a deal of money to cure a hare-shotten lip.

—Mary Webb, *Precious Bane*

On Monday morning, the weather grew wet and blustery
again, matching Viola's mood.

Sitting with Emily in the library, Viola stared at the
fire and sensed her twin watching her. She glanced over and saw
Emily narrow her eyes.

"Why are you not at Westmount today?"

Viola gave a fatalistic shrug. "The major's gone. Gone to have
an awful procedure by that butcher of a surgeon." She had told
Mamma and Emily the news when she'd returned from Westmount. Only Mamma had seemed to understand her deep fears
about the surgeon and the danger he posed to Jack Hutton.

"Already? I didn't realize it was happening so soon. Why are
you not with him?"

"I have no place there. Besides, he knows I don't approve, and
we argued. Heatedly. He doesn't want to see me. And at all events,
it's too late. He's already gone to Exeter."

"Exeter?" Emily echoed in surprise.

"To an operating theatre there. I believe they were leaving early this morning."

Emily stepped to the side window and looked out. "Are you sure? There's a carriage at Westmount's door."

Viola hurried to join her there and squinted across the distance. "That's not the major's carriage. I think that's his father's chaise."

Emily turned to her. "I know I am the last person who should be offering romantic advice after recent events, but I know you. I know you care for this man. Don't you want to be there with him, to support him, even if you disagree with his decision?"

Viola's heart throbbed, and tears threatened. "You are right. I should at least find out what is happening. Perhaps something went wrong with his carriage, so they have been delayed. I will run over and see. Thank you, Em." She pressed her sister's arm, grabbed her hooded mantle, and hurried out the door.

Viola ran down the lawn, along the lane dotted with sprinkling rain, and up the drive to Westmount.

Taggart held the chaise door as the elder Mr. Hutton prepared to step inside.

"Mr. Hutton!"

He turned. "Miss Viola. I didn't expect to see you this morning."

"Has the major already left?"

His father nodded. "A few hours ago. Colin and Armaan went with him."

"But not you?"

He shook his head. "He knew I disapproved of the risky surgery as you did. Said I should return home and they'd send word later. I agreed at first. Now I've changed my mind. I don't feel right leaving at such a time. So I'm going to Exeter, whether he likes it or not. Father's prerogative."

"Take me with you, please. I want to be there too."

When he hesitated, she added, "I have felt terrible ever since we argued. If something were to happen to him . . ."

"I understand perfectly. Will your family mind? I am more than old enough to be your father, so I don't think tongues will wag, yet perhaps . . ."

"I don't care about that. I just want him to be well. I want to be there when it's all over, no matter what."

"So do I."

"Emily knows I am here, but perhaps Taggart could let my family know I've gone with you?"

Taggart nodded. "'Course, miss."

"Very well," Mr. Hutton said. "Do you need anything else, or are you ready to go?"

"I am ready."

Commanding the lead postilion to urge the horses to speed, they set off up the hill and away from Sidmouth. The postilion, taking Mr. Hutton at his word, drove the horses hard, even when the rain worsened. The two sat quietly inside the carriage, Viola praying until the motion of the vehicle lulled her into a fitful sleep.

They arrived in Exeter less than two hours later.

Stopping to ask a local person for directions, they then made their way through the busy streets to the hospital.

Leaving the chaise and weary animals to the postilion's care, they hurried up the walk and into the building, asking a workman with a mop and bucket where they would find the operating theatre.

"Operating theatre?" the elderly man echoed, face puckering in alarm.

"Yes, we are in a hurry, so . . ."

"You knew him, then? I am sorry. Dreadful sorry."

"What?"

The man shook his head. "Beastly business. Poor fellow died on the table. I didn't see it firsthand, thank the Lord, but I saw the students leaving pale faced, and one poor lad retched." He lifted his tools as proof.

"No!" Viola pressed a hand to her mouth.

Mr. Hutton gritted his teeth. "Take us to him."

"I covered him up, proper-like," the man said. "I don't know that you want to see him, truth be told."

"Take us to him," Mr. Hutton repeated, his tone harsh with suppressed emotions.

"Yes, sir. Right this way." The workman set down his tools and turned to lead the way.

They silently followed the man, who walked with a hobbling gait, down a corridor that smelled of antiseptic, sawdust, and blood.

Viola felt sick and her heart pounded painfully hard. She wouldn't, no, couldn't believe it. It could not be true. Yet had she not warned the major about this very possibility? She had told him not to put his life in that charlatan's hands but felt no satisfaction at being right.

As they turned a corner, a door opened a few yards ahead of them. Out of it stepped two men. She recognized one instantly: Abner Cleeves. Beside him was Dr. Davis, whom she had seen with him in Sidmouth.

"You!" Viola shouted, and both men jumped.

All her former fear and powerlessness ignited into white-hot fury. "You liar. Deceiver. Killer."

His colleague turned to him in alarm.

Cleeves scowled at her. "That woman is mad. Get her out of here."

"No!" Viola cried, standing her ground. "This is all your fault, Abner Cleeves!"

A stout older man burst into the corridor from a nearby office, looking right and left. "Cleeves? Abner Cleeves?" Gaze landing on the surgeon, his brows gathered like black storm clouds. "What the devil are you doing here?"

Mr. Cleeves lifted his chin. "Dr. Davis and Mr. Bird granted me permission to use the theatre for two procedures."

"I can't believe you had the gall to return."

Dr. Davis said, "Sir, if you are not aware, Mr. Cleeves is a renowned, highly trained surgeon."

"Balderdash," the stout man snapped. "Abner Cleeves was the worst apprentice it has ever been my misfortune to mentor. And since then, I've received several reports of his misconduct."

Unnoticed by the medical men, the workman opened a door marked *Operating Theatre*. Exchanging glances, Mr. Hutton and Viola quietly slipped away from the ongoing argument and into the room, afraid the others might try to stop them, given a chance.

Inside the room, the sight of a sheet-covered figure and bloody sawdust nearly made her gag.

Mr. Hutton pressed her arm. "Stay here. I'll look first."

She nodded, afraid she would be sick any moment. How much worse must his own father be feeling?

Face pale and grave, Mr. Hutton walked toward the table, approaching the shrouded figure. His hand, when he lifted it, shook.

He pulled the sheet back from the head and looked down.

"Thank God."

Hope tentatively rose. "He is not dead?"

"Oh, he's dead, poor soul. But he's not Jack."

"Are you certain?" She was afraid to believe it. "The man said it was a beastly business."

"I would know my own son. This man is closer to my age than Jack's." He respectfully replaced the covering.

Viola held herself stiffly, still dubious. "I don't understand."

"Nor I. Yet this is good news, for us at least."

"It seems too good to be true. Perhaps he operated on the major first, and this is already a second . . . victim?"

"Come, my dear. Let's get out of here and find Jack and the others."

In the corridor, the stout man awaited them. He introduced himself as William Snede, hospital administrator. "You are looking for your son, I gather?"

"Yes, Major Hutton. Is he all right?"

The administrator nodded. "He was to be next. But Abner Cleeves will not be performing any more experimental surgeries, not if I have anything to say about it. This way."

"Thank God," Viola breathed, finally able to accept that the major was alive and well. No doubt still angry with her, but as long as he was alive, the rest she could deal with later.

Snede opened a door and preceded them inside.

From behind the administrator, she heard the major ask, "Where is Cleeves?"

"He will not be performing any more surgeries here today or ever again, Lord willing—thanks to this young woman, who alerted me to his presence."

"What young woman?"

Snede turned to the side, arm sweeping in her direction. "I am afraid I did not get their names."

Major Hutton frowned. "What is going on here? Papa, if you used your influence to postpone the proceedings, I will not thank you for interfering."

"On the contrary," Snede said. "Their interference was most timely and appreciated. Thank you, Miss . . ." He peered closely at Viola's face and only then did she remember she was not wearing a veil. He said, "I say, that's a tidy little scar. Did Cleeves do that?"

"No. I went to France to have his work repaired."

"Ah. That makes more sense. For a moment, I thought he might have improved, but apparently not." He turned back to the major. "I promise you, sir, you do not want that man and his scalpel anywhere near you."

"Will someone else here perform the procedure, then?"

"No, I don't recommend it. The ancients attempted epidermic transplant, but we have little skill or experience in the present age."

"Then, what am I supposed to do?"

The older man rested a hand on the major's shoulder. "Be glad you are alive, to begin with, and be thankful to have people in your life who love you, as these two clearly do."

After that, they found Colin and Armaan in another waiting room, and explanations were given once again.

"Never liked the man," Armaan said.

Colin shrugged. "Smart dresser, though."

A short while later, they all departed the hospital together.

On the journey home, Colin rode with his father in the chaise. Armaan insisted on riding on the outside of the major's carriage, despite the rain, leaving Viola and Major Hutton alone together inside, although within sight through a small window for propriety's sake, and in calling distance should either of them need anything.

The brass lamps lit, the major handed her a lap rug and settled a second around himself. He stared out the window at the Exeter streets, then out into the passing countryside as daylight began to fade. She wondered if he was still upset with her for arguing and for further interfering today, yet he said nothing either way.

Finally, she asked, "Are you still angry?"

"Only with myself." After a moment he added, "I am sorry I did not listen to you."

"That's all right. I am just glad you are well."

He nodded, and he was silent for a few moments longer.

"Warm enough?" he asked in a low voice.

"Yes," she replied, and an instant later wished back her quick answer, thinking he might have shared his blanket with her, or sat closer, had she said she was cold.

Instead, she sat in quiet regret, and he said nothing more.

Viola began to feel agitated, the words she longed to say bottled up inside her, corked by worries about his regard for her, and fearing his good opinion might have changed.

He returned to staring outside, or perhaps he had even dozed off, head tilted toward the window, his right side toward her.

Could he really not hear out of his right ear? She grew increasingly restless in his silence and the long confinement.

With him focused out the window, or perhaps even asleep, and with the rumble of wheels and horse hooves filling the carriage, she decided to try an experiment.

She leaned close to his right ear and whispered, "Is this the ear you can't hear on?"

He didn't move. Made no sign he'd heard.

She waited a minute, then leaned close again and said, "Jack Hutton, I think you are wonderful just as you are."

He turned abruptly toward her. Her face flamed. Had he heard her after all?

His brows knit. "What did you say?"

"Oh, um, nothing much. Never mind." Embarrassed, she turned to gaze out the opposite window for the remainder of the journey.

When they finally arrived back in Sidmouth, they stopped at Sea View to return Viola home first. Major Hutton alighted ahead of her, offering a hand to help her down. Even when both feet were on the ground, he held on to her hand.

She looked up at him in silent question.

He leaned close to her ear and said, "Viola Summers, I think you are wonderful too."

32

Yesterday and today there has been very boisterous and rainy
weather, with violent wind . . . The waves have been dashing
over the esplanade and running into the town. Mr. Pepperell,
the dairyman, delivered milk to some of his customers by boat.

—Peter Orlando Hutchinson, diary

The wet weather continued the next day, with heavy
drenching rains that soddened the ground and spirits.
Due to the deluge, the Eltons had put off their departure
for another few days, although relations between them and the
family remained chilly.

Meanwhile, Georgiana and Effie spent a lot of time in the attic
rehearsing their play, which they planned to perform at the end
of the week.

Despite the rain, Viola put on a cape, unfurled their largest
umbrella, and hurried across town to visit Mrs. Denby.

The rolled-earth esplanade was puddled, and people huddled
under the awning of Wallis's Marine Library, staring out wistfully
at the sullen skies.

When she arrived at the poor house, she found Mrs. Denby
looking out her solitary window, wearing a worried frown.

She said, "I don't like how that sounds . . . or looks, from what I can see. Too much rain too soon. We've had flooding here before, you know. And this building is very near the river."

"Marsh Chapel is near the river as well. It must be safe enough."

The old woman snorted. "Hardly. Why they built it there, I shall never understand. The Sid bursts its banks every few years, usually starting near the ford just up the street."

She shook her head. "I still remember when the only cross-ing on the river was a tree trunk. When the water rose, debris would collect behind the tree and block the river, forcing it to flow down Mill Lane into the eastern town. Even now that we have the wooden bridge, flooding still happens, especially after storms or heavy rains."

"Well, let us hope the rain stops soon," Viola said, attempting to cheer her. "Shall I read to you, to take your mind off it?"

"No, my dear. I don't want you to stay long. I don't like the thought of you out in this alone."

"I have come this far. Let me read to you for a few minutes, at least."

"Very well. Luke six, verse forty-eight, then."

Viola opened the small New Testament and Psalms she had lent to Mrs. Denby and flipped to the appropriate page. She read, "He is like a man which built an house, and digged deep, and laid the foundation on a rock: and when the flood arose, the stream beat vehemently upon that house, and could not shake it: for it was founded upon a rock."

On the way home a short while later, Viola took the footpath from the church and stopped at Westmount. She wanted to see how the major was faring. She hoped the dismal weather had not depressed his spirits, especially after the distressing trip to Exeter the day before.

His brother greeted her warmly. "Ah, Miss Vi. You are just in time."

"For what?" Viola asked. "If we had an appointment, I've forgotten."

"No, no. But we need a fourth in whist. Most propitious timing!"

Colin led her into the drawing room. "Here is Miss Summers, braving the storm to save us." In the room, his father and Armaan sat at the games table.

"Perhaps Miss Viola might play for us instead," Armaan suggested, with a nod toward the piano, "and drown out the howling wind and rain."

"I am afraid I do not feel much like music at present."

"Then please join us at cards," Colin pleaded. "We've had a deuce of a time getting Jack to come out of his room and out of his doldrums. You are just the tonic he needs."

"Is he very low? I was afraid of that. It's why I stopped by."

"Go and see him," his father urged.

Colin added, "Drag him out by his good ear, if you have to."

Viola walked down the passage, knocked softly, and let herself in.

"Major? It's me."

He sat in the armchair, magazine on his knee, a candle lamp and cup of tea on the side table. When he looked up, pleasure lit his features. "Ah. The 'me' I most wanted to see." He rose, setting the magazine aside. "I was afraid it was Colin come to coerce me into playing cards."

"I just wanted to make sure you were all right," Viola said. "I know grey days can be difficult."

"True. Yet I feel better already, just seeing you."

Pleasure warmed her. Viola sat down, and he resumed his chair.

She said, "To be perfectly honest, I went to visit Mrs. Denby first."

His lip quirked. "Ah. Well, I don't mind being on your list of charitable cases. As long as I am at least your second favorite client."

"At least," she agreed, smiling softly at him.

After a moment, she stirred. "May I bring you anything? Read to you?"

He shook his head. "I have all I need . . . now. Tell me, what's the latest at Sea View?"

She did so, relaying the disagreement with Mrs. Elton and her threat to give a bad report to Mr. Butcher and Mr. Wallis.

"She sounds quite the dragon."

"I agree."

Colin stuck his head into the room. "Vi, really. You were supposed to drag him out of here. We are still down one player for whist."

She rose. "I shall come and play one hand *if* the major will tutor me."

Jack gave a good-natured groan and pushed to his feet. "Oh, very well."

They gathered around the table and the game began. Viola was not skilled, so the major offered helpful hints from time to time. Too thankful to be playing at all, the men did not protest overmuch.

Sometime later, the game halted when the wind violently shook the house. Viola looked toward the rain-splattered windows and said, "I had better go."

"Wait until it lets up. If it does," Mr. Hutton urged.

Armaan frowned. "I hope Chown is all right. He went out for provisions."

A few minutes later the side door banged open and Chown blew in on a gust of wind, water dripping from his slouch hat, face, and clothes.

"Good heavens," Mr. Hutton said. "Did you swim to the shops?"

"It's bad out there, gents. The river overflowed its banks and is flooding the streets. Shopkeepers are boarding up their doors and windows."

"I suppose that means no wine or cheese?" Colin pouted.

"Afraid not. The baker tossed me a loaf before he closed up. Bit sodden now." Chown lifted the drooping bread loaf as proof.

Colin sighed. "Oh well, at least the flooding is in the eastern town. Won't reach us here."

Viola's chest tightened. "The poor house is near the river. I read to one of the residents there. She is frail and does not see well."

"Surely someone will help her and the others, if needed. The vicar or churchwardens or matron?"

Viola rose. "I hope so. But I need to make sure she is safe."

Mr. Hutton frowned. "I admire your spirit, Miss Viola, but what can you do?"

"I don't know, but I must do something. Excuse me."

She hurried toward the door.

Behind her, she heard the major say, "Colin, there's a second storm coat in the upstairs closet. Fetch it, please. I shall get mine."

Colin said, "I don't want to go out in this."

"It's not for you. It's for Miss Summers."

Armaan said, "I will go too. One moment."

The major and Armaan caught up with Viola as she strode down the lane toward the beach.

After helping her into the coat, the three of them hurried along the esplanade toward the eastern town. They passed the Marine Library, deserted now. As they continued past Beach House, Viola drew up short and pointed at a startling sight.

Ahead of them, water ran down the street past the York Hotel and flowed over the esplanade. In the distance, she could see a wider swath of engorged river filling the estuary and encroaching on the shouldering marshlands in its mad rush to the sea.

Their route to the poor house was cut off.

"This way," Viola urged. They would have to go around, to the north. She led them back to angled Silver Street and followed it toward the churchyard. From there they picked their way past puddles and took Church Lane north toward the mill.

Water swamped the bridge at the ford, then ran in an angry, muddy-brown torrent down Mill Lane, spreading into Fore and Back Streets in twin cascades.

Viola's stomach sank. Between them and the poor house flowed roiling water at least a few feet deep and rising fast.

"I'll go," the major offered. "You stay here."

"But I—"

"You can't swim."

"I don't think anyone could swim in that."

"I can. And so can Armaan."

She gripped the major's sleeve. "Be careful."

Suddenly a boat came into view. How strange to see a fishing boat come rowing up the street, past homes and shops, as though on a Venice canal. At the oars sat Tom Cordey, straining hard.

"Tom!" Viola called, waving to him.

He maneuvered the boat in their direction.

"Need a hand?" the major called.

"Could do, aye. Current's strong. Pa and my brother are out in the skiff, so I'm on my own."

He rowed closer.

"I want to come too," Viola said.

The major shook his head. "We'll need room for Mrs. Denby and any others we find stranded. Armaan and I will bring her to you, I promise. You wait for us somewhere safe and dry. Shall we say the church? You can take care of her from there. Until then, maybe find something to cover her with if she's cold and wet. Can you do that?"

Viola nodded, chilled already and glad to have a task.

He gave her hand a reassuring squeeze, then turned, wading into the water in his tall boots. He climbed into the boat, taking up an extra oar. Armaan climbed in after him.

As the men directed the boat down the flooded street, Viola turned and made her way south.

She tried to make it to Broadbridge's to make sure Miss Stirling was safe, but the water blocked her way. She looked across the flooded marketplace and was relieved to see her in a boat with Mr. Farrant and a few others. Seeing her, Miss Stirling waved and called, "We're all right! Go home and be careful!"

Viola nodded and started toward the church. On impulse, she veered right, sloshing her way through a narrow alley ankle-deep in water, to approach Back Street from the rear.

She knocked on the back door of Mrs. Nicholls's shop. When no one answered, she tentatively let herself in, finding herself amid a flurry of activity.

"Oh, miss," the older woman said, catching sight of her. "Can't stop now, I am afraid. So much to do!" Nearby, her daughter hurried up the stairs with an armful of lacework. "Have to move all the lace upstairs, in case the water rises this high."

"May I help?" Viola had some time, she was sure, until the major might feasibly reach the poor house, collect Mrs. Denby and perhaps her neighbors, and return.

"Would you? How kind. Yes, please."

Following the woman's directions, Viola carried up assorted lace, some carefully packaged, some haphazardly stacked. She and the younger Miss Nicholls passed each other on the stairs like runners in a relay.

Now and again, Viola glanced from the upper-story window before rushing back downstairs. The water, dammed in by the wall of unbroken shop fronts, had risen to the ground-floor windows.

Finally, all the lace was out of harm's way.

"Thank you, my dear." Mrs. Nicholls panted from her exertions. "Now, was there something you wanted?"

"Perhaps something to keep Mrs. Denby warm?" Viola asked.

The older woman's eyes widened. "The antique shawl, do you mean?"

"Heavens no. I can't afford that. Nor would lace be practical in this weather. But if I could borrow something plain and warm, like a blanket? I will return it. The men have gone to gather the poor house residents who can't leave on their own or have nowhere else to go. I'm afraid she might be cold."

"Of course." She sent her daughter upstairs with instructions. While they waited, Mrs. Nicholls said, "I saw you with her at church, you know. Your friendship is no doubt a blessing to Jane."

"And to me."

A moment later, the young woman returned with a knitted wool blanket.

"Perfect. Thank you. I had better go."

Viola hurried out the back door, carrying the small blanket under the storm coat. Realizing it would be impossible for Mrs. Denby to walk all the way to Sea View, she stopped at Mr. Radford's. He had already shut up his shop, but answered her knocking, and agreed to let her borrow the Bath chair she'd hired before. Viola thanked him, then pushed it through the rain to the parish church. Reaching it, Viola waited for the others beneath the covered porch.

A familiar voice called to her, "Viola!" Sarah waved and hurried up the path to join her.

"Here you are. Thank God. I worried when I couldn't find you. I stopped at Westmount, but they said you and the major had gone to the poor house, and when I saw all that water blocking the way . . ."

"I am well. I'm sorry to have worried you."

"Where is the major? I hope he's safe too?"

"So do I. He and Armaan went in Tom Cordey's boat to try to reach the poor house."

Sarah nodded her understanding. "Mr. Henshall went with Mr. Puddicombe in his boat to offer assistance as well. I told them to bring anyone needing shelter or a warm meal to Sea View. We certainly have enough food."

Viola nodded. "Good idea. Though the Eltons won't like that."

"Oh, forget the Eltons."

"Huzzah!" Viola exclaimed. "And I mean that as a compliment."

Sarah quickly embraced her, then asked, "Will you be all right here until the men return? I would like to get back and start making preparations."

"Yes, of course. Go on. I shall see you there soon."

A few minutes later, the major and Armaan appeared, their arms around a small figure, heads bowed against the wet wind.

When they joined her under the porch, Viola said, "I am so glad you are safe."

Mrs. Denby looked up, blinking away the rain. "Thanks to these brave, strapping men."

Noticing the chair, the major said, "Good thinking." They helped Mrs. Denby into it, and Viola spread the woolen blanket around her shoulders.

Despite her relief, Viola was surprised no one else was with them.

"What about the other residents?"

"Mr. Cordey senior had already picked up Mr. Banks."

Mrs. Denby spoke up. "Miss Reed would not come. I tried to convince her, but she said if the water swept her away, no one would miss her."

"Oh no."

"Armaan and I will try again," the major said. "Tom is waiting for us with the boat. We'll see if anyone else needs help."

"If they do, please bring them to Sea View for shelter and food."

"Excellent. Thank you."

He turned to go.

Viola reached out and took his hand. "Take care, Major."

For a long moment he held her gaze. "I shall."

Viola yearned to kiss him but, constrained by the presence of others, made do with squeezing his hand.

When Sarah returned to Sea View, wet and winded, she let herself in through the basement door, unfastening her mantle as she went. She hung her wet outer garments and dripping bonnet on pegs in the vestibule, then proceeded into the kitchen.

In the doorway, she halted midstride, stunned to see her mother at the scrubbed oak table, uncovering bowls and platters of the food prepared for the Eltons.

"The beef and smoked salmon we can serve cold along with the salads. But these other dishes will need to be reheated. Are the stove and oven fired?"

Mrs. Besley nodded. "Lowen is stoking them now."

"Good. We'll also need to heat the soup. Just the thing for a cold, wet evening."

"Yes, ma'am."

"I think arranging the serving dishes on the sideboard will be best on this occasion. I will begin slicing the ham and tongue."

Sarah broke in, "Mamma . . . I am delighted you are up and about, but I have not seen you belowstairs before. How did you even get down here?"

"I walked, my dear. How do you think? Here, help me carry this soup pot. It's heavy."

"Yes, of course." Sarah hurried forward. "I can lift it. Don't overtax yourself."

"Very well. I'll slice the bread and set the butter near the stove to soften. No one wants to spread hard, cold butter."

Setting the pot on the stove, Sarah said, "Thank you for helping, Mamma. I doubted we could get everything prepared before people began arriving, but I see you and Mrs. Besley have everything well in hand between you. Where is Jessie?"

"Gathering all the extra cutlery and plates she can find."

Sarah nodded. "I will go up and make sure the sideboard is cleared and lay a clean cloth on the dining table."

Her mother said, "People can eat either there or in the breakfast room, or even the drawing room, if they prefer. This is no time for formality. Let's make everyone comfortable."

"I agree."

Sarah looked at her mother's contented profile and busy hands and felt a lump rise in her throat. On impulse, she leaned forward and kissed her cheek before hurrying upstairs.

33

Such a rushing happiness went through me; And I
felt as if it was so pure and strong it might even cure
me of my ill. There was some truth in it, too, for my
lip did never look quite so bad from that day.

—Mary Webb, *Precious Bane*

Viola paced up and down the Sea View veranda, praying Jack would soon emerge from the darkness. Inside, the house was awash in light and buzzing with voices as guests gathered to get warm, sip hot tea or cider, and exchange stories of the flood.

Outside, the rain slackened at last. Yet Viola's worries did not abate.

Might he have gone home to Westmount without coming to Sea View first? It was possible. Although he must know she would worry about his safety.

Emily stepped out onto the veranda. "He will be all right, Vi."

Viola twisted her fingers. "I hope so."

She was just about to walk down to the beach to discover if the Cordeys had returned or if any of the other fishermen had seen the major when a donkey cart came rumbling up the dim lane. As it neared, she recognized Major Hutton amid its three passengers.

Relief filling her, she grabbed Emily's hand.

When the cart stopped, Major Hutton and Armaan helped an elderly woman alight. This must be Miss Reed, with her veil askew. But at that moment, Viola had eyes only for Jack.

"Who is that with them?" Emily asked.

"Miss Reed, from the poor house, I believe. She didn't want to come."

"Ah. I remember you telling me about her. Leave her to me."

Her sister squeezed her hand, then rushed out to greet the newcomers. "Welcome. Miss Reed, is it?" Emily took the woman's arm. "Allow me to take you inside. Mr. Sagar, if you could assist me? We'll find a quiet corner and get you warm and dry. Are you hungry? The food will be ready soon, and we have far too much of it. You would be doing us a favor. . . ."

Emily chatted away and, with Armaan's help, led the woman into the house without protest. Leave it to Emily to charm even a woman with a heart of stone.

Her thoughts quickly returned to Jack. When had she begun thinking of him by his Christian name? He paid the driver and thanked him, and the donkey cart pulled away.

As the major walked across the wet lawn toward her, Viola stepped to the edge of the veranda. He reached the stairs and paused to look up at her. Two stairs above him, she was slightly taller than he was.

On impulse, she threw her arms around his neck. "Thank God you are safe."

He wrapped his arms around her waist, gathering her close.

Pressing her cheek to his—his scarred cheek—she leaned into him, savoring his warm embrace.

After several aching heartbeats, Viola pulled back slightly, clasping her hands at the back of his neck. His arms loosened but remained at her waist.

"I am so proud of you," she said. It was a new experience to look into his face from such a height. Such proximity. Such tempting access to his mouth.

His gaze kindled like blue fire. Something simmered there. Sparked.

As if of their own volition, her hands curved forward to frame his jaw.

Her focus shifted from his eyes to his mouth. She bent slightly, angled her head, leaned closer.

He inhaled a ragged breath.

She touched her lips to his, finding them cool, soft, and wet with rain. A moment later, that impression evaporated. He tightened his arms around her and kissed her back, his mouth growing warm, firm, passionate.

He broke contact at last, and it was her turn to draw a ragged breath. The hands bracketing her waist set her slightly away from him. He looked into her eyes, a tremulous smile on his lips.

Glibly, he said, "Remind me to rescue elderly ladies more often."

She chuckled.

A moment later he sobered. "Tell me that was more than a thank-you. Tell me you love me as I love you."

"I . . . do." She faltered, then repeated more confidently, "I definitely do."

"Did you mean what you said before? That I am still a man with much to offer? Despite my scars and the fact that I am blind in one eye and all but missing one ear?"

"Yes, I meant it. With all my heart."

"Does this mean you have changed your mind? That you are willing to brave a future with me?" His voice thickened. "Viola . . ." came his hoarse plea. "Say you'll marry me. Hurry. For I long to kiss you again."

"I will." She leaned forward and pressed her mouth to his once more.

In reply, he embraced her, lifting her from the veranda into his arms, her body held to his, his mouth pressed to hers. Then, slowly, slowly, she slid down the length of him until her feet, once again, came reluctantly down to earth.

⌒⌒⌒

Even though Sarah had not been able to help directly with the rescue efforts, she was glad they could at least offer those who had, and those displaced, a haven to get warm, dry, and well-fed.

Mrs. Besley, Jessie, and her mother were putting the final touches on the banquet in the dining room while Georgiana and Effie went around offering hot tea or cider, having ceased their play practice to lend a hand.

Soon the drawing room was crowded with a mismatched jumble of people. There sat Mrs. Denby and Armaan, not far from Mr. Gwilt and his parrot.

And near the fire sat the mysterious newcomer, Miss Reed.

Then arrived Colin and Mr. Hutton from Westmount, come to see if the major and Armaan were safe.

Emily quickly reassured them. "Mr. Sagar is just there. And Major Hutton is perfectly well too. Just, um . . . finishing up outside. He shall be in shortly."

Sarah said, "Do stay and join us. We are about to serve supper and have plenty of food." She gestured toward the dining room.

"Thank you. If you are sure you don't mind uninvited guests."

"Not at all. It is all spur of the moment. Or perhaps I should say, spur of the flood!"

Mr. Henshall came in behind them, followed by a reluctant trio of Cordeys, hats in hand, along with an elderly man from the poor house.

Sarah's spirits lifted to see them, her gaze lingering on Mr. Henshall, clothes damp, hair tousled, face ruddy from the wind. She had never found him more attractive.

Mr. Henshall wiped his feet and advanced into the room, but the fishermen hung back.

Mr. Cordey said, "Don't wanna muck up yer floor."

"Never mind that. Please come in. We're all somewhat bedraggled tonight. Here are towels for each of you, if you'd like to dry off a bit. And Mr. Henshall can show you where the water closet is."

"An indoor water closet?" Mr. Cordey asked, eyes narrowing.

"Yes, just upstairs."

"Have 'ee no privy?"

"We do—it's outside at the back of the garden."

"That'll do fer me. Never used an indoor privy in me life and don't mean to start now."

"Just promise you'll come back. We shall need your help eating a great deal of food. There's beef, ham, pie. . . ."

"Aye, maid'n. That I can do."

Effie approached her stepfather and spread a knitted blanket around his shoulders.

His expression softened. "Thank ye, lass."

Then the Eltons crept tentatively down the stairs.

"Well!" Mrs. Elton lifted her nose. "I see you are making good use of the food we paid for."

"Mr. and Mrs. Elton." Sarah scraped together a final remnant of kindness for the couple. "Will you not join us? These dear people either were stranded by the flood or risked their safety to rescue those who were. It seemed a pity to waste all of this good food."

Mrs. Elton looked from one guest to the next, hesitated on the well-dressed Huttons, then recoiled when her gaze landed on Mr. Cordey.

"I think not. One must have standards. Come, Mr. Elton. Back to our room for one final night of torture. I told you we never should have chosen this place."

Oh dear, Sarah thought. Well. She had tried.

Mr. Banks, from the poor house, had fallen in his first attempt to climb into the boat, so Sarah offered the elderly stranger dry clothes—her father's coat and trousers, and the shirt she had sewn for Peter. It had lain wrapped in tissue in her trunk long enough. She showed the man to an unoccupied room where he could change.

A short while later, at her mother's signal, Sarah summoned their guests into the dining room. "Come, everyone. There is a veritable feast awaiting you. I cannot tell you what a blessing it is to have so many gathered here to partake of it."

———

Some time later, Sarah sat down for a moment's rest, weary from all the preparations but pleased with how everything was going. There was something deeply satisfying about feeding people, she realized.

Nearby, in a high-backed armchair near the fire, Miss Reed sat stiffly, veil over her face.

"May I bring you something to eat or drink?" Emily asked her, and not for the first time.

"No, thank you."

A short while later, Mr. Hornbeam approached the matching chair facing the fire. He touched the back and asked, "Pardon me, is this seat taken?"

The woman either did not hear or ignored him, so Sarah answered, "No. It's free."

He sat down, set his dark glasses on the side table, and rubbed the bridge of his nose.

The woman glanced in his direction, then she turned again, studying his profile in the dim light.

"Simon Hornbeam?"

"Yes?" He turned toward the chair next to his. If one didn't know better, one would think he could see her.

The woman said, "I thought it was you. You probably don't recognize me. I am Miss Reed."

Sarah had not intended to eavesdrop, but she was too interested to move away.

"Not . . . Alvinia Reed?" he asked.

"Yes."

396

"Ah. Your voice is familiar. Are you visiting Sidmouth, as I am?"

"No, I live here. The po— My home was flooded."

"Sorry to hear it. I must say, I am surprised you remember me, when you refused my suit all those years ago—refused even to dance with me."

"And now you no doubt thank your lucky stars that I did so."

"No. I don't thank stars. But I do thank God that, after you rejected me, I met and married my wife, Mary. We were very happy for many years."

"Lucky you."

"I prefer 'blessed.'"

"And I suppose you had children?" Miss Reed said, sounding almost accusatory.

He nodded. "Mary and I had one son. He and I are not close. That was not her fault, though I often feel it is mine."

Georgiana appeared. "Here you go, Mr. Hornbeam. A plate of tarts and biscuits."

"Thank you, Georgiana." He accepted the plate and offered it to Miss Reed. "Will you have one? Miss Sarah is an excellent baker."

"No, thank you."

"Are you not hungry?"

"One cannot eat in a ladylike manner while wearing a veil. And I prefer not to remove it."

"Ah." He paused, and Sarah held her breath. "You had the smallpox, I believe. I remember hearing so, from a mutual friend."

"And you rejoiced in my misery, no doubt. Saw it as my just deserts after I rejected you."

"Not at all." After a brief pause, he asked quietly, "Is it . . . so bad?"

She sniffed. "It was. The scars had faded somewhat but are now magnified by wrinkles and age spots!" Her voice broke, as if confiding a great calamity.

He nodded his understanding, then said, "May I bring you

something to drink? Tea or cider? Georgiana would no doubt be happy to assist me."

"Did you not hear what I said?"

He winced at her sharp tone. "I heard," he replied, then added, "I find we often worry too much about how people see us. When the truth is, everyone else is more worried about how we view them. They might look, even stare, for a moment, but then their focus returns to themselves and their own problems."

Miss Reed studied him in dawning realization. "Are you . . . ? You are blind."

"Yes, I lost my sight some time ago." He picked up his glasses. "These were pinching me, but I can put them back on. I did not intend to fool anyone into thinking I was anything other than I am. Yet here, in these high-backed chairs, facing the fire, I thought it would be all right. No one is looking. No one cares if I remove my glasses, or you, your veil. They are just glad for a warm room, good food, and good company."

Miss Reed glanced surreptitiously around the back of her chair. People did not glance her way. They were all too busy chatting with whomever sat beside them, or enjoying a plate of food.

"Yes, please, Mr. Hornbeam. A cup of tea sounds just the thing. Can you manage it?"

"Easily. I know this house almost as well as my own."

He rose and walked toward the dining room. Miss Reed watched him go, then slowly pushed back the veil from her face— her scarred and lined face.

She lifted a biscuit from the plate, and as she did, her eyes filled. The sheen of tears gave her face a luster, a brilliancy, that made her almost beautiful.

Mr. Hornbeam returned. Georgiana accompanied him, holding a second cup. He handed the one he carried to Miss Reed. "Here you are."

"Thank you."

He settled himself once again in the chair, and Georgiana handed him the second cup. "Thank you, my dear."

They each sipped from their tea.

He said, "You had so many admirers in those days. I was not terribly surprised you did not consider me."

"That was a long time ago. I have no admirers now, I assure you."

"And whose fault is that?"

She gaped. "How dare you? My life was ruined through no fault of my own."

"Of course the disease was not your fault," Mr. Hornbeam said more softly. "But we choose how we respond to life's misfortunes."

"Easy to say now that you can't see me. But you were not blind then, Simon Hornbeam, and would have no doubt joined the other fellows in commiserating with my *poor* betrothed."

"Not I. I cut that man's acquaintance when he cut yours."

She reared her head back. "You imply you would have stayed with me, out of gentlemanly honor. Do you think I wanted someone to marry me out of duty? Charity? So, what? He could be admired for his long-suffering forbearance?"

After a moment he said evenly, "Bitterness is never attractive, Miss Reed. Even to a blind man."

She sucked in a shocked breath. Sarah felt almost sorry for her and regretted eavesdropping.

He gentled his voice. "It is futile to focus on the past, my friend."

"We are not friends."

"No." He shook his head. "Although we could be."

The door knocker sounded again, and Sarah rose to answer it. She was stunned to see upon their threshold the Reverend Edmund Butcher and his wife.

Excitement and trepidation filled her. "Come in, come in. I hope your home was not damaged by the flood?"

"No, no. We, um, learned a few of the poor-house residents were brought here and came to make sure they are all right."

"Yes. Mrs. Denby, Miss Reed, and Mr. Banks are here, and perfectly well. Please, do join us. We have plenty of food, and you are very welcome."

Viola came over to greet them, and together she and Sarah took the couple's damp outer garments and led them into the drawing room, and soon both were comfortably seated with plates of food and warm drinks.

Watching the proceedings, Emily raised both hands in triumph. Sarah feared the gesture premature. With the rooms crowded with coarse-talking fishermen, elderly people wearing blankets, and other bedraggled guests, along with piles of wet boots and coats, she knew Sea View was not looking, nor smelling, its best. *Oh well*, she told herself. Some things were more important.

Georgie glanced around the room and said, "I feel like we are all inside Noah's ark, safe and dry while the rain falls and floodwater rises outside."

Amused by this, people exchanged smiles with those near them. Many seemed to have already paired off in twos and threes by unspoken agreement.

Georgiana nudged Effie beside her, while Sarah found herself exchanging glances with Effie's father.

Across the room, Viola and Major Hutton grinned at each other like besotted fools, as did Mr. Gwilt and Parry. Meanwhile, Miss Reed sent a surreptitious glance toward Mr. Hornbeam.

Emily and Mamma sat near each other. The Huttons and Armaan. Mr. Banks from the poor house and Mrs. Denby. Mr. and Mrs. Butcher. And two pairs of Cordeys: Punch and Tom, Bibi and her father.

All safe and sound.

Gratitude washed over her. *Thank you, Lord.*

Finding herself with a quiet moment while the major talked with his family, Viola crossed the room to see how Mrs. Denby was faring. The old woman was seated alone on one end of the sofa, lap rug over her legs, Bath chair stowed in the hall. Mr. Banks had returned to the dining room to refill his plate.

"All right, Mrs. Denby? Warm enough? May I bring you more tea?"

"No, my dear. I have all I need." She patted the space beside her. "But I have something for you."

She pulled a flat square of folded brown paper from inside her bodice.

Viola sat down and accepted it. "What's this?"

The older woman reached over and unwrapped the paper. "You didn't think I would leave them behind with a flood threatening?"

"Your sprigs!" Viola recognized them as the woman's prized pieces of Honiton lace. The flower, leaves, and birds.

Mrs. Denby held up the flower. "The pattern was supposed to be a pansy, but it *could* be a violet. We'll call it a viola. In any case, I want you to have these. They may not be perfect, yet they're beautiful and give me such pleasure whenever I see them—as you do."

"Oh, Mrs. Denby. I love them, but are you sure? I know how you value them."

She nodded. "I have no daughter or granddaughter—except for you. There is no one I would rather give them to."

Viola squeezed her hand. "Thank you. I think these would look rather well, say, on a bridal veil?"

Mrs. Denby drew in a sharp breath. "Oh, my dear! Now that's one veil I would like to see you wear! I can think of no better place for these to end up."

"You are the first to know, so shh . . ." Viola put a finger to her lips.

"I understand." The woman's eyes shone with delight. "Oh! I am so happy!"

Viola kissed her cheek and then went to tell her mother.

34

The dove came in to him in the evening; and, lo, in her mouth
was an olive leaf . . . so Noah knew that the waters were abated.

—Genesis 8:11

L ate on the night of the flood, people with dry homes awaiting them, including the Cordeys, Butchers, and Huttons,
departed with many thanks for the feast. The poor-house
residents, however, could not yet return home. Mamma insisted
on giving up her room to Mrs. Denby, who was frail and far less
able to manage stairs than she was. Mamma said she felt stronger
than she had in years and would sleep in her husband's former
room. Despite these assurances, Emily noticed her breathing hard
and gripping the railing tight, all but pulling herself up the final
steps. Emily quickly offered an arm to assist her.

They gave Miss Reed the only other unoccupied guest room,
the one vacated by Mr. Stanley several days before and recently
cleaned. Meanwhile Mr. Hornbeam offered the spare bed in his
room—never slept in by his son—to Mr. Banks.

Amid all this bustle, Emily noticed Viola slip into Mamma's
temporary room for a few minutes and guessed what the two might
be talking about. Hopeful anticipation gladdened Emily's heart.

When all their guests were finally settled, she sought out Viola and found her in the quiet kitchen lit by lamps, heating a saucepan of warm milk.

Emily held out her hand, and Viola took it. Her twin's shining gaze latched onto hers like two halves of a locket.

"He asked you, then?"

Viola nodded, lips pressed together in a giddy smile.

"I knew it." Emily grasped her other hand as well. "Well done."

"Well done? It is not as though I set out to capture him."

"Yet you did. And you have me to thank. For I am the one who placed that advertisement, remember."

Viola chuckled. "How could I forget?" She squeezed Emily's hands before releasing them. "I do thank you."

"Though at the time you wanted to throttle me."

"True." Viola retrieved a second cup, divided the milk between them, and set them on the table. She stared dreamily at the flickering candle lamp and slowly shook her head. "I still can't believe it. I thought I would never marry. No one did. While everyone thought you . . ." Viola looked down, lips pressed in a thin line. "Sorry."

"It's all right."

Viola said, "If Charles does not come to his senses, in time some wiser man will."

"Or several! But for now, I am content. Truly. As long as . . ." Emily's teasing voice trailed away, and she tapped her chin.

"As long as what?"

"I get to be your bridesmaid."

Viola grinned. "Who else?"

The next morning, Viola shared her good news with Sarah as well.

"Do you mind that one of your younger sisters shall be married first?" Viola asked, feeling rather nervous.

"Not at all!" Sarah came around the library desk to embrace her. "I am very happy for you and the major both. Besides, it's past time we had a wedding in the family."

Viola tilted her head to regard her. "I was waiting for you to say what you always say—that you have already had one great love in your life and do not expect to have another."

Sarah gave her a closed-lip smile that did not reach her eyes. "I did say that a lot, I know. But now . . . now I wish I had not."

"Because of Mr. Henshall?" Viola whispered.

Sarah shook her head. "Mr. Henshall and Effie leave for Scotland in a few days' time. He has responsibilities there. An estate. People depending on him. Just as I have here."

"Surely there must be some way to manage both. This place and your happiness?"

Sarah sighed and patted Viola's hand. "You are kind to think of me. But wash off that long face. Today we are going to be happy for you."

When Viola left the office, Sarah sat back down at the desk.

A few moments later, Mr. Elton stepped in. "We are taking our leave. I have come to pay for the extra nights."

"Thank you, Mr. Elton."

Sarah glanced behind him but saw no sign of his wife.

After he had settled his bill, Sarah rose to walk him out. Mrs. Elton stood in the entry hall near their piled baggage, spine stiff, face averted.

Sarah took a steadying breath and said, "Safe journey."

The woman refused to look at her.

It struck Sarah as a vivid reminder that she had not only failed to please one of their first guests but had also alienated her. Regret dampened her spirits. She did not like to fail.

A coach and horses arrived, and Lowen carried out the couple's baggage. Mr. Elton opened the door for his wife. Head high, she sniffed and stepped through the door without a backward glance.

With a final apologetic look, her husband dutifully followed her outside.

Sarah watched them go with a heavy heart, wishing their stay had gone better and considering what she might have done differently.

Then, with a mournful exhale, she returned to the office.

In short order, another guest entered and Sarah's mood instantly lightened.

"Good morning, Mr. Hornbeam. What can I do for you?"

"Ah, Miss Sarah," he began. "Just the person I wished to speak to. I've been thinking; might you have the availability and the inclination to extend my stay?"

Sarah's mood brightened all the more. "My dear sir, we have plenty of both where you are concerned. In fact, my entire family will be pleased to learn you are staying on longer."

"Thank you. You are kind to say so."

Sarah privately wondered if this decision had anything to do with Miss Reed but decided not to pry.

Thankfully, the water that had rushed into the poor house during the flood quickly receded. When it did, Viola and her sisters went over to help with the clean-up efforts. Tall Mrs. Fulford was there, organizing, while Mr. Butcher and a few volunteers from his congregation joined them in the work. Even Major Hutton came over to offer his assistance, which only increased Viola's admiration for him.

When all was ready, Viola delivered Mrs. Denby back to her room, with promises to visit again soon.

Mrs. Denby pressed her hand. "Thank you, my dear. And thank you for sharing your home and family with me."

Viola kissed her cheek. "You are family now too."

That night, everyone was back in their own beds, and Sea View had been restored to some semblance of order and normality. Viola was exhausted. Even so, she lay awake in the dressing room off Mamma's bedchamber. The room was small, but the dividing wall gave them both privacy. With the door between them, one could leave her candle burning and stay up reading without bothering the other. Since she'd stopped taking a nightly draught, Mamma sometimes had difficulty sleeping, but tonight, it was Viola who tossed and turned.

She stood and opened the adjoining door. "Mamma? Are you awake?"

Her mother drew in a long breath and yawned. "I am now."

"Oh. Sorry."

"Don't be. I have been sleeping better since I've begun taking more exercise."

"Bathing, do you mean?"

"Well, that, and I've also been walking with Georgiana. Up and down the lanes west of here. With so many hedges about, few see me, which is good since I must look like a feeble old woman, trudging along with my stick. Yet I am slowly getting stronger and can walk farther than I could before."

She studied Viola. "But you did not come in here to talk about that." Mamma patted the mattress in unspoken invitation.

Viola walked over and sat on the edge of the bed. Moonlight from the nearby windows shone on her mother's face, revealing her concerned expression.

"Now, what is it? Are you having doubts about the major already?"

"Not a one. It's not me I'm worried about. It's Sarah."

"What about Sarah?"

"She likes Mr. Henshall—I know she does. And he clearly likes her. But he is about to leave with no hope of his affection being returned, because Sarah believes she can't leave her responsibilities here." Viola raised her hand. "I am not blaming anyone. I just feel bad. There must be something we can do."

"Has he made her an offer of marriage?"

"I don't think so. She has given him too little encouragement."

"They have known each other for less than two months—is that not right?"

"Yes. Six weeks or so. The same amount of time I've known Jack."

Mamma nodded thoughtfully. "Sarah is so much like your father. Both determined to carry everything on their own shoulders, unwilling to ask for help."

"Ha." Viola smirked. "Sarah has no trouble asking her sisters for help. *That* I shan't miss when I become a married woman."

Her mother chuckled.

Viola thought, then added, "Sarah likes to be needed, I know. But it doesn't seem right that she should deny herself another chance at happiness. I am not nearly as noble. I confess I did not give my duty to this house a moment's thought before I accepted the major. Does that make me terribly selfish?"

"No, my dear. Besides, you'll only be moving next door."

"True. And I could continue to help, if I am needed."

Her mother tucked her chin. "I cannot imagine the major's wife coming over to clean our water closet."

"No. That is one task I shan't be volunteering for."

"But I do hope we shall see you both often. After your honeymoon period, of course!"

Viola grinned at the thought, even as her cheeks heated.

Her mother gazed at her wistfully. "You really love him, don't you?"

Viola nodded.

"And it's obvious he loves you. Oh, my dear. You don't know what a pleasure it is to see you so happy. To see your beautiful smile on your beautiful face." She laid a finger beneath Viola's chin, and her voice thickened. "And to know a worthy man has come to recognize what I have always seen in you." She caressed Viola's cheek before releasing her.

"Now, you start thinking about your wedding, and leave Sarah to me. Agreed?"

Heart warm and eyes damp, Viola nodded. "Thank you, Mamma."

In honor of their last full day together, Georgiana and Effie announced they would be performing their play, which they had been rehearsing for some time.

Georgie had wanted to borrow one of the Cordeys' boats as a prop, but Sarah forbade her to ask, reminding her that, first of all, the boats were the men's livelihood. Second, they were heavier than they appeared. And third, she did not want a damp, sandy, smelly boat in their house—even if they could fit it through the door, which she doubted.

So instead, the girls fashioned a boat from a slipper bath wrapped in brown paper and placed in the parlour, the blue velvet curtains a fitting backdrop. Nearby stood a stool covered by a dark cloak. Seven chairs had been set before this makeshift stage, and at the appointed hour, they were filled by Emily, Viola, Mamma, Mr. Hornbeam, Mr. Henshall, Sarah, and Mr. Gwilt on the end. The parrot cage was strangely absent.

Sarah leaned close to Mr. Gwilt and asked, "Where's Parry?"

Eyes shining, he whispered conspiratorially, "Getting ready for his big entrance."

In the play, Effie had cast herself as a ship's captain, sailing the high seas.

A storm blew up and flooded an island, until all that was left was one spot of dry land on a hilltop. Marooned there was a beautiful maiden, portrayed by Georgiana.

It amused Sarah to see her rough-and-tumble sister in an elegant dress, her hair curled and pinned atop her head, wearing a tiara, a necklace, and even a bit of rouge on lips and cheeks. She looked pretty and startlingly grown up.

Effie, meanwhile, wore a borrowed tricorne, one of her father's coats, and a painted-on mustache. She was rather amusing as a swaggering seaman. The unexpected casting required both girls to behave quite differently from themselves, and perhaps that was why they had chosen the parts they had.

Georgiana stood atop the stool and waved a handkerchief, calling in melodramatic style, "Help, help! The water is rising and I shall be swept away!"

"Never fear, I shall rescue ye!" Effie replied. She feigned rowing and then gave Georgiana a hand into the "boat." "Come aboard, fair lady."

Unfortunately, the girls' acting was as unpolished as the script. They ought to have asked Emily to write something for them.

When both girls stood in the boat, they exaggerated swaying to and fro.

Georgie said in a high, affected voice, "Oh dear! The storm has worsened."

Effie raised her hands. "And I have lost the oars."

"Oh no!" Georgie exclaimed. "How shall we reach safe haven now?"

"I can swim. Can *you*?" the captain asked.

"Not one stroke," Georgie replied. "We're doomed."

Suddenly a parrot flew across the water, alighted on the boat, and squawked. This was Parry, carried by Mr. Gwilt, who had been recruited to help in the play. The bird was out of his cage, but permanently attached to his perch.

"Please, Mr. Parrot," Georgie said. "If you can talk, fly to shore and summon help."

"He canna talk," Effie said. "He only squawks."

"Not so, me hearties!" Mr. Gwilt parroted. "I talk. And I shall fly to dry land and bring help."

Mr. Gwilt carried off his bird with a few extra squawks for good measure.

Several more stilted lines of nonsense followed, then the captain clasped the lady's hand and said, "When this is all over, ye must marry me."

"But, sir, we are too different. From different lands with different . . . accents. It would never do."

"Ye mustn't say that. You'll break my heart. Only true love matters. . . ."

Sarah began to grow uncomfortable. Were the girls trying to teach her a lesson, having devised this play to get their point across?

"If the parrot doesna return soon, I must try to swim to shore."

Georgie crossed her hands over her chest and sighed dramatically. "If you don't return, sir, I shall never forget you!"

Drawn by Georgiana's hands, Sarah found herself looking more carefully at the costume necklace she wore, sparkling blue in the lamplight. Wait. Could it be? She glanced over at Mr. Henshall and saw his eyes narrowing on it as well.

Sarah stood and called, "Intermission!"

Georgiana frowned. "What? Sarah, no, there is no intermission."

"There is now. That necklace. Where did you get it?"

Georgiana shrugged. "Upstairs in the nursery with all of the other cast-off toys and things. They're only paste. There were earrings too, but they pinched."

Mr. Henshall walked closer to study the blue gems set in gold.

"That's not paste, lass. That's the real thing."

Effie looked from the necklace to her stepfather. "I dinnae understand. How do ye know?"

"Those belonged to your mother. She . . . left them when we stayed here a few years ago."

Effie's eyes widened and her mouth parted, yet no words emerged.

He touched her shoulder. "I believe she would have wanted ye to have them."

"Ye never mentioned them to me before."

"I did not want to raise your hopes, should we never find them."

Sarah added, "Your father and I have been searching for them, as a matter of fact. We found the case in the nursery, but it was empty."

"I had taken them to my room," Georgie said. "I found them when I moved to the attic and later put them with our costumes."

Georgie turned back to Effie, eyes shining. "I told you it would look better on you." She reached behind herself, undid the clasp, and with ceremonial air, placed the gold chain around her friend's neck as though a laurel wreath.

"From your mamma," she whispered.

Effie gently, reverently touched the necklace, then looked up again, a small smile of wonder on her lips, even as her eyes filled with tears.

35

No piece of Honiton lace is the work of one
lace maker; many hands contributed.
—Carol McFadzean, *Sidmouth's Lace*

Viola returned to the poor house later that day to visit
Mrs. Denby now that she was once again settled into
her room.

When Viola arrived, she handed her two parcels wrapped in
paper.

"What are these? More biscuits?"

Viola shook her head, excitement rippling through her.

Mrs. Denby peeled back the paper of the first. "Ah, the spectacles! You remembered." She slid on the earpieces and looked at
Viola through the oval lenses. "You are even prettier than I thought.
Thank you, my dear."

"Now open this one," Viola urged.

Mrs. Denby opened the larger second parcel. She bent to look
closer, then pressed a hand to her bosom. "The lace shawl . . ."
Her eyes, large behind the lenses, rose to meet Viola's. "It is really
for me?"

"Of course it is."

"But . . . how? It was terribly expensive."

"Mrs. Nicholls gave me a very good price when she learned it was for 'dear Jane.' I had earned extra money taking on another client. And the major insisted on contributing to the gift, as he knows how fond of you I am."

"So kind. All of you."

The older woman carefully fingered the lace sprigs. "I made these birds. My sister, this edging of leaves. My mother, the flowers. And my aunt did the sewing, joining the pieces together. It's as I told you, no finished piece is the work of one person." She stared at the shawl, eyes misty with memory. "A solitary soul can do little. But together . . . what lasting beauty we create."

Mrs. Denby looked up with a watery smile. "Thank you, my dear. I shall treasure it always. And when I am gone, I want you to have it, all right? No arguing. That's as it should be."

Viola's eyes filled. She blinked back tears and squeezed the woman's hand. "Very well, but only if you promise to live for a good long time."

A short while later, as Viola was leaving the poor house, she encountered Mr. Butcher on his way in.

"Ah, Miss Summers. A pleasure to see you again."

"Thank you, sir. It was good of you to help with the cleanup."

"And you." He twisted his mouth in thought and rocked on his heels. "By the way," he said, "I know I declined your sister's invitation to visit Sea View, and that my unplanned visit the night of the flood did not exemplify a usual stay there."

Was that a criticism or a compliment? Viola felt mildly defensive on her family's behalf. "No. It was quite a hodgepodge of people. And the food not our usual fare."

"It was excellent, and the company diverse, diverting, and welcoming. Mrs. Butcher and I enjoyed ourselves immensely."

Relief. "I am glad to hear it. And it was kind of you to make sure the residents were safe."

He dipped his head, looking mildly sheepish. "I know I said

that's why I was there. But the truth is, I came for two other reasons: you and Major Hutton."

"Major Hutton?" she echoed.

He nodded. "He had been putting me off as I had been your sister. At last he invited me over and extolled the virtues of Sea View and its hostesses—insisted I pay a call. And he is not a man easily refused."

She grinned. "As I am very well aware."

"I was still procrastinating when the flood came. So I used the excuse of making sure the residents were faring well, although I had already heard that they were in good hands. In reality, I wanted to see the place for myself."

Viola waited, afraid to hope.

"You may be glad to know that I will be mentioning Sea View in the new edition of my guidebook. And it will be a positive review."

Satisfaction warmed her. "That is good news, indeed. My mother and sisters will be delighted. Thank you, Mr. Butcher."

She held out her hand and he took it.

"You deserve the praise, my dear. I have been impressed with you since our first meeting. Now." He released her hand and straightened. "How is our Mrs. Denby today?"

"She is well. Cheerful. Delightful as usual."

"And Miss Reed?" He looked toward her door, as if steeling himself. "I suppose I should visit her first."

"She is not here," Viola was pleased to report.

"What?" Concern darkened his features. "Where else would she be? I thought she returned with the others."

"She did. But today she is taking tea at Sea View with one of our guests. The two were old friends, apparently, who had fallen out of touch, and met again the night of the flood."

He shook his head in amazement. "And people doubt that miracles still happen."

Early the next morning, Mr. Henshall came out to join Sarah on the veranda one last time.

"All packed?" she asked.

He nodded and sat beside her, looking not at her but at the horizon. Voice low, he said, "I wish I had a great fortune. Then I might end your financial difficulties and the need for the guest house."

She glanced at his pensive profile and replied gently, "Even if you had, we could not accept it."

"Perhaps ye could. If I . . . If we were . . ." He ran a hand over his face. "It's all useless conjecture, in any case, for I havena a great fortune. I have property and means, aye, but am tied to the land."

"I know," she said. Of course he must leave. She had known it all along. "I am sorry, Mr. Henshall. It was a generous thought, though."

Emotions flickered over his face, then he drew a deep breath, schooling his features. "Ah well. I canna expect to win a woman's regard so quickly, especially when she first suspected I was a thief or worse."

Sarah managed a wan chuckle, even as her chest ached. "I wish things were different, but they are not."

"Might I write to ye, at least?"

Sarah hesitated, feeling torn. "To what end?"

He flinched, and she regretted her hasty words. Yet would not a clean break be better—or at least easier—for them both?

Sarah rose, clasping her hands over her roiling insides. "So." She tried to keep her tone light. "What time does your coach depart?"

He rose as well. "Nine. The lad with the donkey cart should soon be here to take us to the inn."

She swallowed and offered her hand. "Then I wish you and Effie a safe journey."

For a moment, he held her gaze. Then he took her hand, pressed a kiss to the back of it, and departed.

Sarah stood there, rubbing the warm spot with her thumb, until the donkey cart arrived and minutes later rumbled away.

Longing for consolation and assurance that she had done the right thing, Sarah was tempted to seek out her mother. Instead, she went into the library to distract herself with her daily list of tasks.

A short while later, she was surprised when her mother came to find her. "Good morning, my dear."

Sarah rose. "Good morning, Mamma. Do you need something? Can I bring you a cup of tea?"

"Sit down, child. You don't need to wait on me every moment. I like your attention, I admit, but you are not my nurse. Nor do I need one any longer."

Sarah's gaze swept over her. "You are looking rather well, I must say."

"Thank you." Her mother stepped to the window. "The Henshalls departed on time?"

"Yes, a short while ago."

"Sorry to see him go?" Her mother turned to her, expression measuring.

"Maybe a little." Sarah tilted her head to study her mother's face. "Why are you looking at me like that? I never set my cap at him, and I never expected anything to come of our . . . friendship. Certainly not romance. I like him, yes. But it's completely impractical to ponder a future between us. He lives in Scotland and I live here. And we have known each other only a short time."

"About the same amount of time Viola and Major Hutton have been acquainted, and they are engaged."

"It is not the same. Viola and the major both live here, and she may give up reading to invalids any time she likes, whereas my responsibilities will continue."

At the thought of the tasks awaiting her, Sarah said, "Mamma, might we talk later? I have a great deal to do today."

"Like?"

"Like discussing this week's menu with Mrs. Besley and writing up orders for the butcher and greengrocer."

"Already done."

"Oh. Then there are the bills and quarterly wages."

"Paid those too."

"You did?"

"Yes. And Georgiana and Bibi have made all the beds. Emily is all caught up on correspondence. And I dusted the parlour myself."

Sarah blinked in surprise.

"I am slowly regaining my strength," Mamma continued. "I admit helping with the feast the night of the flood exhausted me, but I *am* getting better."

"Due to the sea-bathing, do you think?"

Georgiana came in to join them, replying, "That and the long walks we've been taking."

Emily and Viola appeared in the threshold as well.

"I am thankful," Sarah said. "Yet we still need to work out how to attract more guests. If we don't increase our income soon, we will be in trouble."

"Taken care of," Emily said. "Sea View will be mentioned in the new edition of *The Beauties of Sidmouth Displayed*. I asked Mr. Wallis for a peek and copied down the addition." She handed Sarah a slip of paper, which read,

Sea View is a guest house in the western town, owned and managed by Mrs. Summers and her daughters. The Summers family deserve particular commendation and support for adding to the accommodation of visitors by every species of comfort, neatness, and domestic attention. The house is delightfully situated, with charming views of the sea and the surrounding country. Meals plentiful and excellent. Overall, Sea View is a delightful abode for those not wishing the expense of a private lodging house.

Mind wheeling, Sarah read it again, almost afraid to believe it. "But . . . how?"

"Major Hutton put in a good word for us—even insisted Mr. Butcher call here. That's at least part of the reason he came here the night of the flood."

417

Emily regarded her twin with a twinkle of admiration. "Personally, I think it was because he was impressed with our Viola and all her good works."

Sarah slowly sank into the desk chair. Whatever the reason, she was filled with gratitude and relief.

She suddenly sat up straight and tapped the register. "This will probably mean more guests and more work for us all to do. Except for you, of course, Viola."

Sarah considered, then added, "This gives me an idea. Mr. Gwilt told me he would like to stay here as long as he can afford to. I wonder if we might offer him a job. He used to work for a bank, and I need help with the accounts, but we could not justify a dedicated bookkeeper."

"Then perhaps he could help in other ways too," Emily said. "Lowen can barely carry pails of water and valises up all those stairs, let alone heavy trunks."

"True. But how would you all feel about him staying on here in some . . . official capacity?" Sarah looked from face to face, then added gingerly, "Keeping him means keeping Parry, you know."

"Mr. Gwilt is kind for his eccentricities," Emily defended.

Mamma nodded. "I've spent only a little time with him, yet he seems a humble, respectful man."

"True. And I like Parry," Georgiana added. "Though if they stay on, let us hope Chips never catches him out of his cage."

Again Sarah tapped the register. "*If* and when we have a steady stream of guests, we could afford to pay him. In the meantime, perhaps we might reimburse him with room and board, if he is willing. Are we in agreement?"

They all nodded.

"Very well. I shall speak to him."

Emily tipped her head to the side. "Speaking of a 'steady stream of guests,' did Mr. Henshall say anything about coming back next year?"

"No."

"Did you ask him to return?"

"Of course not."

Emily turned to Georgiana. "Did Effie say anything?"

Georgie shook her head. "Mostly she bemoaned the long journey."

"There, you see?" Sarah said. "That is that."

She feigned nonchalance even as regret filled her. Should she have invited him to return? Or at least given him permission to write to her?

Sarah cleared her throat. "I doubt we shall ever see them again."

"That is up to you," Emily said. "We have his direction, after all. What is to stop you from writing to him? In fact, as proprietor of the Sea View guest house, I'd say you are obligated to write to thank him for his stay and let him know he is more than welcome to return." She waggled her eyebrows.

Hope rose until reality quashed it. "It would be terribly brazen of me to write to him."

Emily shrugged. "Then I shall write to him on your behalf. That advertisement I wrote for Viola did a world of good."

"Oh no, you won't!" Sarah shook her head. "If anyone writes to him it shall be me."

Emily grinned. "I am very glad to hear it."

Eventually, her family dispersed. Finding her tasks completed, Sarah went into the parlour to continue embroidering the handkerchief for Mamma.

As she crossed the room, something on her worktable caught her eye. She walked closer, then stilled. There atop the table lay a thistle—green stalk, spiny bulb, purple flower crown—the symbol of Scotland. The image of Callum Henshall sprang to mind, and with it a wistful smile quivered on her lips.

Sarah gingerly reached out. Touching the spiky flower brought a small stab of pain as well as hope. Memento or no, she guessed a certain Scotsman would never be far from her thoughts.

36

The bride was elegantly dressed; the two bridesmaids
were duly inferior; her father gave her away; her mother
stood with salts in her hand, expecting to be agitated.

—Jane Austen, *Mansfield Park*

The next day, Sarah gathered her thoughts and went to talk to Mr. Gwilt. She found him on the veranda, Parry perched on a nearby chair. She sat on his other side, feeling unaccountably nervous.

"Beautiful day, Miss Sarah, is it not?" He glanced at her and then took a deep breath of fresh sea air. "I loves it here, I do."

"I am glad."

Twisting her hands in her apron, she began, "Mr. Gwilt, my family and I have been discussing your situation. And we don't want you to deplete your savings by staying here and paying guest-house rates."

His face creased in a sad smile. "If you don't want us here, then of course, we shall go."

"No, no. You misunderstand me. We are all happy for you to stay. We were only wondering if you might be willing to work for us in exchange for room and board? You mentioned you've been a clerk and bookkeeper, and I could certainly use help in those areas."

His small eyes brightened. "Are you in earnest?"

She added quickly, "I should make it clear this would not be an all-day job, nor can we afford to pay regular wages. Although that is a possibility for the future, if we are successful here. I'm afraid we would have to add other tasks as well, like carrying trunks and bathwater and that sort of thing. Lowen is getting older, so we could use another man around the place. However, I have no wish to offend you, if that seems—"

"Offend me? Not in the least. You honor me. That you would put your trust in me, well . . . I am nearly as speechless as Parry."

Tentatively, she asked, "You would not deem such manual work beneath you?"

"Miss Sarah. If I ever had such unwarranted pride, it has long been driven from me. I would find it a pleasure to serve your family and your guests."

She bit her lip. "We would probably have to ask you to move to a different room. There is a spare room belowstairs—originally meant for a butler—and several small rooms in the attic."

He shook his head. "Wouldn't dream of intruding on Miss Georgiana's privacy, but if the folks belowstairs would not mind an addition to their number, then that would suit us fine. I would warn Parry to keep the noise down, never fear." He winked.

Sarah remained serious. Better to address all of the uncomfortable topics ahead of time so he would know what he was agreeing to. "About Parry . . ." She glanced at the bird and felt a stab of guilt. "He would certainly be welcome in your room, but we would have to ask that he stay there, at least when you're working."

"Right you are, Miss Sarah. I understand. Never fear, I will explain to him, I will."

Sarah exhaled in relief. "Good. Well. We can iron out the particulars later."

The following week, Mamma handed Sarah a large, flat parcel.

"What's this?" Sarah asked.

"It's for you—well, for all of us, really, but I wanted you to see it first. Go on."

Sarah peeled the wrapping from the rectangular box and lifted the lid.

Nestled in tissue lay the china plate rimmed in gold. The heirloom she had broken, with the colorful image of three young girls in Chinese robes, clustered close as a fourth read to them. The gift from their father.

It had somehow been put back together, though faint lines from the repaired cracks were visible if one looked close. Yet it was, again, in one piece.

"How did you manage this?" Sarah asked. "I had given up. It seemed hopeless to me—too badly broken."

"Oh, you know Miss Stirling," Mamma replied. "She knew 'the very person.'"

"Ah. Of course she did."

Her mother traced her finger over one of the repairs. "I know it's not perfect. You can see where a few original pieces are still missing, filled in and repainted as best as he could."

Sarah studied the plate once more. The replacement pieces fashioned by the expert craftsman were fitted precisely into place, lending a beauty of their own.

"It's rather wonderful," Sarah said. "Thank you, Mamma. And I shall have to thank Miss Stirling as well."

"You are welcome."

Staring at the painting of the clustered sisters, Sarah said softly, "Soon another piece of our family will no longer be in place."

"When Viola marries, do you mean?"

"Who else?"

Mamma gave her a knowing look. "Viola will be only next door, assuming she and the major decide to remain in Sidmouth. And if you ever were to, say, move away, I would miss you terribly—we all would. But we would not prevent or begrudge your happiness for all the world."

"Let's not get ahead of ourselves."

Mamma squeezed her hand. "Very well. For now, we have a more pressing matter to attend to. Will you help me organize Viola's wedding breakfast?"

Sarah grinned. "Just try and stop me."

Emily sat down at the writing desk in Mamma's room. It was quieter there than in the office, and Mamma said she was welcome to use the desk whenever she liked. She and Georgie were out for another walk before going sea-bathing again. Meanwhile, Sarah was finishing some small details for the upcoming wedding break-fast, and Viola was visiting the Huttons. So Emily had time, and the room, all to herself.

She stroked the cover of a new bound journal she had bought at Wallis's Marine Library, then opened it and smoothed the first page.

After considering where to start, she dipped a quill pen in ink and began to write.

On the south coast of Devonshire, there lived four sisters. Sisters who never stopped thinking about, and longing for, the fifth, lost to them, but God willing, not forever. . . .

Viola and Major Hutton met with the vicar of the parish church, and soon the banns were read for the first of three times. They planned to marry in late July. The service would be followed by a wedding breakfast held at Sea View for all the friends and neighbors who would wish to celebrate with them.

On a fine summer morning, the happily anticipated event finally arrived.

Viola wore an elegant new gown of ivory silk with a fashionably tapered waist. Miss Stirling curled and arranged her hair, then helped her don the new veil adorned with Mrs. Denby's sprigs of lace.

Emily, as Viola's attendant, chose an understated dress of pale blue satin for the occasion, and Miss Stirling wove flowers into her hair.

As they were dressing, someone knocked on the bedchamber door. Georgiana poked her head into the room, and Sarah stood behind her. "Are sisters welcome?"

Viola turned. "Definitely. Come in." She embraced each sister in turn, missing Claire once more.

"You both look lovely," Sarah announced. "Miss Stirling, you have not lost your touch!"

Fran Stirling bit back a smile, clearly pleased with their flattery. "I could not resist. I had to come and offer my services, for old times' sake."

Viola pressed the woman's hand. "And we are very glad you did."

For good measure, Miss Stirling added a few curls to Sarah's hair as well and repinned Georgie's haphazard chignon, which had already begun to fall loose.

When everyone was dressed and ready, Emily took her twin's hands and beamed at her. "How beautiful you are."

Viola flushed with pleasure.

Then they all went downstairs and joined Mamma, who wore a subdued gown of pale lilac, now that her year and a day of full mourning had passed. Together they went outside and climbed into the Huttons' carriage, waiting near the door, festooned with ribbons and flowers.

When they arrived at the parish church a few minutes later, the major stood looking nervous and handsome in a dark suit of clothes and snowy white cravat. He wore a discreet black band over his ear, but at Viola's request, he wore no eye patch. To her, both of his blue eyes were beautiful even though only one had sight. With it, he watched in awe as Viola joined him at the altar, love and admiration evident in his expression. Viola had never felt prettier or more cherished.

Friends and loved ones filled the first several pews. Mr. Hutton gave her away while Mamma wiped her eyes on her new handkerchief. Emily attended Viola, and Colin and Armaan stood beside the major during the service.

With friends and neighbors looking on, the vicar began, "Dearly beloved, we are gathered together here in the sight of God to join together this man and this woman in holy matrimony; signifying unto us the mystical union that is betwixt Christ and his Church."

Viola's heart beat a happy rhythm. She still could hardly believe this was really happening.

The vicar continued, "First, it was ordained for the procreation of children, to be brought up in the fear and nurture of the Lord."

Would she and Jack have children? Viola wondered yet again. And if they did, would they be healthy and whole? She recalled the major's assurance that, whatever came, they would face it together and love any and all children God chose to give them. His words gave her comfort and courage—then and now.

"John Robert Hutton, wilt thou have this woman to thy wedded wife, to live together after God's ordinance in the holy estate of matrimony? Wilt thou love her, comfort her, honor, and keep her in sickness and in health; and forsaking all others, keep thee only unto her, so long as ye both shall live?"

The major replied in a strong voice, "I will."

The clergyman turned to her and asked her a variation of the same questions.

Blinking back happy tears, Viola nodded. "I will."

Then they repeated their vows, and the major placed a ring on her finger.

"With this ring I thee wed, with my body I thee worship. . . ."

Viola's stomach tingled to hear him say those words in his deep, serious voice.

The vicar prayed over them, blessed them, and pronounced them man and wife.

After the ceremony, Major Hutton and the new Mrs. Hutton departed the church hand in hand, and wedding guests showered them with handfuls of seed and well wishes.

The major helped Viola into his carriage and climbed in beside her. As the horses started off, he leaned close and gave her a long, lingering kiss.

Together, they drove to Sea View, and their families and guests soon joined them, anticipating a festive banquet. In the dining room, a generous meal awaited, prepared by Mrs. Besley, Jessie, Chown, and two extra servants engaged for the occasion. Mr. Gwilt had also insisted on helping.

Soon the guests spilled over into the drawing room and veranda, among them the Huttons, Mrs. Denby, Mr. Hornbeam, the Cordeys in Sunday best, Miss Stirling, Armaan Sagar, Mr. and Mrs. Butcher, and many others.

Although they were surrounded by dozens of people, Viola could not keep her eyes from one person in particular: Jack Hutton. How she loved this man and relished the assurance that he loved her too.

After they had eaten, she and the major rose and crossed the room together to speak to his father, brother, and friend.

"Many blessings," Armaan said, bowing over her hand before embracing Jack.

"Congratulations, my boy." His father clapped his son's shoulder, then leaned down to kiss Viola's cheek. "Welcome to the family, my dear."

Viola smiled from one to the other. "Thank you. I am happy to join your ranks."

Colin kissed her other cheek. "Not as happy as we are. Think you can put up with us, Vi?"

"I think so. After all, I've always wanted a brother."

"And I always wanted a sister."

Viola looked over at hers—Sarah, Georgiana, and Emily. She wished Claire were there too, but was thankful for her renewed closeness with these three.

Her throat tight, she said, "Yes, sisters are pretty wonderful."

Author's Note

Thank you for reading! I hope you enjoyed this book and look forward to more novels in the ON DEVONSHIRE SHORES series. I am eager to return to the Devon seaside, and hopefully you are too.

Now, just a few notes to share with you:

For any readers who wonder why I used *Devonshire* in the series title instead of the now more commonly used *Devon*, that is because I preferred its historical sound and because Jane Austen refers to the county as *Devonshire* in her novel *Sense and Sensibility*.

While I did not find a great deal published about cleft palate repair during the Regency era, I found it eye-opening and heart-rending to read about procedures (and superstitions) from earlier centuries. I am thankful that techniques have greatly advanced and are made available by charitable organizations like Smile Train and Operation Smile.

Did you recognize Mr. and Mrs. Elton, characters from Jane Austen's *Emma*? Mrs. Elton repeats several lines of dialogue from that novel in this one. You may have also noticed a few phrases from *Pride and Prejudice* in the conversation Viola overhears between her two sisters. If so, I hope you enjoyed these fond nods of honor to the great Jane Austen.

Cricket matches between locals and visitors were played in Sidmouth, although some time after the timeframe of this book. Also, while the flood depicted is fictional, Sidmouth has flooded several times over the years, and the rescue scene was partly inspired by grainy black-and-white photographs of boats going through the town streets to help those stranded. Similarly, bathing machine accidents did occur on the English seaside, and men typically swam au naturel, at least until the second half of the nineteenth century.

Edmund Butcher, John Wallis Jr., and Emanuel Lousada are historical figures but appear in the novel in fictionalized form. Other characters are not meant to represent real people.

Sea View as described did not exist in this time period, but most of the other buildings mentioned did.

I would like to sincerely thank Nigel Hyman and Ann Jones of the Sidmouth Museum for all their gracious help in researching and reviewing this novel when travel restrictions prevented me from visiting Sidmouth myself. Along with answering my questions by email, they also recommended (and sent) several books. I am deeply grateful.

Speaking of books, I relied heavily on *The Beauties of Sidmouth Displayed* by the Reverend Edmund Butcher, and also found helpful *Old Sidmouth* by Reginald Lane, *Sidmouth, A History* by the Museum Committee, *Sidmouth's Prints* by Deborah Robertson, *Sidmouth's Literary Connections* by Nigel Hyman, and *The Georgian Seaside* by Louise Allen, among others. And if you are interested in learning more about Honiton lace and a lace maker's life, I recommend the lovely-to-look-at *Sidmouth's Lace* by Carol McFadzean.

I am also thankful for the helpful input I received from first reader Cari Weber, as well as Anna Shay, pianist Stacy Woytcke, author Michelle Griep, and my agent, Wendy Lawton. Warm gratitude also goes to my editors, Karen Schurrer, Rochelle Gloege, and Hannah Ahlfield, as well as to Raela Schoenherr and my entire team at Bethany House Publishers. A special shout-out to Jennifer Parker for the absolutely beautiful cover.

Finally, thank you again for reading my books. I appreciate each and every one of you! For more information about me and my other novels, please follow me on Facebook or Instagram and sign up for my email list via my website, www.julieklassen.com.

Discussion Questions

1. During the last few hundred years, many people have enjoyed holidays at the seaside. Do you share a love of the sea? Why or why not?

2. What was your reaction to the physician's (historically based) advice to not only bathe in salt water, but to drink it as well?

3. Were you familiar with Honiton lace or other types? Have you seen lace made, or made it yourself? What about that cottage industry interested you?

4. Are you a Jane Austen fan? Did you recognize Mr. and Mrs. Elton from Jane Austen's *Emma*, or any other "nods of honor" to that esteemed author?

5. Viola struggles with bitterness over being born with a cleft lip. She believes in God but doesn't "like all His ways." Similarly, Sarah finds it difficult to accept God's will after the loss of loved ones. Can you relate? What would you say to someone struggling in their faith due to loss or disappointment?

6. What did you learn about cleft lip and palate surgeries (and superstitions) from earlier centuries? Are you familiar

433

with charitable organizations like Smile Train and Operation Smile, which perform procedures for people who might otherwise go without?

7. Which Summers sister are you most like and why? Do you share an interest or hobby with one of them?

8. Do you have a sister or sisters of your own? If so, could you relate to any relationships, frictions, or affections depicted in *The Sisters of Sea View*?

9. Did you have a favorite character in the novel? Least favorite? Did your feelings toward any of the characters change as the story progressed?

10. Which sister and/or relationship are you looking forward to reading more about in later books in the ON DEVONSHIRE SHORES series?

Julie Klassen loves all things Jane—*Jane Eyre* and Jane Austen. Her books have sold over a million copies, and she is a three-time recipient of the Christy Award for Historical Romance. *The Secret of Pembrooke Park* was honored with the Minnesota Book Award for Genre Fiction. Julie has also won the Midwest Book Award and Christian Retailing's BEST Award, and has been a finalist in the RITA and Carol Awards. A graduate of the University of Illinois, Julie worked in publishing for sixteen years and now writes full-time. Julie and her husband have two sons and live in a suburb of St. Paul, Minnesota. For more information, you can follow her on Facebook or visit www.julieklassen.com.

Sign Up for Julie's Newsletter

Keep up to date with Julie's news on book releases and events by signing up for her email list at julieklassen.com.

More from Julie Klassen

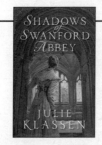

In pursuit of an author who could help get her brother published, Rebecca Lane stays at Swanford Abbey, a grand hotel rumored to be haunted. It is there she encounters Sir Frederick—the man who broke her heart. When a mysterious death occurs, Rebecca is one of the suspects, and Frederick is torn between his feelings for her and his search for the truth.

Shadows of Swanford Abbey

⬧ BETHANYHOUSE

 Stay up to date on your favorite books and authors with our free e-newsletters. Sign up today at bethanyhouse.com.

 facebook.com/bethanyhousepublishers @bethanyhousefiction

OB Free exclusive resources for your book group at bethanyhouseopenbook.com

You May Also Like . . .

Laura Callaway daily walks the windswept Cornwall coast, known for many shipwrecks but few survivors. And when a man with curious wounds and an odd accent is washed ashore, she cares for him while the mystery surrounding him grows. Can their budding attraction survive, and can he be returned to his rightful home when danger pursues them from every side?

A Castaway in Cornwall by Julie Klassen
julieklassen.com

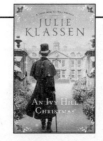

Haunted by an old secret and the shadows of his past, gentleman Richard Brockwell prefers to stay away from Ivy Hill—until his mother threatens to stop funding his carefree life unless he returns for Christmas. Will Christmastime in Ivy Hill, with all of its divine hope, unforeseen surprises, and unexpected romantic encounters, work its magic in his heart?

An Ivy Hill Christmas by Julie Klassen
A Tales from Ivy Hill Novella
julieklassen.com

After uncovering a diary that leads to a secret artifact, Lady Emily Scofield and Bram Sinclair must piece together the mystifying legends while dodging a team of archaeologists. In a race against time, they must decide what makes a hero. Is it fighting valiantly to claim the treasure or sacrificing everything in the name of selfless love?

Worthy of Legend by Roseanna M. White
The Secrets of the Isles #3
roseannamwhite.com

BETHANYHOUSE

More from Bethany House

In 1942, a promise to her brother before he goes off to war puts Avis Montgomery in the unlikely position of head librarian and book club organizer in small-town Maine. The women of her club band together as the war comes dangerously close, but their friendships are tested by secrets, and they must decide whether depending on each other is worth the cost.

The Blackout Book Club by Amy Lynn Green
amygreenbooks.com

Discovered floating in a basket along the canals of Venice, Sebastien Trovato wrestles with questions of his origins. Decades later, on an assignment to translate a rare book, Daniel Goodman finds himself embroiled in a web of secrets carefully kept within the ancient city and in the mystery of the man whose story the book does not finish: Sebastien.

All the Lost Places by Amanda Dykes
amandadykes.com

Captain Marcus Weatherford arrives in Russia on a secret mission with a ballerina posing as his fiancée, but his sense of duty battles his desire to return home to Clare. Clare Danner fears losing her daughter to the father's heartless family, but only Marcus can provide the proof to save her. Can she trust Marcus, or will he shatter her world yet again?

In Love's Time by Kate Breslin
katebreslin.com

◊ BETHANYHOUSE

You Are Invited!

Join like-minded fans in the **Inspirational Regency Readers** group on Facebook.

From book news from popular Regency authors like Kristi Ann Hunter, Michelle Griep, Erica Vetsch, Julie Klassen, and many others, to games and giveaways, to discussions of favorite Regency reads and adaptations new and old, to places we long to travel, you will find plenty of fun and friendship within this growing community.

Free and easy to join, simply search for "Inspirational Regency Readers" on Facebook.

We look forward to seeing you there!

◊ BETHANYHOUSE